DEAD MAN'S DANCE

ALSO BY
ROBERT FERRIGNO

The Cheshire Moon
The Horse Latitudes

DEAD MAN'S DANCE

ROBERT FERRIGNO

G. P. PUTNAM'S SONS • NEW YORK

G. P. PUTNAM'S SONS
Publishers Since 1838
200 Madison Avenue
New York, NY 10016

Library of Congress Cataloging-in-Publication Data
Ferrigno, Robert.
    Dead man's dance / Robert Ferrigno.
        p.   cm.
    ISBN 0-399-14025-5
    Sequel to: The Cheshire moon.
    I. Title.
PS3556.E7259D4   1995   94-38351 CIP
813'.54—dc20

BOOK DESIGN BY JULIE DUQUET

Printed in the United States of America
1   2   3   4   5   6   7   8   9   10

This book is printed on acid-free paper. ∞

ACKNOWLEDGMENTS

Getting by with more than a little help from my friends . . . Thanks to Stacy Creamer, my editor, for her enthusiasm, insight, and clarity of purpose. Thanks also to Mary Evans, my agent, for her brains, creativity, and hard work—I'm grateful she's on my side of the table. Scott Beattie showed me the intricacies of a motor yacht and flew in ten pounds of soft-shelled crabs to set the proper tone for the lesson. Thanks to Ali Marashi for putting me into a dancer's shoes and to Jennifer Clark and the crew at Salon Phoenix. William Ungerman was there for technical advice—I hope I can return the favor. Most of all, I wish to thank Jody. Thanks to Phyllis Grann for giving this book the kind of publishing TLC every author dreams of.

To the sound of kids laughing, yelling . . .
to my Jake, Dani Rose, and Riley Emma.

DEAD MAN'S DANCE

PROLOGUE

He was dancing with his eyes closed, holding her close but not tightly, guiding her through the intricate steps, with gentle touches on her back and elbow, subtle pressures of the hips, and rapid shifts of balance. She partnered him perfectly, the two of them breathing in tandem . . .

He could smell her perfume, hear the rustle of her skirt as they spun across the floor.

Dancing in the dark,
Till the tune ends, we're dancing in the dark,
And it soon ends.
We're waltzing in the wonder of why we're here,
Time hurries by, we're here and gone . . .

He held her hand high, forearms touching, feeling her pulse against his wrist, aroused now, the music wrapped around them. His eyes were still closed, the two of them entwined, ever shifting yet moving as one. Graceful. Perfect.

Her neck brushed against him and he felt the softness of her skin. He kissed her, tasted the sweetness of her as she swayed against him, their passion not so much choreographed as it was utterly in tune with the music.

Looking for the light
Of a new love to brighten up the night.
I have you love, and we can face the music together,
Dancing in the dark . . .

He rolled her away from him in the darkness, brought her back into his arms, right where he wanted her, right where she belonged, the two of them out of breath as the applause rolled around them.

Joe opened his eyes. He was sitting in the darkened living room, the record player skipping at the end of the record. His legs were splayed in the wheelchair, trembling, knees knotted with pain. The room was filled with ashes.

CHAPTER

1

"Last chance . . ." Rick held up the end of his chicken sandwich to Hugo, tantalizing, whispering like someone could overhear.

Last chance for the flesh of dead animals.

"Close your mouth when you chew," said Hugo. He could feel his scalp sweat as he drove the Jacko's Plumbing van toward the guardshack at the entrance to Collingsworth Estates. He waved familiarly as they passed, his hand covering his face. The guard looked up from his newspaper, blinking—an old guy in a starched blue uniform—then went back to reading. Hugo exhaled, not even aware that he had been holding his breath.

They drove down the broad, empty streets, the van silent except for the sound of Rick chewing. No kids riding bicycles, nobody playing on those lush green lawns. It was early evening. Fog drifted in from the ocean, the setting sun turned the air opaque and yellow. Like driving through falling leaves.

"I should have boosted a cleaner truck," said Rick, kicking at the crumpled cigarette packs and greasy Styrofoam containers on the floor of the van. The collar of his new coveralls was turned up, the pantlegs neatly folded. Très chic. Rick nudged a syrupy Big Gulp cup with the toe of his gleaming black combat boots. The laces had tiny red hearts on them. "What was I thinking?"

That was a question without an answer. Hugo downshifted smoothly, his eyes flicking from side to side, noting addresses. The houses were set far back from the street, far apart, safe behind hedges and brick walls, assured of their privacy. The backs of his hands itched through the clear plastic gloves. He wondered if he was having an allergic reaction or an eczema attack. He should have taken a couple of Benedryl before they left.

"You want me to do it?" asked Rick. "It don't make no never mind to me." The pearl grip of the .32 revolver peeked out of his hip pocket. "Might as well be me—I visualized it so many times it's already in my diary."

Rick cut out pictures of red sports cars and Armani suits, taped them to his refrigerator so he could meditate every time he got a can of that iced cappuccino he loved. So far he was still driving a Toyota with a cracked windshield, but Hugo didn't have the heart to point it out.

"I'll do it, Hugo." Rick's head bobbed. "Just say the word."

Hugo didn't say a thing.

Rick shrugged and checked his reflection in the metal dashboard, primping his feathery blonde hair. He was a gangly twenty-year-old with pretty, delicate features and six tiny gold hoops in his left ear. He reminded Hugo of a preening tropical bird, a flamboyant, gold-crested parrot. A parrot with a lady's gun and a bad attitude.

Hugo was a gaunt, gray man somewhere in his thirties, with brooding eyes, thinning hair, and no appetite. No appetite at all. He barely ate anymore, growing stronger every time he pushed aside his untouched plate. He was hard as barbed wire now, all fat and feeling long since stripped away—when he cut himself shaving, he did not bleed.

He turned into the driveway of 411 Brineywood, drove between the high clipped hedges and past a long expanse of lawn, parking in the circular driveway of the sprawling brick house. They moved quickly out of the van, Rick lugging a rusty pipe wrench. Hugo emptied a tiny packet onto the doormat, ground the bits of shell into the fibers of the mat. He had a sour taste in his mouth.

A beefy, older man answered the bell, scowling, wearing a burgundy-striped apron, the sleeves of his dress shirt turned up. Superior Court Judge Theodore Krammerson glared at them from the doorway, a fleshy autocrat with three chins and a full slope of gut. In his fist he cupped a highball glass with little yachts on it.

Hugo smelled chocolate.

"Hey, Betty Crocker." Rick saluted with the pipe wrench, grinning. "Time to get your pipes cleaned."

"I didn't call for a plumber." Ice tinkled in his glass as the judge glowered, jowls quivering, his large head and mane of silvery-white hair giving him a look of primal authority. "Check your work orders, assuming one of you ignoramuses can read." He started to close the door but Hugo shoved it open, knocking the judge backwards into the foyer.

Hugo heard the highball glass shatter on the hardwood floor. He watched a maraschino cherry roll into the sunken living room, leaving a red trail on the white carpet, then quietly closed the door behind them.

"How dare—!" sputtered the judge, scrambling to his feet. "Do you know who I am?"

Rick cracked the judge across the nose with the pipe wrench, knocked him against the wall. "It's a hit, sports fans!" he cheered as the judge slid to the floor, groaning, hands over his face, blood squirting through his clasped fingers. Rick strolled down the hall, bashed a hole in the wall with a two-handed swing with the wrench and kept on walking.

"Yes sir, Your Honor," Hugo said, "we know who you are."

The judge lunged for a security alarm on the wall but Hugo got to him first, dragged him into the living room, and threw him onto the sofa. The judge flopped on the yellow floral-pattern couch, panting, head down. Blood dripped off his chin and onto the yellow-roses pattern of the couch, turning the blossoms a pale pink.

"Tilt your head back."

"Shut up," gasped the judge, complying anyway, chest heaving.

"I didn't know he was going to smack you like that—"

"Fuck you."

"I don't think profanity is called for, Teddy. You mind if I call you Teddy? I'd prefer to keep things informal."

The judge smiled in spite of himself, head still tilted back. "Sure . . . we're pals, you and me." He dabbed his nose with his fingertips, winced. "Your buddy hits like a girl. You, however"—he clenched his jaw—"you're very impressive, Mr. Jack-Sprat-could-eat-no-fat. I'm twice your size, and you carried me in here like a sack of potatoes." He looked directly at Hugo. "What kind of medication are you on?"

Hugo didn't answer. The judge's attitude was unsettling. As if he knew something that Hugo didn't.

The judge twisted around at the sound of breaking glass coming from the rear of the house. Rick's high-pitched squawk echoed through the halls. "What is that asshole's problem?" said the judge. He shook his head. "Let me give you a word of advice"—he gingerly blotted his nose with the edge of the apron—"your buddy is a head case. He's more dangerous to you than he is to me."

"There's nothing wrong with my head." Rick stood in the doorway, indignant, the wrench swinging nervously. "Look at me." He showed his profile. "I got perfect bone structure." He was serious.

The judge looked at Hugo. "Gidget here is going to get you killed."

Hugo stopped Rick with an upraised hand. The judge stayed unconcerned.

"House is clean," said Rick, "just the three of us." He noticed the judge's stained apron and his face brightened. "Looks like the judge spilled his nose all over himself. Most excellent. Just like my visualization."

"Did you check the closets?" asked Hugo. "The shower stall. Did you remember to look under the beds?"

Rick walked into the living room instead, drawn to a large oil painting, a formal portrait of the judge and an attractive, gray-haired woman sitting on a loveseat, holding hands. He pointed at the woman's hair. "Rudolpho, right?"

The judge ignored him.

Rick was hot to be a hairdresser—he liked the glamour of the fancy salon on Melrose where he did shampoos for minimum wage, he liked the gossip and the too-loud music. He even had a little leather shoulder holster made for his styling scissors, which he wore when he gave Hugo his weekly trim.

"Yeah, it's Rudolpho," said Rick, I'd recognize his back-comb technique with my eyes poked out. Still"—he tapped his cheek with a forefinger—"I'd add some lighter streaks, maybe layer the sides for a softer profile." He turned, case closed, sniffed. "Something good's going on in the kitchen," he said, heading out the doorway.

"Stir the chocolate on the double boiler," the judge called after him. "I'm making mocha-mint truffles," he explained to Hugo. "Wouldn't want them to burn."

Hugo was still waiting for the judge to panic. Waiting for him to ask what they wanted. Ask who sent them. Something.

"Hugo," Rick called from the kitchen. "You should see all the shiny copper pots and pans in here. Check it out, I can see myself every place I look." Glass exploded. It sounded like a shelf of crystal being splintered.

The judge grimaced, his hands clenching into fists. His nose was bleeding again.

"He likes breaking things," said Hugo. "Don't worry, you won't have to clean it up."

"Who's worried?" The judge wiped his face with his apron. His eyes didn't leave Hugo's. "You like chocolate? Desserts are my hobby, and you look like you could use fattening up."

"I'm not hungry."

"Wish I could say that just once in my life." The judge patted his ample belly and tried to smile. "I really should get back to my kitchen." His expression darkened at the continuing barrage of breaking glass coming from the kitchen. "How did a guy like you ever get fixed up with somebody like him?" he growled, listening to the crunch of Rick's combat boots marching happily across the floor. "It couldn't have been your idea. I give you too much credit for that."

"He's not so bad."

"Oh yes, he is." The judge absently touched his swollen nose. "You're in over your head, we both know it, so let's not play games. You can still back out . . . I don't hold a grudge. You just get in your truck and drive away, no hard feelings."

"Where would we go, Teddy? It's too early to go home and we're not dressed for the ballet."

The judge stared at Hugo, fascinated. "Have we ever met?"

Hugo smiled. "Don't you think you'd remember me if we had?"

"I think I would, at that," the judge agreed. "You're a breath of fresh air, Hugo—you have no idea of the sheer volume of evasions and duplicity I'm exposed to on a daily basis. All my life I wanted to be a judge, wanted the prestige and decorum of the office, and the power, too, I won't deny that." He shook his head ruefully. "I'm a proud man, and I spend my day directing traffic in a sewer, watching the bullshit float past."

"I am so bored," said Rick, strolling back from the kitchen. He walked over to the ornate gilt mirror like he was being pulled into a whirlpool. "You should see the judge's study . . ." He puckered his lips at his reflection, his face surrounded by gold cherubs. "Books everywhere, floor to ceiling. Who does he think he's kidding? Nobody could read that many books." He suddenly cocked his head from side to side, staring at the mirror. "Hugo, my sideburns look even?"

Hugo rubbed his temples. He had such a headache.

The judge grinned. "A couple of real pros."

Rick circled the spacious living room. He ran his fingers along the curve of a handmade cherrywood rocker, caressed every curlicue of an intricate antique pine armoire, knelt to check the weave of the Chinese rug, all the while murmuring, "Wonderful, wonderful."

Hugo liked to watch Rick when he was like this, his face rapt with joy, giddy with sensation. Rick said human beings were just walking antennae tuned in to pleasure. If that was true, Hugo thought Rick was overly tuned in for his own good, but he envied him nevertheless. All Hugo got was static.

The judge glanced at his watch. "I don't want to rush you," he said to Hugo, his eyes sharp as roofing nails under thick, bushy eyebrows, "but my wife should be back any minute with our bridge club. So unless—"

"Your wife is speaking tonight at the Orange Coast Women's Banquet, seven p.m. to ten p.m., no-host bar," Hugo recited. "I read the society pages. All those party pictures, everybody holding up their drinks for the camera." He saw the judge's eyes widen, and Hugo realized he had pulled the revolver from his coveralls. They stared at each other. Hugo wished he could put it away.

"I get threatened all the time in my line of work," the judge said finally. He spread his arms across the back of the couch, languidly crossed his legs. "Tough guys stand in my courtroom screaming the most vile obscenities and I don't even react. I find myself watching their mouths move, calculating how much their dental care is going to cost the taxpayers . . ." He plucked a speck of lint from his pants, watched it drift onto the floor.

The revolver felt heavier and heavier as the judge

droned on, until Hugo casually slipped it back into his pocket.

"I don't blame the tough guys for their outbursts," the judge said, "in fact, I find their rage entirely reasonable. They're on their way to a ten-by-twelve cell, forty years of mashed-potato sandwiches and sharing farts with their bunky." He smiled at Hugo as though he were looking down from a great height. "Of course, some men might enjoy that . . ."

Hugo was tired. Tired of Rick. Tired of the judge, who was supposed to be scared stupid, not trying to drown them in talk, filling up the room with his jabbering. Did the judge think he was going to hide himself with words? Hugo had lived for years in silence. Words didn't fool him.

"Hey, Judge," chirped Rick, surveying the room. "Did you and the wife hire an interior designer to put this all together? I'm planning to open my own salon, not just hair, more of a total style spa—scalp facials, seaweed body-wraps, reflexology . . ." His voice cracked with excitement. "Maybe aromatherapy . . . anyway, if you went with a designer, I'd like his business card."

"I'm going to tend to my chocolates," the judge said to Hugo, getting up from the couch. "Come with me if you like, you've got your little gun to protect you."

"You really should see what he's got cooking in there, Hugo," said Rick. He pulled an aerosol paint can from his coveralls, shook it and got to work, arms swooping like a symphony conductor, spraying big red letters on those eggshell-white walls.

The judge stopped at the hissing sound, looked back from the doorway, fascinated. His mouth tightened, seeing what was happening to his living room, but he couldn't keep himself from trying to read what Rick was writing. For that instant, Hugo felt sorry for him.

Quinn stood at the mezzanine bar, tapping his foot to the swing music coming over the loudspeakers, listening to the clarinets blaring out a challenge. He licked a spot of blood off the knuckles of his right hand, moving his shoulders to the beat. He smiled. He wasn't a dancer, but he had some moves.

Intermission at the ballroom dance exhibition merely moved the competition into the lobby of the Seal Beach auditorium—it was a fashion face-off, part nostalgia, part nineties romanticism. Glamorous women in shimmering silk dresses fingered ropes of black beads, men in pastel shirts smoothed their slicked-back hair. Patent-leather was everywhere. One idiot even had an ivory cigarette holder clamped between his teeth.

Quinn was the only person in the room whose nose had been broken three times, the only one whose suit smelled of mothballs. He liked his nose just the way it was, but he was going to burn the suit when tonight was over. He ran a hand through his dark, unruly hair as the bartender approached. "My daughter's class is performing tonight," he said proudly. "She's eight years old."

"Congratulations, handsome." She was a chunky blonde in a white nautical jacket with frayed gold epaulettes, and a vaguely interested expression. "So, what can I get you?"

"Two champagnes." Quinn held up a ten for the drinks she poured, added another one. "Double or nothing? You call it."

Her eyes narrowed, considering, then reached into her change pouch, deftly flipped a quarter. Quinn snatched it out of the air, slapped it onto the bar. She covered his hand with hers. "Heads," she said. It was tails.

He handed her the two tens anyway, turned her disappointment into confusion. "It wasn't a fair bet," he said, picking up the plastic flutes of champagne. "I'm on a hot streak. Just wanted to test it out."

He made his way back across the packed room toward Rachel, slipping through the crowd, barely touching anyone, gliding across the polished floor as the music rippled around him. Women glanced over as he passed, nodding absently to their companions while their eyes tracked him.

He missed Jen. She had been gone almost a week and he still hadn't gotten used to sleeping alone. The first few days he had stayed at her apartment, but he couldn't sleep in that bed without her, his face pressed against the pillow, smelling her hair . . . He had moved back into his own place a couple of days ago, taking her pillow with him.

A fat man leaned backwards, gesticulating wildly, making a point—Quinn dipped around him, a drink in each hand, not spilling a drop. You'd have thought it was choreographed. He could see Rachel watching him, her black curly hair brushing her bare shoulders as she swayed to the music. She wore a new dress, a crinkly rayon that followed her every movement, the back cut low to show off the lovely curves of her scapula. He turned, squeezing past a foursome, and Rachel turned along with him, her pale-green dress swirling around her knees like sea foam. Ex-wives shouldn't be allowed to look so good.

Their marriage had been an attraction of opposites. He was an investigative reporter, hot tempered, raw as a blister, more comfortable in the company of criminals than the cognoscenti. She was an art history professor at the university, cool and poised, able to recognize the authentic from the false, and not afraid to say so. He trusted her judgment even more than his own. Their friends were surprised the marriage had lasted six years, even more surprised that they remained such good friends after the divorce.

Quinn angled his way free, Rachel applauding as he reached her unscathed. He handed her the champagne, then stole the strawberry from her glass, popped it into his mouth. An old habit. "To Katie's debut," he said as they touched glasses.

Rachel took a sip. "So, what happened to your hand?"

He slid his hand into his pocket, hiding the battered

knuckles. "I phoned Sacramento a few minutes ago," he said, teasing her, "the state medical board has called a news conference for tomorrow morning. Word is that three doctors on the oversight panel are going to resign."

She kissed him on the cheek. "You nailed them."

Last month, Quinn had written a cover story for *SLAP* magazine detailing the panel's failures. Ostensibly a self-policing body to discipline doctors, the panel usually served to whitewash medical incompetence. His article quoted from their secret discussion of an obstetrician whose botched deliveries were responsible for the deaths of at least five women, all illegal immigrants. The panel had downplayed the deaths, saying the doctor's level of care was as good as the women would have received at one of the third-world clinics in their homeland.

"I still don't understand how you hurt your hand," Rachel said innocently.

Quinn watched the bubbles rising in her glass. "I punched a wall. I was so happy about the news out of Sacramento—"

"Not likely," said Rachel. "You wouldn't waste a punch on a wall. You don't slam doors or write letters to your congressman, either. I know you."

She wasn't going to let it drop. "I ran into somebody," he said, "an acquaintance, spotted him working the room while I was on the phone. Mid-level coke dealer, goldcard clientele. He's not a bad guy—"

"Not a bad guy?"

"Not compared to some doctors." Quinn shrugged. "I

told him there were little kids here tonight, suggested he take his business elsewhere." He flexed his fingers. "We had a slight disagreement about the limits of free-market capitalism."

"It's good to see you like this again." She was beaming.

"Like what?"

"Like you were when we first got married. Charging into trouble, no doubts, no hesitations." She plucked the strawberry from his drink, bit it in half, the remaining flesh bright-red in her pink manicured fingertips. "Maybe it's your new job . . ." She watched him over the rim of her glass. "Maybe it's your new girlfriend. I think Jen has been good for you, if my opinion matters."

"It matters."

"Living with you was . . . an adjustment." Her eyes glinted, remembering. "The phone would ring in the middle of the night and you'd be off to meet some horrible person, so excited you could hardly wait to get dressed. I'd be scared, not wanting you to go, and you'd kiss me, tell me not to worry, say it was only innocent bystanders who got hurt, so you were perfectly safe."

He looked away. "I was wrong," he said softly.

Two years earlier, Quinn had written a series of investigative articles that had gotten a serial killer acquitted—B. K. Groggins, accused of killing two college girls. A few weeks after the verdict, Groggins botched a mini-mart robbery and held the clerk hostage, demanding that Quinn come to the store to broker his surrender. The clerk's name was Doreen. She had terrified eyes and broken-backed shoes and a daughter younger than Katie. Quinn had walked them out of the mini-mart toward the police, stood right beside Doreen, holding her hand while Groggins pressed a gun to her head under the glare of the TV mini-cam lights. "Let her go," Quinn had said. "What are you looking at here, armed robbery? That's chump change."

Groggins had smiled and Quinn felt suddenly sick. "Oh, we're way past armed robbery, partner," said Groggins. "I did some bad shit to my landlady this morning. She was fun . . . but the college girls were even sweeter." The gun went off as Quinn tried to push Doreen aside.

"You made a mistake," said Rachel. "Sometimes I worried that you'd never forgive yourself."

He swallowed his answer, checked the street through the windows. A bag lady clattered past, her shopping cart piled high with flattened aluminum cans and fluorescent-orange traffic cones. No one else. He could see his disappointment reflected in the glass.

"Still waiting for your stepfather?" asked Rachel.

"No," he lied.

"You sent him an announcement, that's all you can do."

"Don't call Teddy my stepfather, okay?" Quinn ground his teeth. "He's the guy my mother married before she skipped out on the both of us. We shared a house and a sense of mutual frustration, which is not usually considered a lasting bond. Call him the honorable Judge Theodore Krammerson. He'd like that."

"He sent you a letter last week at the house. You

should give him your new address. I was going to bring it—"

"It's not a letter, it's a birthday card," said Quinn, the edge in his voice getting sharper with each word. "Every year Teddy sends me a belated birthday card with a note saying 'let's have lunch.' The first few years I actually believed him. Throw it away."

A rat-faced man waved from across the room, then started toward them, pushing his way through the crowd, making slow headway.

"We should go back to our seats," Rachel said quickly, starting toward the auditorium. "The second half is going to start any moment."

"What's the rush?"

The man half-tripped, regained his feet. "Rachel!" He scooted over to them, mouth twitching.

"Oh, hi, Alan."

"Just-just wanted to congratulate you"—the man paused to catch his breath—"the whole department is talking about your good fortune. Not that you don't deserve it," he stumbled, "such an honor, we're all basking in your reflected glory."

Quinn looked at Rachel, not understanding.

"Alan, this is Quinn. I'd love to speak with you, but we have to go inside."

"Perhaps you could put in a good word for me with the division chair," the man called after them. "Someone has to cover your classes, and who better than me. Heh-heh."

The lights in the auditorium were blinking as they

found their seats. "What's the big honor you didn't tell me about?" Quinn said casually, feeling his hands go cold. "Give *me* a chance to bask in your glory. Heh-heh."

"Let's talk about it tomorrow." She didn't look at him. "Tonight is special. Why ruin things?"

"Good news never ruined anything," he said, feeling the cold spreading through him, and wishing he didn't have such good instincts about impending disaster. He was the canary in the mineshaft. The dog that howled before the earthquake. "Tell me now. I can't wait until tomorrow."

"I got an offer," said Rachel. He had to strain to hear her. "From the Sorbonne . . . they want me come to Paris and teach courses in American Folk Art. They offered me a two-year contract."

"Two years . . . ? What about Katie?"

The announcer's voice was fuzzy over the P.A., something about the mambo contest.

"Rachel? Look at me. What about—"

"She'll come with me." She bit her lip. "Happy now?"

The mambo dancers burst onto the stage, three couples twirling in the spotlights in a merry-go-round of red ruffles and Brilliantined hair, all those long legs in perfect syncopation, the steamy Latin beat rolling through the room. The audience leaned forward, fanning themselves, but Quinn was frozen to the back of his seat.

"Just like that, you decide?" Quinn said as applause burst around them like gunfire. "I've got rights."

"You've got a record, I've got custody." She turned to

him, her face pained in the stagelights. "I'm sorry, I didn't mean to say that."

"The charges were dismissed, Rachel."

"I said I was sorry." A net of fine wrinkles creased her high cheekbones, her eyes like black pearls caught forever.

Someone nearby shushed them.

"I haven't decided to take the Sorbonne's offer," Rachel said quietly. "Let's talk about it tomorrow."

He started to respond, but the announcer said something about "talented youngsters" and the two of them stopped, called an unspoken truce as Katie and the rest of her dance class peeked through the curtain.

The line of twelve little girls wound from behind the curtain in frilly white skirts and wrist corsages, tap-dancing to the opening bars of some Janet Jackson song about sexual fantasies. "Shouldn't they be tapping to 'Puttin' on the Ritz' or 'Good Ship Lollipop'?" whispered Quinn, uneasy as the prepubescent chorus line strutted to the beat.

Camcorders whirled as proud parents memorialized the class debut. Katie mouthed "Hi, Daddy" at him, stumbled slightly, then caught herself. She had Rachel's curly hair and his big bones. Quinn swallowed, waved back. Last week he had bought her a new Barbie doll and discovered that Ken now came with an optional earring. Everything was changing.

He tried to imagine his life without Katie for two years. No Sunday afternoons spent watching pro basketball on

TV, Katie shouting "Dunk!" everytime the Lakers got the ball. No more water-balloon hide-and-seek in the backyard, the two of them drenched, Rachel shaking her head in mock disapproval through the kitchen window. Two years. She'd be ten. What would he be?

"Maybe you should take the job," he said, "go to Paris, enjoy yourself. Leave Katie with me. I'll take care of her."

She didn't answer.

The tap dance class finished their number, took a group bow as the applause began, giggling now, their wrist corsages bedraggled, flowers underfoot.

Quinn wiped his eyes, wishing it was darker in the auditorium.

The announcer introduced the judges: a buxom woman in a sequined dress, a short man in a baggy white dinner jacket, and "our very special guest, three-time national ballroom champion . . ." Quinn felt his brow furrow as a handsome older man acknowledged the applause with a nod, his face lean and sensual in the spotlight. There was a red rose in the lapel of his black tuxedo.

"Joe?" Quinn couldn't believe it.

"Mr. Joseph Staducci!"

"Surprise!" Rachel grabbed his arm, pleased with herself. "It was Joe's idea. Why didn't you ever tell me about him before? He came by the house looking for you and heard Katie practicing her tap. The two of them hit it off, which was a shock—you know how she is around strangers."

Quinn was on his feet. "It's Joe Steps." He was smiling

so hard his face hurt, afraid to blink for fear Joe would disappear. "I haven't seen him since I was a kid. I . . . I thought he was dead. Teddy told me he was dead."

Joe Steps blew Rachel a kiss, waved to Quinn. His dark hair was shot with gray, but he moved with the same commanding grace Quinn remembered. Caesar ordering the legions into battle. Basking in the cheers of the populace. It took Quinn a few moments to realize that Joe Steps sat in a wheelchair, its sleek chrome frame glinting in the warm yellow stagelights as though it was made of gold.

CHAPTER

3

Red letters dripped down the living-room wall—WHITE POWER! "Who are you kidding?" the judge snorted, shaking his grand silvery mane. "You expect me to believe you two are Aryan Brotherhood?"

"That's alright, Teddy," said Hugo, "the paint job isn't meant for you." The room was quiet except for the hissing of the aerosol can as Rick started in on another wall. This one would be either ZOG USA! or JEW BABYLON!

"I'm disappointed in you, Hugo," the judge said. "Look at the baggy plastic gloves you're wearing . . ."

"What about them?" Rick said defensively. "We use them at the salon when we do a dye job."

"You should be using surgical gloves," the judge said to Hugo. "You've never killed anyone before, have you? It's not as easy as you think, and getting away with it is even harder. Stick with Gidget here and you're going to the gas chamber."

"Why don't you shut him up, Hugo?"

"Hugo doesn't shut me up because Hugo has a functioning cerebral cortex," the judge explained patiently. "He can project himself beyond the immediate situation. He has the intelligence to entertain doubts. And fears. He can imagine the consequences of harming a sitting judge."

"I'm not afraid of you," said Rick.

The judge rolled his eyes.

"Be quiet, Rick," said Hugo.

"*Me?*"

"It's not too late, Hugo," said the judge. "Don't let him push you into something you'll be sorry for."

The judge's voice was a steady, rumbling growl. He didn't beg. He didn't whine. He still didn't ask who had sent them. Maybe he knew. Or maybe he didn't care. No, the judge had staked out the high ground a long time ago, and regardless of what happened, that's where he was going to make his stand. Hugo found himself wishing again that he and Rick could walk away, just drive off, and not look back.

"What's wrong with you, Hugo?" Rick had stopped in the middle of a word. "Kill him!"

"Do you hear that, Hugo?" the judge said. "That's the voice of the mob shouting at a man on a ledge, telling him to jump. It's a very long way down. Farther than you can possibly imagine." The judge spoke so softly that at first Hugo thought he was talking to himself. "You listen to that voice, you'll fall forever."

Hugo could see a tiny vein throbbing on the side of the judge's head. He wanted to reach out and smooth it.

"Don't just stand there, Hugo!" Rick fumbled for his pistol, snagged it on the lining of his pocket.

"I'm going to take care of my chocolates before they burn," the judge said carefully, slowly walking toward the kitchen. "You want to kill me, you do it in there."

Hugo followed him. He heard the spray can crash into the living-room mirror, and Rick was right behind him, cursing, waving the pistol.

The kitchen was huge, clean, and efficient, with a pink-marble cooking island, the walls lined with copper-bottomed pots and pans. An antique white-pine china cabinet in the corner had been kicked in, the floor littered with broken dishes and shards of crystal. The monkey wrench was embedded in the center of the matching white-pine dining-room table.

The judge had turned his back on the wreckage, standing over the commercial stove, stirring a double boiler. He brought a spoonful of chocolate to his lips and blew on it.

"Almost ruined," he pronounced after a cautious taste. He held out the spoon to Hugo.

Hugo shook his head.

"Skin and bones," the judge chided. "You're going to starve to death if you don't eat something."

"Not me," said Hugo, laughter bubbling up inside him too fast for him to stop it, "I'm living on love."

The judge licked the spoon clean, watching him. For the first time, Hugo thought he looked scared.

The kitchen smelled of butter and chocolate, so rich that the sensation was more tactile than olfactory, a heavy drapery of reeking sweetness. Hugo's mouth watered. The room overwhelmed his senses, overpowered his resistance. He swallowed, feeling dizzy with disgust.

The judge indicated the neat rows of candy on the marble countertop. "Try one from an earlier batch, Hugo. No? You're really missing something. I use almond butter, and bulk chocolate from this specialty outfit in Seattle, with just a touch of framboise liqueur, plus some other things, too, but that's a secret. It took me months of fooling around in the kitchen to get it right. My son loved them when he was a kid. He'd gobble them down while they were still warm, make himself sick."

Hugo glanced toward the front door. "He live here, too?"

"No . . ." The judge stared sadly at the rows of chocolates. "He's all grown up now. I hardly see him at all."

The phone on the wall rang and they all jumped.

"You've got to let me answer it," the judge said to Hugo. "People know I'm home. If I don't answer, they're going to think something is wrong."

"Finish him and let's get out of here." Rick shifted from one foot to the other.

"It might be one of my neighbors," said the judge, "wanting to know why I need a plumber. They could have already—"

Rick picked up the phone, answered with a cheery hello in that fake British accent he affected at the salon.

He smiled at Hugo. "Who am I? Who are you, luv?" He nodded at the receiver, licked chocolate off his glove. "Let me ask you something, missus . . . how much would you pay for a depilatory body sugaring? A complete body sugaring? Hmmm?" He slammed the phone down. "The wifer hung up on me."

"I want to speak to her," the judge said to Hugo.

The phone rang.

"Let me answer it," said the judge. "She'll just keep calling, getting more worried until she calls the cops. You'll have to rush off and where's the fun in that? I won't say anything to her. What good would that do?" The phone rang again. "I won't say anything about you."

"Don't let him, Hugo," yelped Rick.

"Teddy is a man of his word," said Hugo, looking right at the judge. "Besides, he'd hate to have his wife hear the sound of him dying. She'd never forget something like that."

"We're not that different, you and I," said the judge. The phone rang a third time. "We're more alike than you can imagine."

Hugo thought that one over as the judge grabbed the phone. "Hi, honey," the judge crooned, his voice so tender Hugo didn't recognize it. "How is the party? Good. I wish I was there. No, really, I do. Did you see the Chevertons?"

Rick capered near the judge, giggling, quick-drawing his revolver like a gunfighter, fanning the hammer with the side of his hand, making pow-pow-pow sounds as he pretended to shoot the judge.

"I'm almost done with the chocolates," the judge said to his wife. "I think you'll enjoy them." He played with the phone cord, listening. "I am watching my cholesterol, honey, you know me, healthy as a big old bear."

"What are you waiting for?" Rick hissed at Hugo.

The room was brighter. Hugo blinked, thinking for a moment that Rick had turned the lights up, the glare off the white tile so clear and sharp he could hardly stand it. He could see his reflection in the shiny copper bottoms of the cookware on the wall, the pistol glittering in his hand.

"Do it," chanted Rick, "do it, do it, do it."

"It's nothing," the judge said into the phone, "some nonsense on television"—he glanced at Rick—"one of those hemorrhoid commercials." Hugo had to smile. "I've got an idea, honey," the judge said. "Why don't you bring the Chevertons home with you? Ask the Piersons, too. I know it's late but ask them. We'll have cognac and truffles, make it a real party. Good."

Hugo pressed the barrel of the pistol against the judge's forehead until the skin around the barrel turned white. Their eyes stayed locked onto each other, the judge's gaze strangely soothing, luring Hugo into their gray depths.

"I'm fine," the judge said. "I just feel like company." There wasn't a trace of fear in him anymore. "You don't mind, do you? We've got plenty of time to be alone to-gether." He closed his eyes for a moment, opened them. "I love you too. Good-bye." The judge clutched the phone. "Honey!" he cried, yanking his wife back from the party. He swallowed, looked away. He had a quiet smile on his face, the same smile that Hugo knew he would find in the judge's wedding photo album, just after the I-do's. "Drive carefully."

Hugo could hear the dial tone buzz.

"Nighty-night!" yelped Rick.

The judge backhanded Rick with the phone, caught him right in the face, knocking him off his feet. "You have no idea how good that felt," he said to Hugo, breathing hard, his eyes calm as smoke. "Opportunity knocks . . . I always answer."

Hugo's hand shook slightly, unable to tear himself away from the judge's eyes. He could hear Rick groaning, trying to stand.

The judge seemed closer, just inches away from Hugo now. "Put yourself in my place," he said softly.

Put yourself in mine, thought Hugo. So much sadness. He could barely contain it . . .

The pistol jerked in Hugo's hand and there was a fine pink fog in the air—he felt it on his cheeks, a warm pink mist, tasted it at the back of his throat. Then he heard the sound of the shot echoing off the walls, heard the steady beat of phone bouncing against the floor, bobbing up and down on its spiral cord.

Hugo watched the phone until it finally stopped next to where the judge had fallen, just a few inches from his outstretched hand. The judge's legs were splayed at a weird angle. One of his shoes had come off. Hugo could see one sock stretched thin against the big toe, the sight so indecent he couldn't look away.

Then Rick was pulling on his arms, dragging him into

the hallway. Hugo still had the pistol in his hand, it was part of him now. He staggered out the front door, expecting sirens and spotlights. The night was quiet. The houses dim. A neighborhood that minded its own business.

He started into the van, but Rick was begging to drive, pleading that it was his turn and he never got to have any fun and . . . Hugo got into the passenger seat just to shut him up. Rick checked his face in the rearview, whining that the cheekbone was already beginning to swell, it was probably broken. He was wondering what shade of makeup would best cover the bruise. They drove slowly down the silent street, Rick muttering to himself while Hugo folded his hands in his lap and waited for something to go wrong.

As they drove by a large white colonial the automatic lawn sprinklers came on in a rush, the cool, fine spray floating through the open window. All down the block, one after the other, sprinklers switched on as they passed, perfectly synchronized. Hugo and Rick glanced at each other, grinning nervously. The cabin of the van crackled with electricity—Hugo could feel the hair on his arms stand up.

Rick snapped his fingers and another lawn erupted as though on command. Then another. "We're golden, Hugo, golden," he crowed, all thoughts of his swollen face forgotten as they rolled down the block. "We can do whatever we want. Whatever we fucking want."

They pulled up to the guardshack, engine idling. Hugo squinted in the glaring light, staring at his blood-speckled gloves like they belonged to someone else. Rick was talking to the old man in the shack, but Hugo couldn't make out what he was saying. He didn't even know why Rick had stopped. There was no gate. They could just drive through.

There was a series of loud pops from the front seat, then Rick floored the accelerator, burning rubber, giggling.

Hugo rolled the window down, the cool night air rushing in, blowing away the smell of gunpowder. The wind smelled of fresh-cut grass—Hugo rested his head against the back of the seat and closed his eyes.

"Candy?" Rick nudged him with an elbow. "I snagged some from the kitchen. Good, too." He smacked his lips. "You sure you don't want any? That Teddy was some cook."

Hugo kept his eyes closed, listening to the drumming of the tires on the pavement, the sound growing louder, a howling now, drowning out the judge's soft voice when he spoke to his wife, drowning out the gunshots and the cries that had come from Hugo's own throat. There was just the night and the highway stretching out before him.

Hugo slowly opened his eyes, blinked into the oncoming headlights. He reached for the chocolates next to him on the seat. He was hungry.

CHAPTER

4

"Look at that," Rachel said to Quinn, shaking her head in wonder as Joe Steps raced down the pier, wheelchair spinning, Katie on his lap, cheering him on. "She doesn't usually warm up to adults, but she acts like Joe is her new best friend."

The Seal Beach pier shuddered underfoot as the waves crashed against it. Katie had dragged them there right after the dance performance, hardly giving Quinn and Joe a chance to speak. She loved the pier at night, when it was dark and mysterious and strung with tiny lights, a rickety, wooden rollercoaster jutting three hundred feet into the Pacific.

"Teddy lied to me," Quinn said, still trying to comprehend the fact that Joe Steps was alive. He kept turning the good news over and over, knowing that something was hidden inside. "He said Joe had been killed in a car crash." Katie and Joe were far ahead of them now, the wheelchair drumming over the pier's rough-hewn planks, Katie yelling "Faster. Faster!" as they careened past startled seagulls. Quinn turned to Rachel. "Why would Teddy lie?"

"Maybe Teddy didn't know the truth, either. He may be as surprised to see Joe as you were."

"They were best friends, Rachel," he said tightly. "Teddy must have known."

The breeze off the ocean smelled of seaweed and salt and Quinn felt like he was ten years old again, getting the bad news over his cornflakes. Teddy had sat him down at the kitchen table and he got scared, because Teddy smelled of bourbon and it was morning and he never drank before noon.

The last time Teddy had booze for breakfast had been the morning Quinn woke to find his mother gone. Teddy hadn't said a word, just shoved her goodbye note to Quinn across the table. Her note to Teddy lay crumpled on the floor. Joe had showed up a few hours later. He put on a pot of coffee for Teddy, then held Quinn in his arms, letting him cry it out, not saying a word, just smoothing Quinn's hair as he sobbed.

The morning Teddy told him that Joe was dead was worse than the morning his mother left. At least that time Joe was still there. Now there was no one. Quinn remembered hanging on to the table, needing to feel something solid, wanting Teddy to look at him, hold him . . . something. Instead, Teddy stayed drunk for a week while Quinn stayed out of his way.

"Maybe they had a quarrel," said Rachel. "Sometimes when best friends have fights, the fights are forever. Maybe Teddy didn't know how to make you understand why Joe wouldn't be coming back. Ask Teddy. Ask Joe. It took two of them to keep the secret."

Joe popped a wheelie, Katie squealing with delight, hanging on to him as they hurtled back toward Quinn and Rachel, their laughter echoing through the evening, the sound so bright and clear that Quinn smiled, and even the stolid fisherman leaning against the railing turned to watch them.

"Give Teddy a chance to explain." Rachel took his hand as they walked. "Give them both a chance."

Katie hopped off his lap and she and Joe Steps played tag, her hair flying as she ducked and twisted away from him.

"You should have seen him thirty years ago," Quinn said as Joe swiveled around a woman walking with a cane, moving so gracefully you almost forgot he was sitting down. Quinn expected the old woman to be angry, but Joe turned his head as he passed, winked at her, and she grinned like a teenager. "It wasn't just the fancy clothes and cars, Joe had style. Everything he did was effortless— dancing, gambling, even the way he tied his shoes . . . he had these custom-made alligator shoes, and it was like the laces tied themselves. I wanted to be just like him when I grew up."

"You didn't turn out so badly."

"I'm not even close." Quinn shook his head. "The

sunshine was brighter when he was around. Parties got louder. Just being near him made you feel . . . special."

"I know what you mean," agreed Rachel. "He showed up at the front door in this pearl-gray suit, bowed, and said, 'Good afternoon, beautiful, can Slick come out and play?' I never heard anyone call you that, but I knew he was asking about you. I was cautious at first, but that smile . . . and there was the wheelchair, of course, and those warm, brown eyes, not innocent, not at all, but pure somehow." She shrugged. "I invited him in."

Katie hid behind the bronze seal statue that overlooked the surf. She stifled a yawn, looked over at Rachel, hoping she hadn't seen. It was almost 10 p.m. Way past bedtime.

"Joe had a cigar box full of old snapshots," said Rachel. "We spent the whole afternoon looking through them. You must have been four years old in this one photo, wearing a sailor suit . . . such skinny boy legs." The chuckle started low and husky. He loved her laugh. "My favorite was you and Joe clowning around in a big red Cadillac convertible, you pretending to drive, not even able to see over the steering wheel." She threw back her head, her throat white as cream in the murky light.

"We'd drive to Santa Anita with the top down, radio on, me and Joe singing as loud as we could, trying to drown each other out." He could still hear their voices, felt the warmth of the sun on his skin . . .

"Where was the judge while you and Joe were cruising?"

"Right there singing along with us. The Three Caballeros, that's what Teddy called us. Teddy wasn't a judge
then—he was just a guy from the same lousy neighborhood as Joe Steps, working days, going to law school at
night." He shook his head, darkening. "The best times
Teddy and I had were when Joe came to visit. After Joe was
killed . . . after Teddy told me he was killed, I was dumped
at my grandmother's. My mother's mother, Donna.
Bleached-blonde granny. Donna was as surprised to see
me as I was to see her. About as thrilled, too. I remember
her taking money from Teddy, then looking at me and
wiggling her fingers for more." Quinn laughed at the memory, but it hadn't been funny at the time. It wasn't really
funny now. "When Teddy picked me up a few months
later," he said softly, "we had a new house in a new
neighborhood. It was quieter and cleaner and nothing was
any fun."

Fog drifted in from Catalina, slowly blotting out the
stars. Rachel wrapped her long coat around her.

Joe caught up with Katie—she yawned, hanging on to
the wheelchair with one hand. She looked like she was
about to crawl up into Joe Steps's lap and fall asleep.

Rachel walked over and scooped her up. Katie pro-
tested that she wasn't tired, eyes half-closed, then leaned
over to kiss first Joe Steps goodnight, then Quinn.
Rachel kissed them both, too, saying something to Joe
before starting back down the pier, Katie slung over her
shoulder.

"We still need to talk," Quinn called after her. "Parlez-vous tomorrow?" He watched them leave, didn't take his eyes off them until they were safely in their car.

Rachel waved as she drove past.

Joe led the way out to the end of the pier, past the shuttered hamburger shop, leaving the lights and people behind. "You've filled out since the last time I saw you. What are you, six-two, six-three if you stood straight and proper?" He rocked the wheelchair back and forth, keeping himself in constant motion. "Lovely wife, little girl . . . I envy you."

"We're divorced. Almost two years now."

"That's what Rachel said. Doesn't matter, you're still a family. You'll always be a family."

Quinn let it slide. "What happened to you?"

Joe Steps patted the wheelchair. "Arthritis. No big—"

"That's not what I mean."

Joe saw Quinn's expression. "What's the problem? I thought you'd be happy to see me."

"You're twenty-eight years late, Joe." Quinn hadn't realized how angry he was. "We were all supposed to go to Disneyland, the Three Caballeros. Remember? It was a Tuesday, I stayed home from school and you never came and Teddy got a phone call . . . he got this phone call . . ." Quinn could feel a lump in his throat too big to swallow, which was ridiculous. He was thirty-eight years old, he could go to Disneyland any time he wanted.

Back down the pier there was the whirring sound of fishermen casting their lines, spinning out hooks into the darkness.

"Teddy said you had been killed. A head-on collision outside of Las Vegas." Quinn used to imagine the wreck, the scream of brakes, the car turning end over end. In his mind he saw Joe Steps with his eyes closed, sleeping through eternity, his body unscathed, suit pressed, a red rose in his lapel. "Teddy said the funeral was going to be back east, and I couldn't go. And I was glad. I couldn't stand to see you dead."

Joe smiled. "It would have been a wasted trip."

Quinn didn't return it. "Why did Teddy tell me you were dead?"

"Maybe because I was."

"No more games." Quinn grabbed the old man's shoulder. "If you and Teddy had a fight, you could have told me. You could have said good-bye." The black tuxedo wrinkled in his grip, but Joe's arm was solid and unyielding. "I hate him for lying to me, and I hate you even more for letting me believe it. You could have called. You could have written. Even my mother left a note when she took off."

"You got me wrong," Joe said quietly.

"You think you can show up now and we just start where we left off? I'm grown up, Joe. I don't need you anymore."

"I was in prison for the last twenty-eight years, Slick."

Quinn felt like he had been slapped.

Joe Steps's fingers rested on the arms of the wheelchair, his fingernails lightly tapping. It was a familiar rhythm, but Quinn couldn't place it.

"What . . . what did you do?"

Joe Steps stopped. Looked up at Quinn. "Nothing." He said it without expression. "Not a thing." His fingers resumed their tapping, hammering out the same cadence, his eyes burning. "What I was *convicted* of was murder."

Quinn finally recognized the song Joe Steps was tapping. It was the music Katie had been dancing to earlier that evening. He shivered.

"Murder in the first degree." Tap-tap-tap. "Double homicide." Tap-tap-tap. He forced his hands to be silent. "I was on death row when my sentence was reduced to life without possibility of parole." The salty breeze eddied around them and he smiled, but there was no joy in it. "Here I am, twenty-eight years later, free as a bird . . . Kind of shakes your faith in the legal system."

"Did you do it?"

Joe looked hurt. "No."

Quinn dropped to one knee and put his arms around him, ashamed to have even asked the question.

"I did write you," Joe said, cradling Quinn's face in his hands, "but my letters always came back, 'Refused,' and after a while I stopped writing. I don't blame Teddy, he was doing what he thought was best for you."

"You're here, now," said Quinn as Joe patted his hair, his hands rough and callused from the wheelchair, comforting him in a way that Teddy had never been able to. Something was broke, Joe could fix it. Something was lost, Joe could find it. Joe had the touch. They all knew it. "You came back," said Quinn, standing up slowly, feeling the night wrap itself around them. "You came back . . . that's what matters. We'll make up for lost time."

"I'd like that." Joe Steps spun his wheelchair and started back down the pier toward shore. "I remember the first time I saw your byline in the newspaper"—he shook his head, pleased—"I had no idea what you were up to, and there you were all over the front page, writing about that psycho who killed the college girls. You got him off." His expression turned bleak. "Ugly business. Somebody must have given you bum information. That what happened? Somebody set you up?"

They listened to the waves against the pier, each waiting for the other to say something.

"Yeah," said Quinn. "Not that it makes any difference. Somebody lied to me. I didn't have to believe them."

Joe cleared his throat. "I wasn't surprised you became a reporter, you were always poking your nose where it didn't belong. I had to teach you to box because you kept coming home bloody from sticking up for that kid—what was his name? If you're going to have a big heart, you better have quick hands, that's what I told you."

"Good advice," teased Quinn. "I still got beat up."

"Well"—Joe Steps grinned back at him—"there were too many of them, and they were bigger."

"I was just about to quit fighting when you started with the boxing lessons. I was going to take a different route home, let that kid take care of his problems himself, but once you got involved I couldn't run away."

"Sometimes it's better to run away." Joe licked his lips.

"I read about what happened to you a few months ago, the football player who took you apart in that hotel room."

Quinn didn't say anything.

"This football player . . . Liston, right? I remember him. I used to bet college games pretty heavy way back when. He was a linebacker, played pro ball for just a couple of games during the sixties, then got hurt. Got old. Got mean."

"He almost killed me . . ."

"You're alive." Joe Steps plucked at the spokes of his wheelchair. "You're alive and he's dead."

"No thanks to me." Quinn's voice was lost in the wind. There were tiny whitecaps on the water. "Jen . . . my girlfriend shot him. Emptied the gun into him while he held me down, beating me. His fists were so big. I remember hearing my ribs break." His legs were shaking so badly he had to hang on to the railing of the pier.

"Your girlfriend killed him. That's right. I read that. Liston had thrown her against a wall, knocked her out."

Quinn nodded. Sometimes when Jen brushed out her hair he could see the scar along the back of her head.

"So she . . . Jen, right? So Jen comes to, sees this gorilla wailing away on you, and she doesn't run away?"

"No."

"She stays." Joe slapped his leg, delighted. "Stays and blows him away. You're a lucky guy, Slick. Hang on to that one. Don't lose her."

The waves were louder against the pier, the old wood groaning under the blows.

"You should have let me know where you were all these years," Quinn said. "I'd have come to see you."

"I know." Joe sighed. "I never expected to get out. When you're looking at that kind of time, you can't allow yourself to think too much about what's outside the walls. You do that, you go crazy. Let the past stay dead, that's the only way to survive the joint."

"Does Teddy know you're out?"

"Yeah . . . Teddy and I made a start. We've got a lot of catching up to do." His eyes followed a plastic bag billow down the pier, rolling end over end until it was lost from view. "We should all get together, the Three Caballeros riding the range again. Wouldn't that be something?"

"Let me give you a lift," said Quinn. "My car's right around the corner. Where are you staying?"

"Right here in Seal Beach. You can get my number from directory assistance."

"I'll take you home—"

"Give me a raincheck, my ride's here." Joe Steps spun his wheels hard, spurted ahead of Quinn toward the taxi-cab that had pulled up next to the pier.

"I'll call you!" Quinn yelled after him.

The driver got out, popped the trunk for the wheel-chair, and opened the rear door. He watched Quinn as Joe Steps rolled toward him, then easily lifted Joe out of the chair, helped him into the backseat. The man made Quinn uneasy.

Under the amber streetlight, the driver seemed more scarecrow than human, his clothes flapping, his face a pale autumn skull. He nodded slowly, deliberately, at Quinn as he drove off, and Quinn had to fight off the impulse to chase the taxi down and pull Joe Steps free.

CHAPTER

5

"What possible use would you be to me in Paris?" Antonin Napitano sneered at Quinn across the vast expanse of polished ebony, his desk a mirrored black lake between them. The diminutive publisher of *SLAP* magazine rocked gently in a high-backed red leather chair, resplendent in white silk pajamas, spit curls carefully arranged across his brow—a languid emperor dwarfed by his imperial furnishings. He sipped water from a crystal goblet. "What would you do in Paris?"

"I don't know, Nino . . ." Quinn yawned. He sat directly across from the publisher, slouching there in his wrinkled suit, exhausted and irritable. "I could talk to Interpol, ask them how the investigation of you is going."

Napitano continued rocking. "Interpol is vastly overrated."

"Mills of the gods, Nino," smiled Quinn, "grinding slowly but ever so fine."

"Interpol no longer has any interest in me, dear boy." Nino's voice was buttery, but his eyes glittered. "Besides, you would hate Paris—the narrow streets, the sanctimonious intellectualism . . ." He shook his head. "Stay here. Stay where you belong."

Where was that, anyway? Quinn blinked in the early-morning glare from the windows—7 a.m. and nothing was well. He had driven aimlessly all night, unable to sleep, worried about the possibility of Rachel and Katie moving to Europe, overwhelmed with Joe Steps's return from the dead. Bad news and good news. He felt like a jack-in-the-box with somebody else's hand on the crank—he's sitting back, enjoying the music, next thing he knows, his head explodes.

Quinn had pulled into the *SLAP* building as the sun came up, rode the elevator to the twentieth floor, then wandered the empty halls until he stepped into the publisher's suite. He had waved sleepily to Napitano, ambled into the ornate bathroom and squeezed toothpaste on his finger, scrubbing away while Napitano reminded him there was an employees' restroom. Quinn had nodded, then wiped his mouth on one of the monogrammed towels.

"I'm not used to seeing you here so early," Napitano said, peering at him from the other side of the desk, "but then, Ms. Takamura is due back this morning, isn't she?" He steepled his fingers. "A most extraordinary woman,

Jen. I can understand your"—he savored the thought—
"eagerness."

Napitano was the first one there in the morning, the
last to leave at night. When he left. There was a canopy
bed in the suite and a soaking tub in the marble bathroom,
everything done in feverish reds and blacks and purples.
A Francis Bacon painting dominated one whole wall, a
distorted male nude writhing in ecstasy or torment—the
painting seemed right at home in that angry environment.

Jen said Napitano's office was a nasty little boy's wet
dream. Told him to his face, too. Jen was the best photographer at *SLAP*. She said whatever she wanted to. They had
been together for three months now and Quinn still
couldn't believe his luck. Jen was uncharted emotional
terrain, wild and independent and way too young for him.
She was considering getting her navel pierced. Where was
that going to lead, he wanted to know? What else was going
to get pierced? She thought his squeamishness "cute." He
hoped he was cute enough to convince her to go to Paris
with him, if it came to that.

A row of televisions was set into the wall behind
Quinn, sound off—he could see blurred images of five
different news shows reflected in the windows flanking
Napitano.

Napitano sipped his drink. "You know," he said, puck-
ering his lips thoughtfully, "I sometimes imagine what it
must be like, you and Ms. Takamura in bed—"

A familiar face flashed across the windows for a moment, too blurred to recognize—Quinn turned to the TV

sets but there were just commercials and fat weathermen pointing to their maps. He shifted back in his seat.

"Is something wrong?"

Quinn didn't answer, glanced back at the TVs again.

Napitano watched him, swirling his drink, a soft little man with a round, infantile face and eyes like dirty glass.

"You look tired." Napitano pulled a bottle of mineral water from the ice bucket beside his desk, dripping water on the Aubusson as he refilled his goblet. "Would you like an espresso? I have the beans flown in from Perugia every week."

"A double espresso would be great."

"Help yourself." Napitano nodded to the elaborate copper espresso maker that took up one corner of the room, steam tubes hissing.

"I wouldn't know where to begin. It sounds like it's about to explode."

"Pity. Helen doesn't come in until eight-thirty. She makes a lovely doppio."

"Don't you know how?"

"Of course, dear boy, but how would that look?" Napitano held the goblet aloft in the morning light, then drained it. "Me making you a cup of coffee . . ." He tossed his head at the thought, his silky pajamas billowing.

"Who would know? There's just the two of us, Nino."

Napitano belched, not bothering to cover his mouth. "Exactly."

A secretive Italian tabloid king, Napitano had suddenly liquidated his European holdings two years earlier, moving an undisclosed fortune and his vast art collection to Southern California. Bored after three months of perfect sunshine, he decided to launch a new magazine, spending lavishly to create *SLAP*, a chic, upscale monthly specializing in glamour-envy and the scent of blood in high places.

Napitano had recruited Quinn when his career was in ruins, betrayed by a source . . . a friend. Napitano said he liked individuals who were professionally disgraced, people who had risked everything for what they believed in and lost, people willing, nay eager to chop up the lifeboats as the storm gathered—"grand bloody failures" he called them, and Quinn was his favorite.

Derided at first by the mainstream press, condemned by the literati, and ignored by advertisers, *SLAP*'s blank-check exposés had since brought down a bishop of the Roman Catholic church, a network anchorwoman, and last year's #3 male box-office star. Quinn had just missed nailing California's current candidate for governor on a homicide charge. *SLAP* interviewed people who gave no interviews, photographed that which had never been seen. Circulation had quintupled and their ad rates were the highest in the industry. No one laughed at Napitano anymore.

"You still haven't told me why you want to move to Paris." Napitano leaned back in his chair, propping his tiny red velvet slippers up on the desk. "You know you can trust me."

It was true. Napitano was lewd and arrogant, a short

man given to towering rages and petty cruelties, but he was
utterly direct and unflinching in the face of opposition. In
an age when presidents apologized to vagrants and billion-
aires wore wigs and wept in court, Napitano begged no
one's pardon. He and Quinn weren't friends, but there was
a recognition between them, a shared sense of the unravel-
ing of all things, and how little they could do to stop it.
They trusted each other. It was the best they could do.

"Are you and Ms. Takamura having . . . problems?"
Napitano waggled his toes at him, and the gesture seemed
both playful and strangely obscene. "Is that the reason for
your sudden interest in la belle française? You want to get
away from her?" He dipped a small gold spoon into the
round metal tin balanced on his lap, brought it to his lips
brimming with black caviar. "I do hope your difficulties
with the lady aren't . . . sexual in nature. A young woman,
an older man . . ." He slurped the spoon clean, pushing
the caviar against the roof of his mouth with his tongue,
bursting the cold roe.

"Jen and I aren't having any problems." Quinn
watched the TVs reflected in the glass, the reverse images
shimmering and out of focus. "It's full-speed ahead for the
Love Boat."

"Would you like to see my erection?" asked Napitano.

Quinn was caught off guard, but only for a moment.
"No thanks, Nino. I scare easily."

"I'm quite serious." The spoon flashed in the sunlight.
"It's the beluga—I have four ounces every morning, four
ounces of vitamins, minerals, and certain trace elements

not yet understood by science. A full four ounces, which is why I cannot offer you a taste of my breakfast. If you like, however, I will give you the name of my Russian exporter. Beluga is very expensive, but it takes over twenty years for the sturgeon to attain her maturity. So many things can happen in that time, swimming alone in such a dark hungry sea . . ." He shook his head. "How old do you think I am?"

"Fifty-four."

"Yes . . ." Napitano pursed his lips, annoyed. "Regardless, I will match my erection against any man's, regardless of age. Not size, you understand. Size is for barbarians and homosexuals. I refer to the angle of my tumescence." The gold spoon tapped against his front teeth. "My hardness." He leaned forward slightly, his pink soft face glowing with heat. "My erection is adamantine."

"Your secret is safe with me."

Napitano sighed, sat back, and slid another spoonful into his mouth. "You Americans are so fastidious," he said contemptuously, tiny black pearls of caviar squirting onto his lower lip as he chewed.

Quinn toyed with the objects on Napitano's desk—a moon rock from Apollo XI, an inscribed shard of unglazed pottery. He picked up the Roman dagger from its place of honor, admiring the spiral ivory handle inlaid with gold, then tossed it from one hand to the other, enjoying Napitano's wince. The knife flew back and forth. Two thousand years old and its balance was perfect. He wished he could say the same thing for himself.

"Careful, mi pisano."

"Who are you really worried about?" said Quinn, slowly stropping the blade on his throat, the metal cool and sharp against his stubble. Napitano was interested now, watching with a heavy-lidded curiosity. Quinn felt the blade nick his Adam's apple, but he didn't react, wondering instead how many other throats the blade had danced across, howling barbarians and silently praying Christian martyrs. He was blood brothers now with dust and bone, part of an historical atrocity rolling down the millennia.

"I thought I heard you in here"—the woman's voice came from behind him, warm and teasing.

Quinn flipped the dagger onto the desk, turned around and smiled as Jen threw herself into his arms. He lifted her off the floor, burying his face into her thick hair. She smelled of sweat and pine trees and camp fires. She bit his ear as they spun slowly, bit him hard. He licked her neck, tasted salt, felt her nails digging into his back—

"Go ahead, fuck right here on the carpet," said Napitano, his cheeks flushed. He held the spoonful of caviar next to his mouth. "Please, do not let my presence dampen your lubricities." He wagged the spoon at them. "Ignore me."

Jen tenderly kissed Quinn on the lips, barely touching him, breathing into his parted lips. "I'm hungry, she growled, then walked quickly to Napitano's desk. She plucked the can of caviar from Napitano's lap, dug two fingers in and brought them out thick with glistening black roe. Napitano yelped as she sucked her fingers clean, then went back for more, eating until she had scooped the can clean. She licked her lips, her eyes on Quinn.

"I missed you, too," he said softly.

Quinn watched as she retrieved the camera bag she had dropped beside the door, enjoying the way she moved. She was slim, but her hips were ripe—too ripe, she said, but he liked her curves. Her face was smooth, with a full mouth and large eyes. Too *blatant* for the Japanese ideal, she said, blaming her half-white mother. Quinn woke up some nights and just stared at her sleeping on the pillow next to him and wanted to cry she was so beautiful.

She bent over the camera case, her jeans dirty, burrs stuck to the legs. Her t-shirt was smudged, her bare arms scratched. She looked up at him, caught him with those hot green eyes that knew everything.

"It was a pretty crazy week running with the wild womyn," she said. "I could use a long bath and a longer massage." She ran a hand through her tangled black hair. "I got back before sunup, just finished processing my film and printing some proof sheets and headshots . . ." She smiled at Quinn. "Finding you here is a pleasant surprise . . ."

"I'd like to see these proof sheets I paid for," interrupted Napitano, snapping his fingers. "I still have my doubts about this project . . . 'Wild Womyn Workshops,' " he sneered. "Bored suburban wives with too many tennis bracelets and not enough orgasms."

Jen's face hardened. She wordlessly flung a manila

envelope onto the desk. Quinn stood next to her, leaning over Napitano's shoulder as he pulled out the photographs.

Jen had spent the last week at a women's retreat in the Sierras, lugging her cameras up and down the rugged terrain, following the progress of eighteen women who had signed up for the rigorous blend of survival training and self-discovery. Tuition by donation only.

"That's Donna." Jen indicated a photo of a sharp-featured white teenager. "She's a single mother. Works at Burger Chef, and hopes to be a flight attendant because she thinks it's the most glamorous job in the world. Her two children sleep in the bathtub to avoid random gunfire. She left her tennis bracelet in the Mercedes."

Napitano grunted.

"That's Clarissa." Jen nodded at the overweight black woman with a short sculpted Afro. "College professor. Ph.D. in psychology. She threw up after every meal for the first two days. Force of habit."

Napitano was riffling through the pictures faster and faster, a blur of faces, young and old, women with flowers tattooed around their wrists, women with cigarette burns on their arms. Jen pointed out that they all had a similar, wary gaze. The second half of the stack of photos showed the same women, but they looked different somehow . . . exhausted but rested, streaked with dirt but clean. They looked directly into the camera. Some of them even smiled.

"I took those shots at the end of the week," said Jen.

Napitano quietly tucked the photos back into their folder.

"Nino!" Quinn barked, seeing Teddy's face appear on one of the TVs, the official photo of Teddy with his judicial robes on. "Nino! Turn up the sound!"

"Quinn?" said Jen.

Quinn hit the TV controls on the desk, fiddling with the knobs until he turned up the sound.

". . . was found last night murdered at his home in a secluded subdivision of Orange County. The cause of death was a single gunshot to the head. A security guard was also killed." A guardshack was onscreen, one of the glass panels shattered. Something had spilled on the ground.

"What's wrong?" asked Jen. "Did you know this judge?"

He couldn't talk. She was too far away to hear him anyway.

". . . while the authorities have clamped a lid on the investigation, sources close to—"

"Quinn?" Jen said. He felt her hand on his shoulder. Light as a falling leaf. "Did you know him?"

The TV station had cut to a public-service ad-on. Seat belts. Wear them. Save yourself. Save your loved ones.

Quinn nodded his head, unable to look at her. "I knew him."

CHAPTER

6

A TV news helicopter screamed overhead as Quinn
gunned the open 4X4 Jeep onto the Collingsworth Estates
exit ramp, wind howling around him.

"I know you're upset," said Jen, shouting to be heard.

"I'm not upset—" He pumped the brakes, whipped
around a rusted Pinto, spraying gravel. "I'm in a hurry. A
judge being murdered is a big story and I have access . . .
an insight that other reporters won't have. You saw how
excited Napitano got when I told him the judge was my
stepfather. You saw his face."

She squeezed his arm. "Quinn. I saw your face."

"Don't worry about me. I'm tough."

"No you're not. I'm tough, you're strong. Big difference." She took his hand. "I know what it's like to lose a
father." The wind whipped her straight black hair. "I
didn't know about Judge Krammerson . . . you never men-

tioned a stepfather. You said your mother abandoned you—"

"I didn't use that word. I never said 'abandoned.' "

"You said your mother left when you were a kid," Jen said carefully. "You said you never knew your father. The way you acted made me not want to ask you anymore about it. I thought you had been raised by a relative or foster care—"

"Teddy raised me. Tried to, anyway." Quinn kept his eyes on the winding road, wishing Teddy had come to Katie's dance performance last night. Quinn had sent him an announcement, but he should have made the invitation personal, enclosed some photos of Katie in her dance outfit. He should have at least made a phone call, told Teddy how much he would like to see him. Maybe they could all have gone out for ice cream sodas afterwards. Acted like a real family.

Teddy had seen through his equivocation, his "hope to see you there!" scrawled at the bottom of the mimeographed dance announcement. Teddy could have come, anyway. He could have taken that first step. It wouldn't have killed him. Funny. It wouldn't have killed Quinn, either. "Teddy and I . . . we weren't close. Not for a long time."

It had been years. They sent cards on holidays, sent gifts at Christmas, left messages on each other's answering machines, relieved that there was no one home. Quinn didn't remember any single incident that had caused an irrevocable rift. There was just a . . . discomfort, a steady drifting apart and no good reason to come together. Now it was too late.

Collingsworth Estates was visible from the crest of the hill, a mass of vibrant green spread across the dry brown hills overlooking the ocean. There was a drought in Southern California; restaurants no longer served glasses of water unless asked, lawns were left to die or paved over and painted to look like grass. Not in Collingsworth Estates. No wonder they put a brick wall around the place.

Teddy had moved there three years ago, right after he married Marie, and she decided that a superior court judge and his wife deserved a better zip code than the house on Ravenna. Quinn hadn't made it to the housewarming, too busy staking out a wrecking yard that night, working on an auto-repo investigation. He should have gone.

Backyard swimming pools shimmered in the distance, cool and blue. Teddy had asked him once if Katie knew how to swim. "Sure," Quinn had said, then waited for an invitation which never came. Maybe Teddy thought they didn't need one.

It was barely 9:30 a.m. as Quinn and Jen reached the entrance, saw a line of police cars and satellite-dish news vans parked along the side of the road in front of the guard kiosk. Two police cars blocked the way, light-bars flashing blue and red, narrowing it to one lane. A cluster of uniforms leaned against their cruisers, drinking coffee, talking with reporters. Radio probably, or newspapers. Otherwise the cops would be at attention, no coffee or donuts evident.

Police spokesperson Manuel Vargas was doing a stand-up with Allison Tate of KHTS-TV, the camera framing the shattered glass of the guardshack. Quinn could see the chalk outline of a leg sticking out, surrounded by a bloodstain. Allison Tate nodded solemnly into the camera while one hand idly scratched her hip. Vargas was wearing a reassuring expression and a dark blue suit that probably cost a patrolman's monthly salary. Worth every penny of it, too. He could give the department's version of the mistaken arrest and strip search of the pope's grandmother and make it seem justifiable.

A cop held up his hand as Quinn's Jeep neared, then jabbed his thumb toward the side of the road. He was a gruff redheaded veteran with a nasty sunburn. Quinn held up his Press ID but the cop waved it away. "Rancho Shangri-La here is private property—no one goes in who don't live there, or has official business. You want a press update, wait in line for Manny like the rest of 'em."

"I'm . . . family. Judge Krammerson is . . . was my stepfather."

"Yeah, and my stepfather's Clarence Thomas."

"Call it in, officer. Okay?"

The redhead grunted, then took Quinn's ID over to a squad car where he consulted with a bored lieutenant, who was spooning yogurt out of a plastic cup. The lieutenant looked over at Quinn, still eating, chewing with his mouth open, finally picked up his radio mike. He talked in between bites.

Quinn's phone beeped. "Hello." It was Rachel returning his call. "I'm fine," he said as Jen pretended not to listen. "Does Katie know?"

"I told her," said Rachel, "but she didn't seem too upset. She doesn't really remember the judge."

"Teddy wasn't part of her life. That's what happens . . . kids need regular contact, you can't do that long distance . . ." His voice trailed off, wanting her to make the connection, to say she wasn't taking Katie to Paris. She didn't say a word. He saw the lieutenant hang up, then exchange more words with the redhead before going back to his yogurt.

"Quinn . . ." Rachel lowered her voice, and he had to press the receiver against his ear to hear. "I wish I could help . . . but I can't."

Quinn listened to the dial tone, feeling Jen's eyes on him.

The redhead walked over, handed Quinn's ID back. "Go ahead."

"Can you give me directions? I know it's on Forty-seventh."

"Real close-knit family, huh?" the redhead chuckled. "Ok, John-Boy. Take the first right, then a left. You'll see it."

Jen readied her camera equipment while Quinn drove them down the deserted streets, finally spotting what must have been a dozen cars parked in front of a big brick house—regular marked units, the nondescript gray-blue Plymouths the undercover cops preferred and three forensics vans. Five techs in white coveralls crawled on their hands and knees along the winding driveway, another was on the front porch. Parked illegally across the street was a white Rolls Corniche with a GREENPEACE bumper sticker.

Before the Jeep could come to a complete stop, a pair of plainclothes detectives appeared, eyes invisible behind dark glasses, hands on their weapons. The big one in the worn blue corduroy sportcoat leaned against Quinn's door, but Quinn barely glanced at him—he held up his ID, concentrating his attention on the short one who had taken a position next to Jen. A sleek Asian-American cop wearing a black Members-Only nylon jacket.

The big cop pretended to blow his nose on Quinn's ID.

"Boyle?" Quinn wiped off his ID. "Boyle, you suave son of a bitch."

The big cop lifted up his sunglasses, grinning. "At your service."

Sergeant Vince Boyle was an acne-pitted barrel of guts with twelve departmental commendations for bravery, a survivor of three Internal Affairs investigations. Once, after giving a speech at the Police Academy graduation, he had whoopie-cushioned himself—a photo of his shocked innocence made the front page of the Police Guild newsletter that month.

"I can't believe they fell for your 'family of the deceased' horseshit at the gate," guffawed Boyle.

"It's true. Judge Krammerson was my stepfather."

"Oh man . . . I am sorry." Boyle looked pained. "Come on. We got to go in the back way so's we don't track things up."

Quinn hoisted himself out of the Jeep. Jen started to open her door, but the other detective held it shut.

"Stay in the vehicle, miss," Members-Only growled.

"She's with me, detective," said Quinn.

"That's her problem," said Members-Only. He had a pale scar that curved down his neck. "You were cleared through the gate. Not her. She shouldn't even be here."

"Go on, Quinn," said Jen.

Boyle sucked on a tooth.

Quinn and Members-Only stared at each other, the detective rocking on his heels, the scar along his neck pulsing slowly. Quinn outweighed him by fifty pounds, but the man looked like he wanted Quinn to make a move on him.

"It's fine, Quinn," said Jen.

Boyle ducked under the yellow perimeter tape. Quinn looked at Jen, then followed Boyle across the lawn. "I didn't recognize you at first," Quinn said. "You've been eating for two. Two hundred."

Boyle grabbed his thick love handles with two hands. "I think my metabolism must be changing . . . The captain's giving me a hard time, and my old lady's climbed on the bandwagon, too, said she doesn't want to fuck no whale. Ask me, I think she needs to see a marriage counselor."

Quinn saw Members-Only stationed beside Jen's door, following their progress.

"Don't mind Yamada," said Boyle, breathing hard as they made their way up the steep slope of grass, "he'd like to hand you your dentures, but it's not personal. He just don't like to see his cherry blossoms with white guys."

They crested the hill and Jen was lost to sight.

"Yamada always gives away the first punch," said Boyle. "You take your best shot, then he kicks the shit out of you. He even gives a little bow afterwards. Sometimes I think me and Yamada are the last real cops left."

"Sorry if I disappointed you."

"Hey, the day is young. Besides, I seen you fight, you might have surprised him. Either way it would have been worth a peek. Break up the tension. I been to more crime scenes than Carter got pills, and this is the worst party I ever worked. The suits are falling all over themselves, and the forensic nerds brought all their new toys and won't let anybody else play."

A harsh blue light flared from inside Teddy's house and they stopped to watch.

"That's what I'm talking about." Boyle nodded toward the big bay window. "You ever seen a Luma-Light? There's only one in the whole county. It's this hot-shit arc lamp, uses metal vapor—better than a laser—you can spot every eyelash and cum stain in a shag carpet. Nobody's talking, but I think they came up with something on the doormat."

"You're kidding. The bad guys wiped their feet?"

"Happens all the time. Habits"—he patted his stomach—"habits do all of us in." He yawned, scratching his bristly jowls. He needed a shave.

"How long have you been here?"

"Since just before midnight." Boyle yawned again, mouth wide, yellowed teeth on display. "I was the first cop on the scene—caught the call over my radio, popped out the gumball, and ran every light. I saw the mess at the guardshack and knew there wasn't going to be no happy ending. Look at these houses." He waved at the huge homes nearby, the lavish landscaping. "You got a million-dollar neighborhood here, and they hire these ten-dollar-an-hour retired military police to man the front gate." He shook his head, disgusted. "Throwing drunks in the brig don't prepare you for what's out there on the street. Not nowadays."

"If you were first on the scene, how did you draw the valet-parking detail? Why aren't you inside?"

Boyle spit, almost splashed his black crepe-soled shoes. "Don't get me started." His face was getting redder, the deep acne scars flaring purple. "Deputy Chief Feyse shows up around three a.m. in full regalia, takes charge, then asks for my notebook, my fucking notebook, which is a clear violation of departmental rules, and when I tell him I will be happy, sir, to type up a complete report, sir, he tells me to stand out on the street and guard the curb. 'Guard the curb.' That pasty-faced REMF actually told me to guard the fucking curb." He spit again. "Twenty-three years ago my brother asked me to go into the rental appliance business with him. Today, he wakes up in a mansion in Holmby Hills, and I spent the night standing in the gutter someplace where the gardeners make more than I do."

"Yeah, I can see you demonstrating the automatic icemaker of the new Frigidaire."

Boyle laughed, fumbled a crumpled pack of cigarettes out of his pocket, pulled out the last one. It was bent almost in half, but he didn't bother straightening it. Neither of them spoke until he had taken three deep drags, exhaling smoke into the cool clean air. He turned at last to Quinn. "I'm sorry about the judge."

"Me too."

"He ran a good court—no bullshit, no excuses, no mercy."

Quinn watched Boyle smoke. "What happened last night? Was there a break-in? Teddy come home and surprise somebody?"

"Teddy? You call Judge K., Teddy?" Boyle shook his head, coughed, flicked the butt into the grass. It sizzled on the dew.

"Talk to me, Boyle."

Boyle picked a fleck of tobacco off his front tooth, stared at his fingertip. "It wasn't no break-in." He wiped his finger on his jacket. "The sergeant at the gate said you needed directions to get here." He looked at Quinn. "The judge has been living here for three years . . . what's your hurry to visit now?"

They turned at the whomp-whomp-whomp sound, saw the newscopter hovering nearby. "They been flying around all morning," said Boyle, squinting as they followed its slow progress. "If it's not one station it's the other. What the hell they think they're going to see from up there?"

"They don't care what they can see," said Quinn, "they just want to make the viewer think he's part of the action."

"They're not part of nothing," Boyle said. "They're sitting in their living room in their skivvies. We're here, not them. TV turns everybody into a looky-loo." He waved at the helicopter, grinning as it dipped closer, the pilot indistinct behind his plastic bubble, anonymous as a mosquito in the dark. Quinn smiled, seeing that Boyle's friendly wave had turned into a middle-digit salute.

CHAPTER

7

"I could give you a sea-salt rubdown later," chirped Rick, "exfoliate your skin cells, buff up the old aura . . . ?"

Hugo heard the squirt of shampoo, felt Rick working his fingers through the foaming lather. Hugo lay with his eyes closed, wrapped in a white cotton robe in the stylist's chair of the little salon Rick had set up in his living room. Horns beeped from the nearby freeway but Hugo barely noticed, only vaguely aware of Rick swaying against him, singing to himself.

"Nancy Tyler-Tuck did an on-the-spot report from our crime scene early this morning," said Rick. "She dive-bombed the judge's house in the Channel 8 skycopter. You see it?"

Hugo opened one eye. Posters of James Dean and Christian Slater and Wayne Gretsky smirked from the walls.

"You didn't?" Rick was incredulous, slouched in a billowy silk shirt imprinted with red cherries and baggy pleated trousers. There was a faint purple bruise on one cheek where the judge had hit him with the phone. He switched on the TV, scrolled past the game shows and infomercials. No news. "Maybe later. I wonder what one of those skycopters costs?" he mused. "If I had one of those I could land in a client's backyard for a private cut and consultation, drop right down on their tennis court."

Hugo tried to ignore Rick's chatter, focusing on the moment, the infinite now stretching forward and back in time, going round and round and round—

"That fat anchorman from Channel 5 did his stand-up right where I popped the guard," said Rick. "John Corey, that was the guard's name. Retired from the Navy last year. They showed a picture of him in his uniform, saluting. Terrible haircut. I guess that's why they call them jar-heads."

"Swabbies. Sailors are swabbies. Marines are jar-heads."

"Guardshack was totally trashed," said Rick, soaping the nape of Hugo's neck, "blood all over the glass—it looked like a bottle of cherry Coke exploded in there." He nodded, swaying happily. "You'll like this shampoo. It's five percent lamb placenta, really builds up the keratin in your hair, makes it fuller."

Hugo stared at himself in the mirror and didn't recognize his own face. His ascetic cheekbones stood out in high relief like wings of bone. He had seen angel wings in his face yesterday. Now he saw bat wings. Rick bobbed around him, silk shirt fluttering, his pompadour tipped with food-color purple. Hugo always saw Rick as a beautiful bird, a garrulous parrot with bright plumage . . . today he noticed the dead eyes and cruel hooked beak.

"You're quiet," said Rick. "You're thinking all the time. It's like they say about still waters . . . lay down beside the still waters, something like that. It means you're real deep, like that cold lake in Scotland where the sea serpent lives."

Hugo stiffened, hearing footsteps on the stairs— groceries shifted in a paper sack as whoever it was walked past Rick's door and continued down the hall. Hugo had to force himself to exhale. His hands trembled. He was never going to regain his balance, his composure, his perfect stillness, achieved at such cost and so easily shattered.

After they had linked up, he and Rick had moved into a peach-colored apartment complex near the Orange County Airport, their third-floor units directly across from each other, separated by a wide stairwell. Leaning against the rickety iron railing outside his door, Rick could spit into the pink, heart-shaped swimming pool in the courtyard below.

The developer had planned the building as a twenty-four-unit swinging-singles complex, but the sexual economy had soured along with the job market. The tenants were drawn in by the FIRST MONTH'S RENT FREE! sign more than the promise of nude backgammon tournaments. The swimming pool needed cleaning, the jacuzzi was broken, and someone had slashed up the red velour conversation couches in the lounge downstairs.

"You were late last night," said Rick.

"Are you keeping track of me?"

"I was afraid something went wrong after I dropped you off."

"You dumped the van near the bar? You disposed of the coveralls, the shoes, the guns?"

Rick nodded.

"Fine. You did your job, I did mine." Hugo's hands clenched, hearing again the echo of the shot he had fired into the judge's forehead.

"I expected to see your light on when I got back, that's all," said Rick. "It must take forever, lugging old Joe and his wheelchair in and out of your cab, huh?"

Hugo remembered watching Joe Steps talk with the man on the pier . . . Quinn, that's what Joe called him, a big guy who moved easy, standing right next to Joe, like he belonged there. Hugo had watched from the darkness of a side street, wondering if the guy with Joe was a cop, which made no sense, but he worried just the same.

"Is that who we're working for, Hugo? Is old Joe the one who's paying us?"

"We've been over this before—"

"Well, why can't I know? I can keep a secret." He drew his fingers across mouth, zipping his lips.

"I'm the only one who needs to know," Hugo said patiently. "It's safer that way."

"Safer for who?"

So much for the zipper. "Safer for the man we're working for. Who else?"

"Did you see me quick-draw that guard last night?"

Rick said abruptly, distracted by a vagrant thought. "Did you?" He made pow-pow-pow sounds, shooting with one hand, shampoo bubbles dripping off his aimed fingertip. "I almost didn't stop, this was our big getaway and all—then I figured, why should Hugo have all the fun?"

"It wasn't fun."

"That guard never saw it coming," Rick chirped, lathering away. "That first bullet busted through the back cover of the magazine he was reading. He didn't even react at first, he just slowly puts the magazine down and there's blood all over the pages and he stares at the mess like it belongs to somebody else, then he topples off his chair . . ." Rick laughed at the memory. "He looks up at me from the floor, this dumb rent-a-cop with the blotchy skin and big pores, and he put his hands up in front of his face, like that was going to stop me. Now there was a guy who could have used a paraffin-hibiscus masque."

Hugo rose half out of his chair, disgusted.

"Sorry." Rick gently wiped shampoo away from Hugo's eyes, not understanding. "I put a bullet through each palm," Rick preened, "and he got the message quick enough—Western Union calling, you're dead, motherfucker." He tilted the chair back over the sink, started rinsing Hugo's hair.

Hugo closed his eyes.

"Maybe it's just my imagination," said Rick, "but I think I radiate a certain . . . I don't know, intensity, a dangerous, very bankable intensity, like Andre Agassi or Eddie Veder. Once I get my own salon, I bet I get some serious haircare and makeup endorsements."

It hurt to listen to Rick. Particularly after last night. It was easier when Hugo could dismiss him as a garrulous fool who had seen too many action movies. Hugo liked Rick better when he'd thought he was all talk.

"I'm not putting down the way you took out the judge," said Rick, slathering on conditioner, his hands making slippery sounds as he worked it in, "that's who you are, straight and to the point, and let's be honest—you don't really enjoy the work. Me, I'm an artist. Not just hair, everything I do is a work of art. Anybody can pull a trigger—I like to think I used some creativity on the guard, a little imagination. That's what the clients want, high-end clients. You want to cut hair in Beverly Hills, you need imagination."

Hugo slowly sighed, pushing out the screech of existence, the devouring lust . . . another sigh, longer now, one long exhalation, a single stretched note, the only song he knew, resonating from his quiet heart, beyond the dirt of humanity, the bodies, the fears, the endless scuttling. Hugo wanted none of it. Warm water sluiced through his hair, water the temperature of blood, washing him clean.

Rick blotted Hugo's forehead with the towel, feet tapping as he sized up the situation, scissors out, absently clicking, lips puckered in thought. He belted on the leather shoulder-holster he had custom-made for his three silver-plated styling scissors.

"Your hair . . ." Rick plucked at the top of Hugo's head. "All these cowlicks." He whipped out the smallest scissor from its holster, eyes wide as he circled the chair, bits of hair dropping onto Hugo's shoulders. Rick delicately folded one of Hugo's ears down with a fingertip. "You sure you don't want me to do a modified fade? Maybe angle the sideburns? It would make you look younger, more fashion forward—this nuevo-preppy hairstyle of yours is quelle fucking passé."

"I know who I am."

"Lucky you," sneered Rick. "Last train to Dullsville and you're the engineer. Chugga-chugga-chugga." The scissors snapped away, swooping and diving. "I was talking to those guys in 22B"—he spoke with the same lilting rhythm as his shears—"the guys in the metal band, well, not exactly metal, more like industrial romanticism—"

"They work in a juice bar."

"People have a right to dream," Rick said. "You got dreams, right, Hugo?"

Hugo didn't answer.

Rick stopped his scissor work. "I know you do, Hugo." His fingers gently kneaded Hugo's temples, making small circles, and Hugo gave in to it. "You need to share your dreams, advertise them," said Rick, "that's how you make them happen." He nodded toward the kitchen—a new picture was taped to the front of the refrigerator, a photo of a sleek black helicopter torn out of a magazine. "See it, validate it."

"It's just a piece of paper," Hugo said. "I wish it was more than that. We'd all be cutting out paper dolls."

Rick ran a hand through his own hair, preening for the mirror like he was the only person in the room. "The guys in the band told me the honcho from Warners suggested they do something with their look, maybe get different shaped guitars, tart up their hair. I told them I had some ideas." His scissors grazed Hugo's ear but he didn't apologize. "That's why I was so upset when you were late last night. I was still excited about the judge, then I ran into the band in the hallway and they laid some crystal-GHB on me. I thought we could snort a few lines and go dancing."

"I don't like drugs. You know that."

"GHB isn't drug. It's more like an amino acid that fucks you up."

"I had to wait for Joe. Then when he got in the cab he wanted to drive around, look at all the new buildings and shopping centers. He said he hardly recognizes the area, everything is so different. He's lonely . . . I like him."

Rick shoved the scissors into his holster. "Is that what you and old Joe talk about on those long drives? How lonely he is?" Rick's face was hideous in the mirror. "Maybe you should go dancing with him?—give Joe a little spin on the dance floor? That would be a trip."

Hugo grabbed him by the shirt. Buttons popped.

"I'm sorry." Rick placed a hand on Hugo's chest, not pushing, more like pleading. "It's just that I waited for you to come home and when you finally did you didn't even look over and wave or anything, just opened your door and walked inside. You were thinking about somebody, but you weren't thinking about me. I was the furthest thing from your mind. You were thinking about Joe."

In fact, Hugo had been thinking about Quinn. He could still see him standing at the edge of the pier, partially in shadow, watching Hugo help Joe into the cab. Something about Quinn's interest, his concern, had made Hugo uncomfortable. Like he knew where Hugo had been. Like he knew what Hugo had done.

Had he really done that? Did he really stand in a man's warm kitchen, look deep into his eyes and blow his life out like a candle? He remembered staring at his shoes in the van afterwards, seeing the fine red pinheads of blood and knowing nothing was ever going to be the same again.

"You want me to give you a facial? I got this new volcanic mud from Hawaii, supposed to be slightly radioactive."

Hugo shook his head.

"Come on, lighten up," said Rick. "You were the same way about letting me give you a shampoo. How many times did I have to ask? A million? A billion? Now you like it, right? Trust me. I'll put the mud in the microwave, heat it up—" He waved the scissors at the TV, turned up the sound. "It's our crime scene, Hugo! A live remote!"

The helicopter camera panned across a cluster of police cars parked in front of the judge's house, lines of yellow tape flapping in the breeze, the scene barely recognizable from the quiet street of last night.

"That's where I left rubber peeling out the driveway," chattered Rick. "I bet they already ran a make on the tire tread, they got computers can do it. Good luck, Lt. Columbo!" he mocked the screen. The announcer-pilot was describing the brutality of the crime, the murder of the guard. "They haven't said a thing about my spray paint," he pouted. "I told you, I should have marked an outside wall. That way they could see it from the air."

"Shhhh," said Hugo, leaning forward as the camera hovered over two figures walking across the judge's front lawn.

"What did I say?"

The camera zoomed in and Hugo recognized one of the two men squinting up at the helicopter—Quinn. He was wearing the same suit he had on last night. Hugo had watched Joe in the rearview mirror as he drove him home, wondering what this Quinn had said that made Joe so happy. Hugo rubbed his temples as he stared at the TV, his brain boiling with a rage that was as sudden as it was inexplicable.

"You're always getting mad at me," said Rick, "and I never know what I did wrong."

Hugo saw Quinn cock his head, shading his eyes from the sun, and for some reason he reminded Hugo of the judge—Teddy had looked at Hugo with that same frank curiosity. As if he didn't have anything to worry about either.

"What did I do wrong?"

"It's alright," said Hugo. "You're not the one who did anything wrong."

8

Marie Krammerson came from behind the house, striding toward them, black dress boiling around her knees, her hair pulled severely back. Deputy Chief Feyse, a nervous bureaucrat who had never pulled his weapon in the line of duty, tried to keep up, slipping on the grass. His gold epaulets flashed in the sunlight.

"She's been putting Feyse through his paces all morning," Boyle grinned. "He kept trying to get her to sit down, even offered to have his driver take her to a friend's house, but she wouldn't leave. She stayed in the kitchen the whole time they bagged the judge, even yelled at the M.E. for handling the body like a side of beef—that's what one of the forensics guys told me. You believe that?" He patted his greasy hair. "Judge K. knew how to pick 'em. I'd give my left nut for a broad like that."

Marie turned on her heel, said something to the Deputy Chief. He reluctantly started back to the house.

"Take me, Jesus," murmured Boyle, smoothing his jacket as Marie approached them, "I've seen it all now."

Quinn shifted awkwardly, not sure what to do. Her eyes were red-rimmed, drilling into him. He could see tiny pearls embroidered across the bodice of her black evening dress. Teddy must have loved that outfit. He held his arms out to her. "Marie . . ."

She stepped in close, slapped him so hard his ears rang. Slapped him again, even harder this time. He couldn't move his arms, they were nailed to his sides.

Boyle caught her hand as she swung again. She twisted in his grip, her dark eyes so fierce that for a moment Quinn thought she was going to bite him.

"Three strikes and you're out, Mrs. K.," Boyle said good-naturedly, letting her go. "Your son-in-law—"

"You will kindly not refer to this . . . gentleman as my son-in-law," Marie glared at Boyle, her lower lip trembling. "The only reason I acknowledged him as a family member was so that I could slap his face personally."

"What did I do?" said Quinn, rubbing his fiery cheek.

"Don't you dare show up at the judge's funeral," she raged. "If you could not find the time to visit him while he was alive, I will be damned if I will allow you to put in an appearance now that he's . . . gone." She wiped at her eyes, smeared mascara, then drew herself up straight. "You are not going to get off that easily."

Boyle offered her a handkerchief, which she ignored. It looked like he was sucking in his stomach.

"Please, Marie," said Quinn.

Marie's expression shifted between anger and exhaustion, and suddenly she was sobbing. She grabbed the handkerchief from Boyle. "I won't have you at the funeral," she repeated to Quinn, wiping at her eyes. "You don't belong there."

Quinn wished he could argue with her, make her understand why he had never visited, never called Teddy up to see how things were going. It was like they had started playing a game of you-first, and time passed and they forgot it was a game, and now Quinn was the only one left and it was no fun to play anymore.

He had to look away, but seeing the glaring blue light through the living room windows was as bad as seeing the pain in Marie's face. He kept his eyes down, noting the thick roll of the lawn, the neat beds of yellow tulips bordering the house. Teddy loved order and precision, saw them as a barrier against the ragged chaos of the world.

Marie stared at the crumpled handkerchief in her hand, then handed it back to Boyle. "I know you, Officer." She looked surprised. "You were the first one to arrive this morning. Sergeant . . . Boyle, isn't it? You were very helpful. Where did you disappear to?"

Boyle worked his jaw. "Deputy Chief Feyse took over the scene, and I"—he swallowed—"well, he suggested I take up a station outside."

"I was sitting with Jean Cheverton when you walked in the front door. It seemed like only moments since I had dialed 911 and I saw you and thought, who is this disheveled man in my living room? I misjudged you, Officer. I apologize."

"Nothing to apologize for, Mrs. K. Not after what you came home to. Not many women could have kept it together the way you did. Men neither. Men are worse, most of them fall apart like a two-dollar watch. You, you're one cool cucumber."

"I was wrong about you, Sergeant. The officers who arrived later were the ugly ones—all these bright young men and women bustling through our home in their rubber gloves, chattering away as they worked, talking about television shows and sports scores." She dabbed at the corners of her eyes. "Not you, Sergeant. I brought you to the kitchen, and you stayed in the doorway, taking it all in, and when you saw . . . when you saw Teddy, you crossed yourself."

"No, m'am—"

"Don't be coy with me, Sergeant." Marie stamped her foot. "I roomed with a Catholic girl at Stanford, Mary Ellen Byrne. You crossed yourself—you were quick about it, but I saw you. No one else, not one of all those people who saw my husband's body . . . who touched my husband's body, made the slightest show of respect. It was all words from them. 'Sorry.' 'My condolences.' Words, just words."

"Is there anything I can do for you, Mrs. Krammerson?"

"Yes, Sergeant." Marie laid her hand on Boyle's arm, and Quinn could see that she was shaking. "You can walk me to the house. I'm very tired and there is so much to do."

Boyle patted her hand with his paw. "Stay here until I get back," he told Quinn as they walked away. "You wait."

"Marie?" called Quinn. "Did Teddy ever mention a

man named Joe Steps? An old friend, he's in a wheel-chair now."

She didn't even look back.

Quinn waited, just like Boyle said. He waited until they disappeared into the house, then started after them. He imagined Teddy walking across the wet grass in his bare feet, wriggling his toes. Teddy had grown up in an asphalt world; he used to say a lawn was the ultimate luxury.

When he got to the rear of the house Quinn saw three cops standing around the patio, drinking coffee from Styrofoam cups and talking. A female officer wearing a white forensics smock and disposable surgical booties sat on the brick barbecue eating a sandwich, taking dainty bites. Her feet swung back and forth as she chewed, the knees of her trousers smudged with dusting powder.

The conversation eddied as Quinn strode among them, heads turning toward him. He nodded familiarly to the female forensics officer. The crusts had been cut off her sandwich, which was thick with alfalfa sprouts. "Anybody seen Boyle?" he asked, wanting to cut off any questions about who he was and what he was doing there.

A bull-necked sheriff's deputy grunted something about Boyle and they all laughed. Quinn joined in, too, then turned away from them, edged closer to the sliding glass doors. He could see into the dining room, saw a broken pine sideboard and chairs smashed to pieces. A forensics crew worked a grid pattern search on the floor, squatting on their haunches to avoid the strewn broken glass. It hurt to look at the room—Teddy was so particular about his things, hating any kind of waste or sloppiness.

Quinn tried to remember the last time he had seen Teddy. It was over a year ago—they had lunch at a Mexican tacqueria far from the courthouse. Teddy was the only Anglo regular, the only one in the restaurant wearing a three-piece suit. They ate fish tacos laced with jalapeños, washed them down with bottles of Dos Equis, busying themselves eating and drinking. Teddy had to loosen his tie from the heat of the hot peppers. It was a good time. They fought over the check. Teddy won. They never saw each other again.

Quinn blinked as the conversation behind him started up again. The deputy was arguing with one of the uniforms over the way Teddy had died, his voice drowning out the rest of them. "The judge was shot at close range, right, Arlene?"

Quinn heard a woman's voice—it must have been the forensics tech—say something about powder burns and the lack of a contact wound, "six inches maybe," she said, her voice as dainty as her nibbles, "no more than a foot away."

Quinn winced, seeing Teddy staring into the barrel of a gun, waiting for the hammer to fall. He moved along the back of the house until he was facing into the kitchen, a large room ablaze with the high-voltage lamps the medical examiner used. There was red spray paint on the walls—at least he hoped it was spray paint. There were words, but it was hard to read in the glare from the spotlights.

"A foot away," repeated the deputy. "Then the judge wasn't the big man you think he was," he jeered. Any man with the balls God gave him, has to make a grab for a gun that close. Has to. If he don't, he's a pussy, a flat-out pussy."

Quinn turned and stared at the deputy, wanting to shut him up. Teddy was past caring, but he wasn't.

"Give it a rest, Millikin," Arlene said to the deputy. "You don't know what you'd do. None of us do."

Quinn could see a chalk outline on the tile floor of the kitchen, a small puddle of blood outside the chalk border. Such a small stain. Quinn had seen more blood when he cut his thumb laying carpet in Katie's bedroom.

"I know I wouldn't stand there waiting to catch a slug like a B-movie zombie," said the deputy. "The judge didn't make a move on the shooter, did he? He just took it, didn't he?"

"I can't give you a definitive answer until the autopsy," Arlene said wearily, "but it looked like the bullet strike was direct to the forehead, as opposed to a glancing shot."

"So?"

"Which would indicate that the judge was stationary at the moment of impact."

"What I tell you?" crowed the deputy. "Judge went down without a whimper. Christ, you wouldn't see me taking it like that. Like I'm a good little boy and grateful for it. I'd go out kicking and screaming and it damn straight would take more than one round to put me down."

Quinn's fists were so tight that his fingernails left

marks in the palms of his hands. He tried to relax, to turn away from the yellow chalk outline in the kitchen, but he couldn't. He stood there. All that chrome and copper, polished so bright . . . it made his eyes water.

Teddy loved being in the kitchen—he had to learn how to cook after Quinn's mother left, and he also learned that he liked creating a recipe, liked filling a room with good smells. Quinn remembered looking up from his plate, mouth stuffed with steak and fried onions, and seeing Teddy smiling, happy to watch him eat.

This was the kitchen where Teddy had fixed breakfast for himself yesterday, French toast maybe, the kitchen where he brewed his strong coffee with two spoons of sugar . . . and last night, while Quinn was pissed off, waiting for him to show up for Katie's recital, this is where Teddy had died.

In the living room, Quinn could see Marie sitting on a pale-yellow loveseat next to an older man with chiseled, patrician features. That room must have already been vacuumed and dusted, neither of them were wearing surgical smocks or booties. The man wore a dark blue suit, his legs crossed at the knee. He wasn't a cop. He looked like money and power, a man who would own a white Rolls.

Marie sat fingering her wedding band and crying. She wasn't the same woman who had slapped the hell out of him a few minutes ago. She seemed frail now, her shoulders slumped. Quinn wished she had let him comfort her—it might have done them both some good.

The man patted Marie's arm, head nodding sympathetically. He saw something on his shoe, absently wiped it on the loveseat, still nodding, listening to Marie weep. The man looked directly at Quinn, stared right at him, his face impassive, and Quinn took a step backwards, not knowing why, feeling somehow that he had just lost an argument.

There was something faintly familiar about the man— a distant memory, not so much of his face but of his manner, the conflicting signals he sent: concerned and contemptuous as the same time. Quinn kept trying to remember.

"Maybe the judge was a tough customer once upon a time," the deputy said, interrupting Quinn's train of thought, "but he forgot where he came from, living the soft life out here among the richies with their four-car garages and Irish crystal. Well, his fancy crystal is all over the floor; it didn't help him. He'd have been better off packing a piece. That's what I do. On the street, on the crapper—if you see me, I'm armed and dangerous."

Quinn stared at the ruined white walls of the kitchen, trying to ignore the deputy's bluster. Quinn had been lying in a white room the last time he had seen Teddy, lying doped up in the hospital after almost being beaten to death by Emory Roy Liston, a psychotic ex-football player. Quinn had drifted along in that white bed with the sheets tucked in too tightly, dreaming of Liston, the sheer enormity of him, seeing those huge fists raining down. He had cried out in his sleep, opened his eyes and saw Teddy sitting in a chair next to the bed, holding his hand. Quinn had tried to speak but Teddy was already fading, until all that remained was the warmth of his touch.

When Quinn awoke he was alone. The nurses said no one had been in to see him, and Quinn had dismissed it—a missed opportunity, one that would never be made right.

He squinted into the kitchen—he could read the words on the walls now, see the dripping red swastikas. What had Teddy gotten himself into? Whatever it was, Quinn was going to find out. It was the last promise he would make to Teddy.

"You tell me how the hitter got in, Arlene," demanded the deputy. "There was no forced entry. The hitter rang the bell and the judge invited him inside, just rolled out the red carpet. How stupid can even a judge be?"

Quinn was moving across the patio before he was aware of it. His first punch split the deputy's lip, snapped back his head in a spray of blood. The next one caught him under the eye, sent a jolt of pain through Quinn's knuckles. Someone grabbed him before he could hit him again.

Boyle wrapped his arms around Quinn from behind, holding him in an iron grip against his soft belly. "No fair, champ," he whispered. "If anybody's going to knock the shit out of Millikin, it's gonna be me."

The deputy stood unsteadily, clutching the air for support, trying to focus his eyes.

The other cops watched. One had his hand resting on the butt of his pistol. Arlene was hiding a smile behind the last of her alfalfa sprouts.

"You're okay, aren't you, Milly?" said Boyle, leading Quinn off the patio. "Big strong guy like you ain't gonna let some civie cold-cock him. Word gets out, you might as well strap on some tits—no offense, Arlene—and put in for meter maid."

The two of them started up the hill. "I told you to stay put," grumbled Boyle. "You want to end up in jail? I don't know about you, but I got better things to do."

Quinn was walking so fast that Boyle could barely keep up.

CHAPTER

9

Joe Steps could see blue sky and thick white clouds through the canopy of jacaranda branches that overhung the swimming pool. Purple blossoms floated past, tickling his hair, grazing his shoulders as he backstroked slowly through the warm water.

He had planted jacaranda trees when he built the house, thinking their fragrant tropical blooms a perfect complement to the Spanish-style architecture, with its rough stucco walls, high ceilings, and rounded doorways.

By the time he got out of prison the trees had grown tall and tangled, a riot of glossy leaves shadowing the pool, roots cracking the adobe walls that surrounded the house. Joe had sat beside the pool, and had actually considered having the trees cut back. No. The backyard was his own private jungle, and he was of an age when he didn't like to see wild things brought to heel, carved into shape. Let nature run amuck. He wasn't going to do anything to stop it.

His backstroke was smooth and precise, hands slightly bent as they entered the water, pushing it down his sides. Foam floats around his ankles kept his legs up. He couldn't kick. His knees and ankles were too swollen and stiff with arthritis. No complaints. He kept his chin up as he swam, watching the morning sky flow through the trees.

A lap pool was a rarity during the early sixties when every architect in California was committed to those useless, kidney-shaped monstrosities. But Joe had insisted. He had always loved swimming, and loved it even more now—the weightlessness, the fluidity of movement, the freedom. It was as close to dancing as he could get anymore.

The pool was kept at a steady 88 degrees, the gas heater running constantly to keep it at bathwater temperature. Mornings were best for him, the water soothing his knotty, swollen joints, allowing him some semblance of mobility.

He closed his eyes, floating among the flowers. He had once danced with Cyd Charisse on a Bob Hope Special. She had worn a big orchid in her hair, and moved so lightly that he could have lifted her with a smile.

The house had been closed up for almost thirty years. Renovations had amounted to more than twice its original construction cost, but it was worth it. Broken windows were replaced, hardwood floors polished, the walls and ceilings freshly painted. He kept the original fixtures and as much of the furniture as possible, comforted by their evocation of good times past. The handrails in the bathrooms were new. So were the ramps to the front and back porches.

The house. Their house. He had bought it for her—intending it to be a surprise, a celebration of their new life together. It was a nice place, with a large kitchen, just a few blocks from Seal Beach, close enough to smell a storm coming in. Plenty of room there for the two of them. Plenty of room for some kids, too, sooner rather than later. She would have liked that house.

She wasn't a professional dancer, but she had all the right moves. With him, anyway. That's what she said the first time they danced together, his hand fitting perfectly into the small of her back, her cheek on his shoulder as they glided across the floor. Everything between them was easy. Love most of all.

He rolled his shoulders as he swam, the water warm as tears.

They never got to live in the house. He had kept the pool drained and the property vacant while he was in prison, not because he thought he would ever get out, but because he couldn't stand the idea of someone else living there. He had a hefty bank account when he was sentenced, the interest alone was more than enough to keep up the taxes.

Bicycles whirled down the street, children racing to the nearby school, whooping it up. Joe smiled. The sound of kids laughing, yelling . . . he missed that sound more than anything else those long years in prison. More than birds singing. More than live music. Two kids flipping baseball cards against a front stoop, arguing over who was closest. You can't buy anything that good.

The morning sun went behind a cloud as jacaranda petals rained down into the swimming pool. He remembered sitting on the veranda of the Beverly Hills Hotel, watching a Monarch butterfly hovering over the beds of red carnations, making thousand-dollar bets with Hyman Kipp on which flower it would land on. After losing eight thousand dollars, Hyman had accused him of training the butterfly as he angrily scrawled a check.

Thirty years later, the incident still made Joe smile. Hyman was a very wise man, who had made a fortune in penny stocks. He should have known that nobody could train a butterfly. The idea was ridiculous. Painting selected carnations with sugar water . . . that was no problem at all.

Joe touched the edge of the pool, slowly turned his body 180 degrees, his knees and ankles already beginning to throb, and started back the other direction. He floated now, eyes closed, seeing Quinn as a boy—the littlest hustler, a beanpole with big bright eyes trying to mimic Joe's confident walk. He had changed after his mother left for parts unknown, gotten quieter, angrier. Joe had to cajole him into playing nickel-a-hand blackjack, and Quinn was distracted and had trouble keeping track of the cards. Teddy was worse, wandering through the house slamming doors, throwing her clothes into the trash, shiny, sequined dresses overflowing the garbage can like Christmas decorations.

The three of them would get together soon, the Three Caballeros, back for an encore. He had called Teddy at his judicial office last week, said he was downstairs in the lobby—Teddy was silent so long that Joe thought he had hung up, but then he finally said he'd come down. Teddy got tears in his eyes when he saw Joe in the wheelchair. Joe told him to can it, said he wouldn't mention that Teddy had gotten fat if Teddy wouldn't treat him like a cripple. They shook on it. Both of them still had a good grip.

Joe heard his doorbell ring and lifted his head, listening. It couldn't be Quinn or Teddy, they would call first. Hugo was supposed to pick him up this afternoon, and he never came by uninvited. A breeze stirred the surface of the pool, sending the purple blossoms skittering to one side. Joe shivered in the warm water.

Early morning was the perfect time for a house call. That's what the pros called it. He heard the bell again. The good ones always rang first, they never barged in. They liked to see if you were alone, check out the terrain. Using the doorbell established a formal pace, a rhythm. Once you set the rhythm, you could control the flow of events. The best of the pros were dancers, cheek to cheek with Death. The only way to survive was to avoid the expected: establish your own rhythm, take control of the dance. Lead or follow. Joe paddled toward the shallow end of the pool, moving as quietly as possible.

He heard footsteps going down the front steps, crunching along the gravel path leading to the backyard. The back was completely hidden from the street by the adobe wall, but the gate was old, the lock not meant to keep anyone out. Not anyone who wanted in.

Joe swam faster, splashing now, not worried about making noise, angry at his helplessness. As a convicted felon he couldn't own a gun. He was forced to trust the good intentions of his fellow man.

He heard someone rattle the gate as he reached the end of the pool. He unsnapped the floats from his ankles, pulling himself up the steps and onto the concrete apron, hand over hand. His chest was scraped raw by the rough concrete as he crawled to his canes.

The canes were heavy, steel tipped. All he needed was a moment's hesitation from the pro, seeing this old wreck who wobbled in front of him, knees swollen to the size of softballs.

Joe had kept himself alive for twenty-eight years with some of the most dangerous bastards on the planet. He used his wits, his quick reflexes, his charm. Win a pack of cigarettes off a con playing dominoes, you offer him a smoke from that same pack, light it for him. You still cover your back. You keep a shank handy.

The gate shook harder as he reached his canes, pushed himself upright. The tip slipped on the wet cement and he banged one knee. Stifling his cry, he pulled himself up again, water dripping around his flopping, in-turned feet, as he waited for the gate to be knocked off its hinges. The air was sweet, the sky so blue.

Joe flung open the gate. Balanced on one cane, he hooked the other around the startled man's ankle, tripping him, sending his clipboard flying. He drove the steel tip of the cane against the man's throat, leaning into it, crushing his windpipe. Water dripped off Joe's bathing suit onto the concrete as the man thrashed around like a bug.

The man's eyes bulged as he slapped futilely at the cane, trying to speak. He was wearing a beige uniform with an embroidered nametag, "Chris." He was young— pimples on his chin and braces on his teeth. Joe eased up slightly on the cane, leaning closer to hear what the man was trying to say.

"Please," the man hissed between gasps, "don't hurt . . ."

Joe lifted the tip of the cane from his throat and the man rolled onto his side, weeping, gasping for breath. UPS was stenciled across the back of his uniform in big letters. Joe could see a large, brown-wrapped package beside the gate.

"You have ID?" demanded Joe.

Still curled on the ground, the UPS man rubbed at the red welt on his throat.

Joe limped to the gate. His own name and address were on the package. Return address: the California State prison at Vacaville. The Department of Corrections had finally gotten around to sending him the books and papers he hadn't been able to carry out when he was released.

The UPS man got to his feet slowly.

"I . . . uh, don't need any ID," said Joe, offering a hand. "Sorry. We . . . we've had some break-ins around here."

The UPS man nodded, not meeting Joe's eyes, then staggered off toward his truck.

CHAPTER

10

Jen waited until they were back at her apartment before confronting Quinn, instead allowing herself to doze in the open Jeep on the ride back from the judge's house, feeling the gritty wind rush past like a bolt of warm raw silk.

She waited until after her long bath—Quinn scrubbing her back with the loofah, then climbing into the tub with her, rubbing away a week of sleeping on the cold ground from her neck, kneading out the kinks. She suddenly leaned back, pushing him over backwards, the two of them wrestling now, laughing, water sloshing over the sides onto the floor.

Quinn was never inhibited, but today he was totally abandoned, one hand gripping the edge of the tub as he leveraged himself deeper inside her. His passion was more than not having seen her in a week. He was running from Teddy's death, trying to keep ahead of his fears. She covered his hand with her, pushing against him, until their cries echoed off the pink tile walls, leaving them panting, still entwined in the cooling water.

She waited while he dried her off with a thick towel, kissed the blisters on her feet, whispering how much he had missed her. She almost asked him then, but he had already buried his face in her breasts, and his eyelashes were tickling her nipples. It felt too good to interrupt. She put on a gauzy pale green robe, then waited until she had brushed out her hair while he lay on her bed, a towel around his waist, watching . . . then she asked him.

"What did Boyle mean?"

"When?"

She sat at her deco vanity with the glass top, seeing him in the large oval mirror. "As you were getting back into the car, he walked around to my side, leered, and said, 'You got a dirty fighter here, miss. Watch yourself in the clinches.' What did he mean by that?"

He plucked at the towel, a big fluffy one stitched with HOTEL SPLENDID in blue letters. She had taken it from a Beirut hotel last year where the towels were the only thing that qualified as splendid.

"Quinn?"

"I punched out a cop. A deputy sheriff with a big mouth."

She dragged the brush through her thick hair. "That was intelligent."

"I was in an intelligent mood." He pulled at the towel, avoiding her eyes. "Teddy's wife told me she doesn't want me going to the funeral. She said I was a bad son." He shrugged. "Maybe she was right."

"How would she know? You should go to the funeral. You don't need her permission." Jen's hair was damp against her neck. She brought a handful to her face, sniffed—she could still smell woodsmoke, even after shampooing twice. Lots of split ends. She picked up the cut-glass bottle of perfume, sprayed her throat, then opened her robe and sprayed again, the cool mist making her shiver.

"Come to bed," he said.

Afternoon light slanted through the closed blinds— she wasn't going back to work today. She turned away from the mirror, went over and sat beside him. "What's wrong?" She laid her hand on his chest. "I always feel this tension, this undercurrent of frustration inside you. It's like something is chasing you." She could feel his heart beating against the palm of her hand.

"Too much talk radio." He pulled her down on top of him, held her close, her hair swinging against his face. "I'll cut back. Promise."

He looked his age today. She was acutely aware of the fifteen-year distance between them at this moment, seeing the wrinkles around his eyes, the deep laugh lines framing his mouth. Usually he appeared younger—there was a bounce to him, an energy, a brightness that radiated youth. Not today. Not now. It was more than fatigue and the gap between them was more than years.

She took his face in her hands, wanting to protect him

from whatever it was that was after him. She kissed him. "Maybe you should take some time off after the funeral."

"I don't want to take some time off." He lay back, stared at the cracked ceiling. "I'm tired of people being beaten to death with baseball bats for not yielding the right of way. I'm tired of kids being shot because they shoplifted a can of pop or wore the wrong color bandana. I'm tired of mothers killing their babies and husbands killing their wives, and customers killing 7-Eleven clerks who won't make change. I'm tired. I see a shoe by the side of the freeway, just an old sneaker, and my mind fills with terrible thoughts . . . I'm tired of people dying, Jen. I'll never get used to it."

"That's why I love you." She smoothed the worry lines out of his forehead with her fingertips.

"I didn't talk to Teddy for months at a time, and when I did we had nothing to say." He wiped at his eyes. "Now that he's gone, I miss him."

She touched a fingertip to his cheek, drew a wet X on her heart. Neither of them spoke. A breeze clattered the blinds. Horns beeped in the distance.

"I was only ten years old when my father died," Jen said. "I used to go to his repair shop every day after school and we'd talk about math class and movies while he showed me how to rewire toasters and record players . . ." She could still see him bent over his immaculate work bench in his white shirt and tie, wielding a soldering iron like a surgeon. Such beautiful hands. Leonard Takamura never got to go to college, but he dressed like the professional man he had hoped to be. "When he died I was sure it was because of something I had done, some way I had let him down. That didn't make any sense, either, but that's the way I felt."

"Maybe I did let Teddy down." He swallowed. She could see gray hairs sprinkled across his chest. "I tried to help Marie, but she won't even talk to me. I don't blame her. What did I ever do for her? I saw her inside the house with this older man—"

"Fontayne. His name is Ellis Fontayne."

Quinn looked at her. "I know that name . . ."

"He's a top defense attorney," said Jen. "Semiretired now, but he still does plenty of pro bono work, mostly civil rights and opening up educational opportunities."

"He's supposed to be on the short list for the next Supreme Court nomination," said Quinn. "I thought he looked familiar . . ." He shook that idea off. The sight of Fontayne in Teddy's living room this morning had triggered memories older than newspaper photos of potential Supreme Court justices. He wished he could remember where he had seen him before. "Are you sure that's who he is?"

"Sergeant Yamada told me that was Fontayne's Rolls parked across the street from Teddy's house—Yamada called in a traffic cop to write him a ticket for illegal parking. Yamada hates defense attorneys. The better they are, the more he hates them."

"I didn't like Fontayne either," said Quinn. "Nothing definitive . . . he wiped his shoes on Teddy's sofa.

There was such contempt in the way he did it." He sat up. "What would a defense attorney be doing at Teddy's?"

"He and Teddy must have been friends," said Jen. "Sergeant Yamada said Marie called him first thing this morning."

"He made it over fast, too, didn't he? You should have seen Fontayne on the sofa with Marie, drying the widow's tears."

"That's what friends do," said Jen.

"Marie's a very attractive woman," said Quinn, not hearing her. He rubbed his forehead, his eyes masked.

Jen watched him, wondering how they ever got together, glad that they had. They were so different. She was precise and logical, an exacting scientist in the darkroom, factoring exposures in her head. She didn't believe in intuition. It led to sloppy work. Quinn wasn't troubled by such rigorous standards. He operated by impulse— punching a police officer!—and instinct, trusting his feelings, without regard for the consequences. It worked for him, though, she had to admit it. He was often right. Maybe he was also right about Fontayne and Teddy's wife.

Quinn rolled over onto his stomach. "I wish I had taken down the license off the Rolls, I'd run his address—"

"957 PRW."

Quinn nodded. "That's right. You're a high-school dropout with a photographic memory, speak four languages, Mensa member since fourteen—you don't go to meetings but you still get the newsletter."

"Thirteen," corrected Jen. "I was thirteen."

"Obviously I'm not bright enough to make it into the Brainiac club."

"That's okay." She slapped him on his bare ass and he yelled. "You have other charms." She could see her red handprint on his white buttock. He grabbed for her and she slapped him again, left a fiery matching print on the other side of his beautiful ass.

"That hurt," he said, leaning into her.

"I'm sorry." She brushed her lips across his crooked nose, then slapped him again, giggling.

He yelped, straddled her, pinning her arms over her head.

"If it hurts so bad, what's that?" she asked, nodding at his rapidly stiffening erection.

He slid his tongue deep inside her mouth, slowly releasing her arms. He stayed on top of her, pinning her hips against the bed, the two of them tangled in the green robe. He caressed her belly with the back of his fingers. "Have you ever thought of living in Paris?"

She laughed. "Sure, let's go to Mars."

"Venus," he said, rubbing his cheek against her ribs as he slid toward her navel. "I was just thinking. Paris might be nice." He slid his tongue into her belly button and she giggled. He kissed his way lower, inhaling her fresh, soapy, female smell. "I talked to Napitano. He seemed . . . amenable. We could rent separate apartments if you want, that way you can keep your independence, whatever that is. We could live right next door to each other, get a place with an adjoining bath—you know how scared I get, showering by myself."

She lifted her leg slightly toward him, and he laughed, catching her. "What's in Paris?" She jerked as he lightly kissed the inside of her thighs, tilting her pelvis against him, eyes clenched shut, feeling his warm breath.

"Us," he whispered, his face between her legs. "We'd be in Paris." The tip of his tongue touched her. "It's a great place to be in love, that's what I've heard."

She moved slightly closer to his tongue. It was an involuntary act, she was sure of it. "I like being in love right here." She cupped the back of his head in her hands, rocking against him as he caressed her, and she was tearing at his hair, arching double as his hands slid up and pinched her nipples. She was groaning, trying to buck him in deeper but he was holding back and she was clawing at him, and he was right there, and she felt her head snap back, rolling against the pillow as he drank her up, and she was biting her lip to stop herself from crying out how much she loved him, and then she couldn't stop, and what she was crying out wasn't words anyway, none that anyone could understand, none that anyone but he could . . .

When she came back, when she came back to knowing where she was, when she could open her eyes, she saw him lying against her hip, a dreamy, opalescent smile on his face.

She reached down and pulled him up to her, the two of them holding each other, innocent hearts beating a lullaby.

He wrapped his fingers in hers. "Paris would be a good place for a honeymoon—"

She pressed his lips shut with a finger. "Let's not wreck it," she whispered, snuggling into his chest.

"You think getting married would wreck us?"

"Shhh. Last night you saw Rachel and Katie, today you want to get married." She played with the hair on his chest, yawning. He smelled good, smelled of salt and sex and she wished she wasn't so sleepy. "Some men are bachelors, swinging singles, rogue males . . . you, you're a family man. You want to tuck the kids in bed at night, wake up next to the wife in the morning. My God," she laughed, "you carry a little Band-Aid in your wallet in case Katie cuts herself."

"What's wrong with that?"

"Nothing. Not a thing."

"I love you, Jen. We could be a family."

She stroked his hands, strong hands, not at all like her father's . . . she lightly touched the knuckles, knowing she had to give him an answer.

"Jen?"

"I'm not ready for that," she said carefully. "Not now."

He looked pained. "You think we have all the time in the world?" He gripped her shoulders, trembling now, the shaking running through the two of them. "Not now, you say, but now is all we have, right now, right this minute, that's all we're sure of. Teddy and I put off seeing each

other—next week, next month, next birthday. Well, sometimes you don't get a second chance."

Jen took his hand from her shoulder, kissed his open
palm. "You've got a very strong lifeline." She yawned,
curling against him, feeling him stroking her hair as she
drifted into sleep. "A very long lifeline."

CHAPTER

11

Jen slept beside him, her breath warm on his chest. Quinn wished he could stay. He gently untangled himself, quieted her mumbled protests with a kiss, tucking the sheets around her. She pressed his pillow against her belly and slept on.

He dressed quickly, afraid that if he didn't leave immediately he would be pulled back into that beautiful warm bed with her. He checked every window in her apartment, made sure they were locked, then closed the door behind him, turning both dead bolts with his key.

The mid-afternoon traffic on the freeway was still light. Another half-hour and the pace would crawl, the air turning a carcinogenic orange in the sunset. Not now. He made good time, driving hard, tailgating slow drivers in the fast lane—he still couldn't outrun his anger with himself.

For the last three months Jen had turned down his

suggestions that they live together, saying she wasn't ready, that she needed her privacy—what made him think she would be willing to marry him?

He tromped the accelerator, cutting off a blue Camaro, staring down the driver. Go ahead. Pull over. Jen should have said yes. At least to Paris. The two of them in Paris . . . the four of them actually, Rachel and Katie would be living there, of course. Rachel might say she hadn't decided to take the job offer yet, but he knew better. She and Katie were going. He gripped the steering wheel, gunning the Jeep. Horns blared in his wake.

He jabbed the twentieth-floor button in the elevator of the *SLAP* magazine building. The other three people in the elevator edged away from him as the floors passed. He glimpsed himself in the burnished steel surface of the door—windblown hair, rumpled suit, wild eyes. His face was scratched. He couldn't tell if it was from Marie's smacking him this morning or Jen's lovemaking this afternoon.

The editorial offices crackled with activity: writers hunched over their computers, phones propped against their ears as they tapped away. Napitano would be on his tenth espresso by now, making decisions, snapping his fingers at the laziness and stupidity he saw surrounding him. He told Quinn once that he didn't really enjoy firing people, it was just one of life's sad necessities. Right.

A couple of the writers muttered their acknowledgment of the Medical Board resignations. Madalyn, the new fashion editor, gave him a round of solitary applause. She had almost died from a botched appendectomy. Her bill included the charge for the original surgeon, plus the second one who had to clean up the first one's mess.

He hung his jacket over the back of his chair, rolled up his sleeves, and logged on to his computer, scrolling past the messages. Joe's number wasn't in the phonebook, but Directory Assistance had him listed. It must have rung twenty times before he picked it up.

"Yes?" Joe sounded tired.

"It's me. Did you hear about Teddy?"

"What happened?" Joe didn't sound tired anymore.

"He was murdered last night." Quinn could hear Joe breathing on the other end of the line, long deep breaths, steady as the waves hitting the Seal Beach pier. "Joe?"

"I didn't know." There was a catch in his voice. "I was taking a nap . . ."

"I'm sorry." It was weird. All day people had been telling him they were sorry, now he was saying it to Joe.

"Do they know who did it?"

"Not yet."

"I saw Teddy just last week," Joe said. "We made a start . . ."

"I've got a lot to do now, but maybe later . . . tomorrow . . ."

"Anytime, Slick. I'm not going anyplace."

Quinn tried Marie next. Teddy's voice came on the answering machine and he almost hung up. When the beep came, he hurriedly asked Marie to please call him when she got a chance, he understood about this morning.

He called the Orange County Superior Court offices, asked to speak to Teddy's court clerk. The clerk, Daronda Washington, was not available, so Quinn left his name and number, said he was Judge Krammerson's stepson and would like to speak to her for a few minutes.

He ran Fontayne's license plate through the Department of Motor Vehicles. He gave the operator his media clearance number, and less than ten seconds later she recited Fontayne's home address and driving record. He had three vehicles registered, the Rolls Royce, a Jaguar, and a Hyundai. Quinn wondered who drove that. Probably the butler. Fontayne lived at 18 Belford Lane, Balboa. Clean driving record for the last ten years, then two months ago he was cited in a rear-ender.

Quinn thanked the operator, sat there tapping his chin. He looked up Ellis Fontayne in the computer database, found 217 separate entries. He started with the "Who's Who" entry, quickly scrolling down the short paragraphs. Fontayne was sixty-eight. He had looked ten years younger through Teddy's window. Married, three children. Law degree, Yale, 1951. Yale Law Review. President of the American Bar Society, 1983–85. Member of the executive committee of the ACLU. Honored by the NAACP and the American Justice Center for his work in expanding the rights of defendants in criminal proceedings. Argued before the U.S. Supreme Court three times, winning each time. Visiting Professor at the University of Southern California law school.

He grabbed his phone before it finished the first ring.

"This is Daronda Washington," the voice on the phone said. She had been crying.

"Hello, Ms. Washington, I'm—"

"I know who you are," she said. "The judge spoke of you. The judge . . ." she blew her nose. "I'm very sorry. I wasn't going to come in today after I heard . . . then I didn't want to stay home, like I was abandoning my responsibilities. The judge was a stickler . . . but then, you know that."

"Yes . . . of course."

"My heart goes out to you and your family."

"Thank you. The reason I called . . . did the judge have any recent cases involving skinheads or neo-Nazis?"

There was silence on the line for several seconds. "We're not supposed to discuss any of this until the District Attorney makes a formal announcement."

"I understand," Quinn said, "but the judge's past caseload is a matter of public record. It would save me some time if you just could tell me yes or no."

"I . . . I wouldn't want to get into trouble," she said. Quinn could hear typing and conversation in the background.

"Ms. Washington, anything you tell me is confidential. I wouldn't want you to do anything that was wrong."

"You couldn't get me to do anything wrong. I'm a Baptist."

"Yes m'am, I understand, Satan himself couldn't tempt you to jaywalk." She didn't laugh, but he felt the tension ease. "I just hoped you could give me a simple yes or no, did the judge try a case recently involving—"

"Yes."

"Yes." He nodded as if he were looking at her. He always visualized the other person when doing a phone interview. "I just have a couple more questions, Ms. Washington."

"It's Mrs. Washington. I'm a married woman and proud of it."

"I understand."

"I can't talk here," she whispered.

"Can you call me back from someplace you feel more comfortable talking?" Silence on the line. "I'm sorry to ask this of you, but this has been such a shock, and there's some concern that other members of the judge's family might be in danger, and no one will tell me what we're dealing with."

"I'd like to help," she repeated, as though trying to convince herself of something.

Quinn's throat was constricted. "I know you want to do what's right. I do, too. I won't betray your trust in me, Mrs. Washington. You have my promise."

"I'll call you back in a few minutes," she said at last.

Quinn heard a dial tone, hung up, and dialed Boyle's number. The detective who answered said he was off-duty. Quinn tried his home number. Boyle's wife barked, "Vincent!" and dropped the phone. Quinn heard someone yawn into the receiver. "Boyle?"

"Quinn?" Boyle blew his nose. Quinn doubted a Kleenex was involved.

"Sorry to bother you," said Quinn, "but I wanted to

know what happened when Fontayne showed up at Teddy's."

"What happened?"

"How did Marie react?" explained Quinn. "Did she and Fontayne . . . behave inappropriately? You have cop-radar—did anything about the two of them set you off?"

"You got a fucking sick mind, Quinn," growled Boyle. "Mrs. Krammerson . . . Marie, that is one stand-by-your-man broad. She didn't even know Fontayne's phone number. She asked me to get it from Teddy's Rolodex. She said Fontayne was a friend of Teddy's, and she wanted somebody with heavy juice to come by and keep the department from tearing her house apart. I'm no fan of Fontayne, but as soon as he showed up everybody inside was on their best behavior." He laughed. "Assistant Chief Asshole Feyse choked on his Rolaids when the white Rolls pulled up out front. That alone was worth the price of admission."

"Thanks, Boyle." Quinn didn't feel grateful. The phone rang as soon as he hung up.

"This is Daronda Washington."

"Thank you for getting back to me, Mrs. Washington," Quinn said, disappointed after his conversation with Boyle. "How . . . how long ago was this skinhead trial?"

"Maybe ten months ago, right around Halloween. It wasn't much, receiving stolen property, VCRs and guns mostly. The defendant was this surftrash with swastika tattoos on the back of his hands."

"Name?"

"Hatch. Eugene Hatch."

Quinn wrote it down. The magazine database kept a one-year record of all state court proceedings. "Did Hatch threaten Teddy?"

"Not out loud. He spat at me, though, when I swore him in. Told me to go back to Africa. You should have seen the judge's face then," she clucked, "his eyes got that going-to-the-woodshed look. I know you know the one I'm talking about."

Quinn did. "Is Hatch still in jail?"

"The judge maxxed him out good. Eight to ten. The prosecutor only asked for two years. The word is that some of his Aryan buddies"—her voice cracked—"went to see the judge."

"Thank you, Mrs. Washington. I appreciate it."

"The judge . . . he was like family."

Quinn put the phone down. He doodled on a yellow pad with a pencil, making intersecting circles, big ones and small ones, postponing what he knew he was going to do. Joe Steps shows up after nearly thirty years, makes plans with Rachel to surprise him at Katie's dance performance, and that same night somebody murders Teddy. Stranger things had happened, but Quinn wasn't a kid anymore. He was suspicious these days. You lived longer that way.

Quinn tossed the pencil aside and called the L.A. County Felony Files office. They said Lester was on vacation for the next week. He tried the Orange County office and Romero answered, which was just who he wanted to speak to. There was always a backlog of file requests, and dealing with the usual paperwork could take weeks. "Que pasa, Jesús?"

"Quinn? No complaints, hombre. What can I do you for?"

"I need you to run a check on a Joseph Staducci, aka Joe Steps, double-homicide conviction. I'm looking for a summary of the court transcripts and complete probation report. I need it by tomorrow at the latest."

"About how long ago was the conviction?"

Quinn had to check his own memory. "Somewhere around . . . summer, 1964."

Romero whistled. "Computers don't go back that far, amigo. I'm going to have to pull records from the basement. I hate the basement, man. Cock-a-roaches."

"I'll owe you."

"It's dusty down there. Cockroaches and everything. I don't like to get dirty, man, you know that."

"I'll get you a couple of Rams tickets—"

"Everybody gives me Rams tickets. I wipe my ass with Rams tickets."

"Okay." Quinn mentally calculated how much he had left on his credit card limit. "I'll get you a couple of seats to next month's bantamweight championship bout, Herrera and that other guy—"

"Lopez."

"Lopez. Not ringside, but good seats."

"Why not ringside? What do you do with your money?"

"Child support. Mortgage on a house I don't live in . . ."

"Stay with the mother of your children, man. It's cheaper."

"You want the seat, Jesús?"

"Deal."

"Not yet. I'm not sure the trial was in Orange County." Quinn could hear Jesús groan. "If you come up blank, I want you to try L.A. for me. My contact is on vacation—"

"No problema," said Jesús. "My cousin Jorge works there. If I don't find your double homicide, he will. I'll stick Jorge with your Rams tickets. Jorge loves the fucking Rams."

CHAPTER

12

The raw chemical smell burned Quinn's nostrils as he quietly opened the door to the fiberglass room, but he smiled anyway, seeing Gill Wertham bent over the surfboard he was working on. Quinn released the bouquet of helium balloons he was carrying and held out the six-pack of beer. "Happy Birthday, Gill."

Gill looked up, startled. He was a husky, sunburnt man wearing nothing but a pair of low-slung Aussi-print trunks and flip-flops. "It's not my birthday and that's not my name anymore."

Quinn tossed him the beer. "Relax."

The balloons bounced against the low ceiling, the overhead fan sending them scuttling around the small, stifling room. A poster of Heather Locklear in a bikini was taped to one wall—someone had drawn nipple-rings on her full breasts. A radio was tuned to that right-wing loudmouth whose sponsors all sold commodities futures or cassette tapes designed to improve your vocabulary.

"You could get me in trouble coming here." Gill checked the closed door. "You could get me killed."

"Give me some credit," soothed Quinn. "I'm a Beer-Gram deliveryman who screwed up his order and can't remember the name of the birthday boy. I just know he's some shorthair making boards. I've been to seventeen surfshops looking for you; I was about ready—"

"Who told you I was glassing boards?" Gill's face was streaked with sweat, his bleached-white buzzcut caked with wisps of red and green fiberglass, his nostrils rimmed with fluorescent colors. He looked like a National Geographic cover of an aborigine in warpaint.

Quinn examined the surfboard Gill had been working on.

"I asked you a question. Who gave me up?"

"I'm the one who taught you how to hide," Quinn said lightly, sighting down the length of the board. "What makes you think I'd need help to find you?"

They had worked together at the Times-Herald a few years ago. Quinn was the star investigative reporter, Gill stuck on the copy desk with aspirations of front-page glory. They had formed a vague friendship, but Gill grew increasingly bitter and erratic—following Quinn like a puppy one day, the next day challenging the security guard to a fight for making him show his ID badge. When he was laid off, Quinn assumed they'd never see each other again, but a few months later Gill called and asked to meet him.

Quinn barely recognized him. Gill had shaved his head, and his tank top revealed numerous tattoos: dragons and tigers and a busty woman with swastika eyes.

Gill said he had decided to infiltrate the White supremacist scene and write a book about it. A best-seller. He saw himself on "Donahue," talking about the dangers he had faced, the risks he had taken. He wanted to play himself in the movie. He just needed a few suggestions from Quinn about how you went about doing undercover work.

Quinn tried to dissuade him, told him it was dangerous, but Gill was adamant. It wasn't a bad idea, actually. Beneath its crust of glamour and wealth, Orange County bubbled with resentment, a poisonous stew of rich against poor, color against color, and everyone against the new immigrants on the block. Asians ate the neighborhood cats, warned the locals, Latins brought exotic diseases, and Whites fleeing the rust belt were drunks and child abusers. They all worked too cheap.

Under the microwave of sun and smog, the local variety of White supremacists had mutated into something unique to Southern California. They didn't wear sheets or burn crosses. They weren't Bible-reading survivalists stockpiling food and fearing Armageddon. Orange County skins were laid-back dropouts in their teens and twenties, surfers and skateboarders and potheads. They were strip-club Nazis spending Grandma's money on tequila shooters and pussy, tattooed love boys driving VW vans with "nigger-head" gearshifts and "Party Naked" bumper stickers. Orange County skins surfed Trestles in South County all day, then dropped some D Meth and drove up to Laguna Beach for a little gay-bashing under the moonlight.

Quinn had been interested in covering the Aryan scene himself, but he didn't surf, he didn't skate—he was too old to pass. He could still teach Gill a few things about slipping into character though, how to talk the talk, how to ease off and slowly gain people's confidence. Gill got a job at a head shop in Huntington Beach, selling bongs and cherry-flavored rolling papers. He surfed up and down the coast, yelling at Mexican families picnicking on "our beach." After a few months he stopped calling. Quinn had other worries.

"How's the book coming?" asked Quinn. "You sounded like you were making progress the last time we talked."

"I quit." Gill's mouth tightened and he drug his hand across his peeling nose. "There's another book I might write someday . . . they'd never print it though."

Quinn nodded, not sure what he meant. "The cops swept the Screwdriver Tavern yesterday. All those little Nazis led out like a line of ducks—"

"I heard." Gill checked the door again. "You should go."

"The D.A. is charging three of the regulars with murder and conspiracy in the Judge Krammerson homicide. He's going to announce the arrests at a five p.m. press conference—just in time for the six o'clock news. The judge was murdered Sunday night, here it is just Wednesday afternoon and case closed. Fast work, don't you think?"

"Yeah, well, that's what you pay taxes for."

Minute flecks of iridescent fiberglass floated past, prisming the air. "I can hardly breathe in here," said Quinn. "Why don't we go outside, crack some of those beers?"

"I can breathe just fine." Gill stood over the Styrofoam core of the surfboard, slathering on hot acrylic resin, the acrid vapors twisting in the sluggish breeze.

"I'm not trying to step on anything you're working on," Quinn reassured him. "This isn't a news story, this is personal. You know how I get—"

"Yeah, you're a fucking hero." Sweat dripped off Gill's forehead onto the surfboard as he worked.

"I went to a lot of trouble to find you," said Quinn, moving closer.

Gill jumped back. "Quit crowding me!"

Quinn stepped away. "I just want to talk."

"I know how that works," sputtered Gill. "You think I'm stupid? I read your stuff in that fancy-ass magazine." He bent over the board, mouth twisting. "Must be nice, working in an air-conditioned office, babes looking up to you like you're King Shit . . ."

Quinn walked over and turned up the radio. "Is somebody listening? Is that it?"

"You just don't get it." Gill smiled. One of his teeth was missing. "You will. Just wait."

"I talked to your mother—"

"My mother doesn't know where I live. She doesn't know where I work, so don't bring her into this."

"She's worried about you. You used to come home every couple of weeks, drop off a sack of laundry and watch TV with her. Now she doesn't see you for months at a time, and when you do come by she says you talk crazy. The fumes in this room . . . you might as well be sniffing glue. You should give your mom a call—"

"You like my mother's house? Flowers in the front, nice little lawn. I grew up in that house in Garden Grove," said Gill, digging furiously at the surfboard with a long, flat blade, smoothing it out. "It's ruined now," he hissed. "*They* ruined it." The blade tore chunks out of the board, but he didn't seem to notice. " 'Little Saigon,' that's what they call it now. You can't read the fucking signs in the strip malls unless you speak gook. There's more Trangs and Wangs and Changs in the phone book than Smiths." He glared at Quinn. "You think that's right?"

"Gill, working undercover is all about assuming a role, taking on another identity, and that can be as much of a danger as being found out. You have to be careful not to internalize—"

"Save the psycho bullshit." Gill pointed the blade at him. "Don't pretend to be my friend, either. I know who my friends are. You came looking for me because you wanted something, not because you care anything about me."

Quinn watched the shiny glass dust motes dance in the air, finally nodded in agreement. "True." It seemed to satisfy Gill. "One question, then I'll go. Do you think the Screwdriver suspects killed the judge?"

"Those posers?" Gill spit. "The Screwdriver is full of frat boys and jocks talking racial purity Friday night and screwing spics and niggers on Saturday."

Quinn stared at him.

"You don't go for dark meat, do you?" sneered Gill. "No, you stick with sushi, right? That gook photographer I read about. Is that what you like?"

"That's what I like. What can you expect? My mother was Italian. I just look White."

Gill shook his head. "I used to look up to you."

"I used to think you could turn into a real reporter," said Quinn. "We were both deluded." He knew Gill. If he had any information, he wouldn't be able to stop himself from bragging about it.

Gill worked on the board for a little while, then stopped. "I went to the Screwdriver once," he said, a strange smile playing around the corner of his mouth. "Once was plenty."

"Yeah?"

"Yeah." The smile twitched happily.

"They throw you out, is that it? They card you?" Quinn shook his head in dismissal. "All this time undercover and you didn't find out anything." He started toward the door.

"Check out the bartender at the Screwdriver," called Gill. "I figured that would get your attention. Nice lead, huh?" He popped a beer and beer foam rolled over his hand. "I thought the bartender looked familiar when I walked in—I must have shot pool for an hour before I pinned him." He took a long swallow. "Dude was a transfer student at my high school. Right before graduation thirty-four kids were busted. This guy was an undercover cop then, and he probably hasn't made any radical career moves since." He shook his head. "The Screwdriver was a bust. Nobody I know ever went there. Nobody serious."

Quinn nodded his thanks. "These people you know . . . the serious ones you're afraid are going to walk through the door . . . any chance they might have paid a visit to the judge?"

Gill squeezed a long belch out. "That would be premature. Things aren't that bad. Not yet. Besides, the cops are just looking for an excuse to come down on us, wipe us out—cops probably killed the judge. Give the papers a chance to run some more of their 'Honor Diversity' editorials. Tell that to Reginald Denny." The empty beer can bounced against a corner and onto the floor. "You should stick with your own kind."

Quinn smiled sadly. "I'm still looking for my own kind."

"You aren't looking in the right places." For a moment Gill looked like the guy who invited himself to sit down next to Quinn in the *Times-Herald* cafeteria, then didn't know what to say to him.

"Gill . . ."

"Where were you when I got laid off from the paper?" Gill said bitterly. "Why me? Why not the Chiquita who worked next to me? I was hired before she was." He shook his head. "I loved that job."

Quinn spread his hands. "The county is half-Hispanic. The whitebreads on Mahogany Row probably thought it would be a good idea to have a few people on staff who speak Spanish."

Gill spit again. "Race war's coming," he warned, "and sooner than you think, rolling in like a western swell before a storm . . . Get out of here, Quinn. You don't belong."

Quinn didn't move. "Maybe I could put a word in for you at the magazine. It would do you good to make some new friends."

"I like the friends I have just fine." Gill reached for another beer. "I'd offer you a brew, but how would that look? You and me . . . I might have to have to kill you someday. It's going to come to that, you know."

Quinn blinked, allowing his eyes to adjust to the dimness of the ancient movie palace. Thursday, 2:30 in the afternoon, the Rialto Azteca was almost empty, the wheezing of the air-conditioner echoing through the vast twilight space. Cigarette smoke rose from a dozen scattered seats, twisting slowly in the gray projector light. On-screen a handsome young caballero sat astride his horse, reins loose in his hands as he sang sadly to the night sky. The picture was slightly out of focus, the caballero a ghost rider serenading the stars.

He spotted Deputy District Attorney Tina Chavez in the center of the empty back row, mouthing the mournful Spanish lyrics that warbled over the blown loudspeakers. She sat erect, a short, voluptuous woman wearing a black tuxedo jacket and short skirt, dark hair coiled into a knot, three strands of pale coral beads around her neck. Popcorn crunched underfoot as he made his way over.

The floor was sticky with decades of snack-bar detritus, layers of ossified sweetness, an Olduvai Gorge of Southern California's changing demographics—from smeared bonbons at the lowest, most ancient level, up through powdered Pez and spilled cherry cokes to the most recent age of Inca Cola, sugary tamarind drops and flattened deep-fried churos.

He eased down next to her, then quickly stood back up, feeling the seat cushions slashed to bare metal. He saw her nod to someone, turned, and saw a burly bouncer bow his head, the big man slouched in a wicker rocker in the far corner of the theater, a baseball bat balanced across his knees.

"Nice place, Tina." Quinn stepped over her bulging briefcase, settling into the seat on the other side of her. "Little far from the office though, isn't it?"

"I like the atmosphere, and no one from the D.A.'s office is apt to disturb us here."

"Not without a police escort."

Fifty years ago the Rialto Azteca was the Rialto Coliseum, a Long Beach landmark, a classic movie theater with pink marble walls and Ben Hur murals, its fluted white columns rising past the third balcony.

These days the Azteca offered splashy Mexican melodramas—today's feature: *Las Passiones de los Muertos!*—and dubbed gringo action epics. The Roman murals had been painted over, fierce Aztec warriors replacing the proud centurions, a towering step pyramid covering a frenzied chariot race. The plaster columns were crumbling, the cinemascope screen torn in a dozen places, including a neat bullet hole where someone had put a .38 slug through Mel Gibson's bare buttock in *Lethal Weapon.*

"It was good to hear you on my answering machine last night, guapo," she said, her voice husky, with just a trace of an accent. "I lay in bed and played it back a couple of times to make sure it was you. Turned off the lights and played it some more."

"Careful, you don't want to wear yourself out . . ."

"No danger of that," she purred, the words rolling with a bosomy resonance. "I haven't seen you in a long time; we should celebrate." She held out a large paper cup, her red lip print on the rim pointed right at his mouth. "Taste. Don't be afraid. It wouldn't be the first time, would it?"

He was smiling, remembering, as he took a drink and almost choked. "Whoooeee." He wiped his chin. "What is this, straight vodka with a splash of coke?"

"Watch." She nodded at the screen. "This is one of my favorite parts."

The caballero rocked in the saddle, closed his eyes, and began sobbing. The horse shifted under him. "Que bonita, que bonita esta mi amor perdido, que bonita," he choked, tears leaking through his silky lashes.

As Tina recited the words along with the caballero, her hand drifted onto Quinn's knee.

Quinn hadn't seen her in over a year, but her features were as strong and sensuous as he remembered, broad cheekbones and fiery, dark eyes, her lips full, her eyebrows plucked into a thin, sharp arch.

Like most of the three hundred or so prosecutors working for the Orange County D.A.'s office she was smart and aggressive, but there was a passionate, raw humanity in her that he had been attracted to the first time he saw her in court.

Most prosecutors ignored crime victims until they were on the witness stand, treating them like bit players in the complex legal melodrama. Not Tina. She patted them on the back, helped them to a chair, shielded them with her body from the defendants' threatening glares. Rape victims got follow-up phone calls years after her successful prosecutions of their attackers. Families of homicide victims got help with financial-aid forms and letters of recommendation to colleges and trade schools.

"What are you looking at?"

"You," he said gently.

"Don't get me excited, Quinn. Not unless you're going to finish the job."

Quinn blushed and she laughed.

The camera cut away from the lonely caballero to a smokey cantina—Zapata moustaches and sombreros around the tables while a scruffy monkey sat chained to the rafters, nibbling on an orange. A sultry señorita danced on the bar, ruffled skirt bouncing high, castanets clicking as the cantina applauded. She threw back her head, nostrils flared.

"The caballero is waiting for her," Tina whispered, leaning close, grazing his cheek with her own, her breath sweet with rum. "She promised to meet him before the moon rose, but she can't disappoint the wealthy Don Renaldo." A fat man in a white linen suit watched her twirl while he smoked a thin cigar. "The caballero swore he'd kill himself if she didn't come, but she doesn't believe him." Tina sighed, her teeth sharp against her bright lipstick. "Love is hard. I don't know how anyone manages it. How do you do it?"

"Mostly it manages me."

"Why don't you go out to dinner with me anymore?" she pouted. "You scared of Tina?"

"Absolutely."

Her throat rippled with laughter. "I thought maybe you got married again . . ." Her hand was higher now. "Not that it bothers me. I am not a possessive woman." She checked her watch. "You covering the judge's funeral? It's almost time."

Quinn shook his head.

"Really? I thought you were acquainted?" Tina shrugged, crossed her leg. "I would not miss it. Could not, even if I wanted to—District Attorney Barkis is giving one of the eulogies, and he likes to see his troops in attendance. That's what he calls us, you know. His 'troops.'" She drank from the paper cup. "I have found that men who use military metaphors invariably have small penises."

"And has this been an extensive survey, Ms. Chavez?"

She pursed her lips. "Modesty and professionalism do not permit me to divulge exact numbers"—she coyly nibbled the rim of the cup—"but my conclusion is unassailable."

Quinn nodded, waited a moment. "Barkis is rushing the investigation," he said lightly. "I saw his news conference yesterday, and that videotape of the Screwdriver bust he played. Pathetic. What's he running for, Attorney General?"

"Barkis wanted to make some arrests before the judge's funeral. You cannot blame him. Besides, there was enough to round them up. They have no alibi for Sunday night, they threatened Judge K. when he maxxed out their fearless leader, and the evidence team found Brazil nut fragments on the judge's doormat."

Quinn stared at her.

"The Screwdriver has all these ball peen hammers hanging from the ceiling," she explained, "and the bar top is piled with Brazil nuts." Her mouth twisted with disgust. " 'Nigger toes,' the neo-Nazis call them. They sit around drinking, busting toes. The floor is covered with shells. Forensics figures the killers tracked some onto the doormat."

"Any physical evidence that directly ties the defendants to the crime? Finger prints? Hair? Anything?"

"Not that I know of—but, it's not my case."

"I did some checking, Tina. You can't sieg-heil in the Screwdriver without spilling beer on an undercover cop. If there was a plan to kill Teddy, the D.A. would have been waiting inside the house with a SWAT team and a camera crew. I don't care about Brazil nuts on the doormat or swastikas on the walls, these clowns didn't kill Teddy."

She shrugged. "Barkis has enough to put them away

for a year or two awaiting trial. If they don't get a good attorney, it may be enough to send them to the gas chamber. The judiciary doesn't like to see one of their own murdered." He could see her smile in the dim light. "It gives people ideas."

A rat ran down the aisle, stopped, raised up on its hind legs, and sniffed the air.

"I thought you said nobody from the D.A.'s office ever came here," said Quinn.

Tina laughed, took another swallow from the paper cup. "You covered my first homicide trial. Remember? The twelve-year-old gangbanger who made his getaway on a Schwinn. 'Pee Wee's Big Adventure.' That's what they called it around the office, a nothing case, but it meant something to me."

"A nothing case?" said Quinn. "He shot a second-grader who accidentally bumped him with his lunchbox."

"I will never forget how you described me in that article," she said: " 'An elegant predator stalking the courtroom, only her absent tugs at her necklace betraying her nervousness.' " She smiled to herself, fingertips stroking the rough coral beads. " 'An elegant predator,' " she repeated, "such a graceful phrase, so knowing . . ." Her hand moved slowly up his leg like a warm little mouse.

He removed her hand.

"You didn't used to be so shy, guapo," she said softly.

"I'm seeing someone. I'm not shy with her."

"Lucky girl, finding the last honorable man in Southern California. I'm envious." She sighed. "Maybe it's my job, but the men I meet are all tainted somehow. You wouldn't believe the jokes I hear, the grotesque cynicism . . . welfare jokes, dead baby jokes—defense attorneys are the worst, much worse than cops. I should have been a schoolteacher."

"You wouldn't like it." He tugged gently at one of her long earrings. "They don't let you lock up students for not doing their homework."

"Well . . ." She tried to hide her pleasure. "If you didn't call me up because you wanted to have some fun, you must need a favor."

Quinn lowered his voice. "I'm working on a story. Ex-con, just finished thirty years at Vacaville for a double homicide—"

"He should have waited." She demurely covered a hiccup with the palm of her hand. "Double homicide is strictly a ten-year ride these days. Out in six if you comb your hair for the parole board."

"I'd like you to put in a request for his prison file. He's living in Orange County so it's in your jurisdiction; they'll release his jacket to you. I need to see it."

"We all have our needs, don't we?" Her hair brushed against him and he felt his body respond. "How bad do you need it?" she whispered, her lips caressing his neck. "How bad?"

He leaned away from her lips.

"A man with principles," she clucked, "you're a danger to yourself and everyone around you." The theater darkened as the screen cut back to the caballero standing by a campfire, alone under the stars. Quinn could see the flames reflected in Tina's hot black eyes, half-closed now, dreamy. "You really get to me," she said, her voice thick. "Cops fall in love with whores. Prosecutors . . . we like bad boys with heart and soul. I think you are a bad boy who does not know it yet. What do you think?"

"I think I need a favor."

"I could use a favor myself." She tapped a forefinger against her lower lip. "Maybe you should write something nice about me in your magazine . . . ?" The campfire blazed on-screen, the theater brighter now, the metal edges of the seats glowing with cold heat. "You reporters call that a 'stroke piece,' don't you? A stroke piece . . . I like that." She watched the caballero fall to his knees in front of the fire, head bent forward in defeat.

Quinn passed her a slip of paper. "Here's the ex-con's name and case number. The sooner the better."

"I want many photos in my stroke piece"—she delicately drained the cup of vodka, pinky raised to the ceiling, as the caballero reached for his pistola—"and quotes from admiring colleagues. Make sure you mention how much I owe to the example and leadership of D.A. Barkis."

Quinn nodded agreement. "How about a photo of you and Barkis in his big corner office? He could even wear his flak-jacket and shoulder holster—"

"A girl has to look out for herself," she sniffled. "Ever since I lost that Sullivan case I'm on the shitlist. You lose a high-profile homicide . . . sometimes you never get another chance." She stiffened. "I'm sick of prosecuting burglars who leave their own wallet at the crime scene, sick of domestic assaults where the wife drops charges. I want Barkis to give me a glamour case—a celebrity drug bust or a serial killer, a pro athlete caught with a suitcase of kiddy porn. I am thirty-two years old, Quinn, and I am tired of waiting."

Quinn jerked at movement to his right, saw a young couple in the back row kissing, shy kisses, the two of them with their best clothes neatly pressed, a rhinestone pin in the girl's thick black hair.

Tina checked her watch. "I have to go to the judge's funeral. You sure you don't want to come? You can be my date. I won't tell your girlfriend."

Quinn shook his head.

She kissed him, breathing her heat into him. "I'll be in touch." She stood up and headed toward the exit. She staggered a bit at first, but soon got her legs under her.

Hugo felt the ground tremble under his feet as the torrent of eighteen-wheelers roared down the nearby freeway, hot air boiling around them. He listened at the door to Stimmler's tiny aluminum trailer, heard the television buzzing. MTV? The trailer glittered in the blazing desert sun, windows covered with silvery foil to reflect the heat. A rusted air conditioner dripped water into the sand.

The trailer sat behind a cinder-block truckstop on Route 66, beached in that long stretch of nowhere between Barstow and Las Vegas. He checked the back door of the truckstop, saw weeds and crushed oil cans and a scraggly orange cat hunkered down in the shade under the steps with something twitching in its mouth.

Rick tugged at the collar of his wispy, rayon shirt. "It's a microwave out here," he panted, red hibiscus billowing around his chest, baggy khaki shorts limp around his knees. That's the way they were wearing them this year, the "Mission to Burma" look. "How come you never sweat, Hugo? Dressed like a Bible salesman and cool as ice . . ."

Hugo stood quietly in a dark suit, white shirt and tie, his hand on the doorknob. It was unlocked.

They stepped inside, Hugo letting Rick go first so that he could follow and make sure the door was locked after them. Rick wasn't so good with details. They were wearing surgical gloves this time, just like Teddy had suggested. Live and learn.

The man in the recliner lay in the room's cool twilight, blinking from the flash of noon they had let in. He registered their presence, then went back to watching the ancient black and white television propped on a wooden fruit crate. Stimmler fit the description. He sat in his underwear, bare legs like sticks poking through the blue robe. A nightstand overflowing with pill bottles stood on one side of the recliner, an oxygen tank flanked the other side, its thin plastic tube fitted under his nose, hissing.

The trailer reeked of pine disinfectant and lilac air freshener, but Hugo could still detect the sharp, underlying smell of rotting meat. Paper bags full of dirty clothes overflowed onto the stained carpet—Rick kicked a gray sweater out of his way, got it tangled around his ankle, and had to pull it off, grimacing, his shirt a swirl of red, the brightest thing in the room.

"You're early," Stimmler croaked, his breathing labored as he stared at the TV, watching girls in white cotton panties writhe around a pimply guitarist. "My probation visit ain't until next month." He smacked his lips at the TV. "Look at that ass. She's shoving it right in our kissers." He glanced over at them, noticed the surgical gloves. "You from the Health Department?" No answer. "Oh, shit." Stimmler licked his lips, looking from one to the other. "Oh . . . shit."

"Oh . . . shit." Rick mimicked.

"Why bother with me?" The black circles under Stimmler's eyes were sunk so deep that he looked like a terrified raccoon. "I ain't even worth your trouble now."

"No trouble," said Hugo, moving closer, the smell getting stronger as he approached the recliner.

Stimmler shrank back. "Who sent you?"

"Take a guess," said Rick. "Go on. You get one guess."

Stimmler looked from one to the other. "Fontayne?"

"Good answer," Rick clapped, "good answer."

Stimmler watched Hugo. "Was it Joe? Did Joe Steps send you?"

"Good answer," Rick clapped, "good answer."

"Does it matter?" asked Hugo.

"Either way, you're a winner," laughed Rick. "We've got cash and prizes and the take-home version of our game for you."

"First thing I ever won in my life," Stimmler said sourly. He touched the air tube in his nose, making sure it was still there. "It's Fontayne, right?"

"Good answer," Rick clapped.

Whatever was eating Stimmler had started long before the cancer that was killing him now. He was only in his fifties, but he was already used up. Hugo was equally gaunt—you could use his ribs for an abacus—but he radiated strength, a power that didn't need something mutable as flesh to operate.

Rick rooted through the piles of pills on the night-stand, checking labels, knocking bottles onto the floor. Stimmler shifted in his seat, and Rick's nose wrinkled with disgust. "Wash your hair, asshole, you're disgusting." Rick held up a box. "Amyl nitrite, Hugo!" he crowed. "Poppers!"

"Put them back," said Hugo. "They might be missed."

Rick crushed a yellow ampule in his gloved fist, in-haled, and almost fell over. "You're not my boss, Hugo, you're my friend," he said slowly, his voice coming from far away. "Ask me anything, Hugo. Anything. But don't order me around." He leaned against the wall, face flushed, hyperventilating. His eyes were dilated, two black holes in his face. You could look in and not see bottom.

"Leave one in the box," Hugo said. "Please?"

"What's Fontayne worried about after all these years?" Stimmler wailed. His cheeks were glazed red, stiff as pottery. "Look at me, boys. Who would listen to me?"

"Joe Steps," answered Hugo. "He listened, didn't he?"

Stimmler squirmed in his chair. "I'm no snitch," he said. "Don't you stick that label on me. What I did was one con squaring things with another." He licked his cracked lips, waiting for a reaction from Hugo.

Hugo listened to the steady hiss of oxygen in the trailer, the rattle of the air conditioner, the rock music on

TV. It was a John Cage performance: the Black Lung Symphony. Hugo smiled. He wished he could explain that one to Rick.

"I bounced from one lockup to another most of my life," Stimmler said wearily, his voice fading. "Somehow I always knew I'd end up in Vacaville with Joe Steps. He didn't know me from Adam, but I knew him. I used to watch him in the yard—he'd been inside forever by then—he still moved like he was dancing."

"Is that why you talked to him?" asked Hugo. "He was such a good dancer?"

"I thought I was dying," blubbered Stimmler. "Prison doctors had chopped most of my lungs out . . . hospital trustee said it looked like burnt toast inside me." He shook his head. "I should have smoked filters," he said hoarsely, "but who knew?"

Hugo handed him a tissue.

Stimmler dabbed at his nostrils. There was a raw spot under his nose where the constant airflow irritated the membrane. "I wanted to clear the books with Joe Steps before I died. It bothered me, what I done to him. Didn't you ever do something you wanted to take back?"

"Yes, I have," said Hugo.

"There you go," nodded Stimmler. "It's the same with me."

"Maybe you waited too long to ask forgiveness," said Hugo. "All those years . . . that was a long time for Joe to wait."

Stimmler jerked like a marionette. "Joe sent you?" His

hands flopped in his lap, out of his control. "I thought you told me you were working for Fontayne?"

"I didn't tell you anything," Hugo said. "That was merely an inference you made."

"A what?"

Rick slowly straightened up, his mouth still slack with pleasure. He ran both hands through his hair, then checked himself in the built-in mirror, primping his eyebrows with a moistened fingertip. His toilette finished, he turned toward Stimmler, quickly drawing a tiny .22 automatic from under his shirt, racking a bullet into the chamber with one swift motion. You could tell he liked the solid, metallic sound it made. "My turn, right, Hugo?"

"No guns," said Hugo. "We have to be more subtle with Mr. Stimmler."

"Well, I'm not touching that asshole," grimaced Rick.

"Mr. Stimmler. That's a good one." Stimmler trembled. "That's what they call you in court when they sentence you. That's what the doctors call you when they found something bad. Everybody's so polite these days when they fuck you."

"I'd appreciate it, Mr. Stimmler, if you wouldn't use profanity," said Hugo.

"What about him?" whined Stimmler, indicating Rick.

Hugo spread his hands. "Like Rick said, he's my friend."

"Thanks, Hugo, and fuck you, Stimmler," said Rick.

"Get in line," muttered Stimmler. He tried to smile but his teeth were chattering. He bit his lip, tears welling up.

Seeing Stimmler's fear made Hugo think of the judge, bleeding all over his wife's sofa, knowing it was just the beginning and still keeping up with the wisecracks, acting like *he* was the one with the last laugh. Every breath that Stimmler took was an insult to Teddy's dying.

"You kill him, Hugo," said Rick. "He smells like dirty diapers." He sniffed his own shirt. "I'm going to have to throw away these clothes."

"Not my fault," said Stimmler, "there's too much sulphur in the water. It was my baby sister's idea to move me out here after I got released. She runs the truckstop diner, said the desert air would be good for me." He cackled, hacked up balls of black spit. "Look at me. Picture of health, huh?"

"Quit complaining," snapped Rick. "Think about us! We had to drive way out here to Bedrock to find you—no good radio stations and the car I swiped had a broke air conditioner. Look at what the dry air's done to my skin." Rick kicked the recliner. "I'm going to have to double-moisturize when we get back." He kicked the recliner again, reached over, and turned the valve on the oxygen tank. The hissing stopped.

"Hey," Stimmler reached for the valve, clawed at Rick's glove. "Hey, come on."

"Give him back his air," Hugo said to Rick. "And Mr. Stimmler, you give him back his watch."

Stimmler grinned feebly as he pulled Rick's paisley Swatch from the sleeve of his robe.

Rick snatched it back. "How'd you do that?" He was more delighted than angry.

"Professional secret," Stimmler gasped as Rick opened the valve of the tank. "I always had quick hands," he said, his yellowed nails waving an intricate finger-ballet. "I've slowed down some," he said to Hugo. "In the old days you wouldn't have seen me. Joe Steps never felt a thing when I made my move that day at the racetrack—I barely touched his wrist and it was like his watch jumped into my hand. I was good. That's why they didn't kill me— Liggett wanted to, but Fontayne said no, they could use me. Fontayne . . . he could talk the birds out of the trees and into a cage."

"Can you teach me that watch trick?" asked Rick.

Stimmler jerked a thumb at Rick. "Nice kid," he said to Hugo. "I had a punk like him in Soledad . . ." He swallowed, the gray tip of his tongue protruding from his mouth. "Happiest year of my life. I still miss him."

Hugo sat on the arm of the recliner and Stimmler flinched, his bravado suddenly gone.

"I'm not a brave man," whimpered Stimmler, wrapping the blue robe around himself. "Sometimes I think I been waiting for the shit to hit the fan my whole life." He glanced at Hugo. "Sorry. Never had long to wait, either." He adjusted the airhose in his nostrils.

"It's getting late," said Hugo, "and Rick needs to go home and moisturize."

"You young guys," gulped Stimmler, "killing doesn't mean anything to you. People might as well be cockroaches."

"That wristwatch trick," said Rick, "does it work with Rolexes too?"

"Sure," said Stimmler. "Sure, kid, I can show you. Just takes a little practice, that's all."

"Rick will have to make do with a book on sleight-of-hand from the public library," said Hugo.

"I w-want my music box back," stammered Stimmler, "the one I gave to Addie. This one I got now ain't the same—"

"What's he talking about, Hugo?"

"You boys don't know anything, do you? You're hired help, just like I was. Look where it got me." Stimmler fiddled with his airhose, eyes darting back and forth, looking for a way out of his skull. "I can help you. I can tell you things, important things. Take it from me, what you don't know can kill you."

"It's late, Mr. Stimmler, and you overestimate my curiosity."

"Never too late." Stimmler licked his lips. "I'm tired now, why don't you come back tomorrow? I'll tell you everything."

Hugo shook his head.

"Fontayne took me out in his boat to dump Addie's things," said Stimmler, hurrying now, feeling his life slipping away. It wasn't much of a life but it was the only one he had, and maybe if he kept talking no one would cut him off in mid-sentence. "Three a.m., the ocean is flat as glass and I'm seasick, heaving my guts out and Jack Liggett is laughing, cheering me on. You met Liggett yet? No? You got something ugly to look forward to, then." He thought for a moment. "Maybe Jack's got a visit coming he don't know about. That right? I hit the nail? You two are making the rounds," he nodded. "I wish you had started with Liggett, that way you could have told me how it went down. What he said. What he looked like when . . . when you—"

"Why don't you just sit back and relax, Mr. Stimmler? There's no need to upset yourself."

"I'm trying to tell you something," said Stimmler. "There I was, hanging on to the side of the boat, while Fontayne stands behind the wheel like Captain Courageous, telling me how he's 'looking forward to our mutual enterprise, and isn't it a beautiful night?' Bastard." Stimmler had to slow down, gasping for breath. "I threw . . . I threw Addie's things overboard, just like he wanted, but I palmed the music box. I couldn't throw Addie's music box away. I bought it for her. Only thing I ever gave to anybody that I didn't boost. I loved her. Even after what she done to me, I loved her. You ever love anyone?"

Hugo didn't answer.

"Love don't pay," said Stimmler. "Take my word for it."

There was a banging on the door and a woman's voice shouting, "Neil! I got your lunch here. Open up!"

Rick pulled out his gun.

"Neil? You alright?"

"Leave me alone!" squawked Stimmler, his face silently pleading with Rick. "Go on, git!"

"Suit yourself." She sounded tired. "Food's outside."

Rick listened at the door. He looked disappointed.

"Tell Fontayne I'll set up Joe Steps for him," Stimmler said, voice cracking. "I did it once, I can do it again." He looked back and forth from Rick to Hugo. "Or tell Joe Steps I'll set up Fontayne—I don't care who sent you, I'm happy to help you boys."

"Who are we working for, Hugo?" asked Rick. "This old fuck has got me all confused."

"Go on out to the car, Rick," Hugo said gently. "There's still some sodas in the cooler. I'll be right there."

Stimmler craned his neck, looking around on the floor. "You seen my music box? It's a piece of junk compared to the one I bought for Sweetie, but it's all my baby sister could come up with. You seen my music box? I'd like to hear that song."

"I think there's a root beer left," said Rick. "You can have it if you want, Hugo."

"Thanks anyway. You take it."

"I want to hear my song," said Stimmler.

The door closed behind Rick.

"I never got one break in my whole life," said Stimmler. "Not one." He pressed the oxygen tube deeper into his nose. He suddenly felt under the cushion, pulled out a wooden music box. His hands shook as he wound it. He opened the lid and the music tinkled out.

Hugo waited until the music box had run down.

"I hid Sweetie's music box for safekeeping," said Stimmler. "Lot of good it did me. You . . . you ask Joe Steps to give you a listen. He's got it now. Make sure you listen to it. That's a *real* music box."

Hugo leaned over the recliner, gradually shutting the valve of the airtank, while Stimmler stared at him, lips moving soundlessly. Hugo listened to the hissing slow . . . slow . . . then stop. Time measured in molecules. Later he would turn the air back on. Now he watched Stimmler squirm in the chair, the recliner tilted back almost horizontal, his hands fluttering like white butterflies in the silence.

CHAPTER

15

Quinn sat on the hood of the Jeep, leaning against the windshield as he watched the party going on at Rachel's house. Friday night, the nearby houses filled with soft light and television. Music drifted on the breeze, the palm trees shading the street from the stars. He felt the hot metal under him, the engine steaming and overheated, a perfect match for his mood.

The Jeep was parked on the street, three houses down from Rachel's, close enough to get a clear view of the colored lanterns and crepe-paper streamers waving on the porch. Her boyfriend, Mr. Saab Turbo, had parked his car all the way up the driveway, like he owned the place.

Rachel's house. Two years ago it had been their house, an elegant old two-story in Belmont Shore, an upscale enclave of Long Beach. She had put up the down payment, but he kept up his end of things. Still did. They hadn't been able to sell it after the divorce, no one in California was buying houses anymore. Prices had fallen twenty and thirty percent, and still nobody was buying. The smart money was waiting for another riot, when prices would drop even more.

After the divorce, Quinn had moved into the guest house in the back. It was a tiny cabin with a leaky shower and a lumpy sofabed, but living there allowed him to be part of Katie's growing up. A few months ago, after he got involved with Jen, he had found an apartment of his own. He still kept his keys to the house. It was a good thing— the way things were going between him and Jen, he'd be back in the cabin by next week.

Another car pulled up in front of Rachel's. The woman waited for the man to walk around and open her door. Nice frilly white dress getting out, flash of leg. One of her high heels twisted in the gravel and he heard her curse. "Motherfucker." Her date apologized like it was his fault. Way to go, pal, you got a great future as a husband.

He stretched out on the hood, crossed his legs at the ankles. He was wearing boots and jeans and a plain white t-shirt with the sleeves rolled up, the same outfit he had been wearing for the last twenty years. He heard footsteps, and was already turning—

"Quinn?" They were on the sidewalk, a couple of gangly teenagers in madras shorts and black leather jackets, no shirt, and green 14-eyelet Doc Martens that laced up almost to the knee. Their sandy hair was shaved on one side, long and floppy on the top. "Quinn? Wow, I thought that was you."

"Bobby?"

Bobby grinned, pushing hair out of his eyes. Bobby, the neighbor kid who mowed lawns and always ran out of gas, the paper boy who didn't deliver when it rained or was too hot.

"This is Gomer." Bobby indicated the other kid. "Whatcha doing, Quinn? Checking out the old homestead?"

"Something like that."

"Your wife's having a party, huh?" said Bobby, one man of the world to another. "Tough break." He shook his head. "The doofus with the black Saab is over there all the time. He never stays the night, though. You going to kick his ass? That's what I'd do."

"Kick his ass." Gomer peered out from a curtain of hair.

Bobby patted the Jeep. "I always dug this machine. 'Do it in the dirt,' that's my motto." He and Gomer guffawed. With their boots and skinny legs and scraggly goatees, they looked like cartoon hillbillies. "This is the dude I told you about, Gomer. He writes for *SLAP*, hangs out with movie stars and crooks and gets paid for it."

"You know Sharon Stone?" asked Gomer. "She a real blonde?"

"My lips are sealed."

"What's that mean?" asked Gomer. "Is that like dirty?"

"No, man," Bobby chided Gomer, "it's journalism ethics, don't ask, don't tell. Quinn here almost got wasted a few months ago, working on a story. No shit, Sherlock."

"Wicked cool," said Gomer.

"You ever need some help on a stakeout or something," said Bobby, "just say the word. I'm carrying eight units of Police Science at the community college. Gomer here is going to join the Army."

"Marines," said Gomer, rubbing his gums with a forefinger.

"Your name is Gomer," said Quinn, enjoying their silly innocence, "and you're going to join the Marines?"

"Yeah."

"So if you wanted to be a beach bum, your name would be Gilligan?"

"No, man," Gomer explained, "I want to be a Marine. They get to wear swords, right?"

"Just on special occasions," said Quinn.

"Told you," said Bobby.

Bobby stuck a neatly rolled joint into the corner of his mouth. He snapped open a Zippo with a practiced flick of the wrist, ran the flint across his leg. He took a deep hit. "Quinn?" Bobby held out the joint.

Quinn waved him away.

"It's Hawaiian, dude. I pinched it from my dad's stash."

"He don't want to be a bad role model," snickered Gomer.

"Shut up, Gomer." Bobby beckoned to the house. "Katie's not there, if that's what you're worried about. Your wife drove her away this afternoon. Katie was carrying a little suitcase. I notice things . . . practicing my surveillance."

"Thanks for keeping an eye on the place, Bobby." Quinn heard laughter from Rachel's steps. Bobby and Gomer passed the fragrant joint back and forth while the palm fronds rustled overhead.

"You sure the Marines don't let you wear a sword?" Gomer said a few minutes later. He was glassy-eyed now, draped over the Jeep.

Bobby pulled at his wispy goatee. "You want to come with us, Quinn?" He held the roach between his fingertips, sucked it one last time, and tossed it down his throat. "We could cruise Hollywood if you don't mind driving."

"I don't think so, but thanks for asking."

"I wish you hadn't moved away, man," Bobby said, solemnly shaking his hand as they left. "We could have hung together. Don't laugh. You're not that old."

"Yes, I am."

Quinn watched the colored lanterns at Rachel's house sway in the breeze as Otis Redding's "Sittin' on the Dock of the Bay" rolled mournfully through the twilight. He slid off the hood of the Jeep, checked himself in the sideview mirror, and tucked in his shirt. Party time.

Quinn didn't bother knocking. He walked in Rachel's front door like he still belonged there.

The party rolled around him, Jimi Hendrix on CD, slamming out "Purple Haze," people in party clothes standing around in the living room, glassware tinkling as they chattered away. Nobody was dancing. What a waste of good music.

The woman in the frilly white dress from out front watched him as she sipped her drink. When he looked toward her she turned away, then peeked at him over her date's shoulder. There was a new painting of Rachel's in the living room, a portrait of Katie in her ballerina clothes, tugging at her tights in annoyance, hair falling into her face. Quinn smiled. He had seen Katie do that a thousand times.

Quinn spotted Rachel in the kitchen being kissed by Mr. Saab Turbo. She turned her cheek slightly into the kiss. Good for her. She saw him, cocked her head like she wasn't sure he was really there. He waved. She waved back. Mr. Saab Turbo turned to see who she was waving to and Quinn was pleased to see his mouth tighten. Not that the man let himself frown. Mr. Saab Turbo played squash, and squash players were good sports.

Rachel moved toward him, dodging her guests with a sexy swivel of her hips, then she was embracing him, the two of them slowly spinning. "What are you doing here?" she bubbled, a little tipsy. He recognized the symptoms.

When they were first married, he and Rachel played Presidential Scrabble by candlelight after work. Anytime one of them spelled out the name of a U.S. president the other had to take off an article of clothing and drink a glass of champagne. Katie had been conceived shortly after Quinn used "Raygun" for a triple-word score.

"Nice dress," he said, still holding on to her. "A little short, maybe." He could see Mr. Saab Turbo glowering nearby. "Fun party."

"It was Tynan's idea"—she looked around for Mr. Saab Turbo—"he loves organizing these last-minute galas, I think he keeps the caterers on retainer." She finished her champagne. "Katie's at Lucy's house. They're having a slumber party. You remember Lucy?" She was suddenly sober. "I'm sorry about Teddy. I thought we might run into you at the funeral yesterday . . . Katie and I looked for you, but it was so crowded. We saw Jen taking photos—"

"I wasn't there."

"You weren't there?" She looked stunned.

"Personal request from Teddy's wife."

"Jen didn't mention anything about that—"

"She had other things on her mind," he snapped.

"I'm not supposed to talk to your girlfriend?" Rachel looked confused. "Why? Jen and I get along fine."

"It's not your fault." Quinn could see Mr. Saab Turbo wandering off to get a drink. "Monday I suggested to Jen that she and I consider . . . relocating to Paris." Rachel looked surprised. "I hadn't gotten around to mentioning to Jen that you and Katie might be moving to Paris, too, so when you told her about your job offer, it kind of made things . . . interesting when I saw her this afternoon."

"You didn't tell her?"

"It's my fault, not yours."

"Damn right it's your fault," Rachel said. "When are

you going to learn? You and your secrets . . ." She shook her head. "You don't lie to women, that would violate your private little code of conduct, you just don't tell them the truth." Rachel toasted him with her empty glass. "It's none of my business. You're Jen's problem now."

"I hope so. She wasn't too sure the last time we talked." He looked at her, smiled. "Why is it every time a woman comes to her senses she throws me out?"

Rachel didn't return the smile. This was bad. She took both of his hands. Definitely bad. "I wanted to tell you that I've decided to take the professorship at the Sorbonne."

"I expected that," Quinn said. It hurt to breathe. "When are you leaving?"

"I think it's the right decision," said Rachel.

Mr. Saab Turbo was back, carrying a tray of canapés.

"Get away from me," Quinn said to him. Heads turned.

"Let's go for a walk in the backyard," Rachel ordered, steering Quinn through the kitchen. "I'll be right back, Tynan," she called.

"I hate that guy," said Quinn as they stepped outside.

"This is my house," said Rachel, angry now. "You don't live here anymore. Tynan is very good to me. I like him."

"Right, he has great taste in tiger prawns." She turned to leave and he grabbed her arm. "Don't go. Please?" She disengaged his arm but stayed. "When are you leaving?"

"Three weeks."

He thought at first he hadn't heard her correctly.

"I thought if we were going to go, the sooner the better."

"What does Katie think of this? Does she even know?"

"She knows. She's not happy."

"You're not going to let that stop you, are you?"

Rachel tapped her foot before answering. Three times meant she was annoyed. Six times meant she was really angry. He lost count this time. "Being a parent," she said tautly, "being a full-time parent means that you sometimes have to do things that your child doesn't approve of. Sometimes they have to go to bed early. Sometimes they don't get every toy they ask for. You get to be the good guy, Quinn. You get to take her for banana splits and tell her stories and buy her pets that I have to take care of. You've got the easy job. I don't get to be incommunicado for two or three days while I'm 'working on something.' I have to be here. I have to be here when Katie wakes up in the morning. I have to be here when she goes to bed at night. So yes, Katie is very upset that we're moving so far away from you. I'm sorry she's upset, I'm even sorry you're upset, but I'm going to do what I think is best."

"You're right." He said it too quickly to take it back.

"You're not going to make trouble over custody?"

"I said you were right." They had stopped beside the rose bushes. "I just can't believe this is happening," he said. "I mean, I know it's happening, I just can't . . ." He touched a white blossom and it fell apart in his hand. "I'm going to miss you," he whispered. Like it wouldn't hurt so bad if he said it quietly.

"You can visit anytime you want." Rachel took his hand. "Stay as long as you want." She wiped her eyes and pulled him along the stone path he had laid when they first moved in, pointing out the pansies and tulips, the rustic cypress swing set, the stone frogs that Katie had named, giving him a tour of the yard as though he had never seen it.

A breeze lifted the Chinese lanterns strung along the back of the house and he shivered, rubbed his bare arms, feeling goose bumps. "Something is happening," he said, interrupting her, the words tumbling out before he could stop himself. She looked at him, not sure what he was talking about. "These last few days"—he tried to explain—"I've been talking to people I used to know. Or thought I knew." He shivered again. "Something's wrong . . ."

"What do you mean?"

"I don't know." He shook his head. "There was a woman . . ." He glanced at her. "No, it wasn't like that. She's a prosecutor, a good one, very honest, which can be a real drawback . . . she's drinking in the middle of the day now, worried that she's running out of time."

Rachel watched him.

"Remember Gill? The guy who worked at the newspaper with me? I talked about him a few times. Real gung-ho, always hanging around my desk, reading over my shoulder . . ."

"I don't remember him."

"Something's happened to him too. He's scared, talking crazy. Makes me wonder . . . maybe I'm going to look in the mirror someday and not recognize myself."

"Don't worry," teased Rachel. "I'd know you in the dark. Easy."

Quinn blushed. He looked at the big avocado tree in the far corner of the yard. "New bird feeder."

"Supposedly." She shook her head. "Katie and I stock it with sunflower seeds, but the raccoons loot it before the birds get a chance."

"Mother Nature plays favorites." He bent down, smelled the flowers blooming wildly around the orange tree. "Thanks for attending Teddy's funeral. I appreciate it."

"I'm sorry you didn't get to go."

"I'll say my good-byes to Teddy in my own time."

"Channel 5 covered the funeral live," said Rachel. "All those speeches . . . the judge had a lot of friends."

"Yeah. I saw it on TV. Lot of friends." He stood up.

"Who was that man who gave the final eulogy? He was a beautiful speaker."

"His name is Ellis Fontayne." The name left a bitter taste. "He's a big-time attorney . . . friend of the family." The wind had kicked up, sending the Chinese lanterns bobbing, yellow and blue and green spotlights scooting across the lawn. Their private kaleidoscope. "I . . . I better go."

"Why don't you go see Jen?" said Rachel. She slipped her hand in his side pocket as they walked around the side of the house toward the street. "Bring her some flowers and promise her you won't ever do it again."

"You think that will work?"

"It worked on me."

He raised an eyebrow. "It didn't work well enough."

"I gave you so many chances—"

"What are you talking about?"

She punched him in the arm. It was just a little harder than playful. "You are such a jerk, sometimes."

"What chances? I'm serious."

"I know you are," she laughed. "That's what I mean."

"Tell Katie . . . tell her I'll call tomorrow."

"I'm going to miss you." Rachel stood on the sidewalk with her back to the party. "Even after we got divorced, I used to think . . ." She shook her head, dismissing the idea.

"I used to think that too . . ."

She kissed him and they both lingered, tangled up in each other, eyes closed, until they heard footsteps on the porch behind them and broke apart like lovers caught in the act.

16

Quinn rang the doorbell twice before he heard movement in Joe's house. It was dark on the porch and he felt oddly vulnerable standing there, trying to resist the urge to look behind him. He was shaky from his conversation with Rachel, confused by the intimacy that still existed between them. There should be a statute of limitations on feelings.

The door opened and Joe Steps sat there, dapper as a bridegroom in his suit and tie. "Quinn! Come on inside—"

"I should have called—" Quinn stopped, as the cab driver from the pier walked over from the living room and stood behind Joe, his bony hands resting on the back of the wheelchair. "I . . . I didn't know you had company."

"Hugo isn't company, he's a friend. Hugo, this is Quinn, the guy I told you about."

"Pleased to meet you," they both said. Neither of them moved.

"I saw you at the pier Sunday night . . ." Quinn started.

"I saw you too." Hugo's voice was flat and cold as a river rock—it was impossible to determine if he was making a simple declaration of fact or a veiled threat.

"Joe, were you going out?" asked Quinn, watching Hugo. "I don't want to interrupt. I was at Rachel's and—"

"Hugo is off the meter tonight. I told you, he's a friend. Now, come on in, damnit, and close the door." Joe rolled into the living room and Quinn finally stepped inside.

"I'm going to leave," said Hugo.

Joe spun his chair around and faced them, annoyed. "What is it with you two? Shake hands, you make me nervous."

Their hands stabbed out toward each other. Quinn felt like he was touching a frozen leather glove.

"I'm glad you came by," Joe said. "I know Teddy's funeral was yesterday, but I couldn't do it. I didn't belong there."

Quinn felt like he had stepped off a cliff and was falling through the darkness, wind rushing past him. "Me neither."

"You knew Judge Krammerson?" Hugo asked Quinn. He looked surprised.

"Teddy was Quinn's stepfather," said Joe.

Quinn nodded. "Did . . . did you know Teddy?"

Hugo shook his head. "I didn't know the man. I just read about the killing. Terrible." He sagged visibly, his shoulders like sharp sticks. "I am sorry." His voice was the same dry monotone, but Quinn knew with a strange certainty that the man's sympathies were genuine.

"Thank you, Hugo."

"That's better," said Joe, pleased. "Like I said, you two have more in common than you think."

Quinn and Hugo shifted.

"I'm serious," said Joe. "That's how I knew Hugo and I were going to hit it off. The first time I got into Hugo's cab—what was it, couple of months ago?—Hugo's got this little hand-made sign taped up next to his hack license: 'Driver will flip double or nothing for his tip.' Just like you used to do when you were a kid, Slick, remember? I'd send you to the store to get me cigars and you always wanted to go double or nothing for my change. You were one lucky kid. Hugo is lucky, too. I keep trying to get him to play the ponies with me, but he won't. Just wants to play for his tip. I don't understand it."

"I don't like to gamble," Hugo explained to Quinn. "Double or nothing is different, because I'm playing for money I never had in my pocket. You don't miss what you never had."

"Dumbest thing I ever heard," groused Joe. "What you never had is what you miss the most."

"Hugo's right," said Quinn. "You get a taste of something, then it's taken away . . . you can go crazy with hunger."

"I wasn't asking for a vote," said Joe. "I just wanted to point out you two had something in common."

Hugo nodded.

"The reason I stopped by," Quinn said to Joe, "I thought maybe you and I could go out to the graveyard. We'd have the place to ourselves." He glanced over at Hugo. "We could do it another time . . ."

Joe smacked the arms of his wheelchair. "Let's go."

"We don't have to do it right now," Quinn said.

"Why wait? Let's go pay our respects to Teddy. All of us."

"I don't think so," Hugo said. "This is a family matter."

"Teddy wouldn't mind," said Joe. "It's okay, isn't it, Quinn?"

Quinn didn't answer.

"Fine," said Joe, clapping his hands together. "Besides, Rachel told me about the Jeep you drive—that thing would shake my bones apart. Hugo's got his taxi here, a big cushiony land yacht." He rolled toward the door, flung it wide. "Come on boys," he called as he started down the ramp on the front porch, "let's go see Teddy!"

"Careful," Joe said as Hugo lifted him to the top of the brick wall surrounding the cemetery. Quinn reached up from the other side and gently lowered Joe to the ground. Joe hung onto his shoulder, his legs unsteady as Quinn took the folded wheelchair that Hugo passed over to him.

"You're breathing hard, Slick," Joe said, sitting down.

Hugo dropped onto the grass from the top of the wall, putting his hands out to stop himself from tumbling forward.

Joe hoisted himself up in his wheelchair, craning his neck. "Where is it?"

"I'm not sure . . ." Quinn looked around. "There." He pointed toward a low, tree-shaded hill, the crest heaped with bouquets, stacked with floral wreaths.

"I can do it myself," snapped Joe as Quinn started to push him. His hands slipped on the wheels and he cursed, leaning forward for leverage. The wheelchair began moving over the spongy ground, slowly at first, then gaining momentum.

Quinn and Hugo looked at each other, shrugged, and followed.

Looking at Hugo, Quinn was reminded again of a scarecrow, but there was a peacefulness about him, a bright intelligence in his eyes that belied his grim appearance. He wondered if Hugo was sick with AIDS or some other wasting disease, but there was such a robust, energetic quality about him that all thought of illness seemed inappropriate. If Hugo was sick, it didn't show.

"Have you been driving a cab a long time?"

"Not really." Hugo smiled shyly. He had big, uneven teeth. "Joe's my best customer—he hires me by the day, whether we drive or not. I feel bad taking his money."

"He wouldn't pay you if he didn't think it was worth it."

"I expect that's true, but he's the exception." Hugo spoke with a calm formality, a quiet reserve that seemed out of phase with the frantic intimacy of Southern California. No wonder Joe enjoyed his company. "I'm not sure if

I'm really suited for this job," Hugo said apologetically. "I make people nervous. Sometimes a fare will get in my cab, then ask to be let out a block later."

"I've had interviews like that," said Quinn. They were walking together now across the grass. "People think they want to talk, then they worry they're going to say too much and get themselves in trouble. It's not us—people are afraid of themselves."

"It's very kind of you to say that, but I don't think that's the problem. It's my appearance. People think I look spooky. Don't deny it. You don't have to spare my feelings—I've been told that on any number of occasions and I've learned to accept it. Not that I don't appreciate kindness when I encounter it. Your wife, for example . . ."

Quinn slipped on a patch of wet ground, caught himself.

"I dropped Joe off at her house that first time, walked him to the door. She asked him about me later . . . told him that I reminded her of an El Greco painting." Hugo shook his head in wonder. "What a lovely thing to say."

"What did you mean, 'the first time'?" Quinn said lightly.

Hugo shrugged. "I've brought Joe over there twice this week . . . I thought you knew."

"No."

"I hope I haven't said anything to upset you."

"No. Not at all."

"You're very easy to talk to," said Hugo, his eyes sunk so deeply into his face that he appeared to be looking at

Quinn from the bottom of a well. "I'm not much of a conversationalist."

"Could have fooled me, Hugo."

They both flinched as a jetliner came in low overhead, engines roaring, wheels down for its landing approach to the nearby airport: Orange County's John Wayne International, where a larger-than-life bronze statue of the Duke in cowboy regalia guarded the main entrance.

The grass was flattened now, tamped down by the hundreds of feet that had stood there yesterday afternoon: the mourners and the curious, police officers and government officials come to pay their respects, to see and be seen.

Joe struggled up the knoll where Teddy was buried, breathing hard, hair plastered to his forehead. When he finally reached the top, he did a quick 180-degree spin and waited for them, his face flushed and triumphant.

Quinn walked past him and toward Teddy's gravestone, his body growing heavier with each step. The stone was a simple slab of black granite inscribed with his name, his dates of birth and death, and the inscription, LOVING HUSBAND, HONORABLE MAN. The arc of Teddy's life—no mention of fatherhood. Quinn stood there wanting to feel something, at least a sense of finality, the knowledge that he and Teddy were beyond arguments and apologies now . . . let forgiveness reign. Instead he stood silenced by the freshness of the gravesite, the ripe smell of dark earth and wilting flowers.

"I'm going," Hugo said from where he had stopped

below the knoll. "I'll . . . I'll wait back by the wall, give you two a chance to make your peace." He backed away.

Joe watched Hugo hurrying away, watched as Hugo glanced back, then doubled his pace. He followed Hugo's retreat down the slope of grass, turned and pulled a large silver flask out of his jacket. "Enough with the sad face, Slick—the funeral's over, this is the wake." He poured a splash of booze onto the grave, took a drink himself.

"Teddy loved good Scotch," Joe said pensively. "That's all any of us drank in the old days. Scotch, bourbon, maybe a cold Gibson served straight up. A man's drink. I come out of the joint and all you young guys are wearing earrings and drinking these sweet umbrella drinks the color of Easter eggs." He chuckled to himself, held out the flask to Quinn. "That-a-boy," he cheered, his eyes wild in the moonlight as Quinn took a long drink, flask pointed to the stars, "the Three Caballeros ride again!"

CHAPTER

17

Rick watched the party wind down from the front seat of the Mercedes 560SL convertible, saw women in slinky Lagerfeld knockoffs and their J. Crew dates saying goodbye to this Rachel babe on the front porch, exchanging hugs in the dim light. Barely 1 a.m. and they were headed home to their fixed char-peis and their adjustable mortgages. He was never going to get old.

No sign of Hugo. The breeze caressed his hair. He was glad he had put the Mercedes's top down. Rick aimed the 9mm at the Chinese lanterns bobbing in the wind, made pow-pow sounds like he had a silencer. Chinese lanterns were terminally lame. Might as well string up a fucking piñata.

He flipped the safety of the 9mm automatic off and on, off and on, scratching an itch at the back of his head with the barrel, off and on, off and on. Rick had been parked near the house for a half-hour. If he heard another song by Springsteen, U-2, or Roy Orbison, he was going in with guns blazing. Blazing. Yeah, he liked the sound of that. Like he was a forest fire or a napalm strike. Guns blazing. Oh, yeah. And, nobody going to put him out once he got going.

Rick turned the rearview mirror so that he could see himself. He smoothed his right sideburn with his thumb. The jacket of his new suit fit him perfectly, the collar hugging the back of his neck and shoulders. No prole gap. His first tailored suit. An Ungaro. Three-button, side-vented, dark-blue cashmere. Soft as love, that's what the salesman had said. Rick couldn't wait to show it to Hugo, maybe talk him into getting one, too. They had plenty of money now, and more coming. They were ahead of schedule. Wait until Hugo found out. Wouldn't he be surprised.

Where was Hugo? He had said he was going to see Joe tonight . . . a social call, if you could believe that. Couple of pals. Rick had driven by Joe's place but didn't see Hugo's taxi. He'd driven past the pier, just in case. Rachel's house was a long shot—there was no sign of the taxi on her street either—but Rick had waited anyway when he saw the party.

Rick had followed Hugo and Joe here twice this week, to this house with the big porch, keeping well back, each time driving a different car he had boosted. The Camaro Tuesday had taken forty-one seconds from popping the doorlock to driving it away, the VW Jetta Wednesday took thirty-eight. His record was twenty-three seconds for a

1991 Pontiac Firebird. The Mercedes he was driving now—Rick smiled—he hadn't had to boost.

Hugo had told him about the woman who lived in this house—Rachel—said she was really nice, and so was her little girl, whatever the fuck her name was. Rick had seen her talking to Hugo, a real tomboy, scabs on her knees, laughing too loud.

Rick didn't like tomboys, he didn't like dinosaur rock, he didn't like not knowing where Hugo and Joe were. Out having fun, probably, living it up to the extent that either of them could, which wasn't much. A couple of days ago, Rick had watched Joe Steps trying to show the tomboy some intricate dance moves, the geezer looking ridiculous shifting around in his wheelchair like a spazzed-out Ironside. Hugo probably wasn't even thinking about Rick. He played with the safety of the 9mm, trying to imagine what Hugo could be doing without him. Off, on, off, on. D.O.A. Roulette, that's what he called it, a little game he played when he was a kid. Donny played, too. Rick taught him. They used to goof around in Donny's bedroom with his father's .45, a big gun that you needed two hands to hold. Donny had made him take out the magazine that last afternoon, blubbering how he didn't want to play anymore. 'One more time,' Rick had promised, off, on, off, on, pointing the barrel at Donny's forehead. How was he supposed to know there was still a bullet in the chamber? Rick's ears rang for the rest of the day. Bummer. Rick got probation and a lecture from a lady judge with a zit on the end of her nose. The next time it happened, the next time he got caught, he was sent to the California Youth Authority for three years. Good thing they didn't find out about the other times. They'd never have let him out.

Rick tucked the 9mm between the seats, picked up the Mercedes's car phone, and dialed the 900-number of Psychic Soulmate. He jigged the monogrammed leather keycase in the ignition while he waited through the message tape telling him that the call would cost $12.95 for the first minute and $5.95 for each minute thereafter, and that if he wasn't eighteen or older he needed his parents' permission first. Sure. Give me a shovel, I'll ask them.

"Good evening, sir," said the pleasant woman on the line. She hiccupped. "Pardonnez-moi," she giggled, then caught herself. "Do you have a regular Psychic Soulmate?"

"Yeah, but I want to try a new soulmate," said Rick, still watching the front door of the house. "Somebody who knows what they're fucking doing."

"All of our psychics are certified," said the woman, speaking slowly, like they all did, keeping the clock running. "Princess Adriadica is very—"

"She a real princess?"

"Yes . . . yes, I think so. Yes, I'm sure of it," she said, hiccupping. Rick heard paper rustling on the other end.

"Put her on," said Rick. He was on hold a long time. Twenty seconds at least. What was that, four or five dollars for sitting around with the phone next to his ear listening to space music? Not that Rick was going to get the bill, that was going to Mr. Jack Liggett, owner of the Mercedes and the carphone in it. It still pissed him off—Rick didn't like to be made a fool of.

"This is Princess Adriadica—"

"You sound like the girl I was just talking to," said Rick.

"Sir, I am your personal soulmate—"

"You sure you're not her?"

"My name," she said slowly, "is Princess Adriadica. What is your name, and how can I help you?"

"You're the fucking psychic, you tell me."

"I can sense that you are very troubled . . ."

"Totally troubled, princess," said Rick, impressed. "I got a friend . . . sometimes I don't know if he really likes me, or just needs me . . . for stuff."

"I understand completely." Princess Adriadica lowered her voice. "Men can be such pigs. I had this one boyfriend—"

"That's not what I mean."

"Of course. I understand completely. Just a moment, while I consult my higher self . . ." Rick waited. It took a while. "Your friend," said Princess Adriadica, pausing after every word, "he is very sincere. But shy. I don't think you have any reason to doubt him."

"Wow." Rick was relieved.

"I sense that you have more questions," she said quickly.

"Yeah?" Rick thought about it. "Okay. I was thinking of opening a business soon . . ." Princess Adriadica hiccupped in his ear. Rick stared at the phone.

"Yes? Go on," said Princess Adriadica. She hiccupped again. "Pardonnez-moi. Go on, I understand complete-ly—"

Rick beat the phone against the dash, flailing away until the case cracked. He smoothed his hair, still breathing hard, watching the people leaving the party, lingering on the front steps. He picked up the 9mm again as this woman came out onto the porch, hugging everyone she could get her hands on. Must be Rachel. No wonder Hugo liked to hang around here. He had never seen her touch Hugo, but that didn't mean she hadn't. Rick sat back, flipping the 9mm's safety off-on, off-on as he watched her, off-on, off-on, round and round she goes . . .

Rachel stepped off the porch and down the steps, walking her guests onto the sidewalk. He jerked upright as she stopped under the streetlight, her face clearly visible for the first time as she waved good-bye.

It was the woman in the photograph. The one that the judge had kept by the bed. Rick had picked it up the night they killed him, stared at the three smiling faces, wondering who they were, and what the fuck they thought was so funny. He hadn't recognized the tomboy, she was just a baby in the photo. There was a guy holding the kid, a jock with tough eyes and a woman with her arm around him. Rachel. He had slammed the pipe wrench into the photo, shattering it, beating it to pieces, not knowing why it made him angry.

Princess Adriadica wasn't the only one who was psychic.

Rachel turned and walked back up the steps and onto the porch. Nice ass.

Rick could see himself reflected in the tachometer of the Mercedes, the numbers spread across his face like an alarm clock. He smiled at his reflection. What time is it? Time for fun. He aimed the gun at Rachel's back through the windshield and pulled the trigger. Safety on. Lucky girl.

Quinn listened to the faint rush of traffic, the freeway a river of headlights shimmering in the night. He jumped as a plane swooped low from the ocean toward John Wayne Airport, engines screaming as it slowed. He had lost track of how long he had been standing in front of Teddy's grave.

"Hard to believe that Teddy's lying there under all that dirt," said Joe. He shook his head. "Seems like yesterday he and I were youngsters, chasing around after life . . . Your mama thought I was a bad influence on him; she said Teddy spilled more booze with me than he drank with her." He smiled to himself. "Maybe he did." Joe fumbled in his jacket, brought out one of the twisted rum-soaked crooks Quinn remembered him smoking when he was a kid. He lit a wooden match with his thumbnail. "Your mother never liked my cigars, either."

"She liked you though. Anybody could see that. I

never saw her in the kitchen except when you were coming over."

"Well, we went back a ways, your mama and me. She knew what I liked." He flicked away the match, bounced it off a nearby headstone. "I introduced her to Teddy, did you know that? No? Well, I did. I told Teddy he owed me forever." Clouds rolled over the stars. "Forever."

"She always wore her best dresses when you visited, Joe. I remember playing in the backyard and hearing her sing in the bedroom, getting dressed and Teddy in the doorway, watching me, just watching me, the two of us pretending we didn't hear her singing. I was just a kid, Joe, I don't even know why we were pretending, but we were."

"Well, I used to make her laugh, sometimes that's enough to make a husband uncomfortable. Or a son." Joe rested his head against the back of the chair. His grin flashed in the night like lightning. "She had a great laugh. You heard it and you thought you were missing out on something good."

Quinn could see Hugo waiting in the shadow of the brick wall surrounding the graveyard, standing there as immobile as a headstone.

"Did my mother ever talk about my father?"

Joe hesitated, shook his head. "Your mama . . . well, when something was finished with her, it was over." He puffed on the cigar. "I never understood her walking out on the two of you like that. Teddy just gets up one morning and finds a note on the table. He never got over it."

"He wasn't the only one."

Joe's face was wreathed in smoke and sadness. "Maybe I should have left well enough alone and stopped coming around. Maybe she wouldn't have left."

"Maybe." Quinn bit off the word.

The wind rustled the trees around them, rippling through the grass. "I missed the wind when I was inside," Joe said quietly, "missed the way a breeze can stir things up, almost without anyone noticing."

"I saw Rachel tonight. She and Katie have been seeing a lot of you lately."

"Rachel asked me over . . . and I like being there. A kid in the house makes all the difference. Katie keeps asking me what you were like as a boy—were you brave when the house made funny sounds and did you always like to tell stories?" Joe shook his head in wonder. "She's sharp, like you were, weighing everything she's told, not taking anything on credit."

"I've been reading your trial transcripts," Quinn said suddenly.

"I'm not surprised," Joe said, unfazed. "You were always snooping in my things."

"The D.A. had a good case, Joe. A big-time bookie and his bodyguard were shot to death in a warehouse. Close range. Cops found your watch clutched in the bookie's hand—"

"My watch was stolen that morning at the track," said Joe. "Sometime between the sixth and seventh races. I liked that gold Piaget, too—that's what they gave to finalists at the Nationals that year. My partner and I placed

Second. Should have won. Politics. It's all politics." They listened to the traffic sounds, neither of them wanting to speak. "Hard to believe there was a time around here when you could stand outside at night and not hear cars," Joe said at last. "We all used to go for midnight swims at Seal Beach and hardly see a light on shore. Remember that?"

Quinn didn't respond. He was tired of Memory Lane.

"You don't want me to visit your family any more?"

"Your name was in the bookie's notebook. Bookies are like accountants, they keep good records. You were supposed to meet him the night he was murdered. You owed him money."

"I owed him money, I never denied that. I didn't kill him, though," insisted Joe. "I never made it over to the bookie's."

"You had no alibi—"

"That wasn't my fault!" Joe's voice had risen, echoing off the marble tombstones. He caught himself, looked away. When he turned back to Quinn, his tone was softer. "Teddy and I had made plans to get together that night. We were supposed to meet the bookie, then go out for drinks and catch a show at the Pantages Theatre . . . Teddy showed up at my house four hours late. I had already called the bookie to reschedule, but he didn't answer his phone. According to the cops, he was already dead."

"Why was Teddy so late?"

"His car had broke down on the freeway after he dropped you off with a baby-sitter. He sat there watching the traffic whip past, waiting for a cop or a towtruck to drive by. He finally hiked out on his own." Joe shook his head. "I used to think I was lucky. Teddy's Caddy throws a rod and I lose twenty-eight years of my life."

The air was heavy with perfume. Quinn stared at the piled flowers around the gravesite and wanted to kick them to pieces. "You must have been pretty mad at Teddy," he said carefully. "He should have gotten to a phone quicker, not hung you up like that. He could have been your alibi."

"It wasn't Teddy's fault," Joe said. "He blamed himself, though. I think that's why he never wrote me in prison, why he told you I was dead." He examined the cigar, then puffed it back to life. "You should have seen Teddy's face when I showed up at the courthouse a couple of weeks ago," Joe chuckled. "After all those years he was still apologizing."

"Who set you up, Joe? You have to have some idea."

Joe shrugged. He wrapped his coat around himself. "It was a long time ago." He swiveled his head, taking in the full extent of the cemetery. "This place looks different than it did on TV. All those bigshots talking about Teddy like they knew him."

"Ellis Fontayne knew Teddy," Quinn said. "I saw him at Teddy's house the day after the murder, consoling the widow. I didn't even know who he was at the time. He and Teddy must have been close."

"Teddy and Fontayne knew each other," Joe said. "That doesn't mean they were close."

"I'm talking to Fontayne next week. I've got an interview scheduled for Monday."

Joe's face was impassive. "Now why would you do that?"

"I don't know." Quinn was telling the truth. "I saw him sitting in Teddy's house and something about him wasn't right. Being a reporter is a lot like playing poker . . . sometimes you have to play your hunches."

"Be careful." Joe leaned forward. "Watch yourself with him."

"Why would you say that?"

"Just be careful with him."

"I'm careful with everybody, Joe," Quinn said evenly.

"You remind me of your mother when you get that nasty edge in your voice." Joe sat back, happily puffing away on the twisted cigar. "She was a beautiful woman. Fiery Italian girl with waves of thick black hair, and the smoothest skin. Those eyes of hers," he laughed, "she could give you a look that would boil coffee."

Quinn looked around but there was only Hugo, still waiting, well out of earshot. "You know, when you're a kid, and things aren't working out at home"—he licked his lips, feeling like he was ten years old all over again—"you make up stories, make up things that aren't real but you hope they're real, because you want to believe them . . ."

"What's the matter?" asked Joe.

"Joe . . . are you my father?" Quinn had wanted to ask him the question for as long as he could remember. "I looked at my birth records, but there's no father listed."

Joe just looked at him.

"Are you, Joe? It would make things so much easier . . . I'm sorry for Teddy, I loved him . . . loved him as best I could, but I always wished"—the words burned in his throat, a raw insult to Teddy whispered over his grave—"I always wished you were my father."

"I wish I were." The breeze whipped away the cigar smoke and suddenly there were tears brimming in Joe's eyes. "Sometimes I look at you . . . and there she is, staring back at me." A single tear slid down his cheek—in the red glow of the cigar tip it looked like a drop of blood. "I wish that I had had kids," he said hoarsely. "Boy, girl, it wouldn't have mattered. I would like to have seen a piece of myself in someone else's eyes or mouth or the way they held a fork. I would have liked that."

Quinn nodded, unable to speak, not wanting to believe Joe, still hanging on to the hope that the two of them were . . . family. Another plane was coming in for a landing, engines screaming. He imagined Rachel and Katie at LAX, boarding an AirFrance jet, waving good-bye . . . Quinn could feel his life contracting to a hard black lump. Located at the very center of his throat.

CHAPTER

19

Rick drove the Mercedes south on Pacific Coast Highway from Long Beach, keeping to the speed limit, a steady 35 mph. The cool breeze off the ocean rippled his lightly moussed hair. He checked himself in the rearview, smoothed his eyebrows with a forefinger. Some girls in a rusted Mustang beeped at him from the next lane, smiled his way. He waved back, winked at the cute one driving.

It was a beautiful evening, the moon coming up over the water tower in Sunset Beach. The tower had been converted into a private residence, with 360-degree windows and a private elevator. It was on the market for two million. Someday Rick wanted to live in a place like that, public and private at the same time, distinctive, classy. It would be nice to look down on the rest of the world for a change.

He whipped out the yellow silk handkerchief from his

breast pocket, dropped a couple of the amyl nitrate ampules he had taken from the desert rat into the center. The girls in the rusted Mustang were right alongside him, keeping pace, calling to him, holding up a can of beer.

He crushed the ampules in his fist, brought the handkerchief to his nose and inhaled—the pungent smell twisted through his brain, blood rushing through him like a waterfall. He could hear the girls whooping it up as his head flopped back, eyes wide, his penis stiffening, pushing against the soft cashmere of his trousers. The way the girls were shouting, he thought for a moment the Mercedes had become invisible and they were cheering his hard-on.

The Mercedes thudded over the old railroad tracks at the border of Huntington Beach State Park, and Rick heard something wet and heavy bounce against the inside of the trunk. He was speeding. Blame it on the amyl, which slowed everything down, made you think you could keep up, no matter how fast you went. This was no time to be stopped by a cop. Not that it wouldn't be interesting.

He could see fire rings blazing on the beach to his right, surfers huddled around the concrete pits in the sand like fucking cannibals, stragglers dragging over chunks of driftwood and lumber stolen from nearby construction sites. Rick hated the beach, hated the sand getting in your hair, and the greasy lotion that clogged your pores, and most of all what the sun did to your skin. The sun was a time machine with one direction only: *older*.

Newport Beach was quiet—it was after midnight now, the Ferrari dealerships dark, by-appointment-only real estate offices closed, the neon sign turned off at the Yacht Club. Rick in the morning, sailors take warning. Heh-heh.

The girls in the Mustang drew alongside him, beer cans waving. One of them shouted something about a party. He tried to focus, but it wasn't easy with the amyl pounding in his head. He took another hit from the handkerchief, eyes rolling back in his head. The girl driving was doing something with her tongue. The other one . . . his head lolled against the headrest . . . the other one—the oncoming headlights were so bright—the other one was pulling down her blouse, showing off her tiny white breasts.

Rick liked them small. The flatter the better. If he wanted a cow, he'd have been a farmer. He laughed at his own joke. The girls were laughing, too. The three of them were having a regular party. His cock throbbed like a time bomb.

He hit the brakes, cut behind them, and veered off at the Fashion Island exit, the girls in the Mustang turning around, shocked as he waved bye-bye. They looked in pain as he disappeared from view. He knew the feeling.

Fashion Island was the most exclusive mall in Orange County, a tiny island of orderly palm trees, artificial waterfalls, and sidewalks scrubbed daily. No litter. No graffiti. No Muzak at Fashion Island, either—a pianist in top hat and tails tinkled a white concert grand while taut-cheeked matrons flipped out their platinum cards, serene behind their opaque Matsuda shades. The mall was dark now, the piano silent, the pretty salesgirls and salesboys tucked into their soft 120-thread cotton sheets.

Rick drove up one of the narrow winding streets overlooking the mall. He was the only car on the road, the
Mercedes so quiet he seemed to be gliding through the
night. He stopped at the crest of the hill, turned off
the ignition, and tilted back his seat. He could see the
Svenga billboard clearly from where he sat.

The billboard showed two young couples lounging
around a softly lit sunken living room, L.A. by night visible
through the picture window. Plush leather sofa. Thick
white carpet. Matte-black component stereo system.
Chrome Hydro-Gym gleaming in the far corner. Glasses of
clear Svenga liqueur sweated on the black marble coffee-
table. SVENGA: THE WINNERS CHOICE.

The couples wore pajamas made of a clingy, sheer
material that made you think they were moving even
though they were sitting still. One of the men didn't have a
top on, his chest smooth and muscular. They were all
barefoot, pink-toed, and pedicured. He wondered who did
their hair.

Rick licked his lips, settling back into the seat of the
Mercedes, the smell of new leather in his nostrils as he
watched the winners at play: the blonde boys and blonde
girls, all of them long-limbed and tan, sleek as racehorses.
Svenga was his favorite billboard in the world—he drove
out here whenever he was sad and lonely, to remind himself of the things that money could buy.

Rick unzipped his pants, released his penis into the
cool night air. He was hardening by the moment, growing
thicker. He crushed two more amyl nitrate ampules into

the handkerchief and inhaled, one hand wrapped around his penis.

The girls lay casually on the sofa, skin peeking out from their clothes, faces slack and loose with pleasure. The boys sat on the floor, heads resting against the girls' splayed bodies. One boy looked directly at Rick, staring back at him with a little half-smile. "I see you too," he seemed to be saying.

Stars exploded behind Rick's eyes as he stared at the topless boy, wanting to be inside that knowing smile, to be part of that little slumber party, boys and girls together, all of them the same: slick and hard and hot and juicy, creaming with confidence. Rick was squeezing himself so tightly he could hardly breathe.

An airplane came in low, red winglights blinking as it descended toward the nearby airport. John Wayne Airport. Remember the fucking Alamo.

Rick unbuttoned his shirt, caressed his nipples, wanting to join those beautiful boys and girls in that living room, wanting to touch them, all of them, kiss every inch of their perfect skin, brush out their clean, soft hair. He wanted to be a winner too, a winner playing with other winners, smiling sex toys without any thought of love . . . no love at all.

He inhaled from the handkerchief. A warm electric current surged from his anus to the crown of his head, sparks cracking from his fingertips.

Love was a lie. He gasped, head lolling, helpless now. Love was what people said to you when they wanted to fuck you. Everyone wanted to fuck Rick. Not that he minded. Girls were good. Boys were good. What he had with Hugo, though, that was better. No boyfriend games. No girlfriend games. They were friends. Hugo had said so and Hugo never lied. Never.

Hugo let Rick give him facials and shampoos and haircuts, but that was as far as it went. Hugo just stared at him when Rick offered more. Not angry. Blank. Hugo didn't have any appetite. Not for sex. Not for food. Not for drugs. Hugo was the ultimate winner. He didn't need anyone or anything, which made his acceptance of Rick all the more precious. Rick didn't press for anything more between them. What he and Hugo had . . . it was enough. It was more than enough.

Rick groaned with pleasure as he caught the eye of the topless boy and locked on to his ultrawhite smile, using it to make the leap into the living room, that clear, clean place where no one lost or died, and the fun went on forever . . . His hand circled his penis, twisting the skin behind the head, faster now. The pain was so hot it burned. The only place it didn't hurt was inside the cool blue eyes of the Svenga boy. Rick's hips buckled as he splashed the dashboard, but he couldn't turn away from that winner's smile.

It was after 2 a.m. when Rick saw Hugo's cab turn the corner onto Joe Steps's street. He breathed a sigh of relief, scooted down low in his seat, peering out through the steering wheel. He knew if he waited long enough, Hugo would show up to drop off the old man. Then the two of them could go dump the Mercedes and head home. They had a lot to talk about. Rick felt like apologizing and he didn't even know why.

The cab pulled up to the curb and Hugo got out. Then the passenger door opened. Rick leaned forward. Joe always rode in the back, where he had more room.

A big guy in a leather jacket slid out of the passenger side, stepped into the street. Tough guy. Real retro with the engineer boots and tight jeans. He needed a haircut. And a tailor. Hugo helped the old man, carried him in his arms up the steps, while the tough guy followed with Joe's wheelchair.

Rick watched them open the front door and disappear into the house. He couldn't move. He just sat there in the Mercedes, trying to make sense of it. He had seen this tough guy before. In the photo the judge kept by his bed—Rachel, the kid, and this guy. Little family portrait. Blew them a kiss goodnight. Hugo had killed the judge . . . why was he making friends with his relatives?

Rick could hear a faint scratching from the trunk, but he ignored it. He had more important things to think of.

CHAPTER

20

Jen didn't know how long the doorbell had been ringing before she woke up. It said 3:35 on the digital clock beside her bed. She lay there blinking at the ceiling, still half-asleep, trying to remember what time zone she was in.

"Jen?" Quinn's voice: a loud whisper, pleading.

She groaned, remembering, slowly sat up in bed, rubbing her eyes, taking her time.

"Jen? It's me."

She stretched. Raked her hands through her hair, checking the result in her mirror. She considered brushing her teeth. Not a chance. No way. She hit the hall light, saw the front door partially open, restrained by the security chain. Quinn's face was wedged in the gap, watching her with one eye. His key was still in the lock. He held up a handful of flowers for her to see. She yawned.

"I . . . I know it's late—"

"It's early. Too early."

"You look beautiful." He smiled with his half-face and she thought of the jack-of-hearts. She was wearing one of his t-shirts. It was baggy on her, hanging halfway down her thighs, but with the hall light behind her it would be almost transparent. "Are you going to let me in?" he said. "I picked up the Sunday paper—"

"What's the matter, Quinn, aren't you going to spend Sunday morning with the wife and kiddy?"

"Don't be like that."

"What are you doing here knocking on my door? Did you tuck your little family into their nice warm beds already? Kiss them on their cheeks? I guess they don't need you anymore tonight, that's why you're here."

"I told you I was sorry." Quinn pushed the flowers through the narrow space between the jamb, a fragrant offering. "I wasn't completely straight with you about Paris, I admit it. What else—"

She kicked the door shut, decapitating the bouquet. He gently pushed it open again. The bare green stalks looked ridiculous in his hand.

"You didn't admit it," she said. "You were caught."

"I was going to tell you—"

"When? After we got a charming little place near Les Halles?" Her voice was rising. "Something just a short walk from Rachel and Katie? Close enough so they could drop over for fresh croissants?" She stopped before she started screaming. No one was worth that. That's what she told herself anyway.

"I was wrong and I was stupid," said Quinn. "I know you're hurt, but please—"

"I'm not hurt," she insisted, knowing it wasn't true. "I was hurt this afternoon when Rachel called, and I was angry when I spoke with you afterwards. Now I'm just bored."

"I'm sorry, Jen."

She didn't answer.

"Why don't you let me in?" He tried a smile on her. "You'd have more fun hating me up-close-and-personal."

She glanced back over her shoulder. "It's alright, go back to sleep," she called to her bedroom.

Quinn's smile dropped. "Is somebody there?" He jammed his face into the gap, trying to see. "Come on, don't play games with me."

She started to close the door. "Call me this evening," she said, lowering her voice, pleased to see his pained expression. "We need to talk about how we want to handle interviewing Ellis Fontayne tomorrow. I put together some background—"

"Is someone else really there?" He held the door open. His eyes kept trying to see over her shoulder to the bedroom doorway. "I don't have any excuse for what I did, but I didn't plan to deceive you—"

"Let's call it a lie." She kept her voice low. "We're not lawyers. We're lovers. Remember?" He nodded. "So when you asked me to move to Paris and didn't mention that Rachel and Katie were going along for the ride, to me, that qualifies as a lie. So what else have you lied to me about?"

"Nothing." He dropped the flowerstalks onto the floor, reached a hand through the narrow gap to her. "I didn't intend to lie to you," he gestured helplessly. "We were in bed and it felt so good to be with you—I didn't want to lose you, and I didn't want to lose Katie, and the next thing I knew I was asking you about Paris and I'm sorry, Jen. I'm sorry."

That was one big difference between Quinn and the young guys she had gone out with before. He didn't try to downplay the importance of what he had done. The young ones would have squirmed and made excuses and argued that her anger was just PMS or a "chick thing." Not Quinn. He was an easy man to forgive. But she couldn't forget why he had lied to her. He was a family man and he wanted to keep his family together. There was no room in that family for her. She didn't want a family even if there was room. Sooner or later it was going to be impossible to ignore that fact.

"Jen?" He held out his hand to her. "Please let me in."

"Remember when we first met," she asked, "and I told you I never got into physical encounters—"

"Sex," he corrected. "You said you never had sex with anyone over the age of twenty-two. It's burned into my memory."

"You remember my reasons? I said older men got tired too easily and they always have all this junk running through their head, career worries, family worries, erection worries . . . Well, you don't get tired," she admitted. He smiled shyly, and for a moment she weakened. "You've got more than your share of psychic debris, though. All this . . . baggage from your past. I travel light—two cameras, four lenses. No strobe. Natural light only. I keep my life clean and unencumbered—"

"That's not the way life is."

"That's the way it is for me. I make sure of that. You wanted to know how I keep it all together after living in Beirut and Sarajevo and Newark . . . that's how I do it. I look in their dying eyes, feel every wound that will never heal, every need that will never be met, and I take my photographs, I get the shot, and when the job is done and the photos printed, I let it go. All of it. It's over and done with. Then I go on to another assignment."

"Is that who I am?" He pulled back slightly from the door. "Another assignment?"

"No. If you were, then breaking up would be a lot easier."

"I don't want it to be easy," he declared. She could see his Adam's apple bob. "I want it to be so hard you can't do it. Give us another chance, Jen. Katie is part of my life, and Rachel too, because she's part of Katie's life." His eyes looked right into her, steady and unblinking and she couldn't turn away. "I don't know what's going to happen with us . . . I do know that if you close the door we're both going to regret it."

"What happens if I open the door?" She could feel her heart beating and was afraid he could hear it, too. "I may regret that, too."

His mouth moved but no sound came out.

"I don't know what I was thinking when I got involved with you," she said. "I wasn't thinking, that was my mistake—"

"Don't talk like that."

Jen hung on to the doorknob. "We should quit now. We're not ahead, but things aren't so awful that we'll avoid each other at work. We could still have lunch—"

"No we couldn't. I couldn't eat. Couldn't make small talk."

"You don't know what you can do—"

"I love you," said Quinn.

She nodded.

"Jen? Please."

"You're going to break my heart. We both know it."

"No . . ."

"Yes, you are."

He didn't answer this time.

She gently closed the door. She waited ten long beats, torturing him a little, imagining what it would be like to open the door and find him gone. Loving him infuriated her. There was no sense to it, and she prided herself on her sensibility. She had a gift for calculation, but she never seemed to use it when it came to him. She gave it another ten beats before she slid the security chain off and opened the door, just to prove to herself that she didn't need him.

Quinn stared at her, his eyes brimming with tears.

"Come on in," she said, sleepily. "Maybe you can prove to me that I haven't made a big mistake giving you another chance." As he stepped over the threshold she felt a pain in her heart and knew she should have kept the door closed. Should have let him go. She was just prolonging the inevitable by letting him in. It was so obvious.

He kissed her.

She closed the door behind him, wishing just once that she wasn't so smart, hoping she wasn't right.

21

Quinn stood on the open-air patio, hands on his hips, taking in the rolling grounds at the back of Fontayne's oceanfront estate on the Balboa peninsula. The lush lawn was dotted with interconnecting pools, water burbling from one to the other. Fountains shot high into the air, sending rainbows shimmering through the sultry, carcinogenic morning. All the place needed was a couple of peacocks wandering around flashing their asses at the peasants.

"Drought? What drought?" Quinn said to Jen, listening to the sprinklers. "Somebody should revoke Fontayne's EARTHFIRST! bumper sticker."

"It's GREENPEACE, and I'm sure the water is recycled." Jen stood beside him, her eyes against the viewfinder, taking photos of the grounds.

"Sure." Quinn saluted Fontayne's sleek, fifty-foot motor-yacht bobbing serenely at the dock. "And the Queen Mary there runs on solar power."

"What kind of mileage does your Jeep get?" Jen said, leaning over, bracing her elbows on the railing to hold the camera steady, using a slow shutter speed to capture the blur of water geysering from the main fountain. She greeted his silence with a smile, sat down in one of the patio chairs. She was a good winner, but then she had plenty of practice. With him, anyway.

Jen tossed her black hair so that her neck could catch any faint breeze. She wore a gauzy white top and matching, wide-cut shorts, the waist cinched with a black industrial-rubber belt, black welder's boots half-laced. Rebecca of Sunnybrook Farm meets the Road Warrior.

He could feel his heart beating in his chest as he looked at her, remembering the fresh smell of her bed. He wanted to bend down and kiss the tiny lobes of her ears but was afraid to break the spell.

It was Monday, barely 8 a.m. and Quinn was already sweltering in his jeans and a blue dress shirt with the sleeves rolled up. They were early for their interview—traffic had been light for a change coming south on Pacific Coast Highway.

Fontayne's servant, an impassive, older Filipino, glided out of the house and refilled Quinn's glass from a cut-crystal pitcher. Quinn thanked him, but the man didn't respond, merely turned and shoved the pitcher into a sweating silver bowl heaped with crushed ice. The sound reminded Quinn of nuts cracking and he thought of the Screwdriver tavern, Brazil nuts crunching underfoot . . .

Jen rolled her glass of cold juice against her throat,

eyes closed, reveling in the sensation. "Maybe we should take the day off? Why not the whole week?" She stretched in the chair, arms wide. "We both have vacation time coming—we could drive up the coast, check out Big Sur."

Quinn watched the servant leave, then sat beside her, lowering his voice. "I need to find out about Teddy . . . find who killed him." He was so close that he could see the moist dark hairs along the nape of her neck. "I'm not saying Fontayne is involved—"

She opened one eye. "Yes, you are."

He looked away, toward the orange and lemon trees that ringed the property, branches drooping, heavy with fruit. "I've seen Fontayne before. I don't remember where, but it was a long time ago." He turned to her. "I didn't like him then, either."

"Why do you have to make things so complicated?" She shook her head. "The police—"

"The police are wrong."

"You saw the TV this morning," Jen said patiently.

Channel 7 had interrupted their weather report with a breaking story, the anchor breathless, flanked by a computer map of Southern California dotted with happy Mr. Sunshines. She said that the D.A. had scheduled a noon news conference, and unnamed sources had told Channel 7 News that he was going to announce the recovery of the stolen van used by the killers of Judge Theodore Krammerson. Police had made a positive ID from a license-plate notation in the murdered security guard's logbook.

"The van was abandoned less than a mile from the

Screwdriver," said Jen. "The police supposedly found a matchbook from the tavern on the floor. If they get a fingerprint match on one of the suspects, it's over. Quinn? Are you listening? If the police make a fingerprint match, *then* do we get to go to Big Sur?"

"Anybody can plant a matchbook," Quinn insisted. "You walk into the Screwdriver, wait for the biggest racist loudmouth to light a cigarette and palm the matchbook they drop onto the bar. Instant evidence."

"You should have been a defense attorney," a voice said from behind Quinn, startling him. An older man sat down next to him, a well-groomed, professorial type with longish, silver-white hair and dark, flinty eyes peering over his half-glasses. "I'd be happy to recommend a good law school."

Fontayne turned to Jen before Quinn could answer. "Ms. Takamura," he said, shaking her hand with his fingertips, "you have no idea what a pleasure it is to meet you."

Jen smiled back at him.

Fontayne was dressed in a pink polo shirt and khakis, brown tassel Loafers with no socks. An old preppie, slender and fit, with a yachtsman's sunburnt nose, his hair still damp from his shower. His bio said he was sixty-eight, but if it wasn't for the liver spots on the backs of his hands he could have passed for at least ten years younger.

"I trust your orange juice was satisfactory," said Fontayne. "George picked the fruit this morning—he refuses to strain the juice, says it ruins the taste." He spoke with a bouncy, melodic inflection, like he was reciting poetry. He looked at Jen, taking in her gauzy white shorts and unlaced welder's boots. "Ms. Takamura," he purred, "that is a stunning outfit, and beautifully accessorized, I might add."

"Why thank you, Mr. Fontayne," Jen said cooly, stiffening at his syrupy compliments.

"Ellis. Please, call me Ellis."

Jen held his gaze. "I don't think so."

Fontayne laughed with his mouth. "You're tough," he said appreciatively. "I'm going to have to watch myself with you." He turned to Quinn, peering at him over his spectacles. "I do apologize if I've kept you waiting," he said, "but my tennis lesson ran late. I was having a bit of difficulty with my backhand. Ah well, in the grand scheme of things, a weak backhand is a minor character flaw."

"Depends on what stakes you're playing for," Quinn said.

Fontayne nodded, his fine white hair crowned with sunlight. "I'd like to express my deepest condolences on your loss, Quinn. I saw you at Teddy's house that terrible morning, but I didn't recognize you. I wish you had come around to the front, perhaps I could have induced Marie to let you in. I can be very persuasive."

"I'm sure you can." Quinn could still see Fontayne in Teddy's living room, wiping his feet on the furniture.

The three of them were silent. The only sound the steady whoosh of the lawn sprinklers. Jen stirred her orange juice with an index finger.

"On the telephone you spoke of a magazine article on

me," Fontayne said, uncomfortable with the lack of conversation. Words were like oxygen to him.

"I became interested after hearing you speak at Teddy's funeral," said Quinn. "A lot of people think you're being considered for the next opening on the Supreme Court."

Fontayne finished his orange juice. "Many are called," he said, masticating the pulp with his small, even teeth, "but few are chosen. However, I doubt you're really here to interview me about my possible appointment to the high court. Isn't that true?"

"You're too smart for me," said Quinn.

"Time will tell," chuckled Fontayne. He patted Quinn's arm. "I think you've come to see me because you hope to learn more about Teddy. Whatever your reasons, I'm glad you're here. It's a tragedy what happens to fathers and sons, the bitterness, the drifting apart. Teddy and I knew each other for many years, but he rarely spoke of you. I hope that doesn't hurt your feelings?"

"Just a twinge. But then he never mentioned you, either."

"Teddy was a man who kept his confidences," said Fontayne. "I never knew what he was thinking. I used to say that Teddy could be on fire, and no one would know until they smelled the smoke." He crossed his legs, flicked the tassel of his Loafer. "I remember when he first started working for me, fresh out of school, all eyes and ears—"

"Teddy worked for you?" Quinn was startled.

"I assumed you knew," said Fontayne. "Yes, I gave

Teddy his start—he learned more law carrying my brief-case than he did in that second-rate law school he at-tended. I wish he had stayed in my employ longer," he said, his voice like dust. "I am going to miss him."

"So am I." Quinn wasn't sure he had said the words aloud.

"You're not at all what I expected," Fontayne said. "I did some checking on you after your call. Attorneys hate surprises—I hope you don't mind. You have something of a reputation as a hothead, but I don't see it. You're a pleasant surprise."

"Don't be fooled," said Quinn. "I'm on my best behavior."

"It's true," said Jen.

Fontayne applauded, his soft hands barely making a sound. "You two are quite a pair. Makes me wish I was young again." He sighed, serious now. "Quinn, I'm glad to see you in such fine health. I didn't know if there would be any lasting effects from your recent . . . unpleasantness."

"What are you talking about?"

"The ex–football player who almost beat you to death in that hotel room," clucked Fontayne. "What was it, three or four months ago? Quite a news story." He adjusted his glasses. "Liston . . . ? Yes, that was his name. You're fortu-nate to be alive."

"Yes." Quinn's voice was lost.

"Is this too painful to talk about?" asked Fontayne. "I didn't mean to upset you."

"There's really nothing to talk about," said Jen.

"I read that Liston had thrown you against a wall," Fontayne said to Jen, "knocked you out. True?"

Jen shrugged.

"You regained consciousness," recited Fontayne, "still dizzy, and saw this enormous thug throttling Quinn. Most people would have panicked, run away, saved themselves. You stayed." He regarded her over his half-glasses. "You stayed. You picked up the gun on the floor and shot this Liston fellow to death. Remarkable."

Quinn looked at Jen. Lightly touched her leg under the table. "Yes, she is."

Fontayne watched them through his steepled fingers. "By comparison, my life has been tame, but I, too, have known love like that." He stood up abruptly. "Come with me, please. I have something to show you."

Quinn and Jen exchanged glances as they followed Fontayne back into the house. They walked through a long central hallway, past spacious, sunny, precisely balanced rooms, couches and chairs in muted colors, magazines fanned across the coffeetables, walls of pale yellow and eggshell white—with all the soul of a doll house.

Fontayne threw open the double doors at the end of the hallway, waved them inside. High cathedral ceiling. Massive bookcases. Curtains pulled across the windows. Quinn moved closer to Jen without thinking. The desk was elevated, the worn leather desk chair still carrying the imprint of Fontayne's head, a ghost attorney dreaming of appeals and arguments. The wall behind the chair was lined with photos of Fontayne with the famous: Fontayne and Bishop Tutu, Fontayne and Salman Rushdie, Fontayne and Mother Teresa, Fontayne and each of the last three presidents. A visitor would have to sit before that desk and stare up at Fontayne in that constellation of nobility.

Quinn's attention was drawn instead to a small, hand-colored photograph on the desk—a beautiful woman in a delicate pink ballgown. She stared back at him, one eyebrow arched, idly fingering a strand of diamonds. The rigid pose didn't suit her.

"I have a confession to make," announced Fontayne, "I had my own secret agenda for meeting you both . . ."

Quinn turned and saw Jen staring at the wall opposite Fontayne's desk. Framed photographs covered the dark paneling—Jen's entire South-Central Gothic series, black-and-white portraits of young teenage boys and girls formally posed with their favorite guns. As always, Quinn's gaze was drawn by "Tyrone," a smooth-skinned adolescent holding a Mac-11 automatic pistol across his hairless bare chest. He had the calmest eyes Quinn had ever seen.

"I'm a great admirer of yours," Fontayne said to Jen, "your images of Bosnia, Haiti . . . they made me weep. These, though"—he indicated the wall of photos—"your last exhibition, the benefit for Rebuild L.A., are my favorites. I bought the complete set." He adjusted his glasses with a forefinger. "Anonymously, of course."

"I took these shots less than two years ago," Jen said. "Royce, Daryl, and Chaka are in jail. Marbella got married. Phillip is in ROTC. Armand wants to be a police officer. Milton and Tupac are dead. No one knows what happened to Tyrone." Her voice dropped to a whisper. "He just went out one night and never came home."

Quinn wanted to put his arm around her waist, wanted to protect her, but he knew better than to try it. Not here. Not where Fontayne or anyone else could see. Jen didn't like anyone undercutting her professionalism. Quinn just wanted to touch her.

"You're my secret agenda, Jen," said Fontayne. "I hope to interest you in a rather formidable project of mine—"

"The Elena Foundation?" Quinn said, wishing he had kept his mouth shut, but he wanted to interrupt Fontayne's offer to Jen, felt compelled to throw himself between the words. Like that would protect her.

"Why . . . yes," said Fontayne, surprised. "I haven't made a formal announcement yet." He idly flattened the nubby collar of his polo shirt with his fingertips, watching Quinn. "It seems we both have our sources."

The Elena Foundation was a rumor and a wild one at that. Quinn's contact in the mayor's office had overheard a conversation: Fontayne was planning to donate the bulk of his fortune, estimated at over eighty million dollars, to educate poor children.

"There's always a buzz when someone wants to give away a ton of money," said Quinn. "It makes people . . . wonder. It makes me wonder."

"Unfortunately, we live in an age when good intentions are suspect," Fontayne said sharply.

"Don't blame Quinn," said Jen, "I'm curious, too."

"I'm neither a saint nor a fool," insisted Fontayne. "I'm not trying to assuage a troubled conscience or buy my way onto the Supreme Court. The explanation is rather prosaic: I have more money than I could possibly need. My wife . . . my wife, Elena, is deceased, my children grown—I could leave it to my heirs, but inherited wealth debilitates the character. So why not do some good with it?"

Quinn could hear a clock ticking. He wondered who Fontayne was trying to convince.

"My wife's death left something of a hole in my life," Fontayne said to Jen. "I became quite dependent on her love over the years." He straightened, as though steeling himself against an expected blow. "She died of cancer four years ago." He smiled weakly. "If I were a philosopher, I might suggest that the Elena Foundation is my poor attempt to cure the cancer that is devouring our society." He shook his head. "You must forgive me, Jen, I sometimes descend into mawkishness."

"You don't have to apologize," said Jen.

Quinn watched him, reserving judgment.

Fontayne walked to the window, swept back the curtains, and stared out at the vast gardens. "My wife designed this house, and the grounds too. She was a very talented woman," he said wistfully. "She sometimes complained that I worked too hard, that I didn't take time to smell the flowers." He smiled at her portrait. "Now all I have left are her flowers, and their perfume mocks me. I cannot bear their fragrance." His eyes were like stones.

"I loved my wife very much." He sighed, exhaling in perfect time to the ticking of the clock. "Jen, do you think we decide whom we love, or is love something beyond our control?"

"We choose," responded Jen.

"No way," said Quinn.

Fontayne looked at Jen. "I'm afraid Quinn is right." His hand stabbed out as though he had lost his balance.

Jen moved toward him but Quinn stayed put.

CHAPTER

22

It was just after 10 a.m., when Katie saw this boy walking up the walk. She knew what time it was because "Baywatch" had just gone off. Katie hated that show but Natalie insisted on watching it. Monday wasn't Monday unless Natalie got to see a bunch of rich actors running around in red swimsuits pretending to be lifeguards. The whole idea made Katie suspicious about growing up. Adults were bad enough, but Natalie was sixteen, for God's sake. She was supposed to know better.

This boy on the walk was really cute. Like Jason Priestly on "Beverly Hills 90210" or one of Sassy's "ultimate babes" pictorials, not that she was really interested in boys, unlike her friend Erica who was completely insane on the subject.

Natalie noticed the boy, too. She wet her lips as she watched him come up the steps. What a surprise. She had

boy-radar. Most of the time she was a really good sitter—
not a baby-sitter—she played games (although she
couldn't throw a baseball to save her life), she made great
grilled-cheese sandwiches for lunch, and she brought
copies of those weird supermarket newspapers with stories
about UFO babies and Elvis frozen on ice. She was the
best sitter Katie had. She never treated her like a kid.

The cute boy rang the bell, even though he could see
them inside, watching him.

Natalie walked to the open front door, smiled at him
through the latched screen door.

The boy was wearing baggy polka-dot shorts and a
flowered shirt, these weird, clunky black boots and rhinestone sunglasses like movie stars from the olden days
wore. He was so rad she didn't believe he was real. What
was somebody like this doing on her front porch?

"Hi," he said.

"Hi," said Natalie, her voice all low and sultry.

Puke me out, thought Katie.

The boy took off his sunglasses and smiled at Natalie.

Katie felt her mouth drop. She took a step backwards.
The boy's eyes didn't go with the rest of him. They were
cold eyes . . . like a dead fish. Natalie didn't seem to
notice. She just kept staring at his smile and his cheekbones and his slanted sideburns.

"Nice morning," said the boy.

"Y-yes," said Natalie.

"You two ladies are in luck," said the boy, his head
weaving slowly through the air on the far side of the screen

door, tilting back and forth like he was checking his reflection in the mirror.

"Uh-huh," said Natalie.

"We don't want any," said Katie. She started to close the door, but Natalie stopped her.

"Don't mind her," Natalie said to the boy. "What are you selling?" They exchanged smiles.

"I'm Rick," he said with a mock-bow, "and I'm working my way through cosmetology school." He held up a plastic Barbizon tote bag. "I just spent the weekend in an intensive series of seminars, and girl, I am full of goodies."

"Wow," said Natalie. "Let's check it out." She reached up to unlatch the screen door.

"No!" Katie yelled, her voice startling even herself. Natalie's hand hovered over the latch. "Natalie," Katie said, tearing herself away from Rick's stare, "you know Mom's rules—no strangers in the house, for any reason."

"I'm no stranger, little girl," smiled Rick, bending down like she was a midget. "Don't you want me to give you some makeup tips? Don't you want to look pretty for the boys?"

"No."

Rick kept smiling. Between him and Natalie, it was like being stuck in the middle of an endless toothpaste commercial. "Well, don't you want your big sister to look beautiful for the boys?" He glanced at Natalie. "Not that she needs much help."

"She's not my sister."

Natalie's hand hovered around the latch.

"I really like the Juliette Lewis thing you've got going there," Rick said to Natalie, "the perky-pouty-kissible thing. It's working for you, girl," he smiled, eyes flashing.

Natalie touched her hair, beaming.

"You have a real style sense . . . it's Natalie, right?" said Rick. "Too many fashion victims fall for that overprocessed-and-underloved look. Not you. That little blunt-cut is perfect for your features, but make sure you deep-condition it, maybe even hit it with some color, bring out the depth and shine. Yeah," he nodded. "You ever thought of a traverse cut? It's just a little slicing technique, encourages forward movement." He shook his hair, sent it shimmying across his forehead. "See?"

"Pretty," Natalie said softly, dragging one toe behind her.

"What's your favorite band?" Rick asked suddenly.

"Stone Temple Pilots," Natalie responded immediately. You'd have thought she'd been waiting to be asked that question all her life.

"*Ex*-cellent," said Rick. "They're in the studio now, working on a video—"

"I thought they were touring," said Natalie.

"Nope," said Rick. "They got this video. I may get to help with their makeup. If I do, you could come along."

"Definitely," squealed Natalie. Her hand reached for the latch.

"My father is going to be home any minute," Katie lied. "He's not going to like finding somebody in the house."

Natalie jerked her hand off the latch and stepped back.

"That's alright," Rick said smoothly. "I carry a complete line of men's cosmetics, shampoos, and rinses. I have plenty of free samples I'd be happy to leave with you." He reached into his bag, pulled out a handful of tubes and offered them to the closed screen door. "You want to take them? I think your dad would like them. You could surprise him, give him a shampoo tonight. He'd like that, wouldn't he?"

"I don't think so," said Katie, standing directly in front of the door.

Natalie giggled.

Rick's face got red. "Fine. I got a good sunblock moisturizer you could give him. Your dad gets wrinkles or skin cancer, don't blame me. It'll be your fault."

"Leave them outside the door," said Katie.

"Why don't you come back later?" said Natalie. "When her mother . . . mother and father are here. I'm sure—"

"I've got a few more houses to visit before class tonight," Rick smiled at Natalie, "but don't worry"—his voice shifted to a Schwarzenegger baritone—"I'll be back."

Natalie cracked up but Katie didn't say a word.

Rick moved closer, looking directly at Katie, his face almost touching the screen. His eyes were so flat and ugly, it was hard to believe they belonged with the rest of him. "You're a very smart little girl. Careful, too. I bet your mother and father are very proud of you." Before Katie could say anything he had turned and walked quickly down the steps.

Katie watched him hustle down the street, followed him until he was out of sight. He didn't stop at any other houses.

"God, Katie," sighed Natalie, "you are such a baby. That guy was so hot and you ruined it. The Stone Temple Pilots! What would it have hurt to let him in for a minute? Such a fox . . ." She fluffed out her hair. "He said I looked like Juliette Lewis. You're my witness." She shook her finger at Katie. "Someday, when you're older, you'll realize what you did, but it'll be too late. He's never coming back after the way you treated him. He didn't even leave us any samples."

CHAPTER

23

No sign of Deputy D.A. Tina Chavez. Quinn checked out the broad plaza around the Santa Ana courthouse—natty attorneys clustered around the steps, jabbing chili dogs at each other as they argued, faces shiny with sweat in the bright sunshine. Knots of uniformed police in mirrorshades huddled off by themselves, either fresh from testifying or ready to be called to the stand. They stood with their arms crossed, watching the attorneys, their mouths twisted with contempt.

The families of the Hispanic defendants had spread blankets on the dry grass under the shade of the pepper trees: women in long dresses setting out sliced oranges and mangos, stacks of tortillas, yellow plastic margarine tubs filled with beans and fixings. Old women sat on lawn chairs, fanning themselves, watching the children who scampered between the blankets in their best clothes screeching happily.

Quinn was still boiling from his visit with Fontayne this morning—more angry at Jen's reaction than anything else. She *liked* him. She thought he was a charming host. She liked his politics and his bumper stickers and his taste in photography. She said he had an honest face. Where the hell was Tina?

"Are you looking for me, guapo?"

Quinn turned at the honeyed voice, saw Tina standing nearby, hands on her hips. Empty hands. "What's wrong?"

"I thought you were bringing me Joe Staducci's prison file."

"And I thought you'd be happy to see me," pouted Tina, tapping the toe of one of her lilac snakeskin high heels. She wore a pale green dress that emphasized her curves and smooth brown complexion, a tiny gold crucifix around her neck.

In any other place than Southern California, upward mobility would have necessitated conservative attire— defense attorneys could flout the norms with ten-gallon Stetsons and ponytails, leather mini-skirts and hippy bell bottoms, but city attorneys were usually relegated to varying shades of gray. Not here. The local media loved a certain flamboyance even in its public servants. The district attorney himself, Alvin "Attaboy" Barkis, regularly accompanied the police chief on high-profile drug busts, the two of them decked out in tailored black SWAT jumpsuits for the cameras.

"You going to kiss me?" asked Tina. "It's alright, I kiss

all my friends. If you just stand there, people are going to wonder what we have to hide."

Quinn kissed her on the cheek. "Congratulations, Tina. I was in the back of the courtroom this morning."

"I saw you." Tina smiled, then shrugged. "Save your congratulations for a real win, though. Slam dunking shoplifters . . ." She shook her head. "Such a waste."

"Take the easy ones when you get them." Quinn lifted away a single strand of her hair that had fallen across her face. "Thanks for pulling that file, I really appreciate—"

"Such an eager boy," said Tina, looking up at him with those large dark eyes. His skin felt hot under her open gaze, and for a moment he imagined the two of them alone in the dark, warming each other with their breath and their slippery bodies. "You just can't wait to get in there, can you?" she said, enjoying his discomfort. "Can't wait to dig into the file, be a hero. Judge Teddy would be proud of you." She waved to someone behind his back. "Let's get something to eat before we have company," she said, leading him toward one of the All Beef hotdog stands that ringed the plaza.

She chose one of the muscle boy stands, of course. A young hunk in a thong was dishing out the goods. Last year a Cuban-American entrepreneur, "Cubanito" Sanchez, had started out with two All Beef stands, featuring kosher dogs and male and female bodybuilders dressed in the bare minimum. The authorities had filed suit, citing public decency laws, but the entrepreneur had argued the case himself and won. His servers were college students who wore no less than could be seen on a public beach. There was no touching allowed. He was an upstanding member of the community trying to find the American dream. To deny him this opportunity would constitute restraint of trade. The judge agreed.

The bronze muscle boy handed Tina a hotdog layered with sliced jalepeños. Her regular, evidently. She paid him three dollars, plus a dollar tip, daintily holding the bun between her lilac fingernails, a perfect match for her shoes. She watched as he turned hotdogs on the grill, flexing for her, showing off his oiled washboard abdominals.

"Bravo," murmured Tina, taking a big bite.

"Hola, Chica!" said a swarthy, thickly built man in a white linen suit, embracing her, kissing her full on the lips. He fanned his lips. "Que picante!"

Tina pushed him aside, laughing. "You know Quinn?"

"Sure, me and Quinn go way back."

"Que pasa, hombre?" said Quinn.

"Business is good," said Cubanito, eyes narrowing as he kept watch on his other stands. "Be better if you ordered something." He clapped the bodybuilder on the shoulder. "Whasa matter, Quinn, you no like my Baby Huey here? If you wan', we can go over to Cynthia's stand." He indicated a tall blonde showing the muscles of her inner thighs to a trio of admiring attorneys. "She a Physics major, man. She talk these equations and vectors, but it don' matter—your dick still get hard when she slops on that special sauce."

"I can't wait for you to start franchising, Cubanito," said Quinn. "The TV commercials will be . . . unique."

Cubanito beamed.

Within a month after Cubanito's court victory, and making money by the fistful, competitors had moved in. None of them lasted. Maybe it was his business acumen. Cubanito hired only college students with clean records, and no desire to supplement his generous salary package with after-hours prostitution. He flew in the hotdogs from New York, had the condiments custom-made locally. He kept careful track of his inventory, right down to the last bun. No one stole from him. Cubanito had spent time in Castro's worst jails. His prison number was tattooed on the inside of his lower lip. He had eyes that would scare a sewer rat.

"This pay as well as dealing coke?" Quinn said softly, leaning close, Cubanito's Paco Raban so thick that it stung his eyes. "Speaking abstractly, of course."

"Abstractly . . . no." Cubanito spread his strong hands, offering the gods his human frailty and his gratitude. "No, amigo. I'd be lying to you if I said it did. Cash flow isn't as good, and I got to pay the taxes." He sighed at the injustice of it. "Still, I sleep better now that fuckers only try to kill me with a fountain pen."

"Wait until you get your law degree," said Quinn, "you'll be wishing you were facing down Uzis again. You are still studying to be a lawyer, aren't you?"

"Three nights a week, man. Making straight As, too. I got another couple years, three max, then I take the

bar and give D.A. Chavez here"—a smile for Tina—
"something to worry about." His eyes gleamed with a feral
intelligence. Drop Cubanito onto an asteroid and he'd
carve a spaceship out of the bare rock and sell it to E.T. "I
got some trouble with my record"—he glanced from Tina
to Quinn, flashing his new capped teeth—"nothing that
can't be expunged, though. This is America, right? Money
talks and bullshit walks."

Tina finished her hotdog, took Quinn's arm. "Later,
babee," she called to Cubanito, who bowed formally, looking like a southern plantation owner in that vanilla ice
cream suit.

They walked through the crowd, found an empty bench
on the outskirts of the plaza, a vantage point where they
could been seen but not heard. Still no sign of Joe Steps's
file. Maybe Tina was going to have one of the passing
joggers drop it off when she gave the high-sign—a snap of
the fingers would be more like it.

Tina leaned back, watched a thick white cloud edg-
ing across the sun. "This ex-con, this Joseph Staducci . . .
you didn't tell me he knew Judge Teddy," she said
lightly.

"It was a long time ago." Quinn scanned the shifting
scene in the plaza, keeping watch, keeping track.

"A long time ago." Tina smoothed her lip gloss with
the tip of her little finger, licked her lips. "So why are you
so interested in his prison file? Are you studying ancient
history now?"

"Joe . . . Joe is a friend," said Quinn.

She turned her face to the sky, drinking it up. "So now you investigate your friends?"

Quinn had stumbled into a patch of cactus. He was going to have to be very careful to get out without drawing blood. "Gee, Tina, if I had known I was going to be cross-examined this afternoon, I'd have worn my good clothes."

"You look fine, guapo," she reassured him, continuing with the same sweet tone of voice. "This Joseph Staducci wrote Judge Teddy many times from prison, but all of the letters were returned 'Refused.' " She crossed her legs with a crackle of silk. "Maybe this made your friend Joe angry?"

"No. They had a misunderstanding. It was taken care of."

"Judge Teddy is dead and this ex-con is alive," said Tina. "Now there can be no more misunderstandings."

"You're wrong, Tina."

"Perhaps." Tina shrugged. "And perhaps you are too trusting of your friends. I was the same way when I first joined the D.A.'s office. I fixed a few traffic tickets, listened sympathetically to every excuse. I thought people were basically good. I didn't even own a gun—can you believe that? Today, if I buy a pack of gum, I count my change."

"You have to trust someone—"

"If you trust this Joe so much, why did you have me pull his file? You must have had a reason."

The sun had come out from behind the cloud. Quinn could feel the heat in his face like an arc lamp. That's what the forensics team had used at Teddy's house . . . hard to hide from the big bright light.

"I wondered about Joe, that's all," Quinn said. "I've made mistakes before." It was over two years since the mini-mart killing and he could still see the fear in Doreen's eyes, hear Groggins's voice, the gunshots and people crying, still see the sweaty TV reporter shoving a microphone in his face, asking him how it felt. How it felt to have gotten a killer released? Now that the killer. Had killed. Again?

"Quinn?" She looked worried for him.

He wiped cool sweat off his forehead with the back of his hand. "Don't worry about me," he said, grateful for her concern. "I'm like you now. I check people out. I go through their closets, look under the seat of their car, run a credit check. I had you pull the file because I was suspicious of Joe showing up when he did. I was afraid he was too good to be true."

"Maybe he's way too good to be true," said Tina. "Your Joe has a temper. Did you know that? An old man like him . . . arthritis . . . you'd think he'd want to take things easy."

Quinn turned to her. "What are you talking about?"

"After I read the prison file, I made some calls," Tina said. "The Seal Beach police got a complaint about your Joe. Seems he attacked a UPS deliveryman, scared him half to death. Tough old man for a cripple."

"You've been busy," said Quinn. "I didn't think you were interested in Teddy's homicide. You told me the D.A. had a good case on the little Nazis."

"Our District Attorney Barkis does have a good case," said Tina. "Not good enough for you, though. Maybe not good enough for me, either." She snuggled closer, their shoulders and hips touching as they sat on the bench. "To break open a high-profile case like this . . ." Her nostrils flared. She was the perfect prosecutor now, driven more by ambition than moral outrage. He liked her better before.

Quinn watched a woman sitting under a pepper tree peel a tangerine for her children, her long dress modestly tucked under her legs. Her husband was probably squatting in a holding cell, but she carried on, looking exhausted but happy as she passed out the tangerine slices.

"Can you imagine what could happen to Barkis if we prove that he botched the investigation?" said Tina. "A false indictment in the murder of a sitting judge? Power can shift so rapidly these days . . . there's no sense of allegiance or honor. Guapo, anything can happen." She hummed softly to herself as she contemplated the destruction of the D.A.'s career.

"I knew that sitting judge," Quinn said quietly, keeping his eyes on the woman under the pepper tree. "He . . . he was my stepfather."

Tina's face fell. "Pobrecito!" She grabbed his hands, clutched them to her heart. "I had no idea. I am so sorry. You should have told me."

"There was no reason to."

She looked hurt. "Of course there was. You didn't tell me this was family. That makes all the difference in the world. I thought your interest was strictly professional."

She patted his cheek. "Don't worry, guapo. We will find the one who killed Judge Teddy. No matter what it takes. If it is a personal thing for you, it is a personal thing for me, verdad?"

"Tina, do you know Ellis Fontayne?"

"I know of him. He spoke at Judge Teddy's funeral. Why do you ask?"

"I'm not sure. Teddy and Fontayne knew each other from a long time ago. I didn't know anything about it until recently, and I'm curious to know how far the friendship went." He shrugged, wishing he had more specifics. Of course, if he had specifics he wouldn't need her help. "Maybe you could ask around the department, find out if any of the older prosecutors knew Fontayne from the old days."

"I will do what I can, but . . ."

"Thanks, Tina."

Tina checked her watch. "Court is about to start and I have a couple of dime-baggers we're pleading out." She stood up, smoothed her skirt. "The file is at the Information desk in a manila envelope with your name on it."

"Let's take our time," he cautioned. "So far all we have are some possibilities. Let me—"

"The two of us working together," she said, arranging her dark hair with deft swipes of her hand, "that is not so bad, is it?"

"I just don't want you to get your hopes up."

She traced a heart on his chest with one of her lilac-painted nails. Hard enough to hurt. "You take care of your hopes, I'll take care of mine."

He watched her hips swivel as she walked away from him. She didn't look back the way she had in the Azteca Theater. She had better things to do now.

CHAPTER

24

Hugo could hear laughter and music as he climbed the stairs toward his apartment. Every step was an effort, the evening warm and full of ghosts.

He had taken side streets from Joe's, trying to avoid rush-hour traffic, exhausted after spending the day with Joe in one medical office after another, listening to doctors blandly describing the possible "outcomes" of his deterioration. Joe had merely nodded, teeth clenched against the future.

Most men feared death, but Hugo knew that death was a blessing. A balm to suffering when pain became unbearable. A companion when there was no longer any hope for friendship. A comforting darkness when the light brought only tears. Hugo was not afraid of dying. He knew with a certainty beyond all reason that the moment of his death would be of his own choosing. He had known this for as long as he could remember. This knowledge was his most precious secret.

Teddy had not been ready for death when Hugo and Rick had stormed into his home. Not then. In the kitchen, though, the blood drying on his apron and Rick sprawled on the floor, holding his bruised face, Hugo had looked into Teddy's eyes and plucked him like a bouquet of flowers.

A cigarette butt bounced at the top of the landing right in front of Hugo, rolled down the steps spilling hot ashes.

"Sorry, man."

Hugo looked over to Rick's apartment. A bored teenager leaned in the doorway, dark hair dripping around his shoulders, tattoos covering his arms. He fired up another cigarette, cracked a beer, watching Hugo with the dull eyes of an insect.

Inside the apartment, Hugo could see Rick through the window wearing a flamboyant blue suit, a martini glass in his hand. Rick had read somewhere that the martini was making a comeback among the hip, powerbrokers of the world. It wasn't the drink itself, it was the glassware. Rick was laughing at some joke, gesturing wildly, splashing himself in the process. Hugo walked quickly to his apartment, unlocked the door but didn't go inside.

There were four or five people at Rick's, the rock musicians from A-19 who worked at a juice bar and said that learning to play their instruments would "fuck with the raw purity of their sound. Dude."

Rick caught sight of Hugo. He didn't react, waiting for Hugo to make the first move. Hugo nodded at him. Rick beamed, toasted him with the empty martini glass. Hugo waved, went inside his apartment, and closed the door.

He sat on the floor with the lights off, wishing he were far, far away. His life was a series of small steps that somehow had brought him to this loud, jangling place, the land of the perpetual party. He still couldn't believe it.

He wondered what Quinn had wanted to talk to Joe about. It must have been important, the way he looked. Strange to have gone to the graveyard with him, the two of them whispering in the darkness while Joe paid his last respects. Hugo had watched the vein throb in Quinn's forehead, heard the ache in his voice, and wanted to tell him that he had been with Teddy at the end, that Teddy had not hurtled into death alone, Hugo had been there with him, as close as he was to Quinn. Hugo stayed silent, burdened by secrets.

Ten minutes later came a soft rapping on the door. Hugo flipped on the light and opened the door for Rick.

"Hi," said Rick, uneasy, standing there in a sky-blue suit with a yellow shirt and a floppy, polka-dot bow tie, his hair lacquered flat, pulled back into a tiny ponytail. He peeked around Hugo, trying to see into the room.

Hugo wondered what Rick had done now. "Hello, stranger," he said. "I was starting to think you were avoiding me."

"Look who's talking," snapped Rick. He suddenly looked like he was about to cry. "S-sorry, Hugo," he stammered, hurrying inside. "I-I've been busy . . . shopping. Celebrating. Nothing wrong with that, is there?"

"Are you okay?"

"What do you think?" Rick turned slowly, posing for him, one arm cocked against his side. He flicked the bow tie. "Elegant, expensive"—his thumbs slid down the blue jacket lapels—"classic lines, yet with seductive, postmodern accents."

Hugo stared at him. Most of the time, Rick was marginally articulate at best, his speech a mixture of the profane and the uneducated. When he talked about style, though, about fashion, he could spout the most effusive jargon with total confidence. Hugo didn't have a clue what he was talking about, but he couldn't stop himself from listening.

Rick caressed his left ear. "I treated myself to three new studs. Rubies." He tossed his ponytail. "Brings out the red highlights I rinsed in this morning."

"What are you celebrating?"

"Do I need a reason?" demanded Rick.

"You never have," Hugo said, envying Rick's giddy embrace of pleasure, his manic enthusiasm for fun and feeling. Rick didn't need a reason to celebrate. Or an excuse, either. Rick was a beautiful boy snagging dragonflies on a lazy summer morning, tearing off their iridescent wings and braiding them into his hair. A lord of the dawn with a headdress of dead rainbows.

Rick cocked his head. "What are you thinking?"

Hugo's gaze traced the downy curve of Rick's chin, the small, cruel eyes. "Nothing."

Rick shook his head. He looked around at Hugo's bare living room, nose wrinkled with distaste at the stained, orange shag carpet.

The apartment was an unfurnished one-bedroom when Hugo moved in three months ago, and he had left it that way. It was empty except for the thin bedroll Hugo unrolled every night. Rick's apartment had been just as bare when he rented it, but Rick had immediately recarpeted, painted the walls, hung posters and pictures, bought furniture, and set up his mini-salon in the kitchen area. They had each received the same cash down payment three months ago. It was a lot of money. Rick had spent all of his share, then borrowed half of Hugo's. It was okay. Hugo had no interest in money. And he liked to see Rick happy.

"Why don't you come over to my place?" said Rick. "I've got snacks, drinks, music—anything you want."

"I don't want anything." Hugo felt heavy and earthbound listening to Rick. He wished he hadn't seen Quinn this afternoon. The way he came off the porch, ready to take on the world, he reminded Hugo of Teddy.

"Don't worry, the band's already left," Rick said, annoyed. "I know you better than that—'Hugo the hermit, man of mystery, master of negative vibes.'"

"Are we having an argument?" Hugo asked.

"I'm moving next week," said Rick, head bobbing. "Someplace fancy. I'd like to live in a building with a lobby and an elevator and gated underground parking." He lowered his eyes. "If you want, we could look for a place together."

"You're getting a little ahead of yourself," said Hugo. "We still have Liggett—"

"I took care of that." Rick toyed with his bow tie, smirking.

Hugo stared at him.

"Let's get out of here." Rick indicated the overhead light with a toss of his head. "This place of yours makes everything ugly."

"Not yet," commanded Hugo, his tone stopping Rick at the door, hand on the knob. "You killed Liggett?"

"We get another big payment now, right?" said Rick, turning back to him. "I've been working on a business plan for my salon," he jabbered. "I'm thinking of calling it 'Rik's' or 'Rikk's,' something distinctive, exotic. Like Jon Peters. You think Barbra Streisand would have gone to him if he spelled his name J-o-h-n? I don't think so."

"Rick—"

"You have to differentiate yourself, Hugo, that's the secret of making it with the top people, Hollywood people. I want to be more than a stylist to them—I'd like to be more of a . . . spiritual advisor. 'You look good, you feel good, you do good.' That's my philosophy of life."

Music blared from one of the apartments across the way, voices shouting. It sounded like animals caught in a trap.

"What's wrong, Rick?"

Rick's head jerked from side to side, trying to get his bearings in the harsh overhead glare. "I hate an empty room," he swallowed. "Can't we go?"

"No."

"I was mad at you," Rick blubbered, eyes wide.

"What have you done, Rick?"

"Nothing." Rick twitched. "I didn't do nothing." He

touched his bow tie, nervous. He examined his hand. "My cuticles are ragged. I'm going to have to put on some lotion."

"Killing Liggett by yourself was dangerous," said Hugo. "We're supposed to be a team. The two of us, working together."

"You don't act like we're a team," pouted Rick. "You don't act like you want me around, not unless it's time to do some business." He shook his head, ponytail flipping back and forth. "I saw you, Hugo. I fucking saw you."

"What are you talking about?" Hugo said, exasperated. Everytime he seemed about to follow Rick's thought processes to a logical conclusion, Rick suddenly veered off into unexplored terrain.

"You don't go for little weekend drives with me," accused Rick. "Fine. You missed your Tuesday night facial. Fine. Hey, it's your pores—"

"You're not making any sense."

"I saw you Friday night," said Rick, "you and Joe and that guy in the judge's bedside photograph. First it's milk and cookies with Rachel and the brat, and now you're hanging out with the husband, too. One big happy family."

"Are you talking about Quinn?" Hugo could see the pain in Rick's eyes.

"Quinn . . . that's his name? Does Quinn know what you did to the judge, Hugo? Or is Quinn the one we're working for? Did he pay us to whack out his old man?"

" 'Whack out'?" Hugo started to laugh.

"Did I get it right?" said Rick, his head bobbing wildly. "Yeah? Is it Quinn?"

"You're being ridiculous," said Hugo. "I gave Quinn and Joe a ride to the graveyard, that's all."

"I'm not stupid, Hugo."

"I know that. You shouldn't be hanging around Rachel's house, though, or Joe's, either. You're putting yourself at risk."

"Like you care," mumbled Rick.

"I do care," said Hugo. Rick brightened. "You shouldn't have killed Liggett, though," said Hugo. "Not without me."

"I was showing some initiative," insisted Rick, his suit as bright with promise as a robin's egg. "I thought you'd be proud of me."

"Did you wear gloves when you did it?" asked Hugo. "Did you dump the gun you used on Liggett?"

Rick shrugged.

"You have a juvenile record," explained Hugo. "Your prints are in the databank. They have computers that can run a match in less than twenty minutes."

"Gloves make my hands sweat," said Rick. "I get a rash."

Hugo rubbed the sides of his head, squeezing, trying to hold things together. Rick was going to ruin everything. Part of Hugo wished he would. At least it would be over. The world was too loud and the killings just made it worse.

"Don't worry, Hugo, I'd never rat you out," nodded Rick. "You and me, Hugo, you and me . . ."

"Yeah." Hugo was so tired. There was the faint sound of breaking glass. The party had moved into one of the downstairs apartments, the music muffled like distant thunder. More breaking glass. Hugo was back in Teddy's living room again, hearing Rick shattering crystal in the kitchen. Teddy sat on the couch, blinking back the fear . . .

"I should have waited for you with Liggett," agreed Rick, "but an artist needs to . . . express himself." His face went blank for an instant, then reasserted itself. "Everything's going to be fine, Hugo, you'll see. Six months from now I'll be combing out Julia Roberts's hair and giving her advice on her love life. I know you don't care about money, but it will be nice to have a shitload. You'll see."

"It would be nice," said Hugo, unconvinced.

"You can hang out at my salon or just stay home and think," bubbled Rick. "I mean, there's no reason for us to stop seeing each other when this is all over, right?"

"No reason at all."

"Really? We can still be together?"

"Where else could I go?" sighed Hugo.

Rick showed his sharp tiny teeth in a smile and Hugo imagined a vast shrieking. Rick glanced around for a mirror, gave up on finding a reflective surface in Hugo's apartment. "This Quinn guy isn't your friend," he said lightly, almost as an afterthought, "he just wants to cause trouble. Some people just can't leave well enough alone."

CHAPTER

25

"You still haven't found anything that connects Fontayne to your stepfather's murder, have you?" said Jen.

"Not yet."

"Not yet. Does that mean you're getting close?"

"Not yet."

Jen splashed water in his face and he splashed her back, salt spray dripping from her smile.

"I haven't given up," said Quinn.

"Of course not," said Jen, floating on her back now, the two of them fifty yards offshore, the sky a deep blue above, the hot sun glaring off the Pacific, addling their brains, intoxicating. Tuesday morning. The office could wait. Blue water, blue sky—it was easy to lose perspective and forget which way was up.

Quinn dove under, nibbled at her toes, hearing her laugh before coming up for air. He could see Katie treading water a short distance away, giving him dirty looks, then looking away when he beckoned her closer.

"If I was being attacked by a great white shark, your daughter would throw me a bloody steak," said Jen.

"What do you expect? You stole the man of her dreams."

"Wait until her hormones start kicking in, and she discovers boys—"

"I've already reserved a spot for her in this small convent school in Switzerland—"

"It's the call of the wild, Quinn, you're not going to be able to stop her," said Jen, her slim feet happily paddling away. "Nothing will."

"Let's talk about something else."

She sank below the surface, bobbed back immediately, pushing back her hair. "I asked a friend of mine about Teddy and his wife," she said, wiping her eyes. "You were suspicious about her and Fontayne having an affair . . ."

"Jen—"

"I was discreet," she said. "I made it sound more like idle curiosity, which is nothing out of the usual. David shoots photographs for the Orange County society pages and he always has gossip so juicy it quivers."

Quinn watched the water stream down her neck. "So what did he say?"

"He saw Teddy and Marie just a few weeks ago at some Opera Guild event. David said the two of them seemed very much in love. David has a good eye. These society events can be pretty painful, everyone leering at the camera in silly hats, pretending to be having a good time. He said Teddy and Marie were the real thing."

"That may be enough for you, but I'm not—"

"Fontayne has a girlfriend," said Jen, "but it's not Marie. David says Fontayne started dating about a year after his wife died. Very proper period of mourning. The woman is a another blue blood, a wealthy widow—her money is old, she's about forty. She keeps him quite busy. Fontayne wouldn't fool around with a friend's wife. He wouldn't do anything to jeopardize his chances for making it onto the Supreme Court."

"Thanks for your help."

"What's the matter?" said Jen. "I thought you'd be pleased."

"I said thanks." Quinn could see Katie inching closer, straining to hear. He swam to Jen, put his arms around her, and Katie backed off. "So Fontayne and Marie weren't having an affair," he said, keeping his voice low. "Great."

Jen bobbed against him, belly to belly, their private merry-go-round. "You still think he was involved, though."

He wished she wouldn't keep asking. "I saw something at Teddy's house the morning you and I went there—"

"You told me. Fontayne wiped his feet—"

"It wasn't just that," said Quinn. "It was the way he did it, the way he held his head, his attitude. It reminded me of something, but I couldn't remember what. I got the same sensation at his house yesterday morning. The way he sat there, lounging about, the way he waved off his servant— his tone of voice was very polite, but his gesture was pure arrogance. I had seen that before. I knew it, but I still couldn't remember where."

Jen kissed him, tiny kisses circling his mouth. "It'll come back to you. Then maybe you can see things more clear—"

"It did come back to me," Quinn said, pulling back slightly. "Last night I went for a drive. I ended up parked in front of the first house Teddy and I moved into after my mother left. After Joe Steps disappeared. It seemed like Teddy moved us every few years. I think he was trying to find a place where the two of us would be able to get along together, where we would be comfortable." He smiled to himself. "I left home before he found the right spot."

"What did you remember," Jen said softly, her eyes on his.

Quinn looked down. Looked away. Finally came back to her bright green eyes. "I . . . I didn't think it would be this hard talking about it."

"That's alright," she teased, peering at him through half-lowered lashes. "I know most of your secrets by now, one or two more won't shock me."

"It's not about me." Quinn swallowed. "It's about Teddy." He took a deep breath, but instead of diving, he stayed where he was, in Jen's arms, slowly letting it out. "We had been living in the house for about a year. I must have been eleven or twelve years old. I woke up this one night, hearing voices in the living room, and I crept into the hallway. There was a man with Teddy, but the room was dark and I couldn't really see him. He was sitting in

Teddy's chair, this beautiful, high-backed leather chair, smoking a cigarette. All I remember was the way his legs were crossed at the knee and the way he flicked ashes on the carpet like he didn't care if he set the house on fire. It infuriated me. I wanted to run into the living room and hit the man in Teddy's chair, but I didn't."

"What was the man saying to Teddy?"

"I don't know." The sun coming off the water made his eyes burn. "It wasn't what he was saying that mattered, it was the way Teddy was reacting." He shook his head. "Teddy and I . . . we had our problems, but I respected him. He took no crap from anyone."

Jen waited.

"I don't even remember the sound of the man's voice," said Quinn, "but what was clear then . . . and clear now, was Teddy's resentment of the man, and his total surrender to him." Quinn trailed a hand in the water, not able to look at Jen. "It was like the guy had something on him. It was weird. I had never seen Teddy like that."

"You think that man was Fontayne?" Jen looked skeptical.

"Yes." Quinn looked at her. "I sat outside that house last night, and it was like I was a kid again . . . ashamed for Teddy."

"Fontayne said Teddy had worked for him," said Jen. "Maybe he was a demanding boss. Maybe that's what you saw—"

"No," insisted Quinn. "Teddy was on his own by that time. He rented space in a nice office building. He took me there sometimes. It had new furniture and ugly art on the walls. Fontayne wasn't his boss. Besides, Teddy would never have let his boss beat him down like that. He wouldn't."

"Even if it was Fontayne you saw that night, I still don't know what this all means."

"Neither do I." Quinn broke away from her. "Not yet."

"I'm going back to shore," said Jen, keeping her distance. "I'll study those prison records you brought. Okay?"

Quinn nodded, then watched her swim back to shore, the water getting colder with every stroke between them.

A hand grabbed his ankle and pulled him under for an instant. "Race you to the marker buoy," shouted Katie, taking off, her arms a pinwheel of motion.

Quinn watched Jen, waited until she reached the shore before chasing after Katie. He barely beat her to the buoy. Katie was getting faster or he was getting slower. She was getting faster. That had to be it.

When he was growing up, Teddy would get exasperated at him, and say, "When you have kids, I hope you get one just like you." Like a curse. Well, Teddy had gotten his wish, and Quinn couldn't be happier.

He pushed his hair out of his face, watching her practice her backstroke, swimming parallel to the shore. "Chin up," he called, nodding as she corrected her position. Katie was a good swimmer. He had been teaching her since she was two, at first taking her out into the bay, which was a little warmer. Now they swam together in the ocean, partners in the open water, staying out until their lips turned blue.

A brown pelican swooped low over the water, regarding

the two of them, then continued on, circling around the artificial island in the distance. The island was really an oil-drilling platform, its machinery artfully hidden under a series of pastel structures that looked like condominiums. Tourists were actually fooled sometimes. Katie kept wanting to swim out to the nearest one, but he knew better. Maybe when she was older. If they were still swimming together. Two years . . . she was going to be gone two years. Kids and parents get out of practice. Suddenly you're seeing each other on holidays and checking your watch in the silence.

He glanced back to see Jen sunning herself on the blanket. She was wearing a pale-green maillot that showed off her color and her curves, her face sheltered by a long-billed cap as she read through the stack of Joe's trial transcripts and prison records Quinn had brought.

A red Scirroco with tinted windows cruised slowly along the beach, stereo cranked. Third time around. The driver was probably checking out the bikinis while he looked for a parking spot.

He and Jen had argued all the way back from Fontayne's house yesterday. "You trust that smug son of a bitch?" Quinn kept asking.

"I don't have to trust him," Jen had replied. "I don't have to even like him. That's irrelevant. Fontayne is doing good things. The Elena Foundation is a worthwhile project."

Quinn distrusted righteous types, people with flags and bumper stickers and little charts showing that the world was on the brink and they were just the ones to save it.

"What's the matter, daddy? Your face is all red."

Quinn dove under the cool water, rose slowly, trailing bubbles.

A heavily garbed figure moved slowly down the crowded beach, avoiding the blankets and bare bodies, picking cans and bottles out of the trash, dropping them into the string bag around her waist. She wore gloves and long pants, her head covered so only her eyes showed. The teenagers called her "the mummy," but her name was Mai. She was a Cambodian girl their own age, making money collecting throwaways, her stultifying outfit worn to protect her from the sun. She wouldn't want to darken her skin any more than it already was. A Cambodian girl could lose status that way. He wondered what she thought of all these white bodies bronzing in the heat. It had taken Quinn most of last summer to get her to talk to him. One word at a time. He never saw her other features, but her eyes reminded him of a hawk he had seen tethered in a roadside zoo, fierce and determined to get free.

Katie splashed over and hugged him, shivering. She was eight years old, skinny and lithe. He wondered how long she would cling to him like this, out over her head in the cold cold sea, utterly convinced that he would never let anything harm her. Forever, he hoped.

"You want to go back?" he asked.

She glanced at Jen on the shore. "Not yet."

He could see water beads on her eyelashes like pearls

as she clung to him. "I wish you'd give Jen a chance," he said. "I think you'd like her."

Katie snorted.

"I don't know what you have against her. Your mother and I were divorced for over two years before I met Jen."

"Mama still loves you," she said quietly. "Don't you love her?"

"You don't understand, Katie. Adults—"

"You don't understand. I see the way Mama looks at you when you aren't looking."

"Your mother has a boyfriend—"

She stuck her tongue out.

"When you're right, you're right," smiled Quinn, pulling her to his chest, trying to keep her warm.

Katie glared at the beach. "You're not going to marry *her*, are you?" Her breath smelled of bubble gum. "You could marry Mama again, sleep in her room. You don't tell me stories anymore at night. You're so far away now."

"I'm right here." Quinn wiped at his face. He had salt water in his eyes.

Katie shook her head. "Not like before."

"No." They treaded water together. "Not like before."

Jen waved at them from the shore. She had put down the transcripts. He didn't blame her. Reading in the sun gave him a headache, too. Jen sat on her haunches, facing them, combing out her hair.

Katie looked at his face, pushed away from him.

"Mama's as pretty as she is. Prettier."

"Let's go back in."

"Just cause she's got nice hair you think she's prettier than Mama," accused Katie, dark eyes flashing. "Wait'll Mama starts using her special new shampoo."

"Your mother has beautiful hair. I've got the bad hair genes you should be worried about."

"This boy said his shampoo would make our hair thick," nodded Katie. "I didn't like him, but he had nice hair."

Quinn dunked his head under the cold water, shook himself. "What boy?" he said, blowing spray from his lips.

Katie shrugged. "He came by the house yesterday selling shampoo and makeup, but I didn't let him in. He was cute . . . he looked like Dylan on 'Beverly Hills 90210.'" She shook her head at Quinn's ignorance. "I didn't like the way he kept playing with his hair, though. He had dead-fish eyes, too. I didn't let him in."

"That's good."

"This boy had so many earrings," her head bobbed, excited. "Five in one ear." She clung to him. "Becky Cramer got her nose pierced," she confided. Her voice dropped, cajoling, "Dad . . . ?"

"No."

They treaded water together, floating easily, knees bumping.

"I don't want to go to stupid France," she said suddenly, her voice so quiet it jabbed at his heart.

"You'll like it—"

"If it's so good, why aren't you coming with us?"

"You know why."

"Yeah." Katie glanced at Jen, angry. "Race you!" she shouted, face contorted as she turned away, kicking furiously toward the market buoy.

He watched her strong stroke. This time he wasn't going to give her quite so much of a head start.

CHAPTER

26

"Your young man doesn't like me, does he?" said Ellis Fontayne.

"No," Jen said, "Quinn doesn't like you."

"Ah, well," Fontayne nodded. "I did try with him—"

"No, you didn't."

"Well, it was a lost cause, anyone could see that," said Fontayne, reddening. He bent down and picked up a popsicle wrapper from the dirty sidewalk, walked over to an overflowing trash can. "I do hope you and I can be friends."

"Why is that important to you?" Jen said as she peered into the viewfinder. She photographed him dropping the wrapper into the can, caught the sticky, brightly colored paper drifting from his manicure. Late afternoon light, F16, plenty of depth of field, even the background Fatburger was in sharp focus.

"I'm not used to working so hard for someone's approval," said Fontayne, only half-joking.

"I won't tell if you won't," said Jen, enjoying the brief confusion in his eyes. What Fontayne wasn't used to was not being in control—he probably dominated most social situations with his courtesy and caustic wit, a linguistic good-cop, bad-cop routine that was as effective in private life as it had been in court.

"Let's start over," said Fontayne. "Give me another chance. I need your support and to do that I need to excite your imagination." He smiled at her, peering over his half-glasses, dark eyes twinkling. "That wouldn't be so terrible, would it?"

Jen photographed his flirtatious grin. "I'll let you know," she said, noting the way his approach was direct and ambiguous at the same time, leaving her unsure whether he was flattering her or insulting her. Games within games. One thing she was sure of: Fontayne never said anything that he hadn't practiced and rehearsed for maximum effect.

They were walking along Carson Street in Hawaiian Gardens, a seedy inland town on the border of L.A. and Orange County. There never were any Hawaiians in Hawaiian Gardens—real estate developers thought it was an exotic name that would appeal to new arrivals from the South and Midwest, drawn to Southern California by the booming economy. It worked. Hawaiian Gardens had been a good place for blue-collar workers to raise their families, a multiethnic suburb with neat lawns and picnics in the park. Now it was a great place to sell security bars and razor wire and forty-ounce cans of beer.

"You're not going to recognize this area in five years," Fontayne told her as he gestured expansively toward the boarded-up storefronts and concrete-block check-cashing bunkers. He strolled down the street, wearing gray linen trousers and a blue polo shirt buttoned to the top, edged a shattered green bottle of Thunderbird into the gutter with the toe of his Loafers.

Seeing the broken glass reminded her of the Cambodian girl on the beach a few hours ago. Jen had watched her delicately picking through the trash barrels for cans and bottles to recycle, and the girl had suddenly looked at her with those beautiful dark eyes. Jen had experienced a momentary flash of recognition, a kinship beyond logic or reason. She had felt the sensation before, usually in the most incongruous situations, in the lowered glance of an Afghani teenager or the grim smile of a Somali child. It was the recognition of orphans, one to another.

It was different between her and Quinn. They were lovers, but they were drawn together from across a vast divide. Seeing him swimming with Katie, hearing their laughter echoing across the waves, there was a connection between them that Jen couldn't approach. It was the same intimacy she had with her father, and when he had died the connection had been broken.

The stars in the sky were dying. Atoms decayed. Family was a fiction badly written, and all Quinn's good intentions wouldn't alter that fact. The idea of her and Quinn

getting married, settling down, raising their own happy
little family, that nuclear horror show—

"Ms. Takamura . . . ? Jen?"

"I'm sorry." She roughly wiped her eyes. Ridiculous.
"I was daydreaming."

"Ah. Well, I too have dreams, Ms. Takamura." Fontayne acknowledged the waves of three black men standing on the opposite corner. "We start next month!" he called to them. "Make sure you sign up!"

Jen switched to her camera with the telephoto lens, bringing the men in close.

"Those men are unemployed carpenters," he said, as they posed for Jen, flexing their muscles, laughing, "hard workers too, but they've been frozen out of the trade unions. African-Americans hold only six percent of the construction jobs in the U.S.—were you aware of that? I've already talked to those men about the Elena Foundation and our common goals. The project is going to use local labor as much as possible; without the people feeling a stake in the success of the school, we're doomed to failure."

Fontayne talked like he was being paid by the word, but Jen liked what he was saying. She liked what he was doing, too.

They rounded the corner and Fontayne fairly raced ahead of her down the sidewalk, striding over the broken glass.

"There it is, Jen, there is the future," proclaimed Fontayne, pointing to the vast windowless bulk of the

Great Southland Mall. The chain-link fence surrounding the closed mall was rusting, whole sections cut out, hanging open.

Jen saw him through the camera, filling the foreground with his enthusiasm while the abandoned mall loomed over him in the background. His confidence almost convinced her.

The Great Southland Mall was another in a series of real estate fiascoes by a defunct S&L whose chief executive was now serving a 195-year sentence for financial crimes. Built in a crime-ridden location at a cost of over $110 million, the mall had been completed just in time for the collapse of the Southern California economy. The U.S. taxpayer had picked up the tab. It was just what Fontayne was looking for.

"It's going to be called 'The Elena School,' " said Fontayne, hanging on to the fence with his fingertips, gazing raptly at his new purchase. "Isn't it wonderful?"

Fontayne had bought the mall from the Resolution Trust Authority. He paid slightly less than $3 million for the property, then donated it to the Elena Trust.

"Have you read the prospectus I gave you?" he asked. "I've formed a blue-ribbon board of directors—clergy, educators, entrepreneurs—men and women willing to put their money and their time toward this most noble venture. If you decide to help, Jen, you're going to be in very good company."

The prospectus had presented a grand social vision, backed up with color charts illustrating the financial details. It would cost around $20 million to convert the mall into an independent school system, kindergarten through high school. Air-conditioned, spacious, quiet, and safe, the school would be open to all races and religions. Tuition would be free, but parental involvement was required in matters from building maintenance to staffing the cafeteria to providing security. Fontayne estimated an initial enrollment of three thousand students, and the need for an endowment of at least $100 million.

Jen kept Fontayne in the viewfinder, preferring to see him framed by the camera than on his own, without boundaries. That's the way she liked things, with edges and limits and her finger on the button. She felt like a hunter, capturing souls without shedding a drop of blood.

"I'm willing to donate my entire fortune to the cause," said Fontayne, looking small and vulnerable in the viewfinder, "but we'll still need substantial corporate sponsors, both now and in the future, after the initial glow has faded and the hard work really begins. That's why your photographs are so important—they reveal the power and dignity of the human spirit. I want you to document the building of the Elena School. I intend to distribute your portfolio to every member of Congress, to every Fortune 500 CEO, to every newspaper and magazine publisher in the U.S. Our nation is adrift, Jen," he said, voice rising. "It's up to us to provide a beacon of hope."

Jen put down the camera. The two of them were very close now. Fontayne was breathing hard, cheeks flushed, waiting for her to respond to his offer.

"Life is fleeting," said Fontayne, "it's over so fast . . . You're young, you think you have forever, but you'll wake up one morning and you won't recognize yourself in the mirror." He wiped his dusty shoes with a handkerchief.

A car drove slowly past, young men hanging out the windows, cursing, laughing at them, but Fontayne didn't react. His eyes were fixed on Jen.

"I've made a great many mistakes," Fontayne said, "errors in judgment and grand failures." A gasoline truck rumbled by, its dirty wake eddying around them. "We have a whole lifetime to make mistakes," he said, "and just a few short years to try and set things right. There's never enough time. Never. It doesn't seem fair, does it?"

"Welcome to the club," said Jen, annoyed at his self-pity.

Fontayne smiled ruefully. "You've seen terrible things . . . don't you sometimes worry that you're losing your professional distance?"

"I've never had that problem." Jen could feel her jaw tighten. "I'm *here*," she said, tapping her heart. "The terrible things are on the other side of the camera."

"Ah," nodded Fontayne, "how fortunate for you." The lines around his mouth deepened, and Jen could sense the pain underneath the arrogance. "Well, I hope the horror always stays on the other side of the camera." He stared off at the deserted mall. Trash had billowed against the chain-link fence surrounding it, Sunday funnies and fast-food wrappers shiny with grease. "I loved the law. My wife said I loved the law more than her." He shrugged helplessly.

"Who knows? The law is eternal, while we are small and fleeting things. The law can be more than a protector of our rights, our freedoms—the law can nurture our very humanity. I like to think I've helped shape the law to that end."

"You've made a good start," said Jen. "That's why I'm here."

"A start. Yes." Fontayne nodded to himself. "But just a beginning." He looked at her. "Quinn was correct when he said I hoped to be appointed to the Supreme Court. I've received certain indications that such an honor is not out of the question. Imminent, perhaps. I would welcome the opportunity. There is so much wrong in the world, I hardly know where to begin."

"I doubt that," smiled Jen.

Fontayne laughed. "You're a tough one." He took her hand. His skin was warm and dry. "A few days ago you stood in my office and called me a 'philanthropist.' You sounded like a biologist cataloguing a rare species of insect."

"That's unfair, Ellis."

"Perhaps." Fontayne patted her hand. "You've seen that bumper sticker, 'The one who dies with the most toys wins'?" He chuckled. "Such foolishness, but I was foolish once myself. Now I know that it's not what a man dies with that defines him, but what he does with his life. One marvels at the public legacy of Rockefeller, the public record of Earl Warren, while their private indulgences are long forgotten." He moved closer to her. "May I give you some advice? Don't squander yourself in frivolous pursuits. Keep to the eternal verities. Traditional values ... they're not for people like us. I have three children, but truth be told, I rarely think of them. Family is fleeting, Jen. Friends fail us. Even love does not last. Only our good name and good works may yet endure."

Jen thought of Quinn hanging on to the idea of family, trying to hold back the night with some fragile dream of mommy-daddy-baby. Kitchee-kitchee-coo. She wished she could believe in the dream with him. It was a wonderful dream, but she knew better.

"I talk too much," said Fontayne, smiling. "I would apologize, but I will surely commit the same sin again."

"There's no need to apologize."

"Your young man," said Fontayne. "You love each other very much, that's obvious." A cloud passed over the sun, throwing the street into shadow. "He's too emotional for you, though. You're a professional, cool and precise. He's volatile, thrashing about, destroying that which he is trying to save." He slowly shook his head. "It's not going to work. You know that, don't you?"

"Stick to the law, Mr. Fontayne." Jen wasn't sure if she was angrier at his presumptuousness or that her own doubts were so transparent.

"I take no pleasure in my judgment, let me assure you," said Fontayne. "My wife and I ... there was passion, there was love, there were children. It did us no good." He gazed at the graffiti layered on the nearby buildings, the mosaic of illegible posters and peeling paint. "All things must pass, Jen," he said, quoting the Buddha, "what is born will die, what has been gathered will be dispersed—"

"What has been accumulated will be exhausted," answered Jen to Fontayne's surprise.

"What has been built up will collapse," they said in tandem now, "what has been high will be brought low . . ." The two of them stood beside that busy street, horns honking around them.

CHAPTER

27

Quinn checked the clock on the wall. 4:43. He'd wait another few minutes. The trick was to call just before quitting time, when a person would do almost anything to get off the phone and out the door. He sat in the glassed-in conference room at *SLAP*, watching the second hand sweep the dial.

When Tina Chavez had read through Joe Steps's prison file, her attention had been drawn to his connection with Teddy, his unanswered letters, his lack of visitors. She had noted the length of his sentence and gone over the evaluations of his behavior over the long years. She had missed something, though. Quinn had missed it, too. It was easy to overlook, but Jen had spotted it this morning on the beach. It was just a brief notation. A year ago another prisoner, Neil Stimmler, had made a compassionate request to speak to Joe from his hospital bed. Maybe it was nothing. But it was worth checking into.

Quinn saw Napitano on the far side of the editorial offices, the publisher angrily gesticulating at one of the senior editors. He was sporting chinese-print pajamas. A dragon wearing dragons. Quinn slouched down in his chair, hoping to avoid being noticed. He had been AWOL most of last week.

4:47. Almost time. The yellow legal-size pad on his desk was covered with his handwriting, the name "Hugo Ganz" at the top of the page with a box around it. Hugo Ganz: Joe's driver, Joe's friend. The man did look creepy— whoever had made Hugo had run out of flesh before the job was over. That wasn't Hugo's fault. He took good care of Joe, and when he said he was sorry about what had happened to Teddy, Quinn believed him. That hadn't stopped Quinn from coming into the office, using *SLAP*'s computers to check him out.

Quinn checked everyone out. He ran credit checks on corporate attorneys and government officials, scrolled through their driving history, corroborated their educational credentials. All those mail-order university degrees. He told himself he did it to evaluate their information, but he knew it was because he liked having an edge, a glimpse of their secret self. The first time he was in Jen's apartment he had gone through her medicine chest, looked through her linen closet. She had surprised him. There were lightweight tranquilizers in the medicine chest and a heavy-duty vibrator under the towels.

Hugo had only been driving a cab for five months, got his chauffeur's license three weeks before Joe was released. An interesting coincidence. No arrests, not even a traffic ticket. If anything, his credit file was too clean. No outstanding balance on his credit cards, no bounced checks. This morning, Quinn had asked a friend at the Long Beach Police Department, Lt. Esteban Morales, to have Hugo's fingerprints from the chauffeur's license sent to the National Crime Bureau. Esteban had called back a little while ago, said Hugo's prints weren't on any criminal database. "He is as close to an honest man as you will find," mocked Esteban. "Disappointed?"

Quinn almost was. It was so much easier when the bad guys wore nametags.

At 4:55, Quinn phoned the prison, identified himself as working for the Orange County District Attorney's office, and asked for Inmate Records. The faint chatter of voices and computer keys at the *SLAP* office gave his call a proper soundtrack. Napitano spotted him. Shit.

"Here you are, dear boy," said Napitano, barging into the conference room, his pajamas in full sail, making himself comfy on the chair next to Quinn. "I was wondering if I was ever going to see you again. Was the line too long at the welfare office? Hmmm?"

Quinn silenced him with an upraised hand and an imploring look as a woman came on the phone: "Anna Marie Narbold, Records." She sounded slightly out of breath, talking fast.

Quinn took his time answering, remaining polite but

friendly. He said he was Leonard Dale from Assistant D.A. Tina Chavez' office—Napitano raised an eyebrow at that—and gave Tina's personal ID number, reading it off the request that she had made for Joe Steps's records. It was part of Joe's file now, a thick sheaf of papers sitting on his desk.

"I'm sorry, Mr. Dale, is it? I'm just about ready to leave for the day. Why don't you fax me your official request and I'll return your call first thing tomorrow."

"Ms. Narbold, gosh, I apologize for keeping you, but I've already sent a fax," said Quinn, acting confused. He read the Records fax number off the initial request. "That's correct, isn't it? I sent it hours ago. I guess you're as overworked as I am. We've had a hiring freeze for the last two years," he clucked.

Napitano sat forward, his round face flushed with delight.

"Same here," she agreed. "It's so late, though—"

"I really hope you can help me on this, Anna Marie, one wage slave to another. Her nibs is going to be pulling an all-nighter, and if I don't get the information from you, my a-s-s is going to be in a sling, pardon my French."

Napitano pretended to be shocked, covering his mouth with the palm of his hand.

Long sigh from Ms. Narbold. "Go ahead."

"You sent our office a file on a recently paroled inmate, one Joseph Sabino Staducci."

"I remember," she hurried.

"There was a mention of a compassionate request by

another inmate, a Neil T. Stimmler, who was at that time a patient in the infirmary. Assistant D.A. Chavez was curious what Mr. Stimmler was incarcerated for, and what his current status is?"

There was a long silence. Ms. Narbold would be watching the clock in her office, gauging the buildup of traffic on the freeways for every minute she lingered. It was a logarithmic calculation everyone in Southern California practiced. 5:01. She was on her time now. There was a sudden flurry of keystrokes over the phone, and Quinn silently cheered. A few moments later Ms. Narbold's voice said, reading, "Stimmler, Neil T., extensive record for burglary, larceny, possession of a controlled substance, served eight years on the most recent conviction, receiving stolen property. Released April 5, this year. Okay?" She sounded annoyed.

"One more question, please, Anna Marie, and then I'll let you go home to whoever is lucky enough—"

"Make it snappy."

Napitano rolled his eyes.

"Do you have a current address for Mr. Stimmler? Someone our office can contact? It's very important."

More key strokes. "P.O. Box 834, Barstow, California 98238. Sister: Boggs, Harriet. Phone number is 619-827-9983."

Quinn wrote it down. "Thanks—" She had already hung up. Quinn put down the phone.

"Oh my," beamed Napitano, "I had no idea your job was so much fun. Lying, duplicity, unctuous conversation." He smacked his lips over the words like they were the caviar he devoured for breakfast, "I am paying you entirely too much money, dear boy."

"You want to give me a little privacy here, Nino? I've got another call to make. This pans out you're going to get one hell of a story."

"Leave?" Napitano was shocked. "Out of the question." He leaned over the table, holding his chin with both hands, waiting.

Quinn dialed Harriet Boggs. It rang a long time before someone finally answered.

"Yeah?" A male voice, raspy from cigarettes.

"Mr. Boggs?"

"Who the fuck wants to know?"

Quinn heard sniffling, instinctively held the receiver an inch away from his ear. "This is Don Parker, Prison Outreach. May I speak to Mrs. Boggs, please?"

Napitano silently applauded.

"She's at the Tick-Tock."

"Pardon me?" said Quinn.

"The diner. This about my asshole brother-in-law?"

"I'm calling in reference to Mr. Neil Stimmler. Is he available?"

Boggs laughed, sucking in snot. "Sure, Mac," he cleared his throat, spit, "dial 1-800-HELL, he's standing around in asbestos skivvies shoveling coal into the blast furnace."

"Mr. Boggs?" Boggs had hung up. Quinn thought for a moment, then hit the redial button, listening to the numbers beep off while Napitano smiled. "Mr. Boggs," Quinn said quickly, "I have some money—"

"Yeah?"

"Prison Outreach is a non-profit organization devoted to helping ex-convicts make the transition into society—"

"You said something about money."

"Mr. Stimmler is dead?"

A grunt from Boggs.

"How did he die?"

"He stopped breathing," Boggs sneered. "About time, if you ask me. What's this about money?"

"Prison Outreach may be willing to authorize a bereavement benefit—"

Napitano shook his head no.

"What's that mean?"

"If we receive proof of his death, we may be able to cut you a check to cover funeral expenses. Do you have a medical report, police report . . . was an autopsy performed?"

Napitano shook his head harder.

"Yeah, fucking Quincy showed up with the county meat wagon." Boggs hacked up something that sounded like it had been wrapped around his intestines. "Look, Mac, Neil's been dying for years. He finally caught the train last week. There weren't no autopsy, no police. Funeral home just came and bagged him up. You gonna pay me for that? I got a receipt."

"Is Mr. Stimmler buried—"

"Buried?" Boggs guffawed. "He was a convict, not the

fucking king of Egypt. We cremated his ass. Got the plastic urn and it still cost $317, tax included. I wouldn't have paid a nickel, but my wife went and put it on her charge card. Women. You gonna send us that check soon? I'm never going to be able to rent out that trailer again, not the way he left it. Stink to high heaven."

"Has his trailer been disturbed? I might want to drive out and take a look at it."

"What for?"

"Mr. Boggs, are you interested in receiving pay-ment—"

"You want us to put up another ex-con, is that it? Okay by me, but we're talking $350 a month rent and they pay their own utilities. Pretty nice trailer, too. I was just kid-ding about the smell."

"Give me the address, Mr. Boggs, we'll be in touch."

"I heard that before," said Boggs. He gave Quinn the address anyway.

"It's not really so bad," said Harriet Boggs. She opened the door to the rusted trailer, holding a can of Lysol out into the darkness, spraying herself a path inside. "You just got to get used to it."

Quinn followed her inside, his nose burning from the stink. It smelled like burning hair inside the trailer. Dirty hair.

Harriet flipped on the light, walked over the debris of clothes and trash, and switched on the air conditioner. It made a few thumping sounds and stopped. She banged it with the heel of her hand. It started up. Quinn decided to leave the door open anyway.

"The mister said somebody from the prison office called a few hours ago, asking about my brother, Neil," said Harriet, "but he didn't say you were coming by tonight. He's gone to Bingo. I hope you don't mind talking to me."

"Not at all, Mrs. Boggs. In fact, you're the person I wanted to talk with."

"You best call me Harriet." She wiped her hands on her apron, looking pleased. She was a buxom, older woman, with weary eyes and too much fat around her heart. She was still wearing her food-stained uniform from the kitchen at the Tick-Tock, her flesh the color and consistency of wet dough.

Quinn had driven to the desert straight from *SLAP*, but got caught in the rush-hour mess. It should have taken an hour. It took three. Going back would be faster. When he arrived at the diner it was after 8 p.m. and Harriet was just finishing her shift. She made him have a cup of coffee and peach pie before anything else, saying he looked like he had low blood sugar. The pie was good. The coffee wasn't.

The trailer was bare of furniture except for a worn recliner and a single straight-back kitchen chair with a cracked seat. Harriet turned on the television, then switched it off—it was as though she thought he was considering moving in and wanted to show off the facilities. Quinn stood just within the doorway, looking at the bits and pieces of the room while Harriet moved nervously from one place to the other. Her feet were swollen, but she didn't sit down.

"You must have cared a great deal for your brother to take him in," Quinn said. "With his record, a lot of people, even family, would have turned their back on him."

"Oh I couldn't never do that," said Harriet, shaking her head. "The mister . . . he talks rough, but there was no way I was going to let my big brother die alone." She dabbed at her eyes with the edge of her apron. " 'Course, he did die alone, in a manner of speaking—just last Thursday—but I was close by, at least."

"That's something."

"Yes, I think it is."

"Harriet, your brother, had his condition deteriorated in the days before his death?"

"Neil had been poorly for months. That's why the prison let him out. They figured it was cheaper that way."

"Yes, but the last time you saw him, was he worse than usual?"

"It was hard to tell with Neil." She wandered to the tiny sink, picked up a crusted fork, then dropped it back with a clatter. "Neil hardly ever let me in here for more than a few minutes," she said, clearly embarrassed at the mess, "then after he passed on, after that, I still had a hard time coming in here. I should have picked up—"

"It's not so bad," lied Quinn. "There are divorced guys all over the country living just like this."

"You're a nice person," nodded Harriet, "a very nice person. You should have heard the nasty comments about my cleaning from the man who come to pick up the oxygen tank." She straightened up, patted her hair, and faced him. "What did you want to talk to me about anyway? The mister said there might be some money in it for us?"

"I'm a magazine writer," said Quinn, not wanting to lie to her anymore than he had to. "I'd like to ask you some questions about Neil, and I'd be happy to pay you for any help you might give me."

"I don't know . . . Neil never got much respect in life. I'd hate to have all the worst spread out for everyone to see."

"That's not my intention," said Quinn. Both of them were still standing, neither of them touching anything in the room. "I'm working on a related story—I'm not even sure Neil is part of it, but if he is, I think he got a raw deal and I'd like—"

"Oh, he did," said Harriet. "He absolutely did."

"I don't see a phone," said Quinn.

"We never had no phone in here," said Harriet. "The mister wasn't about to let Neil run up any bills to them 900 numbers. Neil would have, too. He couldn't help it."

"Perhaps he made some calls from your home? Collect?"

"Oh my, no."

Quinn walked to the two cabinets in the kitchen. "May I?"

"Ain't nothing in there. Neil said he traveled light."

The cabinets were empty. The shallow closet was piled with dirty laundry. Quinn took a deep breath and went through them, checked every pocket, felt every seam and cuff. Nothing. He had to resist the urge to wash his hands. He looked in the bathroom next, lifted up the tank lid, felt around behind the bowl. Then he washed his hands. Twice.

"If you're looking for dope, Neil couldn't smoke no dope. His lungs were shot, and I wouldn't allow it."

Quinn bent down, started looking over the magazines and newspapers on the floor, wincing at the smell. Stirring things up just made it worse.

"What are you looking for?" said Harriet. "I'll be glad to help. Not just for the money, either."

"I don't know what I'm looking for," admitted Quinn, on his hands and knees now, picking through an over-turned shoebox.

"Is that the way you magazine writers do it?" asked Harriet, holding up a couple of trashy novels for his inspection, "you just flop around until you find something?"

"That's pretty much the way I do it," smiled Quinn, "but it's not the recommended way to go."

She patted his hand. "You're doing just fine, honey."

"Ouch." Quinn picked a tiny shard of glass from his thumb. He mentally reviewed the date of his last tetanus shot. It was a strange bit of glass, very fine, thinner than a lightbulb.

"These mean anything?" Harriet showed him five har-monicas.

"I don't know."

"Neil always had a harmonica in his pocket when he was growing up. Seemed like he had a new one every week." She pretended to be interested in the blank televi-sion. "He always had a musical nature."

"When Neil was in prison this last time," said Quinn, "when he was very sick, he asked to speak to another inmate, a man named Joe Staducci. Did Neil ever talk about him? Joe Staducci? Joe Steps? It's very important, Harriet."

She shook her head.

"What about before? Before he was sick, when he wasn't in prison. Joe was a dancer, a ballroom dancer. Does that ring a bell? He was a gambler, too. Maybe Neil knew him from before he went to prison? Maybe he owed Joe money? I'm trying to find out why Neil would have asked to see Joe when he was in the hospital. They weren't even on the same cellblock—Neil was in minimum security, Joe was doing hard time. There had to be a reason."

"I wish I could help you, honey, but Neil didn't talk much these last few months. He didn't do much of anything." She brightened. "Maybe you should ask this Joe?" she suggested.

Quinn glanced at his watch. He had gotten a call from Bobby just as he was leaving *SLAP*, and had promised to meet the kid at a club in Long Beach sometime after ten. Quinn had tried to put him off, but Bobby was insistent, a little stoned too, saying he had "surveillanced" something that he couldn't talk about over the phone. Bobby was probably just trying for extra credit in his police-science class, but Quinn humored him. Somebody had to.

"Did Neil ever talk about a man named Fontayne?" asked Quinn. "Ellis Fontayne. He's an attorney. Very successful—"

"Neil had plenty of attorneys," said Harriet, "most of them from Legal Aid. They never were successful for Neil. He was just plain unlucky, there's no way around it."

"Thanks, anyway." Quinn scooted forward, reached under the recliner, and pulled out a small wooden box. His excitement dimmed when he saw Lawrence Welk's picture on the lid with the phrase "and a one, and a two" embossed next to the bandleader's baton.

"There it is," cried Harriet, taking it from him. "I was wondering where that went to." She opened the lid and a few bars of music tinkled out, then stopped. "Neil had me drive all over creation looking for this thing. Fresh out of prison and that was all he cared about. Plain pitiful."

"Could I see that, Harriet? Please?"

"Be careful." She passed it over. "That's a keep-sake now."

"I know." He examined the box, but there wasn't anything inside it. "Do you know why Neil was so interested in this particular music box?"

"Is the box important?" Harriet said, excited, the color rising in her neck.

"I have no idea. It sounds like it was important to Neil."

"Oh my, yes, Neil loved that music box. He said it reminded him of one he had a long time ago and then lost. I used to walk in sometimes and Neil would be in the recliner, crying, winding it up for one more listen." Harriet suddenly looked like she had bitten into a rotten apple. "He was thinking about that Sweetie girl, of course. He bought her a music box once, real beautiful one, too, must have cost Neil a pretty penny." Her face jiggled with annoyance. "Neil was always giving her things. Bracelets, clothes . . . I don't know where he got the money. I told him she wasn't no good—she had wild eyes, anybody could see that—Neil about slapped me."

"What's Sweetie's real name?" asked Quinn. "I'd like to—"

"Sweetie's dead. Long time ago. Everything was a long time ago." Harriet sighed. "Poor Neil. She died right after they broke up, too. I think that's when things really went wrong for Neil," she sniffled. "He had been in trouble before, of course . . . that darned marijuana, but that was just because he was so nervous and quick tempered. After she died, though, it was just one jail after another. Poor Neil. No matter how hard he tried, something always went wrong."

"What did Sweetie look like?" asked Quinn. "She's connected to the music box and the music box seemed to be the only thing your brother was interested in—it must mean something."

"Well, I only met her once," said Harriet, "and once was plenty. Me and the mister was living up in Northern California, right outside of Red Bluff. Neil brought her up for Thanksgiving dinner. 'This here's Sweetie,' Neil says, waving around one of those marijuana cigarettes like she's something to be proud of, this skinny little blonde thing with more rings on her fingers than Astor's pet horse, showing off the music box Neil had just bought for her, bragging on how expensive it cost." She shook her head in disgust.

"Harriet?" Quinn said patiently. "Are you sure you

don't remember Sweetie's real name? Neil must have mentioned it."

Harriet scrunched her brow into soft white furrows, thinking. "Nope. All I remember is her saying she didn't like her given name, said it sounded like a little old lady's name. She said her folks started calling her Sweetie when she was growing up, and she liked that better." She shrugged. "That's all I remember about her. That and she told me she didn't like cinnamon in her candied yams. I spent six hours in a hot kitchen making Thanksgiving dinner. What kind of person don't like cinnamon in yams?"

"Do you know how Sweetie died?" Quinn had put off asking long enough.

Harriet leaned close. "She got herself murdered," she whispered. "Strangled. Poor Neil. They weren't even going together anymore and he still cried like a baby when he told me about it. Neil was like that," she clucked. "Always worried about somebody else."

Quinn toyed with the music box, winding it up. "Harriet, sometimes men with that much love in them are also . . . jealous," he said carefully. "They have a hard time letting go. Was Neil like that?"

"Oh my, yes," nodded Harriet. "I'm the same way," she said proudly. "I got expelled from high school for smacking Vonda Carter. Broke one of her teeth. Front one." She tapped an incisor. "Caught her kissing my boyfriend. Served her right. That's the way Neil and I were raised. You don't let nobody take what's yours. If you do, pretty soon you don't have nothing."

"She died in L.A.?" asked Quinn.

"Who?"

"Sweetie." He opened the lid of the box, listened to the music. It was a nice tune. Old fashioned. A one and a two.

"I guess. Yeah, somewhere down there."

"Do you remember when that was?"

"It would have been . . . 1962," she said, tucking a wisp of hair back behind her ear. "Yes, 1962. The mister and I had just celebrated our five-year anniversary. That's the paper anniversary. He got me a box of stationery with my initials on it." She smiled to herself. "Neil called up and he was upset and asking if he could come stay with us. Right away, too. Asked if I could wire him bus fare. 'Course I said yes, but he didn't stay long. My husband, he never really understood Neil." She looked at Quinn. "Honey? You okay?"

Quinn stared at the music box, listening to the tinkling sound. He finally recognized the song. He wasn't tired anymore. He felt so good he was almost airborne. He didn't know much, but he knew enough now to find out who Sweetie was, and there was no telling where that would lead. "Harriet, when Neil sent you looking for the music box, it wasn't this specific box that he wanted, was it?"

"What do you mean? Specific?"

"It didn't have to be a Lawrence Welk music box, did it? That wasn't what Neil asked for. Am I right?"

" 'Course not," she laughed. "Neil never cared for Lawrence Welk. He just said the music box had to play that song. 'Sweet Adeline.' He must have loved that song. Everybody to their own taste, that's what I always say."

Quinn reached in his pocket, handed her all the big bills.

"No, honey," she said, trying to give it back. "This is too much. I didn't do nothing. If I had been able to help you some, that would be different."

Quinn wrapped her fingers around the money.

CHAPTER

29

Quinn hesitated outside The Summer of Love coffee-house, "In a Gadda da Vida" shaking the gamboling unicorns painted on the plate glass windows. Bobby spotted him from inside the club, waved to him, excited. The noise level soared as Quinn pushed open the door, the air thick with pachoulie and vanilla incense. Bobby pumped his hand, shouting, "Glad you could make it, dude" in Quinn's ear, the fringe on his purple buckskin jacket quivering as he did so.

Bobby led him through the crowded room, wobbling on his platform shoes. Quinn tried not to stare, but it was difficult. There were too many bell bottoms, too many tie-dye dresses, too many peace symbols. Girls with straight blonde hair mouthed the words to the music, clove cigarettes crackling between their fingers, while guys in tinted granny-glasses nodded in time to the rhythm, love beads bouncing. Posters on the walls announced concerts by The Doors and Jefferson Airplane, demanded that Nixon Stop the War! Father Ho gazed beatifically over a pretty dark-haired girl wearing a Mexican peasant blouse, who watched them from a table in the corner.

"This is Felicia," said Bobby, introducing him to the girl in the peasant blouse. She wore white frosted lipstick that made her look like one of the undead. She had a small yellow flower painted on her cheek. "Felicia, this is Quinn."

Quinn offered his hand. She stared at it, then giggled like he had curtseyed or something. He sat down. This is what he got for keeping his promise to Bobby. It was after midnight. Quinn had gone back to *SLAP* after leaving Neil Stimmler's trailer to use the magazine's twenty-four-hour line into the California Department of Public Records. His fingers had danced over the keyboard, making music.

The Lava lamp on their table slowly percolated, oily red bubbles rising and falling. The neo-hippies around him bobbed their heads as the drummer for Iron Butterfly flogged his drumset—Bobby rapped the table in time, while Felicia closed her eyes in ecstasy.

Having an old-fashioned name might have bothered Sweetie, but it made it comparatively easy to track her down. According to the state coroner's reports, in 1962 there were 141 women murdered in the six-county region of Southern California, 68 of whom were within Quinn's rough estimate of Sweetie's age at the time of her death.

There was only one Adeline listed: Adeline Gibson,

Caucasian, age twenty, Los Angeles, September 23. Quinn still didn't know what Adeline Gibson's murder had to do with Joe Steps, but the time frame was contiguous to Joe's own murder conviction. Quinn was going to have a little talk with Joe tomorrow, ask him about that bedside visit with Neil Stimmler. Tomorrow. After he got some sleep.

"In a Gadda da Vida" finally ended. If there was a soundtrack to Hell, that was the first song on the tape. Evidently followed by "Horse with No Name." Quinn fought down the urge to bolt for the door.

"Oh, I love this song," said Felicia, mouthing the words with those frosted lips: " 'been to the desert on a horse with no name . . .' It's by America," she whispered to Quinn, as though passing on the location of the Holy Grail.

"I know," Quinn said. "I was there the first time around."

"Quinn was alive during the real Summer of Love," Bobby said proudly. "He was like one of the original hippies."

Felicia stared at Quinn, mouth open, yellow flower frozen.

"Not exactly," said Quinn. "I was eleven years old at the time—little too young for the love-in. I was still play-ing with firecrackers and my GI Joe."

"I don't believe in war toys," declared Felicia.

"Quinn's cool," Bobby said to her. "Not like those geezers walking around in Docs and black leather saying 'def' and 'whazzup, homey?' I hate those guys."

"Groovy," said Quinn.

Bobby looked blank.

"He's teasing us," explained Felicia.

"What did you want to talk to me about, Bobby?" Quinn said.

"You want some orange spice tea?" asked Bobby. "They don't serve alcohol . . . it's a depressant, you know?"

Quinn looked from one to the other. They were so eager and sincere. He hoped they'd never wake up, never read a newspaper, or crack a history book.

"Felicia's in my police-science class at the community college," said Bobby. "So we can talk around her."

"I'm pre-med," Felicia said. "I'm going to be a forensics specialist. My father's an OB/GYN, but the hours are too erratic. Women have babies anytime they feel like it, but autopsies are scheduled," she said, suddenly serious. "Forensics is the way to go—you know when you can party, you know when you have to clock in."

Quinn nodded. She made so much sense it was terrifying.

Bobby hung over the table, purple fringe dragging across the tabletop, as "Horse with No Name" ricocheted off the walls. Kids at the other tables were actually tapping their feet to the music. The horror. "Remember Saturday night?" said Bobby, "you, me, and Gomer?"

"I remember, Bobby. It was only three days ago, I still have a few functioning brain cells left."

"Cool," said Bobby. "Okay, after Gomer and me—"

"Gomer and I," corrected Felicia.

"Okay," shrugged Bobby. "Anyway, after we checked

out Second Street, which was nowhere, Gomer split and I hiked back to my place. Must have been a couple of hours. Party was still going strong at your old lady's place."

Quinn looked at his watch.

"It wasn't until I got up to my room that I scoped the dude in the Mercedes."

That got Quinn's attention.

"Bobby is really good at surveillance," Felicia said proudly. "I think it's neurological, a hair-trigger gestalt sensitivity." She toyed with the fringe on Bobby's rawhide jacket. "Gestalt is high-level pattern recognition," she explained to Quinn, "sort of a—"

"I know what it is."

"It's just something I was born with," Bobby said shyly, "like knowing when 'Partridge Family' reruns are on without checking the *TV Guide.*"

"What about the guy in the Mercedes?"

"I think he was the same dude I had seen a couple days before, checking out your old lady's house."

"You think?"

"He had a different car last time. A red Blazer," said Bobby. "I thought he was just waiting for somebody. Then I saw him again Saturday night. I told your old lady the next day, but she blew me off. She still thinks I'm just the neighborhood kid who never showed up to mow the lawn when he promised. That wasn't my fault, Quinn—I think I'm allergic to gasoline . . . or pollen." He shrugged. "I asked Felicia what I should do. She said to call you. So I did."

"What did he look like?" Quinn kept his voice even.

"It was pretty dark," admitted Bobby. "He parked between the streetlights. Both times. That's pretty weird, don't you think?"

"Not particularly," said Quinn. "You're sure he was watching Rachel's house?"

"I told you, I seen him before," said Bobby.

"Saw him before," corrected Felicia.

Quinn kept thinking about his conversation with Katie at the beach, her nervousness about the boy at the front door selling cosmetics, a cute boy who preened himself while he talked. "Bobby," he said carefully, "were you still pretty stoned when you saw this guy in the Mercedes?"

"Uh . . ." Bobby shrugged, embarrassed.

"Bobby?" Felicia was annoyed.

"Don't rag on me about a few joints, will you, Felicia?"

"Marijuana shows up in a urine test," she clucked.

Quinn felt relieved. "So Bobby, you come home, it's dark, you're tired, a little stoned, you see a guy in a car who looks like another guy, in another car—"

"Listen," hissed Felicia as 'Nights in White Satin' came on, a shimmering dream of ancient history. "I love The Moody Blues." She glared at Quinn. "You are so lucky. You could go to free concerts during the sixties and be naked and no one would bother you. Strangers would give you acid, just give it away, and it was like the best acid in the whole world." The flower painted on her cheek was cracked. Her lower lip trembled, her dark eyes angry. "What did you people do? The whole world is fucked up now. Everything costs too much and none of it's any good."

"Don't blame Quinn," soothed Bobby. He took her hand. The two of them, not a wrinkle between them. "He didn't wreck the world—it was the other ones."

The other ones? "Bobby," said Quinn, trying to get his attention, "the previous time you saw this guy watching Rachel's house—"

"It was early evening," said Bobby, "I got out of my night class and didn't want to start my homework. He was just sitting in this red Blazer watching the house."

"Was Rachel there?"

"Yeah. They all were. Rachel, Katie, the old guy in the wheelchair—"

"Joe was there?" Quinn cocked his head. "A man in a wheelchair?"

"That's what I said. He was on the front porch with your kid. She was tap-dancing for him. Cracked me up. The cabby was there too. Skinny dude looks like he belongs in a Sally Struthers Somalia telethon"—Bobby sucked in his cheeks. "Rachel brought out this plateful of cookies, but he didn't touch them. Katie and the dude in the wheelchair dove right in, though, both hands. You should have seen it," he snickered, "it was like an episode of 'Leave it to Beaver.' "

"I like that show," said Felicia. "There's a proto-suburban angst permeating every episode."

"Yeah," said Bobby. "I like Eddie Haskell, too."

"The guy in the red Blazer, he didn't get out of the car? He just watched the house?"

"Yeah. I didn't think much of it, that first time. It's a free country, right? But when I spotted him again Saturday night, I got suspicious." He glanced at Felicia. "I got a good gestalt."

Felicia caressed his scraggly goatee so tenderly that Quinn had to look away. For a moment he wished that he was young again, starting out fresh. He didn't care if everything cost too much and nothing was any good. Half the fun of being young was thinking you could change all the things that were wrong with the world.

"It was nice meeting you, Felicia." Quinn still wasn't sure whether Bobby had seen anything. "Thanks, Bobby."

"It was the same dude," insisted Bobby. "Different car, same dude. I'm sure of it. I didn't see his face, but I remember his hair. He kept playing with his hair. Both times I saw him."

Quinn stopped.

"Show him your notebook," urged Felicia.

Bobby pulled a small police notebook out of his jacket, riffed through the pages. " 'Young,' " he read, " 'real feathery hair, kind of glam, keeps fluffing it out with his fingers.' " Bobby looked up at Quinn, pleased with himself.

Quinn stood up so fast he knocked his chair over. It was a twenty-minute drive to Rachel's.

"Hey," said Bobby, "don't you want his license plate?" He tore off a page from his notebook. "I wrote down the license number of the Mercedes." He grinned at Quinn. "I told you, man, I got an aptitude for police work."

Rachel must have been getting ready for bed when Quinn rang the bell. She was wearing her striped terrycloth robe belted around her waist. She stared at him through the glass section of the front door, pleasantly surprised to see him, it seemed. When she let him in, Quinn noticed she hadn't even deadbolted the door.

She looked disappointed when he told her why he was there, watching as he went through the house room by room, checking windows and doors, making sure the outside flood lights were on. Then he went upstairs and secured Katie's window. Rachel came in and stood beside him. Neither of them said a word. They just watched Katie breathe. After a while they sat on the stairs together.

"Bobby was stoned," Rachel said. "Right? He said he thought it was the same kid he had seen watching the house last week. Has Bobby ever impressed you as a thinker?"

"A kid fitting the description showed up at your front door Monday. A pretty boy. Katie told me about him at the beach."

"Why would somebody be watching our house?"

Quinn shook his head. "I don't know."

They sat at the top of the stairs, listening to the night. They used to cuddle here at the end of the day when they were married—it was their spot.

Rachel laid her head against his shoulder, and he put his arm around her. It seemed like the most natural thing in the world. Katie stirred in the next room. He started to get up but Rachel kissed him, and he stayed where he was, trying not to think where this was leading, which was someplace dangerous. Their first date she had kissed him goodnight and he had ended up spending the weekend, barely coming up for air.

Kissing Rachel was so different from kissing Jen. Even after three months together, Jen was still unfamiliar— there was a reserve between them, as though each of them was holding back. Rachel parted his lips with her tongue and he blushed. Strange to feel like he was cheating on his girlfriend by kissing his wife. Ex-wife. Maybe if he had to remind himself, he was cheating on Jen.

"Come to bed," Rachel said softly, laying kisses along his jaw. It was like being punched by an angel.

"Daddy?" Katie stood in her bedroom doorway, rubbing her eyes. "Are you staying here tonight?"

He and Rachel nervously moved apart. "Go back to sleep, honey," said Quinn, getting up to help her slide back under the covers, stumbling, overwhelmed with the sudden eruption of passion between him and Rachel. Their feelings for each other had never gone away, but they rarely acknowledged them. It just made their separation worse. When he got back to the landing, Rachel was making up the bed in the guest room. Perfect. Now the two of them could pretend the invitation never happened.

Quinn stood behind her while she worked. "You've been seeing a lot of Joe," he said. "And Hugo."

"Yes?"

"I think you should . . . discourage that for a while," he said. "Bobby first noticed this kid watching the house when the two of them were visiting. There may be a connection."

"You don't live here anymore." Rachel's dark eyes flashed. "I'll decide who visits, not you."

"I'm still checking out Joe and Hugo," Quinn said evenly. "Why don't you wait until I'm finished?"

"You enjoy investigating people," said Rachel, "it gives you a sense of power. You ran a credit check on Tynan, didn't you? Have you done that to all my dates?"

"Just him," said Quinn. "I thought he was special to you."

"You were afraid he was special."

Quinn didn't answer.

"I like Joe, and so does Katie," said Rachel. "Hugo has a tortured face, but I see a kindness in him. They're both welcome in my home. Is that clear? Good. I'm going to bed."

Quinn sat in the living room all night with Katie's squirtgun in his hand. It was a very realistic *Dirty Harry* look-alike, except that it was made of orange plastic. He kept the lights on low—hopefully, anyone checking out the place from the street would see the gun, but not the color.

Just after 3 a.m., a blue RX-7 drove slowly past with its headlights off. Quinn stood up, walked to the door, casually displaying the squirtgun. The RX-7 beeped once and kept driving. No telling who was behind the wheel. No telling if it was just one of the new neighbors. The last time he looked at the clock it was after 5 a.m.

He dreamed of pretty boys with dead eyes, asking if Katie could come out to play . . .

"Why are you sleeping with my water pistol, Daddy?"

Quinn opened his eyes.

Katie stared at him from the doorway of the living room, her hair a tangle of curls in the morning light, standing there in her Wonder Woman pajamas with a hole in one knee.

"Morning, baby." Quinn stretched, stiff from sleeping upright in the chair. He squirted a few shots into his mouth. The water was warm.

"Daddy?"

"It's nothing, Katie. I was just playing a game."

Katie watched him with her mother's skeptical eyes. "Really."

"What kind of a game?" said Katie. She moved next to him, started to crawl into his lap.

"Who wants breakfast?" Rachel said, coming down the stairs in a striped robe, her hair wrapped in a wet towel. She didn't wait for an answer, breezed past him, leaving a faint wake of Nocturnes. She clattered around in the kitchen, making more noise than she had to brewing coffee.

In the bright light of morning, last night's kisses seemed like a dream. A sweet dream.

"Get dressed, Katie," Rachel called.

Katie stayed next to him.

"It's okay," he whispered.

She scampered up the stairs. Quinn squirted her as she reached the third step, Katie squealing with delight.

He walked into the kitchen, watched as Rachel stood with her back to him, cracking eggs into a brown ceramic bowl. He put away the squirtgun. It was too tempting. "I think you and Katie should go visit your sister."

"I'm busy." Rachel whipped the eggs with a fork. "The sitter is coming in an hour—"

"The sitter almost let this kid in Monday," Quinn said. "It's a good thing Katie has some street smarts."

"Katie is a little girl with a healthy suspicion of strangers," said Rachel, flailing the eggs. "That doesn't mean that everyone who rings the bell is a serial killer." The eggs hit the hot iron skillet with a sizzle.

Quinn checked his watch as Rachel jabbed at the eggs with a spatula. The DMV office in Sacramento had just opened. He picked up the phone. "I'm not going to argue with you."

"That'll be a first." She handed him a cup of coffee. Rachel divided the soft omelette into three plates, called to Katie. Quinn took to his regular seat.

Quinn gave the *SLAP* magazine clearance code to the DMV operator, then read her the license plate number Bobby had given him. Five seconds later she read him the name, age, and address of the registered owner of the gray Mercedes as he wrote down the information.

The registered owner was Jack Kyle Liggett, 37 Bay Drive, Newport Beach, born 1-5-37. Fifty-eight years old, definitely not Prettyboy. Quinn wasn't surprised. Prettyboy must steal a car every time he wanted to go for a drive. Next Quinn called the Newport Beach P.D. and asked for the public information officer. It might help if he could find out where the Mercedes had been stolen. Where it had been found.

Katie raced into the kitchen, skirt flying as she sat down. It seemed like only yesterday she hated dresses, insisting on the same jeans-and-t-shirt look that Quinn favored.

"Bill Dudley, public information," said the chipper young voice at the end of the phone.

"Could I speak to officer Avilla?" asked Quinn.

"She's transferred," said Dudley. "How may I help you, sir?"

Quinn identified himself, said he was working on a story for *SLAP* and needed to know if a Mercedes sedan, license number 863 YSA, had been reported stolen.

"I'm a writer myself," Dudley said cheerfully, keystrokes beeping in the background. "Poetry mostly. *SLAP* doesn't publish poetry, does it?"

"Ah . . . no."

"Too bad." There was a moment's silence. "Nope. No GTA report on an 863 YSA. Sorry." He cleared his throat. "Glad to help a fellow writer. Call me anytime. You have the correct spelling of my name? It's D-U-D-L-E-Y. As in 'Doright.' I get a lot of kidding about that around here."

"Hang tough," said Quinn, starting to hang up.

"Wait. Gee, this is embarrassing," said Officer Dudley. "The report was right in front of me, but in my defense, it wasn't a Grand Theft Auto. Are you still there?"

"What's the matter?" said Rachel. "Don't you like the eggs?"

"I'm still here," said Quinn, putting down his fork.

"Early this morning the Santa Ana P.D. found a white Mercedes, California license plate 863 YSA. The car is registered to a Jack Kyle Liggett, but they haven't officially identified the body in the trunk."

"Thank you." Quinn hung up. Pushed aside the eggs. "Do me a favor, Rachel, and take Katie to the campus with you? Just for today. Please?"

"Please, mama," said Katie. "Please, please, please?"

Rachel saw the expression on Quinn's face and nodded.

It looked like a street fair as Quinn approached the dead-end street in Santa Ana where the Mercedes had been found. The road was blocked off with police barricades, throngs of people stood gaping at the cops, calling out insults and suggestions in Spanish, Vietnamese, and English. Pushcart vendors sold fried bananas, mango snowcones, and Asian pastries. The crack dealers had moved a couple streets over, taking the opportunity to work the four-lane Grand Avenue now that the available officers were busy. John D. Rockefeller would be proud of their initiative.

Quinn flashed his press pass to one of the cops stuck with crowd control. "Any word on the guy in the trunk?"

The lanky officer adjusted his Ray-Bans. "White male. Fifties or sixties. Hard to be sure at this point. Looks like he was pistol-whipped, then shot twice in the face." He hitched up his Sam Browne belt, gun bouncing against his hip as he watched the street. "Cooking for a few days in a trunk didn't help his appearance any, either. You ever play Mr. Potato Head when you were a kid? That's him."

"Forensics come up with anything on the vehicle? Prints—"

"How long you think a Mercedes stays a virgin out here?" asked the officer. "Look at it—no tires, no seats, no CD player, no phone. They crowbarred open the trunk, pushed aside the body, and stole the jack and spare. Finders, keepers." He sidled toward the shade, eyeing a girl with a dripping snowcone. "What we got here is another carjacking, and a citizen who didn't hand the keys over fast enough. Stupid. You want to do some good, tell your readers that the coroner sees way too many heroes."

Quinn drifted along the edges of the crowd. He spotted

a chubby white boy, maybe ten years old, wearing cutoffs and a Mickey Mouse t-shirt. He sat on a skateboard, smoking a cigarette butt, holding it with his fingertips like a joint. The boy had a Mercedes hood ornament on a leather thong around his neck. Quinn sat down beside him.

The boy jumped, but Quinn held him in place with one hand.

"I'm not a cop," said Quinn.

"Get your fucking hand off me then." Heads turned.

"Maybe we should call a cop?" said Quinn, not raising his voice. "Show him your necklace?"

"They already done asked me about it," sneered the boy, showing his brown, dirty teeth. Somebody had taken a Magic Marker to his t-shirt so that Mickey had a black eye and vampire fangs. "I told the pigs I found it lying in the street. They can't prove different. Neither can you."

"The way I see it," said Quinn, "the first half hour, nobody would touch the Mercedes, thinking maybe it belonged to a serious player. After a while, though, somebody would come by, maybe cruise past on their skateboard, grab something quick and easy . . ."

"I told you—"

"Yeah. You found it. I'm just saying, if it was me, I'd grab something nice, like a gold-plated hood ornament. The older guys would come later, take the CD and the seats and anything else they could find, but if I was small and smart and quick, if I was the first one on the scene"—he bounced the necklace—"I'd get me one of these."

"Yeah?"

"Yeah." Quinn held out his last twenty. "What did he look like?"

"Who?"

Quinn stood up, put the twenty in his pocket.

"Wait," the boy jumped to his feet. "He was a white dude. Young. Looked like a hustler going to court. You know . . . suit and shoes with laces."

Quinn handed him the twenty. He was going to have to call Rachel, make sure she didn't go home after work.

"Hey, mister?" The boy held out a blood-crusted medallion. "How much for this?"

Quinn took it from him, holding it gingerly. It was a retired police officer emblem.

"I pried it off the rear bumper," the boy said proudly. "It's a real collector's piece. How much you give me?"

Quinn stared at the cracked metal in the palm of his hand. It was still warm from the boy's pocket.

CHAPTER

31

Quinn had been waiting on Joe's porch steps for over an hour in the late-afternoon heat, sweat trickling down the back of his neck. He hardly noticed.

He had called Rachel right after he saw Jack Liggett's Mercedes, and convinced her to go to her sister's house directly from work. Do not go home. Do not collect $200.

Quinn made more calls, learned that Jack Liggett had been a vice cop with the LAPD. Nice car for a retired civil servant. There was still no answer at any of Jen's numbers.

He didn't like it, but it wasn't uncommon for her to work days at a time, sleeping in the darkroom, not answering her pager.

An ice cream truck rolled slowly down Joe's street, the driver speeding up now, clearly uncomfortable with Quinn's stare. Joe lived on a nice block, the houses freshly painted, lawns mowed, birds singing in the trees. Main

Street U.S.A. Wait around long enough and a parade would come by, beauty queens waving to the neighbors. Quinn didn't believe it.

He walked along the side, looked into the backyard through the fence. He could see a chin-up rack, the metal bar shiny from use. A white beach towel was draped over the chaise lounge, purple flowers floating in the murky waters of the swimming pool. Bali Hi. He went back to the front porch.

Quinn had driven to the main library after calling Jen, where he sprinted up the stairs to his usual floor: the reference section. He had spent a lot of time on the twelfth floor, following the paper trail that was part of every story, every criminal investigation.

Ten minutes later, still panting from the stairs, Quinn was seated in the newspaper morgue, scrolling through microfilm copies of thirty-year-old papers, fingers twirling the dials of the machine so rapidly that the print was a blur. He forced himself to slow down, blinking into the screen.

The September 23, 1962, issue of the *L.A. Times* had reported Sweetie's murder on page B3, a brief, two-inch story with a minute photo of the deceased, Adeline Gibson, a corn-fed blonde from Indiana who had moved to California to break into movies. The other two newspapers simply noted the death in their crime wrap-up, not bothering with a photo. It had been a big news day—Chubby Checker was in town, hosting the world's biggest "Twistathon" outside of City Hall.

Two days later the murder got more interesting. And bigger play. It was now a B1 story, above the fold, with three photos. The first photo showed Sweetie in her high-school cap and gown. The second was from her modeling portfolio. She had sleepy eyes and a perfect smile. It was the third photo that warranted the increased coverage— a picture of a handsome, young black man: Jamie Ledbetter, aged twenty-five, described as "the accused, the musician-boyfriend of the murdered starlet." There was no mention of Neil Stimmler.

Sweetie had lived in a one-room apartment in a seedy building, doing temp work during the day while waiting for MGM to call. She had a lover whom no one had ever seen, although the couple next door had frequently banged on the adjoining wall to get them to quit fighting. A week before her murder she had complained to a friend at work that she was breaking up with her "loser boyfriend."

The manager had used her pass key to enter the apartment after complaints of a bad odor in the hallway and found Sweetie lying across the bed, dressed in only a black brassiere. She had been strangled. Since the door was locked, and the deadbolt turned, police concluded that the killer had a key. Though some of Sweetie's personal effects were missing, robbery was not considered the motive.

Jamie Ledbetter's photograph had been found in Sweetie's purse, his phone number written on the back, surrounded by hearts and Xs and Os. The wallet still containing $47 and a laminated perfect-attendance card from St. Peter's Cathedral, Tallon, Indiana.

When he was picked up, Ledbetter had a key to Sweetie's door on his keyring. Although admitting to a relationship with her, he said they hadn't seen each other in a week, a story he recanted after the police informed him that "physical evidence" linking him to the victim was the same as his bloodtype. Ledbetter then admitted to visiting Sweetie the night she was murdered, but swore he was innocent, insisting that he and Sweetie hadn't broken up—in fact, they had never been closer.

At the trial, Ledbetter's police interrogation was trotted out, his lies and equivocations. The prosecutor demanded that Ledbetter return Sweetie's class ring to her grieving parents, seemingly as outraged at Ledbetter's denial as by the murder itself. The defense offered two witnesses, fellow musicians, who testified that Ledbetter had been with them at the time of Sweetie's death. The prosecutor destroyed their credibility with a sneer and a brusque recitation of their minor criminal records. The jury was out less than an hour. They recommended the death penalty. The judge obliged.

Quinn sat with his back against the wall, pulling up blades of grass, splitting them with his thumb without looking, watching both ends of the block. You had to keep your eyes open. If Jamie Ledbetter had been as careful, things would have been different. Sweetie had been a good Catholic girl with two secret lovers: Neil Stimmler and Jamie Ledbetter. A pickpocket and a black man. Hard to explain either of them to the folks back in Indiana. Hard to explain them to each other. Ledbetter never mentioned the existence of another boyfriend at his trial. He hadn't known.

What seemed obvious thirty years later was that Stimmler had killed Sweetie when she ended their relationship, and Jamie Ledbetter was an innocent man sentenced to death.

Just like Joe Steps. Quinn waved away a fat bumblebee. He had left a request on Tina Chavez's voice mail at the D.A.'s office. He wanted to know if Jamie Ledbetter had been as lucky as Joe, if he had gotten his sentence reduced to life imprisonment. Tina would be able to find out fast.

Quinn tossed aside a knotted blade of grass and was on his feet before Hugo's cab had even rounded the corner. He waited while Hugo lifted Joe out of the backseat and into the wheelchair, Joe wincing with every movement. "We need to talk," Quinn said to Joe.

"Yeah? I'm going to take care of my business first," said Joe. He slapped Hugo's hands away from the wheelchair. "Leave me alone, damnit. I'm a cripple, not an infant." He grunted up the ramp, unlocked the front door, shaking with the exertion, then rolled inside and slammed it after him.

"What do you and Joe do all day?" Quinn said to Hugo. "I called the cab company—they said you don't have to submit a daily log since he's paying a flat rate. Must be nice to be on your own."

"Mostly we just drive," Hugo said, "two or three hundred miles some days. Joe wants to catch up on what he had missed, waterfront houses, new freeways, shopping districts. We spent all day at the orthopedist. He's getting worse. I wish he'd complain—I see him in the rearview biting his lip, but he never says a word."

"Maybe you should keep your eyes on the road," said Quinn.

Hugo blinked, uncomprehending.

"You wouldn't want to get into an accident," Quinn said evenly. "Doctors won't touch you without health insurance."

"I think I'm going to go now," said Hugo.

Quinn stared at Hugo, seeing him again that night on the Seal Beach pier, stepping out of his cab, all arms and legs, a scarecrow under the harvest moon.

"I have to go." Hugo shook Quinn's hand with his icy grip, the gesture curiously formal.

Quinn heard the front door open, the sound of the wheelchair going down the ramp, but he didn't turn around until the cab was out of sight. "How well do you know Hugo?" he said as Joe rolled up.

"What are you asking?" said Joe, his hair freshly combed, his eyes suddenly wary. "If I know you, you already looked into the matter. Am I right?"

"You get out of prison, and a few months later the two of you are driving around like Thelma and Louise," said Quinn. "It made me wonder." He checked the street. "Hugo's got no credit problems, no warrants, no criminal record—"

"Hey, don't hold that against him," Joe grinned.

"It's not that simple," Quinn snapped. "There's a hole in Hugo's life, a twenty-year gap. He's got no health insurance, no medical history that I could find. I've seen a fax of his birth certificate, I've seen his elementary school report cards, but his records all stop after fourth grade. I thought maybe the real Hugo Ganz had died—sometimes people who want a fresh identity pick up one from a dead child, but there was no death certificate filed. Then three years ago Hugo pops up like a mushroom after a rainstorm. Where was he?"

Joe watched him. "Hugo is a lifer. He's never been in prison, but he's done time. I recognized that the first time he picked me up."

"What does that mean?"

"Hugo got hit in the head with a baseball bat when he was nine years old," Joe explained. "Getting hit . . . it made his brain not work right. He didn't recognize his mother or anyone else. People would speak to him and he would just stare. Hugo told me words sounded like rushing water." Joe shrugged. "After a while, they dropped him into a nuthouse and forgot about him. A few years ago something clicked in his head. No reason for it, the words just snapped into place again. The state wanted to cut him loose, but there was no place for him to go. Finally, one of those Goody Two-shoes outfits stepped in, put him in a half-way house, paid for a driving course—"

"What was the name of the institution he was in?" said

Quinn. "Where was it? If you gave me the name of the mental institution, maybe I could confirm his story."

Joe's face darkened. "His story doesn't need confirmation. I can spot a phoney. I still have my instincts. What's your problem anyway? You look like somebody shot your dog."

"I don't have a dog," Quinn said. Joe's vagueness and equivocations just made him more suspicious. "Somebody shot Jack Liggett, though. Does that count?"

Joe turned his chair into the setting sun—his eyes were slits as he basked in the golden dying light. "Jack who?"

"Liggett. He was a vice cop in LA about thirty years ago. Up until a few days ago he had a good address and expensive taste in automobiles." Quinn stepped between Joe and the sun. "I thought a big-time gambler like you might have known him, rubbed shoulders at Santa Anita."

"I knew lots of cops, I didn't keep track of them." Joe looked up at him. "This Liggett, he's dead?"

"Very."

"You think I did it?" Joe laughed, rubbed his knees.

"I'm not sure yet," Quinn said seriously, "but something is going on, and I think you know what it is."

"You overestimate me, Slick."

"I don't think so," said Quinn. Someone was dribbling a basketball down the street, but he kept his eyes on Joe. "I was so happy to see you at Katie's dance recital," he said, seeing Joe once again in the spotlight, waving to the applause. "I couldn't believe it—Joe Steps, my hero, come back to life. You remember that night on the pier, Joe? That was the night Teddy was murdered."

"I remember," Joe said softly.

" 'Watch out for Fontayne,' that's what you told me at Teddy's grave," Quinn said bitterly. "I didn't need much encouragement—I didn't like Fontayne, but maybe somebody should have warned me about you, Joe?"

"You're talking crazy—"

"It was your conversation with Neil Stimmler in the prison hospital that got me interested," said Quinn. "I kept wondering, what could have been so important?—guy on his deathbed, he's not going to waste his time talking politics or who's going to the Superbowl. Then when Stimmler turns up dead . . ." Joe looked surprised. Quinn didn't know what to make of that. "You remember Stimmler, don't you Joe? He's the guy who killed Sweetie."

"I know who he is," Joe said cooly. "I didn't know he was dead."

"It's not too late to send flowers," said Quinn, "Stimmler was found dead just last week." He bent over Joe, putting his hands on the arms of the wheelchair, crowding him. "You see a pattern here? First Teddy. Then Stimmler. Now Jack Liggett. How am I doing, Joe? You impressed? Well, don't be, because I'm just getting started. When I figure out why Teddy was killed, why Stimmler, why Liggett was murdered, then you can be impressed."

"Back off, will you."

Quinn stayed where he was, breathing in Joe's face. "I looked into Stimmler, and I found Sweetie. I looked into Sweetie, and I found Jamie Ledbetter." The two of them were inches apart, panting with anger and frustration, neither of them wanting to take the first punch. Two of a kind. "I still don't know what this is all about, Joe, but I think if I keep looking, I'm going to find you."

"I don't know any Jamie Ledbetter or Jack Liggett," said Joe. "Honest to God, Slick."

"What did Neil Stimmler tell you in the hospital?" said Quinn. "What was so important?"

"That's none of your concern."

"Wrong," said Quinn, still leaning on the arms of the wheelchair. "Two days ago, Katie had her first gentleman caller. Young guy, knocking on the front door—more of a boy than a man, but he was man enough to kill Jack Liggett and stuff him into the trunk of his car."

The color drained from Joe's face like a plug had been pulled.

"Katie was home when the boy came by," Quinn said angrily, "just her and the baby-sitter. Katie didn't let him in. What do you think he might have done if she opened the door?"

"You got her someplace safe now?" demanded Joe. "Her and Rachel? You got them out of there?"

"What do you care, Joe?" Quinn taunted. "You don't know anything. Right?"

Joe suddenly smacked Quinn's arms apart. Quinn fell forward into Joe's lap. Joe grabbed his head in his strong hands, held him tightly. "You want me to break your neck for you? Huh? Then you answer me—Katie and Rachel, you got them out of there, didn't you? They're safe?"

Quinn struggled, grunting, but couldn't get any leverage as Joe slowly twisted his head backwards. "Yes!" he gasped and Joe released him. He lay on the ground, the sky spinning.

CHAPTER

32

"Jen?" Quinn listened at the outer door of one of the *SLAP* magazine darkrooms. No answer. He cautiously entered and closed it behind him. Utter darkness, not even a crack of light from outside. He knocked at the inner door. "Jen?" There was only the sound of running water. He opened the door, walked into a dim red haze, the air thick with chemical smells, feeling his way, moving slowly as though through glycerine.

"Just a minute," Jen said.

Quinn saw her bent over a long, stainless-steel trough, slowly rocking a photographic tray. He smiled, imagining her as a prospector panning for gold, knee-deep in a mountain stream.

Jen hung another eight-by-ten on the line, brushing against him as she did. He could smell the citrus tang of stopbath in her hair, saw water dripping off the shadowed prints, falling onto the black rubber mat on the floor.

"Be right there," Jen said over her shoulder, busy now at the enlarger.

Quinn watched her work, enjoying the smooth precision of her movements as she slid photographic paper into the easel under the dim red light. It was a pleasure watching someone good at her job, someone who knew what she was doing, and why, never entertaining any doubts of the value of what she did.

"How did you find me?" asked Jen.

"Armando told me. He saw your car."

"Who's Armando?"

"The new night guard in the parking structure."

Quinn knew the name of all the security guards on every shift, knew which sports teams they followed. He knew all the receptionists and cleaning staff, too, knew their favorite TV shows, and the names of their husbands and kids. He listened to their advice, laughed at their bad jokes, the way they laughed at his.

"I'm not complaining," said Jen, standing on her tiptoes to kiss him. "I'm glad you found me."

He felt her full lips part, his eyes half shut now. He froze.

"What is it?" She pulled back an inch.

He stared at the prints dangling by one corner from the clothesline overhead, saw Fontayne's patrician face gazing back at him. Under the red safelight, Fontayne appeared to be in fire.

"Quinn?"

He pointed to the photographs. "When did you shoot these?"

"Yesterday afternoon. Why?"

Quinn touched the wet photos by the edges. Fontayne was his usual chipper self, but some of the photos showed a softer side, his dapper polo shirt and chinos out of place in the crumbling urban landscape where Jen had photographed him. "I think you should stay away from Fontayne for a while."

"You do, huh?" She pushed his hand away from her photos. "Good. Now when I need someone to schedule my calendar, I'll know who to contact." She turned back to the enlarger. "Until then, keep your suggestions to yourself."

"It's not a suggestion," Quinn said to her back, "it's a request. I'm trying—"

"You're trying to run my life." Jen whirled and Quinn took a step backwards, hitting one of the red safelights that dangled overhead, throwing shadows across the darkroom. "You're trying to tell me who to see, who to photograph. What's next?"

Quinn held his hands up in mock surrender. "It's just that I don't trust Fontayne. He set off alarm bells in me the first time I saw him."

"We've already been through this—"

"I talked to Joe Steps a couple of hours ago," hurried Quinn. "He thinks Fontayne is up to something, too."

"Up to something? Well, that's specific." Jen stood in

the wildly dancing light. "You consider Joe Steps a reliable source? A man convicted of a double homicide?"

"That's not what is important here."

"I'm sure you'll tell me what's important."

"Jen, please—"

"Does Joe Steps have any reason to mistrust Fontayne?" Jen said sarcastically. "Or is he operating purely on gut instinct like you?"

"I don't know," admitted Quinn. "He didn't want to talk about it. He spent a lot of years keeping his own counsel."

"I see," said Jen. She didn't.

Jen walked to the enlarger, opened the paper safe, and took out a sheet of photographic paper. "So you still think Ellis is involved in Teddy's murder—"

"I'm still putting things together," said Quinn.

Jen shoved the photographic paper into the easel, trying to get it to fit. "You know, if anyone looks suspicious here, it's your friend Joe Steps. You told me that he and Teddy had problems—"

"That's not true."

She jabbed the paper into the easel again, her hands strangely clumsy. "Teddy told you Joe Steps had been killed in a car wreck," said Jen. "Teddy refused any contact with him. Would you describe that kind of relationship as close? Would you describe it as honest?"

Quinn didn't have an answer.

"Joe Steps is the one who just got out of prison," said Jen, "not Fontayne."

"I trust Joe Steps," said Quinn, "that's what counts."

The photographic paper creased as she tried to shove it into the easel. She ripped it out, balled it up, and threw it into the waste can. She looked wild in the red light. "Where were you last night, anyway?"

"Is that why you're so mad at me?"

"I thought you were going to come over." The two of them were almost shouting now. They might as well be married. "Something more important come up?"

"What does that mean?"

"Were you at Rachel's last night?"

"Someone had staked out her house," said Quinn. "I think it was the same guy who killed Teddy."

"Now Fontayne wants to kill Rachel, too?" Jen shook her head. "Do you have any idea how idiotic that sounds?"

"I didn't say that." He ran a hand through his hair, shrugged. "I told you, I'm still working on it."

"I'm sure you are," Jen said sarcastically. "I can just see you last night, showing up at Rachel's doorstep to save her from the forces of evil." She batted her eyelashes at him. "There's Rachel, in her pretty little nightie . . ."

The clothesline of Fontayne faces bounced slightly, watching, seemingly enjoying what they were seeing.

"You don't have anything to be jealous of," said Quinn. "I asked you to marry me. Doesn't that mean anything?"

"Oh, thank you. What an honor."

Quinn had to smile.

"You miss your family," said Jen, serious now. "You think you can start over again with me, but I'm not Rachel."

"You're the one I want, Jen." Quinn moved toward her but she pulled back.

"You don't know what you want," said Jen. "Rachel and Katie are going to Paris. Your solution is for us to go to Paris, too." She shook her head. "You don't need me for that. You're going to go there anyway, sooner or later. I'll probably give you a ride to the airport, too. Why not? I'm a big girl."

"You're talking crazy—"

"Leaving your wife is one thing, leaving your kid, that's different. That's not so easy, is it?"

"I didn't leave Rachel. She left me."

"That's your defense?" Jen laughed, tears running down her face. "Oh, that changes everything, now we're really in love. Now we can get married. Somebody call a priest!" He reached for her but she shook him off. "You said someone was staking out Rachel's house," she said fiercely. "Did you think maybe they were waiting for you, Quinn? Maybe they thought you still lived there? Or maybe they knew you spent a lot of time there?"

"I don't—"

"If someone is really after you, then anyone near you could be in danger," said Jen. "I could be in danger." Her voice was low and steady, talking to him like he was standing on a high ledge. "Did you ever think of that?"

"No."

"Do you ever worry about me the way you worry about Rachel and Katie?"

"Jen—"

"If Rachel and Katie were on a plane," she said softly, "and you knew the plane was going to blow up, and there was nothing you could do about it, absolutely nothing—would you want to be on that plane, sitting next to them, holding their hand?"

"That's a stupid question."

"You would, wouldn't you?" she insisted. "Wouldn't you?"

He nodded.

"If it was me on the plane," Jen said, her voice a husky whisper now, "what would you do?"

Quinn didn't answer.

"Exactly," said Jen.

"What would you do if it was me?" demanded Quinn.

She put both hands on his chest and he wasn't sure if she wanted to embrace him or push him away. "I'd stay on the ground," she said, "just like you." She looked up at him with those green eyes and he felt himself lost at sea, the two of them drifting farther and farther apart.

"I won't let anything bad happen to you," he said. "That's why I'm here."

"I don't need you for that," she said sadly. "I can take care of myself. Go home, Quinn. Go back to Rachel and Katie."

"I want to stay with you."

She shook her head. "You're not here, Quinn. You're already gone. You just don't know it."

"Don't throw me out, Jen. Please."

She put a finger to his lips, the two of them crying now.

"I couldn't do that, even if I wanted to. You already decided. Go on, go home."

Quinn held on to her until she stopped crying, burying her tears in his chest. He didn't have anyplace to put his. They stayed like that, in each other's arms, the two of them almost dancing under the red light.

CHAPTER

33

"Where's my burrito?" Vince Boyle said as Quinn slid into the passenger seat of the unmarked police car, a gray Plymouth parked across from the Blue Flu bar. "You said you'd bring breakfast."

Quinn held out a Tic-Tac but Boyle swatted it away.

Even this early, the Laguna Beach traffic was backed up on Pacific Coast Highway. Everyone was looking for a parking spot. Quinn had left his Jeep behind a hippy health-food store, hopefully protecting it from being towed away by plastering the bumper with "Meat Is Murder" and "Death Begins in the Colon" bumper stickers. He kept a supply of different political and social stickers in the dash for these occasions. Boyle had simply commandeered a Handicapped Zone.

"You're going to like Wild Bill." Boyle shook a bag of nacho 'n' sour creme cornchips into his mouth, spilling half of them down his shirt. "Just don't piss him off. You got a way of doing that, anybody ever tell you?"

"Not that I recall, fatso."

"Wise guy." Boyle chewed with his mouth open, belly bouncing against the steering wheel. His head was small on a thick neck, tiny ears flattened against his skull. He wore a wide tie with a crude, hand-painted bathing beauty and the same baggy corduroy sport coat that he had on at Teddy's house. It had been almost two weeks since the murder, the D. A. and the network news teams moving on to other crimes. It still seemed like yesterday to Quinn.

It was a clear, blue Thursday morning, with a cool breeze off the ocean and seagulls wheeling overhead. The beach was a mosaic of colored towels, perfect bodies centered on the terrycloth, shiny with oil. Gangly youths lined the basketball courts, bare-chested pickup players with zinc oxide warpaint squatting on their haunches, waiting for their turn. Quinn knew how they felt.

Boyle dug around in his ear with his pinkie as he tracked a rollerblader in a fuchsia thong. There were cornchips stuck in his grin. "It's a beautiful day in the neighborhood."

Quinn shifted on the sticky plastic seatcovers, sweating in his jeans and black Harley Davidson t-shirt. The t-shirt lowered his IQ fifty points, but he was still too smart for his own good. He had been awake most of last night, replaying what Jen had said to him in the darkroom, telling himself she didn't know what she was talking about. Just this once. "We going to sit here all morning?" he said, impatient to get things moving.

Boyle wiped his mouth with his necktie and opened his door, cornchips falling off his lap and onto the pavement. He didn't even bother to look before crossing the street. Nice to have a charmed life. Or maybe Boyle just didn't care. Seagulls swooped down and fought for the scattered cornchips, squawking, flapping their wings, until only one of them was left, gorging on Boyle's debris.

The Blue Flu was a cop bar, a concrete-block bunker overlooking the swelter of main beach. Inside it was cool and dark. Quinn could see a pool table in the back room, a lazy game in progress. The bartender stared at him from the far end, a hulking man in a pink, pearl-button western shirt, his face in profile.

"That's him," Boyle said, nodding at the bartender.

They sat at the bar, listening to the talk show shrink on the radio as Wild Bill made his way toward them. The shrink used the word "empowerment" three times in one sentence. Quinn counted. A matchstick electric chair sat next to the cash register, a Gumby doll in the hotseat, arms and legs wide. The wall behind the bar was papered with "Wanted" posters with the faces Xed out, signed and dated by the arresting officers. Fourteen of the posters bore the signature of "Bill Adzach," all of them charged with murder.

"Morning, Vincent." Wild Bill poured Boyle a double bourbon, and slid Quinn a cup of black coffee without asking.

Quinn tried not to stare. The left side of the bartender's face, the half that had been turned away before, was a mass of crawling pink scar tissue, his left ear shredded, the left eye . . . Quinn smiled in spite of his revulsion. The eye was fake, a tiny Texas state flag waved where the iris should be.

"Remember the Alamo," Quinn toasted the glass eye with his coffee, grateful for the steam that obscured his vision.

Boyle guffawed. "Bill, this here's—"

"I know who he is." Wild Bill's voice had a moist, spongy quality to it, like he had lost his palate in whatever had cost him half his face. His mouth twisted . . . it vaguely resembled a smile. In the silence, Quinn heard the shrink on the radio telling the caller to "unzip your fears."

"Hey Bill, throw a pizza in the micro," said Boyle.

Wild Bill shook his head. "Not with your cholesterol, Vincent. How about a veggieburger and sliced tomato?"

"You sound like my old lady," growled Boyle, "worried about fat and salt and stress. She's always listening to that know-it-all babe on the radio, too. That's your problem, Bill. You're getting too much free advice."

Two uniformed cops came out from the pool room. The white one hurriedly threw a few dollars on the bar. The black one stopped next to Boyle, flicked his grimy necktie. "That's quite a cravat, Boyle. You're a credit to your race."

Boyle waved his hands, mocking fear. "Please, Mr. Po-leece, can't . . . can't we all just get along?" The uniforms and Boyle roared with laugher, pounding each other on the back while Quinn and Wild Bill stayed silent. "I'm going to escort these two pussies to their cruiser," Boyle said to Quinn, wiping away tears. "You and Bill have your talk."

Quinn waited until the door closed. "Boyle said you

were LAPD during the sixties," he said quietly. "He thought you knew Jack Liggett."

Wild Bill stared at him. There was only the sound of his soggy breathing.

"I don't have time to ask you to the prom first," said Quinn. "I'm tired. You want to help me—"

"I heard you had an attitude." Wild Bill drank from a glass of club soda, bubbles trickling out the side of his mouth. "Yeah, I knew Jack. Feel better now?" He was enjoying himself. "We worked the seventy-seventh division, the two of us fresh from the Academy, ready to save the world. Me, I liked being a street cop—on my own, never the same day twice. Jack"—he took another drink, coughed, blotted his mouth—"Jack preferred rousting hookers and dopers."

"Do you remember a homicide case . . . maybe thirty years ago," asked Quinn, "young woman named Adeline Gibson, killed by her boyfriend?" The name obviously didn't mean anything to Wild Bill. " 'Sweetie'?"

Wild Bill brightened. "Oh, yeah. Black dude . . . I remember."

"His name was Jamie Ledbetter."

"Yeah. He was a musician, I think."

"You have a good memory," said Quinn. "Did Liggett ever bust Jamie Ledbetter?"

Wild Bill shook his head. "Who knows?"

"What about a pickpocket named Neil Stimmler?" Quinn said. "Stimmler was a young guy then, he smoked some pot . . . Did Liggett ever arrest him?"

"Jack made a lot of busts," said Wild Bill, "I didn't keep track of every skank and lowlife he wrote up." His cowboy shirt had six-guns embroidered across the yoke, smoke curling from their barrels, the fabric cut so full that it was hard to tell just how big he was.

"Maybe you should have paid more attention," Quinn said. "Liggett retired early, but he lived in Newport Beach, drove a Mercedes. That's hard to do on half-salary. Hard for a street cop. Evidently not so difficult in Vice."

Wild Bill smiled. His face looked like something Quinn had seen floating in a bell jar at the forensics lab.

"What about Ellis Fontayne—"

"You're full of questions, aren't you?" Wild Bill sipped his club soda, bubbles trickling down his chin. "A real thinker. Too many cops come in here, beaten down, burned out. No brain waves. You . . . I could watch you all day."

"You're easily entertained," Quinn smiled back at him. "Did Liggett know Ellis Fontayne? It's very important—"

"We all knew Fontayne. He was real loose with a round of drinks. Jack drank strictly twenty-year-old cognac on Fontayne's tab. I stuck with beer. I used to see Fontayne at the courthouse." Wild Bill dabbed at his drooping lip. "Other attorneys would be lugging boxes of depositions and lawbooks down the hallway, but not him. He had assistants for that. One of them even carried Fontayne's crocodile briefcase." His good eye gleamed with humor. "Before crocs were endangered, of course. Yeah, Mr. Ellis Fontayne was a man who liked to keep his hands free."

Quinn had an unpleasant image of Teddy following
Fontayne down a marble corrider, footsteps echoing. "I ran
a title search on Liggett's condo," Quinn said hurriedly.
"It's appraised at over $500,000, no mortgage outstanding.
The money had to come from somewhere. Maybe Liggett
did Fontayne a big favor once. Maybe Fontayne was grateful?"

Wild Bill grinned. "Fontayne didn't mess with vice
busts, his clients were heavy hitters, and, if Fontayne
had some private little habit of his own, he had the juice
to keep it private. He didn't need Jack to protect him."
He stared at his reflection in the polished bartop, then
up at Quinn. "You got your daddy's eyes," he said suddenly.

"Teddy?" Quinn was startled. "Teddy was my stepfather."

Wild Bill shook his head. "That's not what I'm saying.
You got Teddy's way of looking. Direct. Civies always find
something else to stare at when I'm around—the floor, the
ceiling. Even cops, even with all they've scraped off the
concrete, a lot of them don't look at me. Except for Boyle,
of course. Boyle will look at anything."

"You knew Teddy?"

"That's how I recognized you. The judge used to come
in sometimes. Late. Always late. I'd close up and we'd get
polluted, bring out our wallets and brag about our kids."
He chuckled to himself. "You need some sleep—you don't
look near as good as your picture."

"If Teddy wanted to go for a drink, he could have

phoned me." Quinn stumbled over his feelings. "I would have come."

"Don't take it personal." Wild Bill patted Quinn on the shoulder. "Fathers and sons, nobody ever gets it right." He glanced at a cracked Little League trophy next to the cash register. "My oldest played second base. He had some arm, a beautiful arm . . ." His breathing deepened. "He's in Chino now—assault. We'll work it out. We got time." He busied himself arranging the bottles on the shelf behind the bar, then looked back at Quinn. "You have kids, don't you?"

"One."

Wild Bill's good eye was warm. "Then you know what it's like."

Quinn could picture Teddy and Wild Bill standing around after closing, sipping bourbon and talking about their families. The lost and found. "Teddy . . . Teddy worked for Fontayne for a while. He was one of those assistants carrying his books. Did you ever see him do that?"

"No," Wild Bill shook his head. "Don't mean nothing, though. Half the attorneys and judges in the city worked for Fontayne at one time or the other. The best ones didn't last. Fontayne had trouble keeping good help."

"Did Teddy . . . did he ever mention a gambler from the old days, Joe Steps?"

Wild Bill slowly shook his head, then stopped. "Joe Steps? Oh, yeah, the dancer, the one who clipped that bookie about a million years ago . . . Buddy Renee, that was the book's name. Yeah, Joe Steps clipped Buddy and his bodyguard. He was supposed to have owed a bundle from what I remember, but you're going way back now." He rested his hands on the bar. "I never heard Teddy talk about him, though."

"It was a long shot."

"I didn't know Joe Steps myself," said Wild Bill. "We moved in different circles. He and Jack, though, they had something in common," he chuckled. "When Joe Steps clipped the bookie, Jack lost his steak 'n' lobster money."

Quinn shivered, feeling the bar's air-conditioning for the first time. "Liggett was on the book's payroll?"

"Strictly part-time. Most books had a regular body-guard, but when there was a heavy payday—Kentucky Derby or the Superbowl—they'd hire a cop to stand next to them when they settled up. We called it 'showing the badge.' " Wild Bill shrugged. "It was a different world then."

Quinn played with his empty coffee cup, turning it round and round. "Bill," he said carefully, "you knew Jack Liggett as well as anyone I've talked to. Do you think he was the kind of guy who could have taken down the bookie himself? Like you said, it was a big payday?"

Wild Bill glared at Quinn, his one eye hot as a matchhead.

"I don't mean to speak badly of the dead," said Quinn.

"Then you should shut up," growled Wild Bill.

"I can't. Jack Liggett wasn't killed by a carjacker and Teddy wasn't killed by neo-Nazis. I'm getting closer to the truth every day, Bill, I'm halfway home now. If you really were Teddy's friend, you'll help me."

The bell over the front door rang as three uniformed cops walked in.

"We're closed!" said Wild Bill.

The three cops stopped in the doorway. "You okay, Bill?" one said, glancing at Quinn, his hand on his revolver.

Wild Bill laughed at the idea. "Thanks boys, but we're closed."

"Peace in the valley," said one of the cops as they backed out the door.

Wild Bill stood there watching Quinn.

Quinn waited for him to say something.

"Jack should have never been a cop—he had good taste, expensive tastes," Wild Bill said at last. "One of our instructors at the Academy used to say it's alright to pick up a few bucks you find lying in the street, just don't grab so much that you split your pockets." He shook his head. "I always wondered how Jack pulled off that early retirement. He told me he made some smart investments, and I gave him the benefit of the doubt."

"You think Jack could have murdered the bookie?"

"Like this." Wild Bill snapped his fingers. His hands were wet from the bartop—Quinn felt the moisture hit his face. "Jack would do it in a second. If he thought he could get away with it. It's not that easy, you know."

"Not that hard, either. Not if you plan it out."

"No," said Wild Bill, "not if you know what you're doing."

CHAPTER

34

Quinn was at LAX, panting up flights of stairs as planes screamed overhead, trying to keep up with Katie and Rachel as they hurried toward Gate 32. The airport was bright, full of soft music and happy people leaving on vacations. He could hear a phone ringing in the distance.

Katie and Rachel walked ahead of him in summer shorts and light jackets, chattering away in French. Katie was wearing the Mickey Mouse ears he had bought her two summers ago and which she hadn't worn since, because they made her look like a "little kid." For some reason it was hard for him to keep up. The floor was like taffy, holding him back. That phone was still ringing. Why didn't someone answer it?

Rachel and Katie reached their gate, joined the crowd of tourists on their way to Europe. They were cleared through with a wave, but Quinn couldn't move, couldn't speak, could only watch as Rachel and Katie strolled away from him. Katie was swinging her Simpsons purse, which he had bought her years ago and which she never liked. Rachel hesitated at the door of the plane, but Katie skipped inside. She never looked back.

Quinn blinked awake, soaked with sweat, grabbing for the phone next to his bed. He knocked it off the cradle, fumbled the phone to his ear.

"Yeah?" Quinn croaked, still seeing Katie and her mouse ears disappear into the airplane. Bon voyage. "Yes?"

"Dear boy," cooed Napitano, "so good to speak with you. This is Antonin Napitano. Your employer. Perhaps you remember me?"

"I remember, Nino." Quinn sat up in bed, cleared his throat. His hair was damp, plastered to his face. He felt like someone had beaten him up while he slept.

"Perhaps you would honor us with your presence sometime in the near future?" said Napitano. "I am thinking of renting out your desk just to get some use out of it."

Quinn hung up. There was a carton of orange juice beside the bed. He shook it up, took a long drink. It was still cool. He must not have been asleep very long. Sunshine warmed the pulled shades. Late afternoon—hottest time of the day, the worst time to sleep. Guaranteed nightmares. The phone rang. Tough.

He had come back from the Blue Flu a few hours ago, called Joe Steps but there was no answer. He had scribbled a few notes, then closed his eyes. Just for a moment. He hated falling asleep with his clothes on. He hated waking up to the sound of Napitano's voice even more. The phone rang. He cooled his cheeks with the carton of orange juice, one side, then the other. Then he answered the phone.

"We seem to have been disconnected, dear boy."

"I'm tired, Nino."

"Fatigue is for weaklings," chided Napitano. "I myself require only three hours of sleep a night."

"Congratulations."

"Did anything come of your little . . . deception in the desert?" asked Napitano, "this dead convict you seemed so interested in?"

"I'm still working on it. I've got to go now."

"Miss Takamura informed me of your contact with Ellis Fontayne on Monday. This grand educational project of his will make a good story. Myself, I cannot imagine giving away my wealth to a swarm of dangerous urchins. Americans," he sneered, "you create a great country, as all great countries are created, by taking it from those who came before you. Then your descendants, racked with guilt over their largess and privilege, proceed to squander their inheritance—either through waste and profligacy, or through charity. I find charity more reprehensible than waste. Charity is an evolutionary fraud, a violation of natural law. The big fish does not share with the little fish. The big fish eats the little fish."

Quinn yawned. "I treasure our philosophical discussions, Nino, but I'm going to go back to sleep."

Rachel wasn't at the university. He tried her sister's

house in Pacific Palisades where she and Katie were staying. No answer there either. They were probably at a movie. Or shopping for their trip. The blood pounded in his temples as he followed the cracks in the ceiling. The phone rang again. He almost jumped out of bed.

"Hola, guapo," Tina Chavez said cheerfully. Quinn heard horns beeping. "Que pasa?"

"Where are you?"

"I'm on the 405. Got done with my casework early and thought I'd head up to L.A. You want to come? I can swing by."

"I'm beat, Tina. Were you able to find anything on Fontayne and Teddy? If there was any gossip—"

"Not much," said Tina. "You knew that Judge Teddy had worked for Fontayne many years ago, yes? The two of them seemed to have a cordial relationship . . . professionally. There was no bad blood that I could find. Are you still there?"

"Yes."

"I didn't have time to check on the status of the inmate you asked me about, this Jamie—"

"I already did that," said Quinn. He had called Tina yesterday and asked her to see if Jamie Ledbetter had been executed or was still in prison. He had told her that he thought there might be a connection to Teddy's murder, but he hadn't been specific. Quinn heard the squeal of brakes from the phone and Tina cursing in Spanish.

"What did—"

"Ledbetter was killed by another inmate," Quinn said, raising his voice to be heard over the Freeway hum. "Stabbed to death twenty-eight years ago in the dining hall. There was an argument over chocolate pudding. One of them evidently wanted seconds."

"It must have been very good pudding," said Tina.

"Ledbetter's trial attorney died a few years ago," said Quinn. "Heart attack. I got an address on Ledbetter's mother and made an appointment to see her tomorrow morning. I don't expect much. I think Jamie Ledbetter was just a guy who ended up falling in love with the wrong woman."

"Another sad caballero," sighed Tina. "Love is dangerous to man and woman alike, but what else is there?"

Quinn reached for the carton of orange juice on the floor and knocked it over, soaking the rug and the legal pad of notes he had made. There goes the damage deposit.

There was the sound of acceleration. "I still think your friend Mr. Joe Steps has been a naughty boy," shouted Tina. "In my experience, prison does not make one kinder or gentler."

"He was framed, Tina."

"Prison is even harder on an innocent man." The phone crackled. "Why don't we have lunch tomorrow?" Tina breezed. "I may have some new information—" Her voice was cut off by a blast of static.

He held the phone against his ear for a long time, listening to the sound of chaos before giving up. Southern California was full of flat spots and static. Another reason to hate cellular phones. You learned to talk fast and fill in the blanks. Sometimes you still missed out on the most important parts of the conversation and there was no way to retrieve them.

He shook orange juice off his notes, stared at the diagrams and scenarios he had written out before falling asleep. Trying to make sense of Teddy's murder was like reconstructing a garbled cellular conversation—Quinn had individual words and phrases, but nothing to connect them into a semblance of meaning.

The phone rang.

"You sound sleepy . . . I guess you been staying up late, guarding the old homestead, huh?"

Quinn sat up. He had never heard the voice before, but he knew immediately who it was.

"You should slice up some cucumbers for those bags under your eyes." Giggles. Nasty giggles. Prettyboy was a real cutup. "Seriously, though . . ." More giggles. What was he on?

"How did you get this number?" demanded Quinn.

"You think you're the only one with a brain," said Prettyboy. "I just told the receptionist at *SLAP* that I had to get in touch with you, it was an emergency." His voice was suddenly desperate. "Please m'am, his wife and little girl have been in a terrible accident . . ."

"That's pretty good," Quinn said tightly, "maybe you and I could get together, talk about it."

"Your little girl is a real bitch-in-training," said Prettyboy. "Somebody should teach her some manners."

"We could talk about that, too," Quinn said amiably. "Anyplace you want, just the two of us."

"Two's company, right? Three ... that's something else," said Prettyboy.

Quinn listened to the dial tone. It sounded like an alarm clock going off.

Her portable phone beeped just as Tina Chavez opened the door to her car. She cursed under her breath but never considered not answering it. The District Attorney's office didn't care that it was her day off—if some lowlife in the county lockup read his horoscope in the morning paper and suddenly decided to turn state's evidence, Tina was expected to drop whatever she was doing and race over to depose him. She was supposed to ignore his mossy teeth and stinking coveralls to say "thank you for your coopera-tion" while the lowlife ratted out his friends and family. She kept mouthwash in the dash, a change of clothes in the trunk of her car, and her phone in her purse.

"Mi guapo," she squealed happily, hearing Quinn's "Hello." Dios mio, he had a voice that wrapped around her like a pair of strong arms. She glanced at her watch. "We are still on for lunch, yes? Where are you?"

"Getting ready to visit with Jamie Ledbetter's mother. She's in a retirement home in Costa Mesa—Redeemer's Arms."

"That's not very far from where I am now." Tina primped in the rearview, wanting to look good for him. Damn. There was a small sty in the corner of her right eye—too much staring at fine print. "There's a Vietnamese cafe near here," she said, reaching for her eyedrops, "just a hole in the wall, but the food is good and they have tables and umbrellas outside . . . do you know it? No? Well, meet me here and I'll drive." She gave him the address of the apartment complex, told him she would meet him in the parking lot.

"Who are you seeing?"

She blinked back the eyedrops, blotted her mascara with a tissue. "Don't be jealous. This is business. Our business, guapo, Judge Teddy's murder. Why don't you tell me what you found out." She didn't bother to reach for the notebook she kept on the dash. She knew him better than that. Quinn wasn't going to tell her anything, not over the phone. He liked to control what he had discovered, keep it to himself, release it in bits and pieces, just enough to string her along. She was the same way. Knowledge was power. You share it, you weaken it. Knowledge was for trading, not for sharing.

"We'll talk over lunch," said Quinn. "I'll see you as soon as I'm done here. Maybe if we pool our information, we can decide what to do next."

She smiled at her reflection in the rearview. "It will be such pleasure working together, you and I."

"Be careful," said Quinn. "Teddy's not the only one who's been killed. There's a regular list somewhere, and somebody is scratching the names off one at a time."

"Such a dramatic turn of phrase . . ." Tina felt her skin grow warm as though in the sunlight. "You should write my summation speeches."

"I'm serious, Tina, be careful."

"Adios." She broke the connection, tucked the flip phone into her purse, right next to the pearl-handled .38 snubby. A ladies' gun, according to the fat fool who headed the D.A.'s personal security detail. A ladies' gun packed with hollow-point hotloads. Tina didn't like her purse weighed down with some awkward magnum, but she appreciated stopping power as much as anyone.

She locked her car, looked for the stairs. Hugo Ganz lived in apartment #311, according to Yellowtone Cab. She had run a check of Joseph Staducci's bank accounts. There was nothing exceptional: a longtime savings account which had grown substantially over the last thirty years, and a checking account with very few transactions, many of them written to the Yellowtone Cab. He had a regular account with them, paid by the week. The dispatcher at the cab company said Hugo Ganz was Joe's regular driver, by request.

Tina started up the steps, trying not to let her eagerness carry her away. She didn't want to trip. Terrible to bloody her nose before she met Quinn. She smiled, imagining the look on his face. Why was she always attracted to men who were out of reach? Her first love had been a young priest at her church, Father Jalisco. An unrequited love to be sure, but what a handsome man. Those hands as he placed the host on her outstretched tongue . . . She still thought of him sometimes when she . . . she grabbed for the railing, stumbling, caught herself. Careful, Tina.

The dispatcher said Hugo Ganz was a hard worker, always on time, never took a sick day. No tickets and he always left his cab clean. Perhaps Hugo had noticed something about Joe, seen someone at his house when he dropped him off or picked him up. Joe Steps paid a flat rate so there was no log kept of his cab rides. Flat rate was expensive, but with his arthritis, he evidently needed to have a cab on call. Maybe Hugo could recall some of their regular stops.

Tina had interviewed many people in the course of her job. The ones who thought themselves important were usually the least informative, the least helpful. Doctors and lawyers were the worst, they noticed only their own state of mind, never what was going on around them. Little people—gardeners, supermarket checkers, cabbies— these were the ones who would dredge their memories to be of service, to please, to be important for a brief moment. Her father had been a waiter . . . he could tell you the kind of watch every one of his regular customers wore. Papa . . . she wiped her eyes. He had lived just long enough to see her get her law degree. God is good.

She knocked on #311. No answer. She knocked again. Listened at the door. The cab company said he wasn't scheduled to work today. She hadn't called Mr. Ganz beforehand. It was better to surprise, let them stare at her official ID with the state seal. Let them ask what they could do to help. She knocked again, already making plans to come back later. After lunch.

"He's not home."

She turned. A boy on the other side of the stairwell waved to her. Que bonito. He leaned against the railing, a slender, bare-chested boy wearing tiger-striped boxer shorts. She could feel a growl starting in her belly.

"Hugo's not home." What a beautiful smile he had. An angel, no, not with those wicked eyes and rings in his ears, flimsy boxer shorts rippling in the breeze. A devil.

Tina walked toward him. She did love her bad boys. "Do you know Mr. Ganz?"

The boy shrugged. He ran his eyes over her, taking his time.

"My name is Tina Chavez," she said, enjoying his interest. "I'm a Deputy District Attorney for Orange County."

The boy smiled. "Wowie-zowie." He turned and leaned his hands against the wall, looked back at her. "You want to frisk me, boss?" he said coquettishly.

She looked him over. Such a nice ass. "Maybe later," she said. "If you're nice."

"I'm better than nice, boss," he smiled. He faced her again, ran his hands through his hair, showing off his thin chest. Not a hair on it.

"Do you have any idea when Mr. Ganz will be back?"

"Mr. Ganz? I saw him leave about an hour ago," said

the boy. "You can come into my place and wait for him. He usually stays close to home on the weekends." His fingers played at the waistband of his boxer shorts. "He doesn't have what you'd call an active social life."

"That's too bad," said Tina, watching his fingers.

"Different strokes," said the boy. He lounged against the doorway of his apartment. "Why don't you come on in? I won't bite."

"That's disappointing," said Tina.

The boy giggled. The sunlight flashed off the gold hoops in his ears. There must have been five or six in each ear. He looked like a young god, smooth and supple and utterly knowing. Keeper of the secrets of good and evil. "My name is Rick. Come on, we can leave the door open." He smiled. "You'll be able to see Hugo as soon as he comes back."

Tina smiled and went to join him.

CHAPTER

36

"Miz Ledbetter doesn't get many visitors," said Patricia, the wan nurse's aide who led Quinn down the hallway of the Redeemer's Arms Retirement Home. "She's a real sweet lady—gives me a Bible verse everytime I run an errand for her. Not that I couldn't use cash money even more."

The hallway smelled of soap and lilac water. It had taken several days to track down the current address of Mrs. Bertha Ledbetter. According to his contact at the Social Security office she had been a resident at Redeemer's Arms for two years.

Redeemer's Arms was clean and well staffed. Pictures of Jesus holding small children and leading flocks of sheep hung from the freshly painted walls. Quinn wasn't much for religion but he liked these kindly-Jesus images. It was the crown-of-thorns-Jesus, the bleeding-Jesus that he had

problems with. He had been in too many churches that
looked like crime scenes.

Patricia knocked on room #117. "Miz Ledbetter?"

Quinn heard footsteps, then the door swung open. A
small black woman peered up at him with bright, inquisi-
tive eyes. She wore a neat pale-yellow dress. Her white
hair was cropped close to her head. In her hand she held a
book. He expected it to be a well-thumbed Bible but it was
the latest Elmore Leonard novel. Hardback too.

"Good morning, Mrs. Ledbetter, my name is Quinn.
We spoke yesterday."

"I have a very good memory, young man," said Mrs.
Ledbetter, her mouth tightening at the corners. "I taught
geography for thirty-eight years. I can still recite the
names of all the state capitals and the original members of
the United Nations. This was before all this nonsense of
trying to teach self-esteem and cooperation."

"I flunked those courses, too." Quinn smiled at her.

Mrs. Ledbetter snorted. "Thank you, Patricia," she
said, opening the door wide for Quinn. "You'll have to ask
your questions quickly," she said to him, indicating one of
the matching upholstered chairs in the small room. She sat
in the other. "My baseball game starts shortly on the big-
screen TV in the rec room, and there are several individuals here—I won't name names, but they know who
they are—who think nothing about taking someone's
regular spot."

"Yes, m'am." Mrs. Ledbetter had the schoolmarm
power—she made him feel like he should be practicing

his penmanship in study hall. The bed was covered with an intricate quilt, the pattern of praying hands endlessly repeated. The walls were covered with framed family photographs. He noticed several of a young Jamie Ledbetter, a thin, happy boy usually featured playing a musical instrument—sitting at a piano, holding a guitar, blowing a trumpet, cheeks puffed out.

"My Jamie had a gift," said Mrs. Ledbetter, her expression darkening. She folded her hands in her lap. "He could wring music out of a stone. Mr. Ledbetter and I raised four children and I loved every one of them, every blessed one, but a mother always has her favorite." She smiled to herself. "That was Jamie," she said softly.

"I'm sorry, Mrs. Ledbetter," said Quinn. "I know your son was innocent—"

"I don't need you to tell me what I already know," she said. "That was a long time ago, but there isn't a day that I don't think of what might have been if he'd never taken up with that girl, that white trash girl." She glanced at the dark-skinned Jesus on the opposite wall. "I'm a good Baptist. I believe that the Lord judges the guilty in His own time and His own way. I know that He taught us to turn the other cheek, to love those who curse us." Her whole body shook with anger—she clasped her hands in her lap, hanging on as though caught in a storm.

"Mrs. Ledbetter? One of the police officers who arrested your son was named Jack Liggett. Did Jamie ever have dealings with this man before that? I wondered if maybe Jamie did something to make this officer mad at him?"

"My Jamie was a good boy. Police always looking for a reason to blame the black man." Her mouth twisted. "I was taught to forgive my enemies, to forgive those that smite me, even on to seven times seven, but the Lord must understand," she said, eyes blazing, "that there are some things a mother simply can not do."

"Did Jamie know a man named Joe Staducci?" Quinn said, aware that she was no longer listening. "Joe Staducci . . . Joe Steps. He was a dancer. They might have known each other professionally."

"They killed my baby," said Mrs. Ledbetter. "How do I forgive that? I've prayed and I've prayed and I've prayed, but I can't get past it. They killed my baby."

Quinn stood up. "I couldn't forgive that, either, Mrs. Ledbetter," he said gently. "I apologize for disturbing—" He picked up a small photograph from the bookcase and stared at the man in the photo, a serious man in a fine gray suit standing next to a gleaming automobile. The photo must have been taken twenty or thirty years ago.

"Mrs. Ledbetter?" Quinn held up the photograph. His hand shook. "Is this Ellis Fontayne?"

She nodded. "Best white man I ever met."

"How . . . how did you know him?"

She looked up at him. "Mr. Ledbetter and I took a second mortgage on our house to get Jamie a good attorney, and it didn't do any good at all. Mr. Ledbetter worked a second job for the next five years, he put himself in an early grave paying off that good attorney."

"Fontayne wasn't your attorney," said Quinn. "I've read the court documents."

Mrs. Ledbetter got up and took the photograph from Quinn. "Mr. Fontayne handled Jamie's appeal," she said, looking at Fontayne's photo with a sweetness that transformed her face. "He volunteered to do it, and never charged us a blessed cent. Paid for everything out of his own pocket. He said Jamie should never even been brought to trial, said the police violated the Constitution." She sighed. "I could have told him that." She wiped dust off the frame of the photograph with her fingertips, then carefully replaced it on the bookcase. "It took over two years for Jamie's case to work its way through the courts, one appeal after the other. We were close, too. Then I got the telegram from the prison and it was all for nothing. Mr. Fontayne sat beside me at Jamie's funeral, holding my hand. He cried like he was a member of the family."

Quinn couldn't move.

"You go on now," said Mrs. Ledbetter. "My ballgame is about to begin." She wagged a finger at him. "Just make sure you don't say anything bad about my baby or Mr. Fontayne in your magazine," she commanded. "You do, you'll roast in Hell, that's certain."

Quinn walked out the door and down the hallway lined with compassionate Jesuses, hurrying now, almost running.

CHAPTER

37

"I hope Hugo's not in some kind of trouble," said Rick, ushering Tina into his apartment, his hand warm and airy as a spotlight on the small of her back. "He seems like a good guy. Quiet, maybe, not what you'd call a party person." He flashed another one of his knowing smiles.

"I just want to ask him some questions," said Tina, checking out the small living room, idly pacing off the blue-green op-art carpet. Nice furnishings. Much nicer than the building. Dark green leather sofa, soft as chamois. She swayed slightly to the slow, electronic music. She had danced to this same CD at the Buzz Klub last weekend— hearing it made her think of fucking in elevators.

There were too many mirrors in the room. Other Tinas stared back at her from all over the room: wary Tinas, curious Tinas, now an excited Tina with a flush in her neck, spotting the boy behind her, dancing along with her.

The air was edged with electricity—she could feel it crackling down her spine. She wished she hadn't told Quinn to come by so soon. She wanted to take her time here.

"What do you do for a living?" she said, as Rick started fixing them drinks. She hadn't asked for a drink. She liked the idea of him taking the lead, anticipating her wants. "Are you a model?"

"I thought about modeling once," Rick beamed, "but it's all about who you know, who you blow. Besides," he shrugged, "I got another career now." He handed her a campari and soda, the tall glass filled with cracked ice. It looked like strawberry soda. Elegantly bitter. They clicked glasses.

Tina felt like she was a girl again, having a cocktail party with her girlfriends, pretending to be debutantes. She took another long drink, shivering with pleasure. Rick refilled their glasses and she didn't even think to stop him. Vodka was her drink of choice during the week, but today was Saturday, and she was on her own time. No need to worry about her breath smelling of alcohol.

Rick had made no effort to put on a shirt, or pants for that matter, content to pad around barefoot in the flagrant tiger-striped boxers. A framed movie poster from *Saturday Night Fever* hovered beside a beauty salon swivel-chair in the kitchen. She walked over and stood before the poster. John Travolta stared blankly back at her, poised in his white suit on the dance floor, one hand pointing skyward.

He must have seen her expression. "Hey," Rick said

defensively, moving beside her, "disco is back. I paid a lot for that poster. It's signed by the BeeGees."

"I won't hold it against you," laughed Tina.

"Sit down," said Rick, indicating the swivel chair. "I can show you some styling tips that will make you even more beautiful." He patted his cheeks. "Look at my skin. Perfect, right? That's my business. I'm like a beauty coach. So let me help you. The door is open, you can see Hugo if he comes home. Why not get a makeover while you wait?"

Tina took another drink. The front door was wide open. "I haven't got much time."

Rick patted the seat of the chair. "Then we better hurry," he grinned. She sat, stared at herself in the mirror. She laid her handbag on the counter. He smiled. "You're not going to recognize yourself when I get through with you."

Tina glanced at her watch.

"Hugo should be back anytime," said Rick, leaning close, the two of them cheek to cheek in the mirror. He smelled *good*. She was going to have to ask him what cologne he was wearing—maybe she'd get some for Quinn. "With your skin color, you should be wearing a slightly pinker shade of lipstick." His fingers lightly outlined her lips and she was overwhelmed with an erotic rush. "Just a couple of shades toward the pink palette." He patted blush onto her cheekbones, smoothing it out until it was barely visible. He moved around her in his tiger stripes, his tiny boy nipples brushing against her as he worked. "What do you think?" Rick said, stepping back.

She stared at herself in the mirror. She looked . . . younger, prettier. Her eyes were bigger, brighter. "I . . . like it."

"This is nothing," said Rick. "I don't know who cuts your hair, but he doesn't know what he was doing." He shook his head, dismissive. "You deserve a cut that emphasizes your strong jaw and elegant forehead." He slipped on a leather shoulder holster and she had to stifle a giggle, pretending to cough. There were three scissors stuck in the holster. He slid one out. "Relax. I know what I'm doing." He pulled her hair from the nape of her neck, his touch light and knowing, utterly confident. "I'm going to open my own salon soon. I want you to come in for a full treatment."

She nodded, feeling him beside her as he surveyed her face.

He examined a few strands of hair, snipped off the ends. "You're going to have to change your shampoo," he sniffed. "I've got some samples I can give you."

She settled back into the chair, closed her eyes, enjoying the attention. "Let me know if you see Hugo come in."

"What do you want to talk to Hugo about anyway?" asked Rick, click-click-clicking. She could feel her hair drifting down like mist. "It must be something important to get you out here on a Saturday."

"I don't know if it's important," said Tina. "That's why I need to talk with Hugo."

"If he was up to no good, I'd be the first to know," said Rick, sculpting her hair with his fingers, measuring the length. "I notice everything." His fingertips gently kneaded the notch at the base of her skull where the tension built up. "It's a gift."

She groaned as he dug in, the sensation somewhere between pain and pleasure. She let her head loll against his taut stomach, humming along to the music, barely hearing him. The campari and soda had hit her harder than she expected. That's what she got for drinking on an empty stomach.

"You like my new couch?" Rick lifted her hair, precisely snipping away a millimeter at a time. "I like making love on leather," he said matter-of-factly.

Tina opened her eyes. "I prefer satin sheets myself."

"See that rough spot on the arm?" Rick pointed to the couch. "Teeth marks." He winked at her. "Now, I'm not saying it was my teeth made the marks, or somebody else's . . ." He cocked his head. "You can test for things like that, right? You got crime labs can tell who took the bite, don't you? I seen that on 'NYPD Blue.' " He chewed his lip. "Maybe it was 'Star Trek'? I forget." He shrugged. "You have nice tight pores. What are you using?"

"Ah . . . glycerine soap."

Rick winced. "I pity your pH balance." He tossed his head, sent his hoop earrings wriggling. "It's lucky for you we ran into each other."

"What makes you think luck had anything to do with it?" Tina said coyly. "I've had my eye on you for a long time." She thought she was being flirtatious, but Rick must have misunderstood.

"W-what do you mean?" he stammered.

"Nothing," said Tina, forcing the smile. "Just kidding." She recognized that vocal cue, the faint, uncertain quaver that signaled guilt. Maybe Rick had a few overdue parking tickets. Or a few grams of coke in his top drawer.

Rick's face was stretched too tight, his eyes narrowed to sharp points. "People think I'm stupid. That's a mistake."

"I don't think you're stupid," Tina said carefully, slowly sitting up in the chair.

"Now you're being patronizing," accused Rick. "I bet you didn't even think I knew what that word meant, did you?"

"I bet you're full of surprises," Tina said seductively. Her hand edged toward her purse with the revolver tucked inside. She was stone sober now.

"Don't move," ordered Rick. "I almost nicked you." He waved the scissors in front of her face. An inch from her nose. Click-click-click. She thought of lobsters scuttling across the bottom of a cold dark sea.

The phone in her purse beeped.

"They'll call back," Rick said. Click-click-click.

"That's my office," Tina said. "I have to answer it. They'll think something is wrong if I don't."

"Nothing's wrong." Rick snapped at her hair with the shears, his movements angry and jerky now. "Who said anything is wrong? You trying to entrap me?"

"Somebody is meeting me here," said Tina. Swallowing was painful, her throat was so tight from tension. Her hand could almost touch her purse now. "He should be here any minute." She struggled to maintain eye contact in the mirror with him. "I'll come back later and let you finish."

"Stay where you are," said Rick.

"Look, junior," Tina said gruffly. He didn't back off. She grabbed her purse. "I have official business to take care of. Move your ass aside before—"

"Before what?" Rick loomed over her in the mirror, one hand on her shoulder, the other holding the scissors. "Who you gonna call? GHOSTBUSTERS?" he giggled, voice cracking.

She fumbled at the latch to her purse, but he slapped it out of her hand and onto the floor.

"I'm like totally disappointed in you, Tina. No shit."

"Tina!" It was Quinn calling from far below. Too far.

She cried out, but Rick grabbed her hair, pulled her head backwards, exposing her throat. "We got company coming?" Rick asked sweetly, poking her with the tip of the scissors, not quite breaking the skin. "Goody."

"I told you," she gasped, feeling the point bounce against her throat, "I've got a friend downstairs, a cop. You better take off while you can."

"I'm fucking terrified," Rick whispered in her ear.

"Tina!" Quinn sounded closer now. "Tina! It's Quinn!"

"It's Quinn," Rick repeated. He slid his tongue in her ear, the scissors pressing harder against her throat. She could feel a trickle of blood run down her neck. "He's no cop. You think I'm stupid?"

She looked toward the open doorway, letting her right arm drop to her side.

"Not a sound," hissed Rick, maintaining his grip on her hair. He stretched his bare foot toward her open purse.

"Tina!" Quinn was on the second floor.

She reached behind her, grabbed Rick's testicles through his silk boxers and twisted. Hard. He shrieked. "Quinn!" she shouted as the scissors plunged into her chest. She squeezed harder. He stabbed her again and again. She remembered thinking it was funny that he was the one screaming with pain instead of her.

Rick fell to the floor, cursing, holding himself, moaning, but Tina stayed in the chair, not saying a word. She felt cold. There was a funny bubbly sound when she breathed.

Rick held onto the chair, unsteady, yelling at her, looking like some crazy buccaneer with his earrings and shoulder holster, waving the bloody scissors. He crawled behind the sofa on his hands and knees, trying to throw up.

She saw herself in the mirror. She didn't remember her dress being red. It was a light blue dress, she was sure of it. She felt warmer now, but her face was so pale . . . she was going to have to get some sun. People in the barrio were going to think she was Anglo.

"Tina?" Quinn stood in the doorway, then rushed toward her. She called his name but no sound came out as he eased her onto the floor, pressing his hands over her chest, trying to stop the bleeding. Might as well try to staunch the sea. Pobrecito, he looked scared for her. It was easier to breathe now, with his hands on her. The air tasted sweet.

She saw Rick come from behind the sofa, his eyes wild. She tried to warn Quinn, but he shushed her, told her not to worry. Quinn's mouth flew open as the scissors drove into his back, Rick squalking happily as he slashed away, blood flying everywhere.

Quinn stood up, punched Rick in the face. What a beautiful sound. He hit him again, buckled his knees, then grabbed him by that stupid shoulder holster and threw him across the room. Rick crashed into the wall, slid down, groaning.

It was darker in the room now, harder to breathe, as though her mouth was covered with a wet warm blanket. So nice to sleep . . . Quinn staggered back to her, sealed the hole in her chest with his hands, and it got easier to breathe. She could touch her purse on the floor beside her. It was open, but she didn't have the strength to pull it toward her.

Quinn held one hand on her chest, pulled the phone off the counter with the other. He must have dialed 911. The average response time in this part of the county was over eight minutes. Forever. Quinn was over her, his face filling her field of vision. "Don't die, Tina," he said. She wanted to laugh, but he was so serious. "It's going to be okay," said Quinn. "They'll be right here." His shirt was bloody. Bad boys like Rick shouldn't be allowed to play with sharp things.

It was so dark. Quinn was shouting at her. She'd talk to him later. After she got some sleep. "Tina!" Okay, okay, I'm coming. Her eyes fluttered open. He looked like he was going to cry. What was he so upset about? She was the one . . . she was the one who was dying.

"Tina!" Her mouth wasn't working. "Tina!" I'm right here. You don't have to shout. She imagined what it would have been like to make love with Quinn, the two of them in some big bed, a four-poster, with a frilly lace canopy and a pitcher of margueritas. She liked a big man who wasn't rough. That was Quinn. A big man with tender eyes. She had never even seen him naked. One more reason to stay alive. A girl could hope. There was always hope . . .

She blinked, tried to speak. Rick had gotten to his feet and was lurching toward them. She clutched at her purse, the gun bouncing out. Quinn turned as Rick stabbed down with the scissors, tried to fend him off. She saw the scissors go clear through his outstretched left hand, the point protruding right below his ring finger.

Rick pulled the scissors out, flailing at him, but Quinn didn't leave her. He kept his right hand on her, maintaining pressure as he tried to dodge Rick's attack.

She tried to pick up the gun, but it was so slippery, the pearl handle coated with red . . . Quinn took the gun from her. It quivered in his shredded left hand. He was right-handed but he needed his good hand to plug up the leaks in her chest. Don't worry about me, guapo, just kill him. Kill him. Rick laughed, the scissors raised high. There was a gunshot and breaking glass. Missed. Rick scrambled for the door. He was laughing again. Quinn tried to hold the gun steady, but his hand wasn't closing right. Rick swayed in the doorway in those tiger-striped boxer shorts.

She wanted to tell Quinn to hold the gun with his good hand, to let her go, she could breathe some other time, but he kept the pressure on. She heard the gun fire, and Rick howled, stumbled against the outside railing. The gun dropped from Quinn's torn hand. What was that sound? Like metal groaning. Rick screamed, arms cartwheeling as the railing gave way and he fell backwards, out of sight. Then the screaming stopped.

She had noticed a small heart-shaped swimming pool at the base of the stairs when she first came into the building. She imagined Rick sprawled on the concrete, his broken head in the pool, turning the water pink. An ugly valentine.

Quinn was over her, pinching off her nostrils, breathing into her. One, two, three, four . . . she lost count. Her eyes drooped. It was too much effort to keep them open. His lips covered her mouth again. He was a good kisser. She liked the idea of the two of them sharing breath. Heart to heart. Who knew where it could lead?

CHAPTER

38

"You're a lucky man," said the E.R. doctor, stitching up Quinn's back. "An inch over and you'd have a punctured lung."

Quinn didn't feel lucky. He felt tired and sluggish. "How's Tina?" He could feel the needle bite into his flesh as the doctor finished off the stitches, but it seemed far away, like it was happening to someone else. "Tina . . . the woman who was brought in with me. Is she okay?"

"Wrap him up, nurse." The doctor peeled off his surgical gloves with a pop, tossed them into the trash. He left through the sheer curtains that hung next to the bed without even looking at Quinn.

"He's a good doctor," said the nurse, laying bandages across Quinn's back, "but he's got the bedside manner of a coroner."

Quinn stared at his left hand, which had swollen

to twice its size and was crisscrossed with stitches. The anesthetic must be wearing off the way it throbbed. "Do you know how the woman . . . how Tina is doing?"

"Sorry," said the nurse, deftly taping his back and shoulder. "Don't worry, we have a fine chest trauma team. If anyone can save her, they will."

Quinn clamped his mouth shut, listening to her rip off sections of adhesive tape. He tried to concentrate on what he had learned this morning, but his mind was fuzzy. Fontayne had been handling Jamie Ledbetter's appeal. Why would Fontayne sell out his client? He must have known that Neil Stimmler had killed Sweetie. Wasn't that what Stimmler told Joe? It hurt to think.

A sullen detective in his mid-forties pushed through the curtain, his notebook already open. He smelled of sweat and cigarettes. "Hey pal," he said to Quinn, sitting on the end of the bed with a groan. "Hemorrhoids," he winked humorlessly at the nurse. "Maybe you could put some cream on them for me."

"Just cut down on the jelly donuts, Kojack, you'll be fine," she said, starting in on Quinn's hand. He winced but she didn't seem to notice.

"Everybody's a comedian," said the detective. He had dull eyes and a long, expressionless face, a gray man in a gray suit and black Reeboks.

"How's Tina?" repeated Quinn. His voice sounded even weaker than he felt.

"Still in a coma," the detective said, disinterested, riffling through his notebook. "She's got so many tubes coming out of her she looks like a Freeway interchange."

"What's her condition?" persisted Quinn. "Is she in ICU?"

"I ask the questions," grumbled the detective. "What were you two doing at that apartment, anyway? You and Tina stop off for a little nooner?"

"What?"

The detective jerked back like he could read Quinn's mind. "Hey pal, I just need to know if it was business or pleasure for Tina."

Quinn stared at him. "I already gave my statement to the uniform."

"So now you can give it to me," said the detective. "I guess Tina likes you hard types, huh? That what she goes for? Little walk on the wild side?"

"Did Tina turn you down once?" asked Quinn. "Is that it? You should be used to women slamming the door on your dick."

The nurse laughed. "All done," she said to Quinn, still smiling.

Quinn turned his hand over, admiring the nurse's work. "Thanks," he said to her. His bandaged hand was the size of an oven mitt. "Is Prettyboy dead?" he asked the detective. "I didn't see him on the pavement when they carried me down the steps, and the uniform I talked to didn't know, either."

"Prettyboy?"

"The kid who stabbed Tina." Quinn leaned forward, pain lancing through his shoulder. He could still hear

Prettyboy laughing as he plunged the scissors down. "He stabbed me too. He fell over the railing—"

"We didn't find anybody," said the detective, "but that railing was an accident waiting to happen. "The support bolts were rusted clear through. Somebody's going to have one hell of a lawsuit."

"You must have found him," Quinn insisted. "He was wearing these tiger-striped undies . . ."

The detective shook his head. "We did find a pair of scissors in the swimming pool . . . Tiger-striped undies, huh? You three must have been having a grand old time."

Quinn felt dizzy.

"The uniforms are still doing interviews, but the residents aren't very cooperative. Nobody was home. Nobody was awake. Nobody heard nothing." He referred to his notebook. "That apartment was rented to a Rick Eichorn. Is that the kid in tiger-stripes?"

"I don't know his name." Quinn glanced at the curtains, half-expecting Prettyboy to come rushing through like Anthony Perkins.

"You going to tell me why this kid tried to make hamburger out of you and Tina?" The detective crossed his legs, lounging on the bed like he owned it. Quinn could see a hole in one knee of the man's suitpants. "We found dope in the apartment . . . was he fucked up? What about you? What about Tina?" he leered. "We're going to run blood tests, you might as well make it easy."

"Like I told the uniform, I went there to meet Tina," Quinn said, exhausted. "We were going to have lunch. I found her on the floor, bleeding, then the kid jumped me. I don't know why." He didn't want to tell the detective anymore than he had to. Not that Quinn didn't have plenty of questions of his own. How did Tina track down Prettyboy? And why would she just walk into his apartment by herself? "Did you find Tina's notebook?" he asked the detective. "Maybe she wrote something down that would help us."

"What do you mean 'us'?" sneered the detective. "Look, pal, borrow a shirt and get down to the Santa Ana Station. I got some business to take care of first, but I'll meet you there later. If Rick Eichorn has a record, I'll pull his jacket and maybe you can ID him." He turned to the nurse. "Is 'our hero' patched up enough to leave?"

"Not for a while," said the nurse. "He shouldn't drive, either—he's lost some blood and the percodan's going to make him woozy."

The detective slid off the bed. "He'll be okay. Big strong guy like him." His pasty-white face looked like it had melted in the sun, elongating in the heat. "You get yourself down to the station ASAP, pal. Pronto."

"Pronto? Where do you think we are," Quinn said, "Fort Apache?"

The detective grumbled his way through the curtains.

"You lie down for a while," the nurse said to Quinn. "No arguments."

Quinn wouldn't consider it. He closed his eyes, grateful for the silence. It seemed like only a moment later that the same nurse was gently awakening him.

"I'm sorry," she said. "We need the bed; there was a five-car pileup on Laguna Canyon Road and the E.R. is jammed." She eased him into a baggy blue scrubshirt. His bloody t-shirt had been tossed into the waste container— the HAZARDOUS sticker on the side of the aluminum canister vaguely insulting. He couldn't read her nametag. The letters were blurry. "I wish people would stop riding in the back of pickup trucks," she said, helping him down.

He almost fell over, his head spinning. She grabbed his arm and he cried out.

"Sorry," she said. She slid a wheelchair under him and he sat down heavily, sweat beading across his eyebrows. He tried to get up, somehow terrified of the wheelchair, as though he would never be able to get out. He thought of Joe Steps, the way he and Katie had raced down the Seal Beach pier that first night. The nurse wheeled him through the curtains and out into the crowded waiting room. It was hard to stay awake. He glimpsed people slumped on plastic chairs, bloody towels pressed to their heads, and a torn "Hang in there Baby!" poster of a dangling cat.

Ambulance attendants raced past, carrying an old woman on a gurney, one of them holding aloft an IV bottle. Her head lolled to the side and she looked right at Quinn, her eyes terrified. "Wait here," the nurse said, pushing the wheelchair into a corner, "I'll check back with you when things lighten up."

"Nurse!" he called after her. "Could you make a phone call for me?" She was already wheeling a gurney down the corridor. Quinn closed his eyes. He could hear children crying and adults grumbling, demanding to see a doctor. Someone was asking about insurance. He was tired.

He awoke to the sensation of movement, blinking, his eyelids sticky, still groggy, conversation rolling past him. Muzak burbled overhead, "Smells Like Teen Spirit." Poor Nirvana. "Coming through," said a familiar voice. The automatic doors of the E.R. slid open, the breeze warm on his face. Quinn turned around in the chair, winced at the pain in his shoulder. "H-Hugo? What are you doing here?"

"I was taking a fare to the airport and saw your 4X4 parked behind the apartments," said Hugo, his baggy black suit flapping as he walked. "All those cop cars . . . I thought you might be in trouble."

Quinn looked up into Hugo's cool dark eyes, saw his own anxious reflection. "I . . . I don't like this."

"I don't blame you," Hugo said, pushing him faster.

Quinn could see the taxi parked nearby. He tried to get up, but Hugo put a hand on him, drove him back into his seat, the pain shooting through him.

An ambulance driver leaned against the fender of his wagon, smoking a cigarette. He watched them with a bland, disinterested expression.

"Help me," Quinn said to the driver. His voice was so weak. It sounded like he was talking in his sleep.

The ambulance driver dragged on his cigarette as they passed, ashes spilling onto his white trousers.

Hugo threw open the back door to the cab, lifted Quinn easily out of the wheelchair, and slid him into the back seat. Hugo smelled faintly of cologne. Prettyboy's cologne.

Quinn could see the empty wheelchair rolling slowly down the sidewalk.

"I want to go," said Quinn, grabbing for the door, the pain shooting through him from the sudden movement, his vision darkening around the edges. "I want to get out of here." Hugo cinched the seatbelt around him. "Hugo . . ." he waved at the bloodstains on Hugo's pants, trying to focus. His bandages must be leaking. "Sorry," he mumbled, feeling himself drifting, his tongue thick. "I got blood on you."

"Don't worry about it," Hugo said softly, the darkness rolling in, blotting out the sun, "I'm used to it."

CHAPTER

39

It was dark. An engine rumbled through the blackness, set up a vibration that made Quinn's shoulder hurt. And his head. And his hand. Quinn remembered struggling to get out of the cab and Hugo whacking him across the back of the head with something hard. Slapjack probably, the cabbie's friend. Now he was lying on a cushioned surface, one that moved rhythmically under him, a steady undulation which should have been soothing, but wasn't. He could smell the sea. He was below deck, on a boat. Probably Fontayne's motor yacht.

He sat up slowly, dizzy, red painspots bursting across his vision. It would be so easy to give up, to lie back down and let the boat rock him to sleep.

No. Teddy didn't raise any quitters, that was the lecture anyway. Quinn had come home from football tryouts, his nose flattened, packed in gauze, one eye swollen shut and told Teddy he was thinking of lettering in Ping-Pong instead. Teddy almost smacked him, said, "Why not just go out for cheerleading?" Quinn shivered, remembering the freezing cold as Teddy iced his bruises, saying, "When you quit the game, what you really give up on is you." Quinn was grateful for the lesson, but Teddy, were you talking to me or talking to my mother . . . or talking to yourself?

Quinn's eyes were adjusting. The darkness was gray and amorphous now, a palpable, suffocating presence in the compartment, like the cargo of a ghost ship. Stars were visible through the tiny windows along the low ceiling—it had been late afternoon when Hugo picked him up at the hospital.

He listened but couldn't hear anything but the throb of the engines. The compartment was small and filled with shadows, a bench-bunk running along each wall. He could smell the cologne from the apartment now, Prettyboy's cologne, the same fragrance he had smelled on Hugo in the cab. He stood up from the bunk, ran his hands along the walls, trying to find a light switch as the floor bucked under his feet. His fingers flipped the switch, just as a big swell hit, sending him sprawling, blind from the sudden light, onto the other bunk. Someone was already there.

He shrieked, staring into the face of Prettyboy. The kid lay on the bunk beside him, the two of them cheek to cheek now, the boy's slack features a grotesque mask. Fish eyes, that was what Katie had said. Quinn tried to pull away but he was still groggy, and the boy was grabbing at him with rubbery arms and legs, tangling him up. Quinn pushed against him, punching now, a scream starting . . .

"Get your hands off him," Hugo said from the doorway, moving closer, throwing Quinn onto the floor. "You don't deserve to touch him." He carefully arranged Prettyboy on the bunk, folding his hands across his stomach.

The kid was still wearing the tiger-skin briefs from the apartment. One of the gold hoops in the boy's ears had torn loose and hung by a thread of skin. Quinn looked into those blank eyes, saw the crusted trickle of dried blood from one side of the boy's mouth and knew that he was dead.

"Rick was still alive when I got to him," Hugo said, smoothing back the kid's hair. "A fall like that, and hardly a mark on him—I half expected him to get up and start laughing, but he didn't. He was lying on his back, just like now, and I picked him up and carried him to the cab, and he was so light . . . it was like carrying an angel."

Quinn stared at the two of them.

Hugo smiled to himself. "The last thing Rick said, as I held him in my arms, was, 'How do I look?' I told him he looked perfect." Hugo swallowed. "He did, too." Hugo looked at Quinn. "I don't think vanity is a sin for the truly beautiful." He tenderly wiped Rick's mouth with a damp cloth, cleaning away the blood. "It's ironic, I used to wish that I could shut Rick up, and now . . . now I'd give anything to hear his voice again."

"Your little angel called me yesterday and threatened

my family," said Quinn. "He said he was going to teach Katie some manners."

"I didn't know about that." Hugo was still wearing that threadbare black suit, his gnarled wrists popping out of the frayed sleeves. "I would have stopped him. Rick . . . he got carried away sometimes."

"Yeah, he was a real excitable boy," said Quinn. "I could tell by the way he swung the scissors, just chopping away with that silly little giggle of his."

"You didn't know Rick," Hugo said solemnly, his head brushing the low ceiling as he gazed upon Rick's broken body. "He was just playing a part, pretending to be somebody else. He loved big, dumb action movies, anything with lots of machine guns and buildings exploding and bad guys and good guys who say funny things when they kill people. He liked that most of all. He knew the dialogue to all the 'Die Hard' movies, he would recite whole scenes while he cut my hair, he'd play all the parts."

Quinn could hear the boat's engines slow.

"Rick had wonderful dreams," said Hugo, "extravagant dreams, dreams enough for the both of us, and you took them away. You did that, Quinn. Now, what do I do? You're smart. What do I do now? Tell me."

"You dream your own dreams," said Quinn.

Hugo solemnly shook his head. "I can't."

"Then fake it, just like the rest of us." Quinn got to his feet, hanging on to the wall as he looked out the window. In the distance he could see the faint glow of lights on the shore.

"Oh, you're a long way from home," Hugo said softly, "miles and miles. We all are." He looked at Quinn, his gaze remote and cold and utterly lost. At another time and place, Quinn would have felt sorry for him. Not now.

"Did Rick kill Teddy, or was that you?" Quinn needed to know.

"That was me." The words were flat and heavy. They made the room seem even smaller.

Quinn nodded. Hugo was the last one to see Teddy alive. The last one to hear his voice, see his face . . .

"Teddy went out fighting, if that makes any difference."

"No, Hugo, it doesn't make any difference, none at all," Quinn said. "There are no style points in death." He nodded at Rick's body. "Your buddy there went over the balcony screaming, eyes wide, grasping at the air like a roach on its back, but that didn't change anything. He's just as dead as Teddy, no more, no less. I wish it made a difference," he said. "I'd like to think that there was somebody watching, keeping score, applauding for the ones who die on their feet, with a wisecrack on their lips. I'd like that. Then there could be one spot for guys like Teddy, and another place for gutless bastards who see too many movies and think it's real life."

Hugo opened his mouth but decided not to say anything.

Quinn let his eyes slide across the compartment. The polished walls were dark wood, the same color as the floor. The room was mostly cushions. There—a small fire extinguisher was clipped to one wall. Waiting for an emergency. This qualified.

"Where's Joe?" said Quinn, moving a half-step closer to the fire extinguisher. "Have you killed him yet?"

"It may not come to that."

"Sure, it will, Hugo." Quinn took another step. "You're going to have to kill Joe and me, and then what happens to you, Hugo? You think Fontayne is going to let you live?"

"Do you think I care?" Hugo said, his voice trailing off, a stone sinking into icy water, falling beyond the light.

"Where . . . where is Joe?" said Quinn, momentarily shaken by Hugo's fatalism.

"Mr. Fontayne wants me to throw Rick over the side," said Hugo. "I'm supposed to tie a couple of cinderblocks around his neck and just dump him overboard." He ran a hand lightly across Rick's smooth, hairless chest as though reading a message in braille. "Mr. Fontayne never appreciated Rick."

"Where's Joe?" Quinn said, louder now.

"Joe . . . ? He's topside, talking with Mr. Fontayne." Hugo peered at him. "You don't look so good. Why don't you sit down and I'll bring you a glass of water."

"Were you this helpful to Teddy, Hugo? Did you get him a couple aspirin before you shot him in the head?"

"No, I didn't." Hugo was a walking shadow, marooned between life and death. A sad man in a sad place.

"Did Teddy say anything," Quinn said tightly. "At the end, did he say anything?"

"About you?" Hugo thought about it. "Not really . . .

well, he was making chocolate truffles the night Rick and I showed up. He told me he used to make them for his son when he was growing up. Was that you?"

"Yes." Quinn could still see the tiny kitchen of their old house: Teddy leaning against the stove, sipping Scotch as he watched Quinn gobble chocolates. One of the best times. "Thank you, Hugo."

"You're wel—"

Quinn grabbed the fire extinguisher off the wall, swung it hard, hitting Hugo square against the side of the head, knocking him down and sending the fire extinguisher flying. Quinn howled with pain, feeling the stitches in his back and shoulder tear, but Hugo never made a sound.

Hugo got to his feet, unhurried. There was a deep gash in his head, the scalp peeled back, but hardly any blood.

Quinn picked up the fire extinguisher and stood there at the ready, gasping, waiting for Hugo to do something.

"That stung," Hugo said, gingerly touching his lacerated scalp. "Don't look so disappointed. You're plenty strong, but I've had a lot of experience being hit. They used to call me the human punching bag in my dormitory at Fairhaven—'Hit him and he comes back for more. Hit him and hit him and hit him again. Make him talk, make him say something.' " His bony fingers touched the lapels of his suit jacket, skidded down his ribs. "Children can be so cruel. I have cigarette burns crisscrossing my chest and back like a vast tattoo. One of my nipples was burned off, can you imagine that?" He could have been discussing the weather for all the emotion he showed. "I never said a word. Never cried. It's worse when you cry."

Hugo's long, thin face was eroding before Quinn's eyes, a scarecrow caught in a high wind. Soon only his eyes would remain, black glass, shiny and hard. With a single, salty tear at their centers.

Quinn wanted to cajole Hugo, promise him anything, tell him it wasn't too late to back down, back off, save himself, think of his family—He had heard a SWAT team negotiator use those same bland phrases to talk a suicidal medical student from blowing up himself and the professor who had flunked him. He had seen a beat cop hustle a bank robber out of his hostages with a hot pizza and a six-pack of cold beer. Quinn didn't say anything. Talk wasn't going to work on Hugo. Neither was pizza. Nothing was going to work on Hugo.

"I've encountered very little kindness in this life," said Hugo. "There was Rick." He reached out to touch the kid but pulled back at the last minute. "And there was Mr. Fontayne. Mr. Fontayne got me released from Fairhaven when no one else was interested. He introduced me to Rick. I agreed to . . . help Mr. Fontayne out of gratitude, but I don't think gratitude would have been enough to do what was required. It's not easy to kill someone. Not the first time. Even for me." The floor rolled underfoot and Hugo had to reach out to steady himself. "You want to take another swing at me, go ahead, I won't stop you."

Quinn didn't move, hemmed in by the narrow walls

and low ceiling, trapped by Hugo's dense, imperturbable calm.

"Just as well," said Hugo, "it wouldn't have done you any good." He slammed his fist into the wall. He didn't even wince, watching Quinn. The other fist hit the teak paneling, cracked the wood. "It was hard that first time, to look into Teddy's eyes and have to blow out the light. I almost ran away, but Rick was there cheering me on, and it was so important to him . . . I think that's what Mr. Fontayne was counting on. That's why he put Rick and me together. He's very intelligent, Mr. Fontayne, very good with people."

Quinn held himself back.

Hugo looked at his hands. The skin on his knuckles had split, and one of his fingers was clearly broken. "No feeling," he said, "none at all. No dreams. No fears. No love. No hate." He shook his head, then sat down on the bunk beside Rick. "Rick felt everything—the wind in the palm trees, the smell of a new shampoo, the very music of life. I used to envy his youthful exuberance, even when it got him in trouble, even when it made him seem foolish. Now he's dead." He smoothed one of Rick's eyebrows with a fingertip. "I still envy him," he said softly.

Quinn swung the fire extinguisher with both hands against the back of Hugo's head, swung it as hard as he could, again and again until Hugo fell to the floor and Quinn was too tired to hit him anymore.

CHAPTER

40

"Here he is," Fontayne said, turning away from a cluster of video screens as Quinn peeked out from the top of the spiral staircase. "Come on up," Fontayne beckoned with a pistol.

Quinn stepped out onto the open area at the rear of the yacht. It was dark topside, lit only by a slice of moon and the boat's dim, yellow running lights. The yacht rocked gently, engine rumbling.

"Where's Hugo?" Fontayne said, looking past him.

"Resting."

"Ah, resting." Fontayne glowered from a high-backed "fighting-chair," legs crossed, trying to hide his shock. The chair was heavily padded and steel reinforced, bolted to the deck, designed for combat with 2,000-pound black marlin and yellowfin tuna. Fontayne sat there in his immaculate nautical whites and skipper's cap, the cuffs of his pants rolled.

A bank of small black-and-white video screens beside Fontayne showed the yacht's interior: deserted corridors and stairwells. There was no one at the helm—just the lights of the Nav-center blinking steadily, electronically piloting the yacht's course while Fontayne slouched in the chair, a seaman without interest in the sea.

Quinn took a deep breath, grateful to be outside after the oppressive atmosphere below, Rick's sweet cologne mingling with the stink of death. He let the breeze wash over him. He could see Joe's overturned wheelchair against the stern, Joe lying helpless, his wrists and ankles adhesive-taped to the chair. Quinn went to help him.

"Don't be in such a hurry to die," said Fontayne, the pistol pointed at Quinn's chest. "Stay with me."

"How are you doing, Joe?" called Quinn.

"I'm on Easy Street, Slick. What happened to your mitt?"

Quinn held up his bandaged left hand. "I cut myself on a pair of scissors."

Fontayne fingered the gold buttons on his white jacket. "Joe tried to convince me you didn't really know anything, but I knew better." He polished the buttons with his thumb. "Mrs. Ledbetter called me this morning—she said a reporter had come to see her, asking about her son. She's a grand lady, Quinn, you shouldn't upset her."

"Think how upset she'd be if she knew you let her son die in prison. You had all the proof you needed to get Jamie Ledbetter released and you sat on it."

"Spare me your moral superiority," said Fontayne, his

white clothes like tarnished silver in the dim light. "Jamie was in no danger. My appeal . . . *Jamie's* appeal was a flawless piece of work. I would have gotten him acquitted, you can be certain of that." His head drooped. "Then, of course, Jamie was murdered. Plain bad luck. There was no way I could have foreseen that happening."

"Yeah, tough break for you, Jamie getting himself killed like that," said Quinn. "Sounds like Jack Liggett was the only one who made out. He was the one who put you on to Stimmler and the music box, wasn't he?"

"Aren't you the bright, young man." Fontayne crossed his legs at the knee. Uncrossed them. "It was raining the night Liggett showed up at my door, looking like a drowned rat. A sewer rat. He had rousted Stimmler that evening, found Sweetie's music box in his room and recognized it from the police reports." He grimaced. "A few hours later, Liggett sat in my office, water dripping from his cheap suit, demanding a $20,000 'arrest gratuity,' or he was going to let Stimmler walk. He acted like it happened all the time. Perhaps it did. Liggett assumed I'd be happy to pay for the evidence that would free Jamie—"

"You weren't happy, though," interrupted Quinn. "You had your appeal argument all worked out. Flawlessly. You didn't need Stimmler or the music box."

"No." Fontayne's face was a smooth mask. "I didn't."

"So you made Liggett a counteroffer," said Quinn, goading him, waiting for him to make a mistake. "To frame Joe—"

"To remove him," said Fontayne. "To excise him." He

plucked at his gold buttons, lost in thought. "You should
have seen him at our charity functions, moving about with
his fine clothes and proper manners, pretending he was as
good as the rest of us." His hand clenched. "He soiled our
company with his very presence."

Joe lay on his side, struggling to free himself.

Fontayne idly watched Joe strain against the loops
of adhesive tape. "Then one night I saw my wife dancing
with him, her head thrown back as he held her in his
arms . . . and I knew. I knew." His face flushed. "I was a
young man once, too. Imagine my shame. The whole room
was staring at them. I felt as though my skin were on
fire."

"Elena was wasted on you," Joe spat. "You should
have given her a divorce."

Fontayne's laugh cracked. "You overestimate the
power of your charm. Your kind always does. My wife . . .
my wife would have never left me. The harm was already
done, though. That night, the insult of your dancing together like that . . ."

He raised the pistol, aimed it at Joe.

Quinn moved forward, distracting Fontayne.

"I have always been a very deliberate man," Fontayne
said to Quinn, "a very cautious man, but the night that
Liggett came to my door, I was impulsive. That night I was
bold." He looked at Joe, his smile icy. "You have no idea of
the pleasure it gave me to destroy you. I think I even
surprised Jack Liggett." He peered at the videoscreens.
"Ah, here's Hugo, now, carrying Rick . . . He's going the

wrong way." He flipped on the intercom. "Hugo! You're going . . ." He shrugged. "He'll find his way soon enough."

Quinn leaned against the side railing, surprised that Hugo was able to stand, let alone walk. "You're not going to get away with this, Fontayne."

Fontayne smiled. "It's a beautiful evening, isn't it?"

"You think we're not going to be missed?"

Fontayne shrugged. *"You'll* be missed, but there's an easy explanation for your disappearance. The hospital security cameras will show you being taken away by a taxidriver who will be later identified as a friend of the man you killed at the apartment house. Hugo will never be found, of course. Neither will you, I'm afraid. Unless . . ."

The breeze tasted like copper at the back of Quinn's throat. "Unless what?" He knew asking the question was a mistake as soon as he said it.

Fontayne smiled again, then hit a switch and the transom-panels in the stern slid back, leaving a six-foot opening. The transom allowed large fish to be more easily dragged on board, but things on deck could just as easily slide off into the deep.

Quinn could see the yacht's wake through the gap in the stern, the water iridescent in the moonlight. He saw fear on Joe's face, too. Joe caught himself. Looked away from Quinn. When he turned back he was calm again.

"One push and your problems are over," Fontayne said to Quinn. "One push and we cease being enemies, and become partners. All things considered, I would prefer to keep you alive. There's the whole question of Ms. Takamura. She won't accept your disappearance, no matter what the evidence. She's a very capable woman, very tenacious. Why not save us all a great deal of trouble—"

"Not a chance," said Quinn. He moved closer to Fontayne. "You're going to have to use that gun yourself this time. Hugo isn't much good anymore. I think one of his screws popped loose."

"Tell that to Hugo," said Fontayne, the gun trembling. "He should be here any moment now." He checked the videoscreens. "Joe Steps is the one you should be angry with for your current predicament. He started this— calling me up, playing that damned music box, threatening me, saying he would go to the police, the newspapers, the tabloid television shows. I offered him money, but he didn't want money. What was I supposed to do?"

Quinn inched toward Fontayne, moving in time with the rocking of the boat. A wind was rising.

"He called Jack Liggett, too," said Fontayne, "threw him into a blind panic. Liggett wanted to kill Joe immediately, but that would have been risky." He jabbed the pistol at Joe. "No telling what he might have left behind— some nasty letter to be opened in the event of his death, making wild charges, naming names."

Quinn hesitated. Joe had told him that he didn't know who Liggett was. He glanced over to where Joe lay bound to the overturned wheelchair.

"I wrote that letter you're so scared of," Joe called to Fontayne. "I told where I hid Sweetie's music box, too."

"The music box no longer poses a threat," Fontayne

said airily, "and neither do you. There's no one left to corroborate your accusations. Neo-Nazis killed Teddy. Stimmler died of natural causes, and Liggett was murdered during a carjacking. None of their deaths can be connected to me." His crossed leg bounced happily. "All the loose ends have been trimmed away, Joe. You'll be viewed as just an ex-con who tried to extort money from me and failed."

"Teddy was no loose end," snapped Quinn. He could feel the deck tremble under him. The yacht was surrounded by whitecaps now, the wind whipping the flag atop the tower.

"It's a little late to be defending the family honor, don't you think?" said Fontayne.

"You didn't have to kill Teddy," Joe said. "I showed him the music box, told him about Stimmler. Teddy said it was flimsy and circumstantial at best—"

"I'm aware of what Teddy told you," sighed Fontayne. "Still, you'd be amazed how quickly even a well-kept secret can unravel. Stimmler was a weakling and Detective Liggett, well, let's just say retirement had made him soft." He smoothed his jacket. "I had to protect myself. A Supreme Court appointment would be my life's crowning achievement, and even a whiff of scandal . . ."

Quinn edged toward Fontayne while Joe kept him occupied. The engine labored harder. The yacht was barely moving. He measured the distance to where Fontayne sat.

"Teddy was different," said Fontayne. "He was resolute. Unflinching. He was never really comfortable with what he had done, though. What we had done. It bothered him. A weak man blames the world. A strong man thinks he could have acted differently . . . he blames himself. Teddy was the one I was most worried about. More than Stimmler. More than Liggett. Deep down, I think Teddy still thought he and Joe were friends. That's why I had Hugo start with him."

The pistol fired as Quinn launched himself—a near miss that seared his cheek as he crashed into Fontayne. The gun flew across the deck as he punched Fontayne with his good hand. He hit him until he was out of breath, Joe cheering every blow.

Fontayne lolled in the captain's chair, bleary-eyed, his white jacket sprayed with blood. One of his gold buttons had been torn off.

Quinn's legs shook as he stood over Fontayne. "What . . . what were you saying about Teddy? It didn't make any sense."

Fontayne picked his cap up, replaced it on his head. Adjusted the brim. "Teddy . . . helped me with the frame." He blotted his lip with the back of his hand.

"Liar!" screamed Joe.

Fontayne's smile was a mess. "I needed Stimmler to pick your wristwatch so I could plant it with the bookie," he said to Joe, "but I had to make sure you were alone when the bookie was murdered. I wanted you someplace where you wouldn't have an alibi. Teddy took care of that. You were supposed to go out that night, just the two of you.

Remember? You waited hours for him to come to your house ... such patience. It's your one truly admirable quality, Joe."

"Teddy wouldn't have done that," said Quinn.

"You're a big boy, Quinn," said Fontayne. "It's time to put away childish things and see the world as it is."

"Teddy wouldn't sell Joe out," insisted Quinn.

"Do you actually think I'm the only jealous man on the planet?" laughed Fontayne. "Joe has all the useless qualities that appeal to women: the looks, the charm, that swarthy flirtatiousness. You must have noticed that even as a boy, Quinn. Don't you think there were nights when Teddy lay awake, wondering about his good friend and his loving wife? Wondering why she left so suddenly? Well, don't you?"

Quinn felt dizzy. He wanted to shut Fontayne up.

"Don't believe him!" said Joe. "He's trying to—"

Fontayne shoved the throttle full-forward and the yacht jerked ahead, engine roaring as Quinn tumbled backwards onto the deck. The wheelchair skidded toward the open transom, still on its side, as Joe cried out.

Quinn grabbed the wheelchair, bracing himself against the stern with his shoulder, holding the chair in place.

"If you really cared about the family honor, you'd let him go," counseled Fontayne. "Let Teddy rest in peace."

"Do it, Slick," said Joe. "It's your only chance."

Fontayne nodded at the open transom. "Time to decide

which side you're on, Quinn." His eyes searched for
the gun.

"I know where I belong," grunted Quinn as he dragged
the wheelchair away from the brink. He tried to set it
upright, but it was too hard with his bad hand.

The engines throbbed, cylinders misfiring before suddenly quitting. No one said anything in the abrupt silence.
Then an alarm screeched. "Hugo!" Fontayne shouted as
the yacht tilted hard to port, sinking. "Hugo! What's
going on?"

The wheelchair slid along the slope of the deck. Quinn
bent over, unwinding the adhesive tape around Joe's
wrists.

"Hugo!" Fontayne beat on the video screens.

"Hello, Mr. Fontayne . . ." Hugo's voice crackled over
the intercom. "I put Rick in the master suite, tucked him
in. It's a beautiful room. Rick would like . . . here . . . two
of us . . . long rest." Static popped. ". . . opened sea cocks,
but I didn't think . . . would happen so fast . . . couldn't
throw Rick overboard like garbage . . . Couldn't."

Joe's hand slipped free and he and Quinn worked on
the other hand together. The two of them exhausted. Giddy.

"This boat is perfect for Rick," said Hugo, his voice so
clear that Quinn thought he was standing beside them.
"Rick would really appreciate the polished wood and
shiny brass. He could see himself everywhere."

Fontayne scampered up the ladder to the wheelhouse,
cursing, his foot slipping on the rungs.

"Joe?" said Hugo. "You still here? I'm sorry . . ."
There was a burst of static. The running lights went out.

The yacht was awash. Waves tickled Quinn's legs as he listened to Fontayne crash around in the darkened wheelhouse, trying to switch the communications gear to battery power. S.O.S. Good luck. He and Joe lay next to each other in the dark, cold water splashing around them. Quinn had never seen so many stars.

"Remember that Fred Astaire movie we saw once?" said Quinn. "The one where Fred dances with the hatrack? You told me only a great dancer could partner a hatrack, move it around as though it were alive, and make it look graceful."

Joe coughed. "You have a weird sense of timing, Slick."

"You're a great dancer, Joe. You trotted Fontayne all around the floor, and your touch was so light he didn't even feel your hands."

Joe watched him in the dim light.

"You lied to me about knowing Jack Liggett," said Quinn. "You called Fontayne, then you called Liggett. You kept calling, too. You knew Fontayne. You knew he'd have to protect his interests. You gambled that he'd kill his cohorts before he'd go after you. Pretty risky."

Joe patted his cheek with his free hand. "What did I have to lose, Slick?" His face darkened. "Teddy, though . . ." He shook his head, eyes wet with tears. "I never expected that to happen," he said hoarsely. "I never thought he was part of the frame-up. I still don't believe it. Fontayne is a liar. He killed Teddy because of what I had told him. Not because of what Teddy already knew."

The yacht lay dead in the water, waves rolling across

the tilted deck. Quinn got to his feet, heaved the wheel-chair upright. Pain shot through his injured hand. "Why didn't you tell me what was going on?"

"I wanted to keep you out of this. To protect you," said Joe, the two of them unwrapping the tape around his other wrist. "This was never your fight."

"You should have gone to the police," said Quinn.

"With what?" said Joe, tugging at his wrist. "Teddy was right. I didn't have anything that would stand up in court. Fontayne's precious reputation might have been ruined, but I wanted more than that. Not after what he did to me. What they all did to me." He tore at the adhesive tape with his teeth and his hand came loose. He held both hands up, wriggling his fingers to restore the circulation.

Fontayne splashed across the deck, dragging a yellow liferaft. He slipped, the raft skipping across the water. Fontayne stood up, dazed, and Joe rolled over to him, grabbed him, wrapped his arms around him.

The yacht was going down stern-first—the wheel-chair rolled backwards, Joe dragging Fontayne along for the ride.

"Let go!" Fontayne yelled, punching Joe in the face.

"What's your hurry?" Joe laughed. The water was almost to his knees.

"Damn you!" Fontayne flailed away, but Joe held him too tightly for him to do any real damage. "Let me go!" screamed Fontayne, clawing at Joe's chest, desperate now, the ocean swirling around his waist.

Quinn felt under the water for the tape that still bound Joe's ankles to the chair but couldn't find the starting point. The liferaft was bobbing further away now.

"How does it feel?" Joe said to Fontayne, holding him by the hair, looking him right in the eye. "How does it feel to be trapped? Nothing you can do . . . no matter how hard you try. All you can do is wait. And wait. And wait."

"Please—"

Joe pulled back Fontayne's head, shutting off his words. "You should listen for a change." Fontayne thrashed against him as they slid into deeper water, the whitecaps lapping at their chins, but Joe didn't loosen his grip. "Do you hear that, Fontayne?" he said, the water rushing around them. "Do you? It's music. They're playing our song."

"Joe!" Quinn pulled at the wheelchair, treading water, kicking furiously, trying to hold them up. "Let him go. I can get us to the raft."

"You go—you go home," Joe sputtered. "Go home."

Quinn shivered. "Not without you."

Joe pushed Fontayne's head under water, held it there. He looked at Quinn, taking his time, as though seeing him for the first time. "I missed out on you growing up, sonny." He smiled. "You turned out just like I hoped."

"Joe . . . ? What are you saying?"

"Go home . . . son," said Joe, his arms still clamped around Fontayne, cheek to cheek as they sank beneath the waves.

Quinn grabbed for them, but they were beyond his

reach. Beyond all answers. He floated alone under the stars. Seat cushions and other items from the yacht bobbed on the oily surface. Fontayne's white skipper's cap drifted slowly past, gold braid dangling in the dark water.

He headed for the raft.

EPILOGUE

"You didn't have to do this," said Quinn.

"I know." Jen weaved her white Corvette through tiny gaps in the late evening traffic, driving so smoothly that she never had to hit her brakes, so precisely that no one ever honked or gave her the finger.

"I could take a cab," he said. Jen glanced at him and they both winced. "Well, maybe a limo. I didn't expect you to drive me."

"It was a slow day at the magazine," said Jen. She must have felt his eyes on her. "And I wanted to."

"Okay," said Quinn.

"Okay."

They drove in silence for a few miles, the two of them safe behind their sunglasses. "How is Tina Chavez?" said Jen. She was trying to make conversation and Quinn was grateful. "Is she back at the D.A.'s office yet?"

"She started work on Monday," said Quinn. He could see the pale white scars on his left hand. "She's going to be in therapy for a few more months, but her doctors are optimistic."

"Good."

"Yeah."

"Is she going to get a promotion for helping solve Teddy's murder?" asked Jen.

Quinn shook his head. "She's lucky she didn't get fired. District Attorney Barkis doesn't like his people free-lancing, and he wasn't thrilled to have to cut loose the White supremacists he had so publicly arrested. She's going to have to watch herself with him."

"I met Tina," said Jen, whipping down the fastlane, "I think Barkis is the one who should be worried."

Quinn's article about Fontayne and the frame-up of Joe Steps had come out in *SLAP* magazine three weeks ago. He had turned down all TV interviews and several movie-of-the-week offers. Bertha Ledbetter, Jamie's mother, had consented to speak with Willard Scott, the folksy weather-man on the "Today" show, proudly displaying Jamie's pardon which had been hastily signed by the governor. Jen took the airport exit.

"It's not too late," Quinn blurted out. "You have a passport. I can wait. We could take a flight tomorrow. There's plenty of room in Paris for all of us."

"One of the things I'm going to miss the most about you," said Jen, "is your idiotic optimism, this totally unre-alistic belief that everything is going to work out."

"It *could* work out."

"Not in a million years."

"That's not—"

"Not in a billion years."

"Fine." Quinn was hoping to maintain the banter until the last minute, then dash out of the car and into the airport. As usual, she was too smart for him.

"Be happy, Quinn," Jen said solemnly.

He wiped tears from his eyes. "You're very cruel." He took off his sunglasses, dragged the back of his hands across his cheeks.

"I mean it," she said, pulling up into the drop-off zone of his airline.

"I know you mean it." The two of them stared straight ahead, not moving.

"Are you going to kiss me goodbye?" she said, still looking through the windshield.

"Very cruel," he said. "Vicious."

She turned to him, took off her sunglasses. Her green eyes shimmered with tears.

He kissed her and she kissed him back. Horns beeped behind them, but they stayed pressed against each other.

Jen finally separated from him. "You're going to miss your plane," she said softly.

"Jen . . ." his voice broke.

"Go on," said Jen. "Your family is waiting for you."

He nodded. "Yeah." He got out of her car, grabbed his bag, and just stood there.

"Be happy," she said.

"I will." They waved goodbye at the same time. Quinn turned and hurried into the terminal.

The takeoff was smooth but Quinn still kept a death grip on the armrest. He hated flying.

Yesterday he had gone back to the graveyard where Teddy was buried. He had to resist the impulse to duck every time a plane came in low to land at John Wayne airport.

Someone had left fresh flowers on the grave. Marie, probably. Quinn laid his bouquet next to hers. He was glad he had decided not to investigate Teddy's judicial appointment. Not to explore his true relationship with Fontayne.

Quinn had stood there staring at Teddy's tombstone: LOVING HUSBAND, HONORABLE MAN. Joe hadn't believed that Teddy had set him up—he was convinced they were friends. Friends to the end. If the tombstone was a lie, so be it. Graveyards were full of lies. Quinn preferred to rely on his own memories of Teddy—a man who had taken care of him when no one else wanted to. Teddy might have done the job grudgingly, but he did it. And if he and Quinn had had their differences, well, that's the way it was with fathers and sons.

Fathers and sons. Quinn wasn't sure about that, either. All he knew was that Joe and Teddy were both dead. Double or nothing. Sometimes you end up with nothing but memories.

He saw the lights of Los Angeles spread out below as the jumbo jet ascended over the Pacific, a glittering web brighter than the stars. The HOLLYWOOD sign was floodlit against the distant hills, an invitation and a warning. He peered out the window but the moon was behind him, out of sight. He settled back into his seat, closed his eyes. It was going to be a long flight.